The Quince Project

ALSO BY
JESSICA PARRA

Rubi Ramos's Recipe for Success

The Quince Project

A NOVEL

JESSICA PARRA

WEDNESDAY BOOKS
NEW YORK

This is a work of fiction. All of the characters, organizations, and events portrayed in this novel are either products of the author's imagination or are used fictitiously.

First published in the United States by Wednesday Books, an imprint of St. Martin's Publishing Group

For information, address St. Martin's Publishing Group, 120 Broadway, New York, NY 10271.

www.wednesdaybooks.com

Designed by Devan Norman

The Library of Congress Cataloging-in-Publication Data is available upon request.

ISBN 978-1-250-88851-8 (trade paperback)
ISBN 978-1-250-86277-8 (hardcover)
ISBN 978-1-250-86278-5 (ebook)

First Edition: 2024

10 9 8 7 6 5 4 3 2 1

To Stephanie Dodson, Hoda Agharazi, and Vanessa Aguirre:
You are the Fauna, Flora, and Merryweather to my Maleficent.

And to Juno, Jolie, and Arwen:
Thank you for having filled my life with more magic
than any fairy godmother could.

The Quince Project

CHAPTER ONE

If the devil's in the details, then el diablo loved to cha-cha on Spanish accent marks. A dash over the *a* in tonight's side dish, for example, and party guests would get a baked *dad*—instead of a baked potato—to accompany their filet mignon.

I checked the menu card one more time.

All clear. A quick scan down the rest of tonight's other courses—thankfully none of those spellings needed acute accents, dieresis . . . or the dreaded tilde.

Nothing spelled disaster more than a missing squiggly mustache mark over the *n* in *años*.

Having watched Po's birthday banner drop, only for it to wish my sister *happy fifteen buttholes* instead of *happy fifteen years*, I spoke from experience.

I lowered the perfectly spelled menu onto the middle of the gold-rimmed plate with shaky fingers. Flashbacks of that night knocked against my chest. But the memories of the months leading up to it walloped hardest. Threatening to bust my heart open like a piñata.

I shook my head and pulled my planner from my bag. Thumbed through the pages filled with student body association calendar events until I hit the *Angie Montes Bday Party Final Checklist* tab.

Going down the rest of the list, I surveyed the ballroom. Head table set to perfection? Check. White roses and pink hydrangeas brimming from the center of the other tables? Check.

As our school's event-planning chair, I'd gone down similar lists countless times. Every checkmark of the pencil usually steadied my pulse. No such luck tonight.

Probably because this wasn't a Matteo Beach High winter formal, prom, or fundraiser but my first solo(ish) attempt at party planning. As if starting a side hustle wasn't stressful enough, of course the first party out the gates had to be a quince.

Sure, this fiesta celebrated a rite of passage for the birthday girl. But it could be one for me, too.

Because if tonight went off without a hitch, I could keep checking off boxes for both my short- and long-term goals this summer, starting with Angie recommending my services to our classmates and ending with the party-planning experience I needed to apply to Mandy Whitmore and Associates' fairy godmother internship.

I shut the planner and hugged it close, whispering Mandy's mission statement: "With the wave of a magic stylus—plus a few hands-on tricks of the trade—my team of fairy godmother's apprentices and I will make your event storybook stunning."

Closing my eyes, I recited the last sentence: "Happily ever afters are our business."

Like a spell working its magic, pieces of my HEA painted themselves behind my eyelids.

A calendar stuffed with tons of picture-perfect parties. Acceptance into a great college with a stellar hospitality management major and PR minor. Preferably one with a kick-ass volleyball team, so Po could also go there.

Before I slotted in my wishes for Dad, Juno's voice shattered my Torres-family vision board.

"We're good to go, Cas!"

I glanced across the gilded room to Juno, my AP chemistry lab partner moonlighting as the DJ. I flicked the gold-ringed eraser end of my pencil at them.

And just like that, the first step to my family's HEA had liftoff.

Now the rest of the party needed to unfold perfectly for it to keep soaring.

I tucked the pencil behind my ear. Pressed the side of the ancient walkie-talkie, relics from Po's and my Pokémon-catching days. Even with the bumblebee-yellow plastic, it looked super professional—so long as I kept the side with the Pikachu speakers down. "It's almost time to open the floodgates, Callie. Are the assets in position?"

A burst of crackles, then a drumroll emitted from the speaker. Probably her tapping her nails against the walkie-talkie. At student body association meetings, she always thrummed them against her binder before delivering bad news. "Sorry, Cas, Tweedledee and Tweedledum have gone AWOL. Again."

Every chance they got, Ishaan and Sarah sneaked off for an impromptu make-out session. I should've forced them to share their location when I had the chance.

"I'll track them down," I grumbled. "What about Angie? Is she finally ready?"

"Um. About that."

My knuckles clenched the planner's edges. "What now?"

"She's locked herself in the bridal suite and won't let me in."

Ugh. "Fine. I'll handle it." I always did. "I'm going to open the doors. Can you come back here and let me know if anything else happens?"

"Roger."

"Over and out." I gave Juno the signal. A second later, an instrumental version of "My Heart Will Go On" filled the ballroom. I opened the set of double doors, smiling at the flurry of guests blurring past.

Stepping into the hotel's lobby, I broke into a sprint. No signs of the two quince court members gone missing. No skinny-dipping in the pool out back either. Right when my fingers curled around Pikachu's tail—er, the talk button—ready to order Callie to come help with the manhunt, there, through the hotel's tall arches that led to its beautiful Spanish courtyard, they stood.

Their necks defied geometric principles. Even the AP ones I'd learned last year. Blame it on the chismosa part of me—definitely not on the never-been-kissed part—I stepped closer for a better look. With all that teeth gnashing, how were their Invisalign staying in place?

As over-the-top as this PDA was, though, I couldn't deny this spot did scream "perfect background for making out." Burgundy roses rustled in the warm breeze. An eager moon shone silver from a darkening sky, bathing these lovebirds in extra-shimmery light.

They weren't even *the* couple of the night. And although I'd witnessed more of these stolen moments than I could count (both in person and in the rom-coms Mom used to watch to perfect her English), a bunch of butterflies fluttered through me. I threw back my shoulders, flinging off the romantic in me, and stepped into the courtyard. "Hey, you two!"

The couple broke apart. Moonbeams caught on Sarah's plastic aligners. The moonlight didn't similarly bounce off Ishaan's. Not with all of Sarah's lipstick smudged over them. "We were just—" they mumbled at the same time.

I put up a hand. "Ishaan, fix your tie and wipe your Invisalign.

And Sarah—" I reached under my blazer into my utility bag, pulled out my hand, and flung a tube of lipstick that every dama in the court was wearing tonight. "Catch."

Captain of the softball team, she caught MAC's Ballet Slipper in a manicured hand like a pro. "Now, hurry," I said. "The procession starts in ten."

One problem down, one more to go. My body vibrated with purpose. With a plan. There was nothing I loved more than a plan.

I sprinted forward, scrunching smoothing serum on the split ends of some fellow classmates, pointing tipsy tíos the right way. I narrowly avoided crashing into Angie's abuelita.

"Sorry, Señora Montes!"

"¡Wachale, niña!" She squinted at me before gesturing to the floor—no, her gold-spiked kitten heels. Way more dangerous than embroidered-cloth and rubber-soled chanclas worn by less bougie grandmothers. By the look on her face, she'd have zero qualms about using them on my behind if I didn't watch where I was going.

"Why hasn't my granddaughter come down yet?" *Okay, she'd also use the sandals on me if Angie missed the grand entrance.* "Do you even know where she is?"

"Of course I do." Only because Callie told me a second ago. "There's nothing to worry about, I promise." My loud gulp made her eyebrows draw tighter. "Please make your way to the ballroom and enjoy the hors d'oeuvres. Angie will be down any second." I broke into a run before she could say anything else.

Too bad I couldn't outpace Angie's cousin Fernando. "Cas! Wait!"

But if time waited for no one, neither would I. No matter how cute Fer was, or how many times he'd asked me to be his date for a cousin's wedding, you know what they say.

Always a planner, never a plus-one.

Not to mention I'd never been a date since, well, ever.

I ran through one of the hotel's kitchens, losing him in a maze of chefs, hissing grills, and boiling pots. By the time I reached the bridal suite, my thighs burned. I leaned against the door and tried to turn the knob.

It refused to budge. I knocked. No answer.

Great. Angie had gone full-on quincezilla.

"Open the door. It's me—Cas."

Still nothing. I pressed my ear to the door. No TV or music from the other side. Just the *click-click-click* of stilettos pacing across marble floors.

"Angie, if you don't open this door right now"—since we were both too old to believe in El Cucuy, I reached for the other monster Latines feared until they died—"I'll go get your abuelita."

A huge gasp from the other side of the door. But hey, desperate times called for desperate measures. The door creaked open; Angie grabbed my pink blouse and dragged me in. "Careful, Ang! This is my lucky shirt."

She locked the door behind us. "Sorry. If I tore anything, I'll buy you a new one."

I brushed my hands down my blouse. Every pearl button had stayed put. No tears in the pink silk. The shirt I planned to wear to Mandy's fairy godmother internship interview one day was still intact. I blew out a sigh of relief. "It's fine."

"I'm glad one of us is." The top of her bronzed and contoured chest rose and fell. The Swarovski crystals beading her bodice sprayed tiny rainbows on the walls.

"Why are you freaking out now, Angie? You've worked your butt off learning all the routines." Contrary to stereotype, not all Latinas had rhythm. In exchange for Spanish tutoring,

Marcus Bennett, our school's captain of the dance team, agreed to choreograph the dances. Except, to get them down, Angie had put in the ten thousand hours herself. "You could do the father-daughter dance, the group waltz, and el baile de sorpresa blindfolded."

"I wish I was blindfolded."

"And mess up your makeup?"

She jabbed me on the shoulder. "I'm serious, Cas. I know we practiced everything for weeks now . . ." She didn't have to finish telling me. I'd spent the last month of the spring semester and the first week of summer vacation prepping this party. "Except we didn't practice"—Angie dropped her chin to the neckline of her gown—"how it's going to feel having everyone staring at me."

I swallowed a chuckle. Most prom queens and homecoming kings couldn't wait for the one night that guaranteed all eyes on them.

"How did you handle it for your quince? Was it as big as this?"

"Well, I actually—" My voice broke off, then vanished.

"Let me guess. It was an outdoor venue, wasn't it?"

A lump lodged itself in my throat. Over a year ago, my fifteenth birthday's venue had been outdoors, all right.

"I knew it." She stomped her foot.

"Careful with that." I crouched to the floor, checking the heel. "Your mom's going to kill me if another pair of Louboutins gets ruined on my watch." Even worse, one more complaint from Mami Dearest and she'd probably bad-mouth me to all her friends. I didn't even want to entertain how the bad reviews could impact this side hustle. Or, by extension, the internship.

My shoulders tensed before relaxing. "Thankfully, the heel's intact."

Angie stuck her tongue out at me.

"Real adult behavior from someone who is about to become a woman." The moment I said it, the walkie-talkie crackled from my back pocket. Either an electric volt from Pikachu or an incoming message from Callie. Both probably warnings that Mami Dearest or—*gasp*—Abuelita stormed this way.

I rose up and spun Angie around toward the mirror. Pinned up a tendril that had already come loose. "Showtime," I said, dragging her by the elbow.

Except she dug in her high heels. "A daytime quince was my first choice, you know. Outdoors, like yours." Her voice got soft, faraway. "But Abuelita didn't want me to get even darker."

I bit my lips. Protested silently by letting another ringlet stay outside the perfectly sculpted bun.

"And what about the flowers?" Angie asked, probably to keep stalling. "Which kinds did you have?"

"All types." Technically not a lie. But ugh. That damn lump kept swelling.

"Probably in every arrangement imaginable?"

"Yup." Also true. Only they'd been placed on the ground, not across the middles of exquisitely decorated tables.

A wistful sigh escaped her lips, as if she were watching a memory reel inside my head. Before she realized the true story, I bent down again. Rearranged gigantic swaths of pink tulle swallowing the lower half of her body.

"Marble floors?"

"Uh-huh." More like blocks of marble, atop perfectly cut grass. Engraved with names, dashes between dates. Adjectives. And so many nouns. I rolled some of the fabric between my fingers. Swore *Beloved Wife* and *Mother* skimmed my skin.

My eyes went misty. As if it couldn't get any worse, I stood up, only to discover her peepers followed suit before turning red. *Kill me now.*

I reached under my blazer for my utility bag. Dug into the top pocket where I kept the travel-size bottle of Visine and my silk hanky. "Angie, we need to move." Out of this room, before her mom and granny tore down the doors. Before more memories rushed in uninvited.

"Oh, Cas. I'm scared."

"It's scary." I stared at myself in the mirror when I said it. Grief apparently took cues from vampires because that Mom-shaped hole in the middle of my chest cast no reflection.

I flicked my gaze back to Angie. "Look up." I squeezed a drop into each eye. Beads of water clung to her faux lashes. The glint matched the gleam coming off the diamonds looping around her neck. "I'm not going to lie. There are going to be hundreds of eyes on you." One hundred and twenty-eight, to be exact. "If you can, try to focus on just one pair of them."

I pictured Mom's eyes. So dark yet filled with so much fire. Like stars burning over an endless desert. Like candlelight beaming under a rolling blackout. Their brightness started to dim two years ago, fading slowly until no light remained.

I squirted my own eyes with sprays of Visine. "Especially when you're giving the thank-you speech."

Angie shrieked. Exactly like I knew she would. "Cálmate. I have one right here." Speech writing wasn't my forte. Still, I couldn't pass up a chance to write this one. Not when it felt like fanfic of what I wished I would've told Mom at my quince . . . if I'd had one.

I pulled the speech from my pocket. She plucked it from my fingers. False lashes fluttered as she scanned each line. "Thank you for coming and helping me celebrate my fifteenth birthday. Tonight, Papi put a new pair of heels on me. I'm sure my little brother tried his hardest to hide my last doll—"

"Pause for laughter," I said, drawing the pencil from the

back of my ear. While it had a long way to go before becoming like Mandy's magic stylus, I flicked it at Angie anyway, motioning for her to continue.

She gave a small nod. "After finding it, I'll pass it down to my little sister. These rituals will mark my transition from girl to woman. Even without these traditions, I'd still be standing here in all of my womanhood. Because one person has taught me how." Her eyes shimmered with tears. "Mamá, your light illuminates everything it touches . . ."

I mouthed the rest of the speech with her. Every word made my eyes burn. Each one also packed that massive hole in my chest. Made the constant emptiness a little less heavy.

The internship couldn't get here soon enough. Then I'd stuff this void with so many fairy-tale moments that every empty crevice would fill up.

"Cas, this is beautiful." She chuckled. "But will anyone believe it's about *my* mom?"

"Tonight is about magic and—" Before I said "happily ever afters," Mami Dearest threw the doors open and barged in.

I shielded Angie from her wrath. "Señora Montes, we were just on our way down."

"Really, Castillo? Because my mother-in-law said you were running like a chicken with its head cut off looking for my daughter."

And here I thought our classmate Gianna took the title for Orange County's biggest gossipmonger—but et tu, Abuelita?

"I knew Angelica made a mistake by hiring you. We should've hired a real planner. Not a classmate playing dress-up," she hissed, conveniently forgetting her daughter was swaddled in layers of tulle, with a tiara topping her tresses. I didn't point this out, though. No way I'd ruin this moment for Angie. Or my future plans. "¡Apúrense! Everyone's waiting," Mami Dearest said.

"Mamá, stop." Angie walked around me. One small step for her. Yet she cast me a glance, as if knowing this tiny footstep was actually a huge leap. "Cas has everything under control." She faced her mother head-on. "Only someone young, like us, knows the importance of making a fashionably late entrance."

Thank you, I mouthed. Maybe there was something deeper to these parties than the glitz and glamor. Because while she was dressed like a Disney princess, she acted all warrior.

The transition must've been palpable because Mami Dearest blinked and blinked, grabbing her daughter's hands. Angie clasped them.

They held on tighter than the zippers and hems holding them in in all the right places. The soft light hit their profiles. When I tilted my head at just the right angle, they no longer resembled mother and daughter. They were people vowing to be best friends for the rest of their lives.

A tear rolled down my cheek. I let myself out as quickly as I could. Like any future fairy godmother worth her weight, a good quince planner excelled at prepping the belle of the ball to take center stage.

But they were even better at knowing when to disappear behind the curtains.

CHAPTER TWO

According to image quotes on the internet that are probably wrong, Albert Einstein's definition of insanity was doing the same thing over and over but expecting a different result. With my car's headlights beaming up the street, I drove past dark houses. The familiar jealously over their pitch-black front windows crept in. As did the stubborn hope of ours being unlit, too.

But when I pulled up to our house, lights flickered through the slats in the blinds.

All that excitement that swelled my chest like helium balloons less than an hour ago? Popped and deflated by Dad still playing video games well past midnight.

I turned off the ignition. Hung my head heavy against the steering wheel for a minute before trudging up the driveway and into our house.

I slammed the door. Hard.

The *pew-pew-pews* of blaster shots drowned it out. So did the chorus of electric twangs from a lightsaber. The only thing loud enough to cut through this noise was the voice of the world's most famous theoretical physicist ringing inside my head: *You know that spot on your vision board where your papá's acting more like a father and less like a Jedi?*

"Shut it, Einstein," I muttered on the way to the living room.

In the good ol' days, a baby-blue love seat with sunshine-yellow pillows took center stage here. After Mom, Dad stashed it inside the garage. Replaced it with a gaming chair equipped with thick, black leather pads and curved armrests he alleged were designed for "ergonomic support."

Four wheels supported the monstrosity, complete with a 360-degree swivel. He didn't bother to use that feature, though. Not even when I stopped a few feet behind it and said, "Dad, I'm home." I cleared my throat to correct myself. "I mean, I'm back."

Because After Mom, this place flipped from "home" to "house."

A few blaster shots later and still no answer. The wireless headset squashing down a spray of curls stayed glued in the direction of the screen.

Something acidic danced on my tongue, stronger than the shots of espresso we'd handed out to Angie's departing guests. Mandy's Insta grid flashed inside my mind. Especially the candid photos of fathers doting on their daughters.

Once upon a time, he'd showered Po and me with attention. That version of him only lived inside my HEA board now. I didn't know how exactly I'd get him to kiss gaming adiós, transforming him from frog to princely Dad again.

If Mandy Whitmore could train swans to perform synchronized routines for Taylor Swift's last Christmas party, and make Selena Gomez's wedding gown shift from blue to pink à la Princess Aurora as she sashayed down the aisle, surely she'd have some ideas.

Until then, I stepped in front of the TV and waved my arms. "Dad! I'm back."

He tilted his head to the left and kept playing. Apparently, my scrawny frame hardly did anything to block out the onscreen action. "It's past curfew, kiddo. Should I ground you?" he teased.

My arms flapped at my sides. "It's not curfew if it's an event, remember?"

"You're always working school events, kiddo." He groaned. Whether from me putting the *extra* back into *extracurricular* or his avatar getting zapped by a stormtrooper, I couldn't tell. "Can't you take the summer off and have some fun for a change?"

"Dad, you know I can't. I've told you I need more experience before applying to Mandy Whit—" I threw my head up.

With the tall ceilings, exposed beams, and ocean-blue and sand-colored decor, our living room fit perfectly inside a "modern beach farmhouse" mood board. Airy vibes for days. On top of the huge glass doors propped open, letting a salt breeze in.

The atmosphere pressed down on my shoulders anyway, firm and heavy.

What was the point of reminding him about the fairy godmother internship? Or that Angie's quince was my first time planning a party outside of school?

Either he was incapable of paying attention to anything or he was intent on forgetting everything. Both options forced out a sigh like an air horn on its last leg.

"Okay, okay." The lights of the game bounced off his dark hair. "No need to get all riled up. I'm proud of you, event chair."

The Monday after Po's quince-gone-wrong, I'd beelined to SBA's event-planning meeting. Every member who'd witnessed the banner debacle firsthand—or heard about it from Gianna's gossip-girl-wannabe TikTok, HotGoss—turned to stare when I asked if it was too late to join. "I just want to make sure disasters like Po's never happen again, okay?"

The event chair back then reddened, slowly nodding her

head. She tasked Callie, one of the only other freshmen in the committee, to get me up to speed. And soon, I was hooked. Turned out creating events that people remembered for the right reasons beat them being memorable for the wrong ones.

Dad's voice pulled me back into the room. "Youngest chair in Matteo High's history, eh?"

Listing my accomplishments mollified me. Slightly. "Don't you forget it." Seriously, at the very least, remember that.

"All I'm saying is all work and no play makes Jack a dull boy, Cas."

"What about all play and no work?"

Dad winced. Uh-oh. Hit by the stormtrooper's blaster again? Or by me shooting too much judgment into the joke?

Great. Besides frustration, now guilt joined the party. Dad never stopped working. Only now his gaming all-nighters never stopped either. With his candle burning at both ends, wouldn't he eventually get scorched?

Mandy's internship couldn't come any sooner. She'd teach me how to manage—better yet, streamline—her client's jam-packed schedules. Tricks I could hardly wait to use on Dad. Since I wasn't a fairy godmother's apprentice yet, I stepped closer and reached for the next best thing: the Xbox controller.

He slid away from me, clutching the wireless controller against his robed chest. Oh, so now he used the chair's wheels. "A few more minutes, Castillo. I won't stay up too late. Lo prometo."

I shook my head at his empty vow. When he saw I wasn't going to make another move to disrupt his gameplay, he sunk even deeper inside the well-worn crevices of his gaming chair and settled into the place he loved living in most: a galaxy far, far away.

Fine. If I couldn't fix his gaming habit right now, the very least I could do was clean up the mess on the TV tray. I grabbed the two empty bottles of kombucha, a bitter and yeasty tea he started chugging After Mom for its "beneficial health properties."

I didn't have to lift one to my nose for the reek of fermented ginger to make me gag. After chucking the bottles into the kitchen recycling bin, I headed down the hallway.

Woven seagrass frames covered both sides of the walls. Special family events hung here. Per usual, I stopped at my favorite.

Mom, in all her gap-toothed glory, stood in front of *Guantanamera,* her first catering truck. Sunshine glimmered on skin a few shades darker than mine. Her corkscrew curls coiled instead of frizzed (unlike mine). Dad stood next to her, kissing the side of her round cheeks. I traced a fingertip over her dimples, moving over to Dad.

No bags heavier than my utility bag under his eyes. No stubble covering up the strong jaw he'd passed down to me.

Before my stomach twisted more than the thorny brambles surrounding every cursed fairy-tale castle, I tore myself away from the picture. Stepped to the photo of them bringing a newborn Po home from the hospital. Then me. The Christmases we spent in Hawaii. Every picture onward, our smiles shined brightly.

Until they didn't.

I sped up. The only thing worse than the disappearance of our picture-perfect portraits was the snapshots hinting at the beginning of the end.

Photos tracking Mom's hair thinning. Her curvy body following suit. And finally, the single photo without her in it: the one taken a mere month and a half After.

Surprisingly, the last-minute photographer Dad found on Facebook had done a nice job of making Po's trying-on-the-tiara quince moment look natural. Minutes after the shot, the eleventh-hour DJ she'd hired off Insta announced her grand entrance. Her coming through the curtains was the cue for the confetti to rain over guests. For the huge banner to drop, proclaiming Po's happy birthday for even those sitting at the back of the banquet hall to see.

The confetti went off without a hitch. Except the slapdash printer Po found forgot the tilde.

There was lots of laughter. Mortified, I didn't take a poll to figure out if the "laughing at" guests outnumbered those "laughing with." While Po shrugged off her *happy fifteen buttholes,* her blasé attitude didn't stop the all-night muffled snickers or pitying looks. The latter stung a million times worse.

Surprise, surprise, Dad stopped hanging pictures after that.

I avoided eye contact with the blank sections of the walls, picturing Mandy Whitmore's Insta grid instead. Color-coordinated photos impeccably arranged inside a symmetrical grid. I could scroll for hours and never reach the bottom of all the graduations . . . birthday parties . . . all sorts of happily ever afters. Visualizing them made it easier for me to pretend I was strolling past these walls instead of running from them.

The faster I moved away, the more my heartbeat mellowed. The Chewbacca roars and blaster shots receded—only to be replaced by the swell of the newest K-pop melodies spilling from my door. A side of cackles followed the chorus. Whiffs of palo santo trailed right behind.

Hurricane Po was in full force tonight. Lovely.

CHAPTER THREE

Po sat against her headboard, a gold-embroidered silk duster wrapped around her curves. Stickers coated every inch of the laptop perched on her knees. The back of the screen panel blocked most of her face from view.

"When are you going to move your bed back into your room? It's right across the hallway, in case you forgot." I kicked off my loafers and threw myself onto my bed. Sinking into the mattress, I felt sixteen going on sixty . . . because as much as I wanted to tell her how awesome tonight had been, parts of my HEA began to paint themselves behind my drooping eyelids again.

I pulled a pillow over my eyes, darkening the canvas. The images slotted into place, glowing brighter.

The fairy godmother's internship.

Po back on track with college planning.

Dad, well, dad-ing again.

Po's mattress squeaked. Pounding steps. A pillow ripping off my face. The blinding light sent the pieces of my vision board scurrying down the Mom-size hole inside my chest.

"Argh! Mariposa!" Calling her by her full name meant peak annoyance. "I was just beginning to fall asleep!"

"Uh-uh-uh. Not until you tell me how the party went."

I squinted one eye at her. Having spent my entire life with my sister, I knew how to decode her moods via her lipstick shade alone. Purple translated to "extra good."

And extra-good mood implied she'd keep me up for another hour. At least. "And PS, I'm not going back to my room anytime soon. It's cozy in here with the two of us." She spiked the pillow toward the wall. "Soo . . . about the party? Dish."

Her interest reinflated the excitement balloons inside my chest, propping me onto my elbows. "It went off without a hitch." Well, none that I didn't nip in the bud. "I think I have a knack for this."

After giving me a round of applause, she skipped to her bed. Flopped onto the only patch not littered with mounds of rainbow-colored or animal-print athleisure. "You have a knack for lots of things, BTW."

She gestured toward the closet. To the exact spot where I'd stashed my old watercolor supplies. "If you're referring to me painting . . ." Another life, another me. "I prefer less messy activities to fill my time now, thank you very much. While we're on the topic of messy—"

I walked over to her, lifted my thumb to her mouth, and wiped the lipstick smudge on her lower lip. "There. Now on to the next items. Organizing," I said, shoving a pile of clothes to the edge of her bed. "And planning." I lowered myself onto the mattress. "Have you carved out time in your schedule tomorrow to start your college applications?"

She tsk-tsked. "Yesterday's history. Tomorrow's a mystery. But today's a gift." A dramatic pause. "That's why it's called the present."

I rolled my eyes. There she went, breezing past my question. Fine. Like Elsa in *Frozen*, I'd let it go—for a few minutes. "Is that an original 'Poverb'? Or did you read it off a meme?"

She clutched her chest in faux pain. "Well, if you're going to nag me about applications, then I'll return the favor. Now that you've got a fiesta in the books, can you finally apply to that internship?"

I recited the fairy godmother requirements by heart. "'Leadership position in school extracurricular.'" *Event chair—check.* "'Minimum GPA of three point five.'" *I raise you a 4.0, Ms. Whitmore.* "'Able to lift thirty pounds as needed.'" I scooped an armload of Po's clothes over my head. "'Ability to work with difficult people.'" I jutted my chin at her.

Although I wasn't really joking, it earned me a laugh anyway. "What else?" she asked.

An unwavering belief in happily ever afters. I kept that one to myself, not wanting her to rebut this prerequisite with one of her aphorisms. As if to compensate, I projected my voice loudly when I got to the end of the list. "'Party-planning experience preferred.' If this party hustle continues to take off, I can apply by the end of summer."

With my plans on track, I went back to her summer agenda. "Did you look through the college PowerPoint presentations I emailed you earlier? Both schools have great volleyball teams."

Po glanced down to a mound of sports bras. "UCI ain't going to happen, Cas. Alma even less."

Before Mom, the four of us would joke about how Po and me were like those trains that math word problems loved so much: Departing at different times. Heading to awesome collegiate destinations. Ending up at the same one, eventually.

But After Mom, Po dropped out of Future Leaders of OC. Paired the early exit with less-than-stellar grades throughout the whole of sophomore year. She did manage to stay on the volleyball team, rising to become captain of our school's nationally award-winning squad. Plus, she'd held her position at In-N-Out for over a year now.

Heading into senior year this coming fall, she'd have a semester and a half to raise her GPA back to Before Mom levels.

"Both schools are still very much in play, Po." Not to mention interchangeable for my vision board.

I pulled some of her shorts and sports bras closer, folding them into the fancy shapes I picked up from a Martha Stewart YouTube tutorial. "If you stick to my plan, you'll get into UCI or Alma. Then, when I'm a senior, it'll be my turn to do the same."

"Cas!" Po grabbed another pillow, squeezing it so hard I was shocked goose feathers didn't shoot out of it like a party popper. "Are we really going to talk about colleges now when we should celebrate you killing it at Angie's party?"

"I help arrange events and celebrations for other people. Patting myself on the back for my role in planning them, though? Hard pass."

Po put up her hands. "Fine. If you don't want to toot your own kite, then at the very least, step away from my shorts." She pulled my hands away from the Lycra. Without my thumbs to keep the fabric in place, the neatly angled folds I'd created came undone.

"These keep the chub rub away like no one's business," she said, before flinging them to the side. "C'mere. Watch this video I found."

"I've reached my quota of hairless cats playing piano," I said, groaning.

"No, no, no. I found a new lifestyle channel, and I'm obsessed." Ever since summer started, she'd slowly started swapping kitty videos for lifestyle ones.

"Don't you think it's a little shallow, indulgent even, to document slash perform your life for views?" I asked.

"Charola calling the olla black much? How is this any different than that Maisey Whitemore woman you're obsessed with?" She puckered her mouth like she'd had a swig of Dad's kombucha. "Isn't she the poster child for emceeing keggers for the overly privileged?"

I bunched some of the sheets between my fists. Reducing Mandy's genius to a ringmaster for parties of the rich and famous irked me. "Firstly, her name is Mandy Whitmore. Secondly, she convinced Bad Bunny out of retirement to perform at Governor Kardashian's inauguration. And hello, JLo's current marriage? It's not a coincidence that Mandy planned the only matrimony of hers that's lasted."

Mandy understood the power of creating magical memories. The power one perfectly crafted moment had in unfurling the next.

"Thirdly, just because her Insta is literally picture-perfect doesn't mean it's shallow." After Mom, I'd needed a reminder that beauty and joy remained in the world. That happily ever afters did, in fact, exist. Thankfully, my algorithm led me to Mandy's account.

The images didn't fill the Mom-shaped hole completely. But they did pad the sharp edges.

Huh . . . I narrowed my eyes at Po. Maybe watching cats, or the day-to-day of strangers' lives, comforted her the way Mandy's flawlessly executed events comforted me.

I released my grip on the sheets. "Okay. I'll watch the video."

She squealed and flipped the laptop over. Paused on the screen was someone our age. And totally Po's type.

Tall, dark, and extremely good-looking.

My eyes widened at the hundred thousand views before going to the gold nameplate necklace clasped around the YouTuber's neck that spelled *Paulina*. My eyeballs bugged out more at the ginormous chocolate-covered banana she was . . . eating?

Po's laughter filled the room. "Her whole shtick is going to Disneyland to try secret menu items every week. Cool, huh? We should totally go back to try some of them out. Whaddya say?" Po drummed her fingers on the keys, waiting for a response.

She'd have to keep waiting. Because the word *Disneyland* set my head spinning faster than LED projection lights.

She knew I always froze at the Matterhorn rising from behind the 5 whenever we drove down that stretch of freeway. So to have the guts to suggest watching a video, filmed inside Mom's happiest place on earth? Then follow it up with an invite to go back, in such an easy, breezy way?

Then again, this was Hurricane Po. She handled all aspects of life, especially the tough ones, by throwing caution to gale-force winds. I scratched at my blouse's lowest pearl button, trying to stave off the churn of anxiety and annoyance picking up speed inside my stomach.

Why couldn't one good day stay that way, all the way through?

She jabbed me in the ribs. "Earth to Cas! A Disney return? Secret menu items?"

After Mom, we stopped sharing two things: makeup and most feelings. Instead of telling her how I felt about returning there, I said, "Uh-huh. Secret menu items. Cuz we all know about your passion for making them at work." I rolled over, intent on heading back to my own bed. Except Po locked me in her arms, preventing my escape. "Stop!" I yelled. "I don't want to be suffocated by your flesh beasts!"

She laughed. I squirmed. "You're never going to be too old

for a cuddle." She swore she was ten years older than me, not ten months. "No matter how old you get, you'll always be my Little Cuchara."

It wasn't that I didn't want to be her little spoon anymore. But Mom's death cut me so deeply, left too many jagged edges. Made it impossible for my angles to fit snugly against her curves like they used to.

Even with the back of my elbows pushing against the round of her belly, Po squeezed tighter, pressing the side of her cheek to mine. A whiff of fries and the onions she'd probably spent all afternoon grilling curled up my nose. I inhaled deeply, hoping to catch a phantom smell of the garlic mojo Mom would make.

Nothing, and yet . . . I retracted my elbows. A little.

"Cas, Dad keeps harping on us about having fun this summer." Apparently, he'd not even spared his first-born from his spiel. "Considering he's kept on renewing our Magic Keys . . . don't you think we should, I don't know, use them?"

Thankfully I was turned in the opposite direction. That way she couldn't see me frown at the suggestion. Wrapping all the reasons I didn't want to go back to Disneyland with my hypothesis for why she did, I said, "Why? So you can run into your new crush?"

"Noo," she protested a little too forcibly. "So we can try those frozen bananas."

"I don't think my jaw can open that wide."

She cackled, squeezing me so tightly one of my vertebrae cracked.

"But seriously, think about it. We haven't been there since—" Her voice broke off. "Mom."

The space between her big cuchara and my little spoon filled with more loss and memory.

Two things I tried hardest to keep at bay.

Two things she usually blew past.

Now she wanted to start chipping away at our unspoken we-don't-talk-about-Mom rule? What the hell was happening?

Part of the reason I loved planning so much was to avoid treading unknown waters.

I extended an arm, reaching for my phone. For Mandy's grid, the life preserver to keep me from getting dragged underwater. Except Po drew back my shaky hand and used it to hit Play on the laptop.

Paulina bit into the banana. She held her lips tightly as she chewed, almost like she wanted to hold in groans of delight. A few slipped out anyway. She zoomed in on what was left of the snack, then cut away to her riding Tiana's Bayou Adventure.

"Ah, don't you miss that smell?" Po said.

Mom used to love the damp and musty scents inside the Disney water attractions. *Bromine*, she'd said. That's what made the gallons of recycled water smell so weirdly good. "Yeah." A huge gulp. "I do," I said, keeping my eyes fixed on the screen.

Paulina's log splashed through swamps, caves, and backwoods of the bayou. She didn't squeeze her red-glitter-lined eyes shut when the log tipped over waterfalls. Or when it charged down the biggie—a fifty-two-foot drop. About halfway down the dip, she shot her arms into the air. Water hit her in all the right places.

Even though she tried to keep her face still, her nostrils flared on a quick inhale. Wait, was that twitch an attempt at a smile? Paulina blotted the water from her chest.

Po angled closer. "Wow. No hands on the drop. That's tons of courage right there."

More like tons of cleavage, I wanted to say but didn't. Not when I found myself inching closer to get a better look at the all-black clothing.

The color palette (or lack thereof) was another interesting juxtaposition. Not only against the rich hues of the attractions and throng of guests she moved past after the ride, but especially next to the Winnie the Pooh she took a selfie with.

No amount of lip biting could bridle her smile then. Stepping away from the character, she flipped long locks behind her shoulders, like she was pleased that at least the grin hadn't grown wide enough to show teeth.

She ended the vlog with a walk down Main Street, U.S.A., pointing out some of its secret history. How the shade of the bricks paving the ground was meant to resemble red carpets welcoming guests to the park. Her voice lowered a bit when she talked about how several names painted on the windows were dedications to Disney family members. Like the *Walt* on the last window.

His older sibling, Roy, put it there so Walt would always have a view of Sleeping Beauty's castle. Paulina snapped another selfie, capturing the castle in the background.

Like we'd done with Mom countless times. Despite the summertime heat slipping in through the windows, every inch of me froze.

"I know it'll be hard to go back," Po said.

A banquet hall of emotions swirled inside me. At its center, a tango between loss and fear. Could I really go back to the hub of so many memories?

"C'mon, Cas. You can't tell me this"—she pointed to the screen, to Paulina—"doesn't look fun."

"If that's what you're calling it these days," I said.

Her chuckle swelled to a laugh. "Aren't, like, half of our school events—events *you're* in charge of planning—Disney themed?"

"'Under the Sea.' 'A Whole New World.' 'Villains Night.'" The words tumbled out without permission. If our SBA events weren't straight-up Disney rip-offs, they were fairy-tale adjacent for sure.

"Your subconscious must've soaked it up with every visit there."

Dang it. Po was right. Over a decade of Disney-movie marathons with Mom, semesters filled with trips with her to the park—all of it had embedded into my cells. Dormant but not gone, like a dragon sleeping beneath a castle.

Not that I would admit any of this to Po.

"Since that Mandy woman's office is in OC, I bet her parties are also Disney inspired," she said.

I dragged the laptop closer. Split the screen by opening another tab and scrolled through Mandy's grid.

The latest wedding took place at a chateau. The bride donned heels that'd make Cinderella do a double take. Of course, there was the matter of Mandy calling herself a fairy godmother.

And she made HEAs come true.

Apparently, acing AP precalculus bore no correlation to being able to put two and two together. Because clearly SBA wasn't the only Disney stan. I glanced at Po.

"I'm in no rush to go back to the place we spent so many days with Mom." A sigh blew out of me, like helium shooting out of the pinched end of a balloon. "Including our last good day with her."

Po nodded. After what felt like an eternity, she said, "Same." One word, yet her voice shook with the intensity of a magnitude seven quake. "Except, what if . . ." She gestured to the screen. "What if we adopted the adage 'The difference between a former Splash Mountain and an anthill is our perception'?"

"Molehill," I said, correcting her latest miswording.

"The specific word doesn't matter. What matters is our ability to look at Disneyland less like a triggering place and more like"—her eyes flicked to the section of the screen filled with Mandy's grid—"an opportunity for future growth."

It was impossible to deny going back would serve as good prep for future Pinterest boards. Ones I could show to classmates. And ones to attach to my Mandy application when the time finally came.

Hmm . . . If I could change my outlook on the park from past hurt to future planning like Po suggested, would I be able to handle venturing back? "RSVPing 'maybe' to your invite."

"If that logic isn't enough to get a yes, have you ever heard the saying 'Happy sister, happy life'?" Po readjusted herself, jamming her knees into my kidneys.

"You really want to check out this vlogger in person, don't you?"

"No, I want to hang with you. But also, yeah? A crush a day keeps the doctor away."

"I'm pretty sure it's *apples*."

"No apples are as juicy as—"

I yanked the laptop away from her and slammed it shut before her drool short-circuited it. "My virgin ears!"

She narrowed her eyes as if to say, *Your virgin everything,* before bursting with laughter again. "Last time I checked, it wasn't illegal to have a crush. You should try it sometime."

Between making these high school events happen, growing my side hustle, college planning for both of us . . . my schedule didn't allow for a crush. Even if I wanted one.

My stomach growled, catching another whiff of the scents clinging to her skin. "Hey, did you sneak any burgers home tonight?"

Her body tensed.

"Fries? A shake?" Planning extravaganzas didn't translate to feasting with the guests. Usually she brought me a literal midnight snack when her shifts overlapped with my events. "Anything?"

The mattress squeaked as she peeled away from me. Propping herself against the headboard, she said, "Promise you won't get mad."

I rolled over to face her. "I promise nothing."

She grunted, wiping the purple off her lips with the back of her hand. Reaching over to her nightstand, she dipped her fingers into a bowl of lipsticks. "I didn't bring animal-style fries home. Or a Neapolitan shake."

My pulse drumrolled against my temples as she coated her mouth red.

As in code red.

"I got fired, Cas." She gulped. "The ketchup and Thousand Island train is over."

CHAPTER FOUR

One of the shiniest centerpieces of her resume, gone. I grabbed the laptop and opened another tab.

"Are you really not going to ask what happened?" Po said, slingshotting a sports bra at my head.

"Busy here trying to salvage your future college applications." And by extension, rescuing a component of my Torres family HEA vision board. I chewed my lips, scrolling through our high school's summer internship and jobs portal.

"'Persistently going against the pre-set menus,'" she grumbled. "'Too many onions on fries'? Is that even possible?"

Onions weren't just a staple in Cuban cuisine. Back when Cuban food rotated regularly inside our kitchen, Mom made sure they were our household's major food group. I peeked over the screen's rim. "Look. I agree. There can *never* be enough onions. But, Po. You can't make up your own menu whenever you feel like it."

She blew the ends of her bob off her face. "Whatever. What does my manager know about food anyway?"

Typical Po, blowing past everything. She patted my hand when she caught me balling her sports bra between my fists.

"Chill out. I'll find something else this summer."

"Really? Because the deadlines for any UCI- or Alma-worthy

extracurriculars are long gone." My voice came out harsh, exactly as intended.

For once she stayed silent. The enormity of this loss probably, finally, sinking in.

"I'll take care of this, okay?" I said. Fixing her future college admission situation would (fingers crossed) be way easier than solving Dad's current gaming one. "In the meantime, you're helping at the school fundraiser this weekend."

Her jaw dropped. "Seriously?"

Nodding, I crossed the room to get my planner. I flipped to the tab labeled *Hot Dog / Dog Wash*. With my pencil, I went down the list of members. "Cari dropped out," I lied.

Po crossed her arms. "What? Idle hands are Po's playground, or something?"

I neither confirmed nor denied her suspicions. "Who knows? You may like working SBA events. If you do, I'll use my clout on the committee to pull some strings. Get you in for the rest of the summer." OC's main currencies were nepotism and cash. I had no qualms about using the former to help my sister.

"Fine." She straightened her posture. "I'll do it. *If* you go to Disneyland with me tomorrow."

"I don't negotiate with—" A string of phone notifications cut in before I finished.

"Who's blowing you up at this hour?" Po teased, looking toward my bed.

I grabbed my phone. "Angie tagged me in quince photos." Hashtagged lots of them #best #partyplanner #ever. Classmates I've known since kindergarten finally followed me back on Insta. Even SBA's event account had more followers than this morning.

The next tag broadened my smile into a grin. "And Hot Goss's IG reposted a TikTok." Nine times out of ten, Gianna's not-so-anonymous accounts featured student scandals. Once in a blue moon, though . . .

> Is our event chair ready to sit on the party-planner throne? From school proms to after-hours fiestas, sure looks that way! #letsgetthepartystarted

New DMs flooded my inbox. One classmate requested a planner for a younger sibling's period party. Another wanted help for their graduation reception. Someone from AP chemistry asked about an I-got-my-first-car bash.

More notifications flashed across my screen. None exploded as intensely as the fireworks going off inside me. These events could pad my portfolio . . . But would they be the type of party experience Mandy required?

I went to her account again, scanning her grid once more. The fireworks died out. Another big birthday party. That's what I needed to pique her attention and land the fairy godmother internship.

On the phone's next ping, every atom of oxygen flew from my lungs.

"Do I need to run into the kitchen and grab a brown paper bag?" Po asked. "Because it sounds like you're hyperventilating."

"Melina just messaged me." I showed Po the screen so she could confirm this wasn't a dream.

"'Maybe you can plan my sweet sixteen?'" Po squealed before continuing to read off the screen. "'I want it to be bigger than Angie's quince. Chat about it soon? Eye emoji, celebrating-face emoji!'" She threw an armful of clothes toward the ceiling, letting them tumble around us like streamers.

For once, I curbed the instinct to clean up her mess.

"Operation side hustle officially has liftoff," she said.

"To infinity and beyond." I cracked up at the Disney reference slip.

Po slapped her hand on my shoulder. "That settles it. We're celebrating. Me. You. And Disneyland."

Wide awake at 3:00 a.m., thanks to Po's snoring. Well, maybe not completely because of that.

After Mom, sleeping soundly didn't come as easily. I pulled the duvet over my head. Under the covers, I could work without waking Po. And take shelter from any more Mom-related thoughts.

I pointed the phone's flashlight at my planner. Flipped to a blank page.

Once upon a time, I used to love these wide-open canvases. Now the vacant space gnawed at me. It reminded me too much of that void inside my chest.

"Time to fill you up," I whispered. At the top of the page, I wrote *Melina party prep.*

If Angie was the big fish of the freshmen, Mel was the queen bee of the sophomores. Booking two big parties to follow up Hot Goss's boost? Word of my side hustle would spread faster than a California wildfire. All before Mandy's application window closed.

"Let's get a better sense of your aesthetics," I whispered, scrolling down Mel's IG grid. Sapphire oceans, cobalt clothes, teal hair. Lots of velvet headbands crowning her locks. More than half of the pictures featured her on spiraled staircases, posing with a white bunny named Alice.

Through the Looking-Glass / Wonderland vibes, I jotted.

I tapped on her stories next. Rubbed my eyes waiting for them to clear, but nope.

Tomorrow, she was going to "Disneyland Day It Up."

I thanked my lucky stars. Instead of messaging her Pinterest pics, I could show her my ideas and pitch my services in person if—

If I stepped foot into Mom's happiest place on earth.

Something washed over me. Not so much the firework sensations from earlier. More like the cloying plumes of smoke that lingered after a pyrotechnics show.

I pulled the covers back down. Sucked in mouthfuls of the breeze coming through the window. For a few seconds, the room didn't seem to have enough air, until . . .

Honeysuckle? The scent probably wafted in from our next-door neighbor's hedges. I hugged the pillow. Pretended I was melting into Mom's arms, sniffing the top notes from her favorite perfume.

"Is this your way of telling me it's okay to go back?" I whispered deep into the pillowcase. "That it's okay to go back without you?"

I would've preferred dipping a toe into the shallow end first: watching more of that vlogger's videos, or going on a trip to Downtown Disney.

Still.

With Po at my side and with "book Mel's party" on my agenda, maybe I'd have the floaties I needed before diving into the deep end. I let go of the pillow and rolled onto my side.

A folded arm bookended one side of Po's face. A leopard-print sports bra, the other. Her mouth sucked in and blew away crumpled tresses with every snore.

My sister was definitely not the safest flotation device around. Except the only way to apply to the internship *this* summer—to have Mandy teach me how to turn fantasies into a reality now—was to get another party in the books. Stat.

Like Cinderella's tattered dress turning into a ball gown, my previous RSVP of "maybe" transformed into a "yes."

CHAPTER FIVE

A marching band rumbled in the distance. Hooves clomped on the concrete as draft horses towed a trolley. The murmur of the crowd. The cacophony barely drowned out my pounding heart.

Po grabbed my hand. We zigzagged through the horde of park-goers. With her leading the way, dodging strollers, wheelchairs, and streamers pulled taut by helium balloons, it was easier to keep my gaze away from our old haunts lining Main Street, U.S.A.

Memories flashed through my mind anyway: chowing down fried pickles, having our portraits done at the silhouette studio, watching a slew of parades, getting our fortunes told.

Granted, I had to look up and glare at Esmeralda, the "psychic" in the fortune teller booth inside the Penny Arcade. *What a hack you turned out to be, Esme.*

Mom never got better.

"You okay?" Po asked.

"Yup." Despite the ache in my chest, I couldn't deny being proud of my ability to stand here without dissolving into a puddle of tears.

"Cool, then I'll be right back." Po bolted into the nearest

bathroom without asking if I needed to go, too. While Po peed, I prepped.

Leaning against a railing, I checked Mel's IG again.

Eek! Her story from three minutes ago showed her slipping into one of Pirates' boats. Hurry up, I texted Po.

Po

Hold your ponies.

I couldn't hold my "ponies." Not with the Pinterest boards on my phone burning holes in my palms. If memory served me right, Pirates took ten to fifteen minutes.

HURRY! I texted again. If Po hustled, I'd have ample opportunity to run over there and "bump" into Mel right as she exited the ride. Then show off the *Alice in Wonderland*–themed aesthetics I curated for her—and voilà, book her party.

I took a victory breath. Scents of popcorn, corn dogs, and sunscreen curled around me. The enchantment cast by the smells was so intoxicating I couldn't help but pull my face from my phone screen.

I swallowed hard.

I'm really back here.

Victorian facades. Pastel painted porches. Perfectly carved awnings topping every store. I'd forgotten how beautiful these buildings were. Especially the one up ahead, towering over everything inside the park's central hub.

The Sleeping Beauty Castle.

Had Mom named me Castillo after this one? Or some other she'd seen in a travel magazine? There must've been a reason why she chose *castle* for my namesake.

I never got the chance to ask her about it.

To distract myself from how much the tightness in my chest

grew, I busied myself by counting some of the castle's blue and lavender bricks. Studied the way their perfect alignment formed tall towers, letting the pink turrets climb high, every peak racing to reach a cloudless sky.

Gold pixie dust sprinkled the center of the castle's cobalt-shingled roof. Surely, a present from Tinker Bell, rewarding the castillo for remaining upright and sturdy, no matter the weather.

I snapped a picture of it. To add to my collection of mood board prep, obviously.

Not because the building could be a nice image to paint. My watercolor days were long gone.

The hard thumps of Po's combat boots cut through my thoughts. She bounced down the steps with more bronzer contouring her already ample cleavage and a new coat of lipstick.

Pink lipstick. Despite myself, I smiled at the freshened look for her not-so-secret flirting agenda. Too bad her plan played second to mine. "Let's head to New Orleans Square first."

Po arched a brow. "I'm shocked that you, Miss Always Thinking About Mañana, don't want to hit up Tomorrowland first." With hands still wet with sink water, she latched on to my arm and tugged me onward. "C'mon. Space Mountain."

I dug my loafers into the ground. "I'm equally shocked that you, Miss Refuses to Grow Up, don't want to go on Peter Pan's Flight first." While she cracked up, I pushed my game plan. "Pirates."

Po let go of my arm. "It's impossible for you to go with the flow, isn't it?"

"Considering we live at the beach, shouldn't you know that eighty percent of lifeguard rescues are directly attributed to getting caught in a current? Going with the flow isn't all it's cracked up to be."

Po huffed. Her fingers disappeared inside her fringed cross-body purse. Her eyes shot down to what I assumed was her phone. Was she checking her crush's YouTube channel for a live stream or something?

Huh. I should do the same thing.

Argh. Mel was already off Pirates . . . and heading to Space Mountain. "You know what? On second thought, let's have it your way. Nothing like a roller coaster to start our day."

Po gasped so loud that people—and the ducks canvassing the ground for broken-off pieces of churros—turned in our direction.

"What? Isn't this what you wanted?" I tapped my loafer against the ground. "For me to 'go with the flow'?"

Her eyes narrowed at me. Then slowly, any suspicions gave way to an enormous smile. "I knew I'd rub off on you eventually, Little Cuchara." She trotted off. "To the flow!"

"To the flow." Luckily for me, I was directing the current exactly where I needed it to go.

The soles of our shoes squeaked to a stop as we narrowly avoided crashing into a cast member. "Try back later," he said, stringing a chain across Space Mountain's entrance.

"I forgot how often the rides break down here," Po said.

"Same." I sighed. "Well, all that running made me hungry. Let's grab a snack while we figure out what ride to try next." In other words, figure out where Mel was headed since I'd missed her again.

"Yes." Po bolted toward the food carts. "Pretzels, por favor."

"One of your YouTube hottie's favorite snacks, I presume?" I teased, hustling to keep up.

Po glanced back. "Dog's outta the bag, eh? You might think

looking for Paulina's like trying to find a needle in a camel's back, but hey." She broke her stride, stepping into the back of the very long pretzel-cart line. "My chances of bumping into her are as good as your chances of bumping into Melina."

"I'm that obvious, huh?"

She shrugged. "Takes one to know one."

"Hey!" I held out my palm to high-five her. "You actually got that saying right."

Her hand slapped mine, the warm contact momentarily making me forget I was supposed to be on a mission. "I think I got this right, too." Po chewed her top lip, erasing most of the pink makeup. "You can totally tell me if I went too far."

Before I could ask her what the hell she was talking about, she grabbed my hand.

Did she want another high five? Or to tug me forward because the pretzel line moved again? Instead, she placed something inside my palm. Curled her fingers around mine before I could sneak a peek.

Cool to the touch. Smooth surface.

I didn't have to unfurl my fist to know what it was.

The parade's music down Main Street, the squeals ebbing and flowing from the Matterhorn above us—every sound pressed around me. Exactly the way my grip did across the circular button.

One by one, I pried my fingers open.

There, in the middle of my hand, was a button of Goofy holding a bunch of balloons. Underneath him, bold font said, I'M CELEBRATING.

My fingers skimmed the blank space below it, an empty slot to write something celebratory.

"'Life's a collection of tiny celebrations.'" It slipped out without meaning to.

"Mom's fave motto." Po's lighter skin flushed. She fanned her face with both hands. "It's hotter than a witch's tit out here."

Yes, it was. Except I doubt the bright sun caused this much sweat to dot her forehead.

I held the button to my chest as if that could calm my pulse. But its touch only unlocked more memories. Like the first stop whenever Mom brought us here—before any ride or (Po's) bathroom break—would always be Main Street's City Hall to get four of these *I'm Celebrating* pins.

Three for us to fill out during our visit. One for Dad to fill out later.

My mind flashed to the olden days of Po scrawling *boobs* or other body parts. To me jotting the A on whatever test I'd just aced. Most of the time, Mom wrote *mi familia*, in cursive so fancy it could double as calligraphy. After work, Dad would always scribble *Jedi Knights* or something *Star Wars* related.

Mom stored our pins in a huge Danish cookie tin that doubled as our kitchen's fruit platter. Someone must've accidentally thrown it away after the wake, because the next morning, I couldn't find it.

The people in front of us moved. I took a giant step forward, putting much-needed distance between me and that day.

I fiddled with the back of the button, trying to pin it onto my blouse. "Ow!" I stuck my finger in my mouth, pressing my tongue against the pierced skin.

The sting of the lance eased. The sting of everything else . . . not so much.

"Hey, before you prick yourself and pull a Sleeping Beauty on me," Po said, rubbing my shoulder, "you have to write something on it."

I chuckled despite myself, eyeing the crowd. No cute guy

around to kiss me for the first time. To wake me up from this bad dream, let alone break the curse of memory.

"I don't have a Sharpie." Lies. I had one stashed inside my utility bag, right next to my pencil.

"No worries." She grabbed the pin from me before reaching into her cross-body. "I have something better." She uncapped the black liquid eyeliner with her teeth. The marker's felt tip squeaked against the pin as she wrote across its surface. "Plus, I even know what you should write. Ta-da!" She pushed the button back into my hand.

I'M CELEBRATING: *Getting the Mandy Whitmore Internship!!!*

Probably in response to my eyebrows drawing together, she said, "Believing is seeing," as she shuffled up the pretzel line.

There she went again, mixing up her pearls of hashtag-y wisdom, and yet . . . backward and all, her latest mix-up struck in all the right places.

If I believed I'd book more parties, maybe it'd sprinkle me with enough boldness to convince Matteo Beach High's most popular to trust me with their special occasions. And eventually, my resume would teem with enough proof of my fairy godmother skills to win over Mandy Whitmore.

I threw my arms around Po. She hugged me back so hard it dammed off everything else. Hunting for internet crushes. Melina. Getting on the next ride. Salty treats. All of it sunk to the bottom of our agendas. Even when the line moved again and the people from behind tried to jostle us forward, we stayed locked in our embrace.

For one shiny second, this moment was Disneyland's main attraction.

The vendor handed Po a giant Mickey-shaped pretzel. "Sorry, folks—that's it for this batch," he said, placing a SOLD OUT sign on the front of the display case. A chorus of unhappy groans rippled behind us.

Po shimmied over to a small bench and plopped down. She coated her lips with sticky, clear gloss. Not the best choice before wolfing down a pretzel coated with crushed Flamin' Hot Cheetos. "Before you bite into it," I said, walking over to join her, "let's send a pic to Dad." I offered her a makeup wipe while gesturing to her mouth.

"Good thinking," she said, handing the pretzel over before taking the wipe. "You're better with the aesthetic stuff." Instead of removing the gloss, she used the wipe to sharpen the contour lines amplifying her cleavage.

Typical. I took a few steps closer to Space Mountain. Held up the Mickey-shaped pretzel. Made sure both the mouse ears and the white spired dome of the ride fit perfectly inside the frame before snapping a pic.

We took you up on the summer-fun sales pitch. Wish you were here. I hit Send.

Gray bubbles appeared immediately.

They vanished just as quickly.

If anything could push past the lump in my throat, it'd surely be a mouthful of Cheeto-dusted and cream-cheese-filled dough. I lifted the pretzel to my lips.

Po's voice rang from behind "Cas, wait!"

I pivoted back. Po's duster flapped across her curves like wings. The soles of her boots squeaked when she stopped in front of me.

She grabbed my hand—no, the pretzel—and snatched it away.

"I was about to eat that." I reached for it. But she kept it high over her head.

"Someone else might need it more." Her chest rose and fell as she tried to catch her breath.

"What are you—"

She jutted her chin over my shoulder.

"Omigawd, omigawd, omigawd," I chanted—the mantra reserved for the shocked and awed.

"I know," Po whisper-squealed in my ear.

She'd been right. Believing *was* seeing. Because there, cutting through the crowd, with rays of sunshine falling on her like personal spotlights, strode that YouTuber.

And she was headed straight toward us.

CHAPTER SIX

Paulina's eyes darted from Po to me before landing on the pretzel clutched between Po's fingers. "Mike said he sold you the last one."

Of course she was on a first-name basis with the vendors here. She was a Disneyland food vlogger.

"I don't know if there's a non-bizarre way to ask this, but would it be possible to borrow your pretzel for a few minutes?" She made praying hands. "I promise I'll give it back. After I take a bite from it for a vlog. Maybe two?" She leaned forward.

Po drew back. Anyone else would've thought she was putting some distance between her and a stranger's wild request. In reality, she probably didn't want Paulina to hear how hard her heart was probably thudding."You know what? Never mind." Paulina shook her head. Her gold hoops bounced against her sleek, black hair. "I'm acting like a complete weirdo. Pretend this never happened." She settled into that stoic look I recognized from her vlog and turned on wedged Jordans.

Po opened and closed her mouth like she wanted to say something but couldn't. She stuck her free hand into her cross-body. Lipstick tubes knocked against each other. When her hand came back up, nada.

Apparently, the shade for *say something quick* didn't exist in her palette yet.

Po's squirming at Paulina's retreat tugged at something. Fragments of a past Disney day rose to my mind.

Mom, Po, and I sitting on a curb watching the Main Street Electrical Parade. Instead of taking in the hundreds of lights covering so many fantastic floats, or reveling in the soundtracks of so many iconic Disney songs, Mom lasered in on the park-goer next to us: Cuban legend Andy García. Not getting a selfie with him filled our household with soliloquies of regret which lasted for days.

Shyness didn't necessarily run in our family. Still. A huge gap separated imagining how something's going to unfold and it actually happening in real life.

Right now, Po floundered at that juncture.

Paulina disappeared into the crowd. Po's sigh rang hollow, like a piñata devoid of any candy. My pulse beat against my eardrums. I imagined it thumping in Morse code: *fix this now.*

So what if Po scoring a selfie wasn't big enough to include in my HEA? Shouldn't I try to help her anyway?

It'd put a smile on her face and earn me sisterly brownie points. The latter would come in handy when I nagged her about college applications again. The former I simply liked to see.

I plucked the pretzel from her hand and pushed through the crowd. "Paulina, wait!"

She turned, her hair swishing like layers of a prom dress. I handed her the pretzel. "Be our guest." Po's combat boots clomped behind me. I sneaked a wink at her as she sidled up next to me. "Anything to help one of our favorite Disney vloggers."

If Po was shocked by how smoothly my lie slipped out, she didn't say anything. Her brain was probably still busy rebooting.

"Wow, thank you." Paulina pursed her lips like she did in her videos. Slowly, she released a tiny smile. Did the small favor from a "fan" begin to crack her laid-back veneer? Or was it Po's Jack Skellington–size grin at her? "I swear I'm not this big of a weirdo," she added, her attention on Po. "Most of the time."

Po coughed out a laugh, which made Paulina's smile grow. The wattage of her pearly whites outshone the Matterhorn's snowy peaks.

Oh boy. If I looked up *swooning* in the dictionary, I'd find a picture of Po right then. Her giddiness was so palpable, so uncharacteristically cute, that I pretended to snap a picture of Buzz Lightyear dancing, while in reality, I captured my sister.

A photo like this needed to go on a "flirty" mood board. And if we had still lived in the Before era, hell, maybe it would have even been turned into a watercolor portrait.

While I slipped my phone back into my utility bag, Po rummaged for something in her cross-body. She lifted a studded tube of lipstick. Glossy coral.

Her color of choice to summon courage.

"Are you reviewing the new pretzel for a vlog?" Aaannnd she was back. "Don't new flavors drop every week?"

"Yes. They do." Paulina's voice bubbled more in real life. "And I really need to film today's because Mom wants me to meet with—" A shadow flickered across her dark eyes.

If I had to pin-the-tail-on-the-donkey on it, maybe sadness? Regret?

Was that why she lined her eyelids with so much sparkle? An attempt at convincing her subscribers that all that glittered *was,* in fact, gold?

"Never mind about my mom," she said, lifting the pretzel. "And sorry for the snack-snatching divaness, but as the great philosopher Wayne Gretzky once said, 'You miss one hundred percent of the shots you don't take.'"

Po's side-glance screamed, *She's fluent in quotes?*

Mine: *Plus, she got it right?*

"I don't know how to thank you for this," Paulina said.

"How about letting us watch you film your vlog?" Po said, batting her eyelashes.

"Deal." Once more, Paulina's smile seemed reserved only for Po.

I took one step back, then another. While Po was occupied with this flirt fest, she wouldn't even notice my momentary absence.

By the looks of Mel's newest story, she was about to board Star Tours. If I loitered around its exit, maybe I'd finally be able to cross off *book another party.*

Even if Po had no idea I was giving them the slip, Paulina sure did.

"Hold on." She threw her hands up. Flamin' Hot Cheeto dust swirled around her like red-orange confetti. "You're. A. Party. Planner. At. Mandy. Whitmore?" Her voice rose on every word. "Didn't she just do JLo's sixth wedding?!"

"Actually, it was her fifth." My eyebrows shot higher than the Space Mountain's spires. Why did she think I already worked for Mandy?

Po draped an arm across my shoulders and flicked my *I'm Celebrating* pin.

Oh—that's why.

"Technically, I'm the event chair for Matteo Beach High's student body association—" A group of squealing kids rushed past us. Mom and Dad always harped on never selling ourselves short, so I continued. "But yes, I've recently started party planning on the side." I waited until the Monorail finished whooshing by before straightening her misunderstanding.

Only she jumped in again. "No way. I'm about to have a quinceañera. Mandy Whitmore and Associates are La Mera Mera's top choice for planners, FYI."

Huh. Maybe it was the clothes and makeup that made Paulina look older than the cusp of fifteen.

"In her words, 'We are *rich* now, PauPau. Una fiesta grandísima.'" She brushed Cheeto dust off her hands. "That's the type of party that's expected of us.'"

"Urgh," Po said.

I nodded. Through dealing with Angie's Mami Dearest, I'd experienced these displays of newfound wealth myself. As much as the phenomenon soured my stomach, better a showy mamá than no mom, so.

Paulina continued imitating her mother's Mexico City (I presumed) accent and said, "'Can you imagine how jealous a Whitmore-planned extravaganza would make Tía Mari?'" She tugged at her gold necklace. "Come to find out Mandy has a two-year-long wait list."

"The gestation period for the African elephant," Po said, balling her fists in commiseration.

"That's exactly what I said." Paulina shared a look with Po before shining her attention on me. "Can you believe the wait?" She face-palmed, then quickly composed herself. "Of course you can—you work there." She inched closer. "Waiting blows so much, doesn't it? It'd mean so much to me and my mom if, um, you and I maybe . . ." She ran her tongue across her teeth.

Ah, I got it. Tiptoeing around asking for another favor? One much bigger than a Mickey Mouse–shaped pretzel.

I dropped my gaze to the *I'm Celebrating* button and shook my head. "Paulina, I'm not—"

"Say no more—I get it," she said, rushing in again. "You're not an associate planner yet. That's fine. I prefer working with people my age anyway. Considering how many culturally specific rituals quinceañeras include, a fellow Latine planner's a must, too. Except—" She fidgeted with the cursive script on her necklace. "I also want it to be experimental. And innovative."

"Well, what do you know? *Innovative* happens to be the middle name of my talented younger sister, Castillo Torres," Po said. "I'm Po."

"*Mariposa*, I don't have a middle name." It was easier to correct my sister than a stranger.

Suddenly, Po knocked against me and reached into my bag without permission.

What were her fingers poking around for? Considering her nose was starting to look shinier than her lip gloss, maybe the oil blotters?

That was when my soul exited my body.

Po not only pulled out my planner, but also started flipping to the back of it.

After SBA events, I posted a few pics to the event committee's socials. For my personal—and private—use however, I sometimes sketched said pics on these blank pages.

My tongue fell out of my mouth. It didn't hang all the way out like the Pluto walking by. But enough to make it hard to ask how she knew about this secret section.

And even harder to protest Po inviting Paulina to take a look.

With a fingernail, Paulina traced the messy outlines of Zooey and Julie getting crowned homecoming royalty on the football field. The sharp (and not perfectly drawn) angles of Callie's face, smiling at the wad of one-dollar bills after the winter bake sale. The hasty sketch of Sarah surrounded by softball bats topped with pink flowers while Ishaan was on bended knee, promposing junior year.

The drawings were more rough outlines than accurate likenesses. I'd gone wild with the shapes and proportions. The grays in the color palette were brighter or darker depending on how hard I'd pressed on the pencil.

A silly art hobby carried over from what felt like a different lifetime. A pastime I should've stopped when I hung up watercoloring.

But here it was, out in the open.

Somehow, I lifted a loafer. Purposefully stepped on Po's foot on the way to retaking the planner. Surrounded by little kids, she was forced to swallow a curse.

I let a laugh loose. Paulina looked up.

While reaching for the planner, I extended my phone. "Here. The mood boards and Canva collages are much more professional examples of my work than those drawings."

Paulina gave the planner back but made zero attempts to take the phone. "Your sketches . . ." Her voice was as delicate as crepe paper. "Are amazing."

Mom used to always say the same thing. My fingertips, especially the recently pin-pricked one, tingled. "Really?"

"Yes, really." The sparkle in Paulina's eyes almost encouraged me to hand the planner back so she could flip through more.

I shook my head, snapping out of it. "I haven't taken an art class since eighth grade." I wiggled the phone at her. "Like I mentioned, these are higher-caliber."

What better way to boost my confidence before showing them to Mel, or any of my other classmates, than by getting the stamp of approval from someone as glamorous as Paulina?

"No. I don't need to see those." She perked up. "My mind's already made. I want you to plan my party."

All of Tomorrowland folded in on me. When I regained the ability to speak, I said, "NO."

I should've known Po would choose that exact moment to yell "YES!"

CHAPTER SEVEN

"Both of us need to confer for a minute, Paulina." Po grabbed me by the elbow. "Ohhh, look at that! The line for Space Mountain opened up again. Two birds, one rock. Feel free to vlog without us. Wouldn't want that pretzel to get cold."

"I'll be waiting." Paulina's eyes twinkled. And no—it didn't come from her glitter eyeliner.

Po's knees wobbled, yet she somehow mustered the strength to drag me through the line's entrance.

I shook off her grip and charged up the ramp, outpacing her and this new mess she'd created. "What's with showing her my sketches without my consent?" I hissed over the crowd's hum. "And telling her I'd plan her quince just to keep flirting with her? You don't even know if she's into girls."

"I guess we'll find out, because you *are* doing her party." Po's face flushed. "Who cares if I want to keep flirting with her? That doesn't mean this opportunity doesn't benefit you, either. You know what they say . . ." She wiggled her eyebrows. "What's good for the goose is good for the duck."

I tore a hand through my frizzing hair. "No one says that. Plus, the only reason she wants me to plan her party is because she thinks I work for Mandy."

A buzzer sound flew from her lips. "Wrong. She's impressed by your instinctual party-planning visions."

"Let's test your hypothesis, then. I'll go over there right now and tell her I'm not a Mandy intern." Yet. "Wanna bet how fast she revokes her offer?" I turned around, ready to plow through the suddenly packed line.

Po snatched the back of my blouse. "Not so fast, Little Cuchara. There's only one way out of this line."

Before I could protest, her hand traveled to mine. I was caught off guard by how much of my frustrations she dislodged with that little pump she gave me.

"Fine," I said. With the long queue of people crammed behind us, I supposed the most efficient way out was through. "But the second we get off this thing, I'm telling her I'm not doing it." I yanked my hand away. "You better keep your trap shut this time."

I stepped into the hallway leading to the indoor portion of the queue. The sci-fi-inspired melodies of the ride's soundtrack emanated from invisible speakers. A perfect excuse to refrain from arguing with her. Soothing blue-and-purple light glowed through the last hallway, beckoning us into the loading area.

We zipped through the last part of the queue in record time, but the park guests in the Lightning Lane moved even quicker. Some of them had started to pile into the designed-to-look-like-a-rocket-ship roller coaster. The coaster hissed and clicked, its riders cheering as it took off without us.

Po must've glimpsed my jealousy. She pointed to the next group jetting past us and said, "That's what I was trying to say. Paulina could be your 'lightning lane' to the internship." She leaned over the railing, holding the weight of her chin on the back of her hand. "If Mandy's as fancy as you say, she'll probably care more about quality over quantity. Booking a niche famous YouTuber's quince?" She gave a little whistle. "She'd have to be impressed by that more than by doing a few classmates' shindigs, no?"

I hated how my pulse quickened. At this rate, Po should fill that empty extracurricular slot on her schedule with debate team. Because she was convincing me this party could be a good—no, great—idea.

"Even if Mandy does care about quantity over quality," Po continued, "Paulina's channel—"

With Paulina's subscriber count flashing inside my head, I blurted, "Would be the best advertising ever."

She tapped her temple. "Bingo."

We weren't even on the ride yet, and already I felt like I was flying. Equally as quickly, my conscience dragged me down to earth again. "I mean, no. Not doing it."

We stepped through the turnstile and slid into the rocket ship's seats. A cast member pushed down the padded safety bar across my stomach, then Po's. "What do you mean 'no'? This could totally work."

The tightness in my stomach began to build. Not because of the lap bar digging into my belly button, either.

The rocket thrust forward. Gained speed.

As much as I didn't want it to—so did Po's proposal.

A swirling solar field of lights flashed over the walls. I imagined similar projections swirling over Paulina and her court. The space soundtrack swelled, but all I heard was a waltz.

The coaster nose-dived down, shattering my fantasy.

"No, it can't!" I yelled over the *click-click-click* of the ride climbing up the tracks again. "Need I remind you that the Lightning Lane's pay-for-play? Are you suggesting I foot this masquerade's bill with my moral fiber?"

I couldn't gauge Po's reaction. Not when the only light came from flickering stars. While the coaster zipped through the cosmos, I went through more reasons on my this-is-a-bad-idea list.

"What if Paulina finds out I'm not an intern yet?"

Po answered with a scream. So did everyone on the coaster as we plunged down another dip. I let loose a shriek of my own. An appropriate reaction to my planner reputation getting ruined.

"Even worse," I yelled. "What if this gambit got back to Mandy?"

No more parties. No more fairy godmother's apprentice robes. No master class in creating HEAs.

The road back to my family's own HEA, lost forever.

I white-knuckled the lap bar, holding on for dear life. Po, on the other hand, squealed with glee. "Nail the party—which you will because you're *you*—and you'll get the internship." If anyone could continue gabbing through the g-force of the next set of twists and turns, it was her. "As far as Paulina and Mandy go, what they don't know won't kill them."

She howled through the next drop. "If that doesn't convince you, what about '*With great risks come great rewards*'?"

It took all my neck muscles to face her. "You got that pearl of wisdom right."

"I'm right about lots of things. This especially." She shut her eyes, shooting her arms straight into the air, like she wanted to soar down every inch of this free fall.

I didn't let go of the lap bar. Shrieking one more time, I didn't know what surprised me more:

Po being so persuasive, or me wanting to be persuaded.

When the coaster pulled back into the loading area, Po jumped out of the rocket ship and sprinted to the monitors displaying the picture snapped on the coaster's last turn.

Po's face was picture-perfect. Mine showed off a scream worthy of an Edvard Munch painting. Except the curves of my lips did hint at a smile.

Po snapped a pic of our photo and said, "Admit it. You had fun."

With an exaggerated eye-roll, I said, "Yes, it was fun." I meant it, too.

"Ooh, you said the f-word!" She draped her arm over my shoulder. "Are you ready to have more fun?" She gestured toward the area where we'd left Paulina vlogging. She started to say something else.

Her voice fell away as my senses zeroed in on Melina, walking out of the bathrooms ahead. A stack of brightly colored teacups rose between the mouse ears of her Mickey headband. Yes! She was going to love the *Alice in Wonderland*–themed Pinterest boards I'd made.

I rushed forward like the White Rabbit. *Do not be late for this very important date.*

No matter how much Po's scheme made sense, *this* was the planned path. The road more safely traveled.

I expected to keep moving in this direction. Only, as soon as I stepped back into the sunshine, I stopped midstep.

Space Mountain's line had quadrupled in ten minutes tops. The queue stretched so long that cast members had to add extra partitions along the side of the building. Park-goers inched forward slower than a snail's pace. Trudging through a never-ending and windy road.

The line looked too much like what I'd been feeling since After Mom. I wiped my sweaty palms on my blouse, eyeing the Lightning Lane.

The sight of people walking straight into the attraction made my broken heart yearn. No waiting in long queues. Skipping the crap and heading directly to the fun parts.

I wanted that for my family. I wanted that for myself. And I wanted it now.

If planning Paulina's party could fast-track Mandy teaching me the tricks of the HEA trade, so be it. Nothing else mattered.

In the distance, Melina was quickly getting lost in the crowd.

When my loafers lifted, they pivoted away from her teacup Mickey headband and headed toward Paulina and the half-eaten pretzel.

It was probably cold by now, but her party was about to heat up.

CHAPTER EIGHT

I threw the blankets off me. Swung my feet over the bed and reached for my phone. I blinked and blinked. How could it only be 50 percent charged?

Oh. Po's electric toothbrush—that's how. Sometime during the night she'd unplugged my phone and hijacked the socket. "Ugh!" I leaned over, fixing the situation. Scrolled through my notifications as the battery juiced up.

More likes on Angie's quince photos. Two more party requests: A sophomore's pool party. A junior's cat's first birthday. Every option seemed fun. Except neither screamed Mandy material. Especially since—

The phone pinged inside my hands.

Paulina

Excited for our first planning session later 💃

I squirmed against the mattress. Without iconic Disney soundtracks, characters walking by, or any of the enchantments of the happiest place on earth to lose myself in, the realities of my plan sunk in.

This party *had* to go off without a single hitch. Or else adiós to everything I'd worked for. Buh-bye, everything I was hoping to achieve.

With shaky fingers, I typed, ME TOO.

Technically, not a lie. In fact, if Po were here, she'd probably say something like, *Excitement and anxiety are two sides of the same nickel.*

New plan: solely focus on the excitement part of said nickel.

Another ping, followed by a chorus more.

Callie

Want to grab an acai bowl after the event?

I flicked her text away to text Po You better not be late for the fundraiser to cover my bases.

Po

Doggos will be washed on time. I'll head over after I finish spiking these balls.

GAH! THAT SOUNDS SO GROSS 😉

It's at 11? Or 1? I know there's a 1 in it.

Ohhhh and I took your car 😬 Dad's working this weekend so use my bike.

Hauling the fundraiser's rip-away banner and the extra flyers inside of a backpack, which I'd have to strap on my back like a pack mule? Peachy.

I checked the time. Flipped through my planner. Hovered the pencil over *hair wash and flatiron*. Considering it'd now take me three times longer to get to school, I had no option but to cross that out.

Gritting my teeth, I tapped out a text. FUNDRAISER STARTS AT 12. As an extra precaution, I added the event to our shared family calendar and set an alert for two hours before the event. DON'T BE LATE OR I WILL FIRE YOU AS MY ASSISTANT FOR PAULINA'S PARTY. SRSLY MARIPOSA.

Po

😮

The idea for tweaking the dog-wash fundraiser came to me freshman year. Why not sell hot dogs while owners waited for their dogs to be washed? A win for them *and* more cash for the photography club.

I rushed down the hallway, crammed backpack knocking against my spine and planner and pencil in hand as I ran through today's checklist. Extra tubs, shampoos, towels, brushes, dryers. Some of these items were currently inside my car.

The one Po had carjacked. My stomach sank. I waved the pencil over the list, as if sprinkling it with fairy dust. "Po's going to be on time. Po's going to be on time."

I moved on to the next items: King's Hawaiian hot dog buns, Angus beef franks, and condiments. At least these were (safely) stored inside the cafeteria. I made a sharp turn into the kitchen. My loafers squeaked against the floor in an attempt to avoid a collision with Dad.

He swerved, causing most of his Cuban coffee to geyser up—and out—the yellow demitasse cup. It splashed on the floor, luckily missing his white button-down shirt. And my pink blouse. The Tide wipes inside my utility bag were good, but not enough to bleach Cuban rocket fuel from garments.

"Whoa, there, kiddo." He grabbed a paper towel from the dispenser and bent down to mop the puddle between us. "The way you shot in here, I thought you were Po."

I scrunched my nose. He cracked up, his laughter a mix between donkey bray and dolphin squeak. Ridiculous, yes. But the melody sounded better than any song played at Angie's quince. Better than the songs at any of the school dances this year.

"You should do that more." I plucked a red apple from the fruit bowl and took hurried bites.

"What? Compare you to your sister?"

"Ew, no." Although the sweetness of the Gala coated my tongue, my mouth puckered like I'd tasted mojo sauce heavy on garlic and light on orange juice. "I meant laugh more." With the quintessential Cuban condiment on my mind, I said, "While we're at it, you should cook more, too."

Once upon a time, Mom used to experiment with her catered menus here. Using us as her most trusted taste-testers. The kitchen always swam in Cuban scents and flavors. Phantom smells washed over me, rousing echoes of past conversations. *Who taught you how to cook such simple dishes with such big flavors, Mom?* Po had asked.

Castro, she'd snorted.

In exile, Mom had morphed her passion for cooking into a thriving business. I could almost hear her raspy voice say, *These are my ways of staying connected to La Islita. Rabo encendido, congri, vaca frita.*

I licked my lips, wishing for the taste of lime-marinated crispy beef. The only Cuban staple in regular rotation now was coffee.

That's the thing about loss. You lose not only a person, but the tether to so many things about their past—about the places they'd come from.

I spun around before he caught my eyes misting. Busied myself with pouring some cafecito into a cup of my own.

He stepped next to me to refill his. "I'll take the cooking suggestion under consideration," he said. "In the meantime, don't look so glum. There are worse things than being compared to your sister, you know?"

"Doubt it. And if I look 'glum,' it's because . . ." I brought the cup to my lips, hoping he could finish my sentence. Hoping we could finally talk about the absence that crowded every inch of this house, though we pretended it didn't.

If Po and I had been able to talk about Mom the other night—heck, if we could venture back to her happy place—shouldn't I take another stab at a Mom-related convo with Dad?

I took a sip of the coffee for some liquid courage. The drink went down my throat, hot and bitter. "I miss—"

I hadn't even said her name, and all the color drained from Dad's face as he tugged his collar.

Got it. The Madrigals didn't talk about Bruno. And Diego Torres didn't talk about Mom.

I cleared my throat to reset the words. "I miss Cuban food. Like I said . . . um, maybe you should cook more?"

"I miss Cuban food, too." He scratched at the stubble growing against his jawline. "I can't promise I'll be any good at it, but how about I try making us some tostones this week?"

His plantain slices would probably turn out super uneven. So long as we spent time together, I supposed their symmetry didn't really matter.

"Deal." My heart ballooned to triple its size. "Adding dinner to our family calendar right now."

He grabbed his briefcase from the table and kissed the top of my head. "What do you have stashed back here, kiddo?" He jiggled the top of the rolled banner sticking through the top of my backpack. "A lightsaber?"

"Ha ha," I deadpanned. Apparently, Dad couldn't veer too far away from his favorite galaxy. Still. It felt good to know he was capable of making some pit stops in this one.

On the other side of the bike path, golden sand stretched far into the low tide. Strobing sunlight rippled across the ocean's surface, creating a runway of sparkles stretching to the horizon. The faster I rode, the more salty air raked through my hair.

The speed and humidity probably expanded the frizz. A huge price for not having hid my car keys from Po. With a sigh, I revved the throttle.

Sidewalk joggers blurred past. So did the rows of steel posts holding up volleyball nets. I slowed down, craning my neck.

No Po spiking balls to be found. Good—though not a guarantee that she was currently inside our school's parking lot, setting up doggie tubs like she'd promised.

I pressed on the throttle again. Eased up only at the sight of a dog walker up ahead. A pack of leashed pups yanked him forward, like Roger getting dragged by all 101 Dalmatians.

I slowed to a stop and pulled one of the flyers from my pocket. Handing it over, I said, "Enjoy some Angus franks while we wash your dogs."

"Sweet. I'll head over when it starts."

Despite this morning's setback, I was back on track.

I inhaled a victory breath. I even—*gasp*—gulped in another.

Wait. Was this "stopping to smell the tulips"? One Disney day with my sister and her Poverbs had started to grow on me. I cracked up. What if Dad was onto something?

Maybe being a bit like Po wasn't a bad thing.

I pressed the throttle again. Scents ribboned around me. The soundtrack of crashing waves, yapping Chihuahuas, and squawking gulls drifted from every corner of the beach. Colors blended.

It was as if I'd stepped into one of my old paintings.

The urge to capture this moment buzzed though me. I pulled my phone from my back pocket. Using the other hand to ease up on the throttle, I snapped a photo.

A collection of neon streaks with nothing in focus.

I didn't delete it or try for a picture-perfect take. This one contained its own type of charm.

Okay. Enough tulip smelling. Besides pulling off Paulina's party, I'd still need to excel as SBA's event chair. Mandy required both before gracing me with fairy godmother apprentice robes. I clutched the throttle. Uh—

Why wasn't the bike speeding up?

Nothing flashed on the battery indicator. Hold on. Where was the dang thing?

I ran my fingers over the handlebars. Stickers coated every inch of them. Down each curve of the bike. All the way to the rectangular box by the pedals.

An edge of a pastel purple volleyball sticker had peeled off just enough to let a red light blink through.

"No, no, no!"

Yesterday, a part of me wanted to smooch Po. Today, all of me wanted to strangle her. "Come on, come on. You can do it," I coaxed the bike. But no amount of cheerleading kept its motor from sputtering.

I'd always thought of myself as a fairy godmother in training. For the first time in my life, I felt like a Disney princess.

Cinderella, specifically, watching her carriage morph back into a pumpkin with each tick-tock closer to midnight.

If I didn't get to the fundraiser before noon, something was bound to go astray. And by "something," I mostly meant Po. Her distracting the committee from the tasks at hand. Trying to adopt the dogs instead of washing them.

Remember how to breathe.

If the battery was on its last legs, it simply meant I'd have to pump mine a little harder.

I glanced down to check if Matteo Beach's strand hadn't suddenly transformed into the La Brea Tar Pits. But no. Turned out pedaling an electric bike took tons more effort than riding a regular one.

Cyclists swerved around me, serving me dirty looks. Their wheels kicked back tendrils of sand. Great. This impromptu Tour de France was quickly turning into the 405 during rush hour.

Joggers—even walkers—zipped by.

"Get off the road, kid!" Not what I expected from a grandpa clad in neon spandex. I took his "suggestion" before becoming roadkill and hopped off the bicycle. With a grunt, I lugged the bike off the pavement. Plowed it through hot sand which quickly began to fill my loafers. Another problem to fix after dealing with the battery.

Propping the bike against a double set of trash cans, I crouched to my knees. Ugh. My portable charger couldn't power this type of battery. I'd need another ride to get to the fundraiser. I tugged my phone from my back pocket. The trash cans cast enough shade onto the screen for the notifications to beam brighter.

Callie

36 mins until kickoff! ETA?

CAS?! Where are you? We need to hang up the banner ASAP. The photo club's on their way!

Po

How is it possible that I'm here before YOU? 

Callie

Your sister said you okayed her being behind the grills today instead of at the washtubs. She brought her own condiments and is handing out recipes for "secret menu" items

Po

IF THE CORPORATE OVERLORDS OF IN-N-OUT CAN'T APPRECIATE MY COOKING SKILLS, I HAVE FULL FAITH THAT THE DOG OWNERS OF MATTEO BEACH WILL!

How did the phone screen not break with how hard I hit the call button?

"Pick up, Po," I rasped between trills. What was the point of having a phone only to leave it on silent?

One more ring and I'd call Callie. Have her put Po on the phone and then make her come get me.

"Little Cuchara! Where you at?"

The knot in my chest loosened. For a second. "Where. Am. I?" I forced through clenched teeth. "Stranded on the side of the bike path."

"Battery give out again?" She tsk-tsked. "Just tell me what lifeguard tower's nearby and I'll pick you up. No problema."

I had ninety-nine problems, and Po was quickly becoming all of them.

I wanted to unleash my fury, yes. But I wanted to get to the fundraiser on time even more. I pushed off the sand. "Let me check."

Midturn toward the lifeguard towers, someone yelled, "Watch out!"

The shout blared so loudly it rooted me in place.

A *bang* across my backpack. The strike hit hard enough to tip me forward. Then a *pop* followed by an explosion of icy wetness slapping the nape of my neck.

What. The. F—

My hand flew back. My fingers came away moistened by brownish liquid.

Since I'd been holding the phone to my ear, the same fluid trickled over its edges and—oh no—onto its screen.

I broke into a string of curses. Both in English and Spanish. If the little kids building sandcastles nearby heard me, que será será.

"Cas? What happened?"

"A seagull pooped on me!" I shivered at the chorro flowing down my back. "This bird must've flown in from Antarctica or something, because its feces are colder than icicles." I cocked my head, nostrils flaring at a familiar scent. "Did this beast stop at Starbucks on the way north? Because its crap reeks of iced mocha."

Po guffawed, sharing some expletives of her own. I couldn't catch all of them because her voice sounded like it was sinking farther and farther underwater—before vanishing altogether.

A voice behind me took its place. "Oh my gosh, I'm so sorry!"

I didn't immediately turn around to see who it belonged to. Not when I was too busy tapping the phone's screen, squeezing its edges in a desperate attempt to revive it.

A guy shuffled around me. He bent down and grabbed a massive (and empty) Starbucks cup by my loafers. That hadn't been there a second ago, had it?

The muscles in his tan calves bulged as he rose up. He was

around my age and way taller than me. So much so that my nose was almost level with his collarbones.

I looked up.

The lingering coffee scent must've been messing with me, because his brown eyes reminded me of chocolate syrup drizzled over a mocha.

Similarly dark waves, with ends bleached lighter by the sun, curved from under a red cap. An *OC Junior Lifeguard* patch was stitched in the middle. The same patch was sewn over the left side of his red board shorts. And above his left pec on the matching rash guard. Its fabric so tight it left little to the imagination.

"I swear I didn't see you back there." His thick brows knitted together. "Are you hurt?"

My back stung from the ice. But my insides were melting.

"Is everything okay?"

Now I felt like another Disney princess. Voiceless. Weak-kneed. Under the spell of someone who probably spent many hours at sea.

I scanned the sand, but alas—a musically inclined crab eager to warn about the dangers of swooning over a hottie was nowhere to be found.

CHAPTER NINE

Lifeguard Dude wiggled the huge cup. The siren's smirk on the thirty-one-ounce trenta flashed against the sunlight. "You popped out of nowhere when I tried to dunk it."

He prattled off a bunch of other stuff. How in the fall he'd be a junior, which meant he'd go from playing on Lazarus High's JV basketball team to varsity. To prep for the big leagues, he'd been honing his dunking skills by taking every shot he could.

"I'm particularly fond of practicing with these." He raised the cup. "My best friend keeps bringing them for me during lunch breaks, but blech—I've had so many I can't stomach them anymore."

In this life, his hooded eyelids, chiseled jaw, and tan skin made him ethnically ambiguous. In a past life, though? Lifeguard Dude had 100 percent been a Latine granny. No one else divulged these many details upon meeting, er, "dunking," a stranger with coffee.

"Gonna try again," he said, tossing the cup into the trash can. "Yes!" He raised his arms in a victory stance. The gesture would've been bro-ey if it didn't look so cheesy.

Or cute.

He reeled off more stuff. How he liked playing basketball

more than watching it. He'd rather spend those two and a half hours of couch time bingeing a show with his mom or a movie with his best bud. I didn't catch the titles he mentioned. Between the roar of the waves and my stalling brain, everything coming out of his mouth sounded as warbly as Po's voice right before my phone died.

Phone.

The magic word to break this spell.

"Where's your phone? I need it to call my sister."

"It's back at the lifeguard tower over there." He pointed to tower eighteen. "I'll totally let you borrow it, but it's almost out of juice. We can go plug it in at the aquarium at the end of the pier to charge it, though."

"No time," I said. "I have a portable battery." Being prepared always paid off. "It's right here—"

Goose bumps prickled my skin when I patted the backpack. I swung it around and . . . FML.

The iced mocha hadn't dunked only my back. Or my backpack.

But also the fundraiser's banner.

The top half of it drooped like a wilted flower stem. Different-colored inks bled through the white cardstock. "Please don't be ruined," I whispered, opening the zipper carefully.

The lower half of the banner was drier than the top. "Okay, I can work with this," I muttered. Relief washed over me when I patted the bottom of the backpack.

Mercifully, my planner had been spared. Along with my blow-dryer I'd brought as backup for the dog wash.

Regretfully, the extra flyers on top of it hadn't been as fortunate. The iced coffee caused them to swell and stick together, damaging them beyond repair.

Unspool and blow-dry the banner ASAP, or it will suffer a similar fate.

I yanked the towel draped around Lifeguard Dude's neck, spreading it over the trash cans. There. A tablecloth for a makeshift table. "I need to act fast. Keep watch for more people 'dunking' drinks, will you?"

He motioned to his red junior lifeguard patch over his pec—uh, heart. "Lucky for you, keeping watch is my summer job."

"Really?" I shook my head, gently pulling the banner from the backpack. "Seems you're more inclined to drown people, and their personal property, than rescue them."

"It was an accident. One minute you weren't there, and the next—" He squinted. "Does *poof* have a synonym?"

"Materialized, popped up, magically appeared." Why was I helping him prep for the SAT when he should have been helping me fix this mess? I motioned to the binoculars hanging around his neck. "Spot me."

Amusement danced in his eyes before he scanned the beach for rogue projectiles.

This gave me the perfect opportunity to tug at my bra strap. A handful of half-melted ice cubes plopped onto the sand. When Junior Lifeguard turned back, his megawatt smile put the ice's gleam to shame.

Something fluttered in my stomach. Nerves over unfurling the banner, obviously.

"All clear." He stepped closer. "Can I help? It's the very least I could do."

With the banner growing more bloated by the second, I curbed my instincts to take charge of the situation solo. As much as I hated to admit it, in this moment the Poverb "*Four hands work better than two*" rang true.

I moved over a bit. "You unspool to the left; I'll go to the right."

His smile grew, showcasing a single dimple. A shiver went through me. An aftereffect of the mocha's ice, obviously.

We stood shoulder to shoulder. Metaphorically speaking, since his shoulders hovered an entire foot over mine. More flutters.

What was happening? Those worms with wings constantly flittered in Po's stomach—never mine.

"I'm Javier, by the way. Javier Luna." So he *was* Latine! "But my friends call me Javi." He extended a hand.

Instead of shaking it, I brought my hand onto the corner of the banner. "We've got matters to attend to, Javier. Meet and greets aren't one of them." To my surprise, he looked more charmed than offended. Still.

On account of needing his help with the unfurling, perhaps scaling back the aloofness wouldn't be a bad idea. "But if you must know, I'm Castillo. My friends . . ." I trailed off.

Before Mom I had plenty of friends. After . . . Grief, it turned out, wasn't a popular item to bring to sleepovers. Callie stayed my friend. Sort of. Outside of SBA events, or helping me with Angie's quince, we didn't really hang out anymore.

Between school, the after-school events I spearheaded, and now this party side hustle . . . my calendar didn't have much free time for friends anyway.

As for Po? Sisterhood didn't automatically translate to friendship, either.

"You can call me Castillo Torres."

"Castle Towers is a cool name."

"¿Hablas español?" I tilted my chin at him. His tan skin nearly matched the strips of wet sand by the shore, and his eyelashes stretched almost as long as Paulina's faux ones. I bit the insides of my cheeks. "Never mind."

Checking this guy out was not on today's agenda. Neither was opening the door to non-essential convos. I took my attention back to the task at hand. "We unspool this gently on the count of three, got it?"

He nodded. "To answer your previous question, un poquito." His smile shrunk a little. "I used to practice it more with my pops. He was Guatemalan."

My fingers twitched at the banner's edge. Less at the wetness and more at him speaking Parental Past Tense. At the slight brittleness behind his words, like hairline fractures running through glass slippers. But mostly at how much acceptance brimmed from it, too.

He probably spoke about his dad often. Po and I only began talking about Mom recently. Dad was nowhere ready to.

Would I ever gain conversational fluency in Parental Past Tense?

"My mom was Cuban," I said, practicing it.

"I'm sorry. Losing a parent sucks. A lot."

"It does." Two strangers, a few words. Talking about Mom didn't fill her absence. But it lifted some of the constant heaviness pressing on my chest. I motioned to the banner. "Ready?"

He nodded, his smile growing full-size. Popping out that dimple on his right cheek.

Once more, my head went floaty. I shook it, resetting to planner mode. "One. Two. Three." I pulled the top corner without tearing the cardstock. "Gently. Think of separating wet curls without breaking up the spiral."

"I have no idea what that means, but I think I understand." Javier's fingers moved with surprising agility for being so thick. "My mom loves to cook but leaves all the onion and garlic peeling to me."

Sheesh. Just when I thought he couldn't get any cuter. Swooning had to wait, though. At least until we finished the unrolling part of this rescue mission.

Beads of sweat trickled down my temples. The more we unspooled, the more damage revealed itself.

Streaky colors bled into each other. The clean outlines of the dog inside a washtub, its cute tongue hanging out, the floating bubbles—splotched and smudged. The ALL DOGS WELCOME above the drawings? Completely illegible.

How were we supposed to take a photography club and SBA event committee group photo under this? Or hang this over the parking lot?

Much less have the dogs run and break through it.

That was the fundraiser's most important moment. The way we always closed the event. And I'd ruined it.

I scraped my teeth over my bottom lip. Would this go on my event chair's permanent record? Give Mandy pause about my abilities?

Javier's voice cut through my thoughts. "It's going to be fine." The confidence behind his words buoyed me with hope. If anyone could help me save this drowned mess, surely a junior lifeguard could.

I sipped in some air. "Okay. Let's keep moving."

Our finger rolls synched up like a choreographed waltz. Only a few more inches to go.

There. All done.

At least most of MATTEO BEACH HIGH'S 3RD ANNUAL HOT-DOG AND DOG-WASH FUNDRAISER stenciled on the upper half of the banner remained intact. But dear god. The same couldn't be said for its lower half.

Pieces of the banner's cardstock had crumbled away, dissolved by the combo of water, chocolate syrup, and espresso.

And that's when I saw it.

The missing *0* in the 100%.

The *g*, vanished from ANGUS BEEF.

I figured the derrière deities would've spared me from a lifetime of butt phrases ruining banners considering what'd happened at Po's quince. Then again, I—of all people—should've known what'd happen when I *ass*umed.

The only silver lining? There was no possible way this catastrophe could get any worse. Only, of course it did.

"What's the other ninety percent?" Javier asked, roaring with laughter. He grabbed the sides of his rash guard, bracing himself.

Where was the Big One Californians always yammered about? Because I could have really used a fault line opening up to swallow me whole.

Javier glanced at me, still cracking up. And then he snorted.

A lot.

A guy chiseled like a Disney prince but who grunted like Moana's potbellied pig? The absurdity of it—and of another banner fiasco—made me chuckle.

It came out slowly at first. Like Space Mountain's cart chugging up the tracks before picking up momentum. I laughed harder than I had in months, so much that my eyes teared up.

Huh . . . I'd grown so used to them doing this because of sadness I'd completely forgotten laughter could make them water just as easily.

My giggles and his snorts floated into the salty air, scattering over the rest of the beach. As our laughter tapered, a lightness swept over me, making it easier for backup plans to rush in.

I mashed the banner into a ball. Not the exact size of a basketball, but it didn't matter.

I whipped the towel/tablecloth off the trash can and tossed it to Javier. I took the makeshift basketball between my hands, stepped back to angle myself before shooting it toward the trash can reserved for recyclables.

It *swooshed* in, dead center.

"Nice swish, Castle Towers." Javier's eyes went wide. Exactly the way Angie's guests' had when she'd stepped under the spotlight at her quince.

No spotlight here.

Only the brightness of the sun and the flash of Javi's single-dimpled grin. I reveled under both, momentarily forgetting about fixing the banner. Clearing my throat to refocus, I said, "You know those beach warning flags? Where do you keep them? And how many can you spare?"

CHAPTER TEN

The inside of lifeguard tower eighteen thrummed with a flurry of hands and markers. Javier dotted the *i* in *fundraiser*. The black marker squeaked across nylon as I put finishing touches on several dog sketches.

Without SBA's stencils or photos to trace, Javier's lettering wasn't precise, and my drawings leaned more 2D than 3D. But on the red, yellow, and green lifeguard flags, his loopy letters coupled with my freestyle sketches did exude a cool, street-art vibe.

Scanning the rectangular and triangular flags strewn around us, I asked, "Are you sure borrowing this many won't be an issue?"

"Positive." With the way he kept glancing over his shoulder, though, vandalizing and loaning beach property was probably a bigger problem than he let on.

As big of an issue as me not getting to the fundraiser on time. My shoulders slumped.

"What is it?" Javier asked, lowering the marker.

"The banner problem is fixed." I recapped the marker. Snuck a peek at the dial hands ticking upward on the watch strapped to his wrist. "But it's T-minus ten until dogs get washed and grilled—"

Javier gasped, telenovela style, before chuckling. "Teasing!"

I threw the marker at him. He tried to catch it but missed. It rolled on the floor, bumping up against a blue sling bag. A vinyl Mickey appliqué decorated the front compartment. Cord extenders were hooked onto the zip pulls.

I should add those to my utility bag. He must've thought I was staring at the grinning Mickey patch instead of the cord extenders because he said, "I got it at Disneyland." He shrugged. "I like the idea of always taking a smile with me wherever I go."

Even if his sentiment did hit a little saccharine for my taste, I couldn't deny its sweetness. Or its usefulness.

It'd taken me forever to smile After Mom. Having an example of one nearby would've probably helped me remember how to much quicker. "Do you wear it over the shoulder or cross-body?"

"Cross-body," he said, gathering the markers for me. "My best friend trolls me whenever I even wear it as a fanny pack, but hey, it frees up more space that way."

I pressed my lips to hide a smile. Fought the urge to retrieve my utility bag lying at the bottom of my backpack, belt it around my waist, and show it off as a symbol of recognition.

Focus. If this lifeguard tower became a stage for show-and-tell, I'd never get to school. "As I was saying, the fundraiser starts in ten, and I'm stranded here with a dead bike." I shoved the markers into my backpack's front compartment. "And a drowned phone."

Javier swallowed loudly. "Use mine."

School *was* only a mile away. But even if Po did rush over, what about traffic? In SoCal, distance bore zero relation to ETAs. Especially by the beach at the start of summer. "Never mind. It will probably take too long for my sister to pick me up." Ugh. I should've called Po *before* going Picasso on these flags.

"Well . . ." Javier scratched the back of his head. "I'm still on my lunch break, so what about"—were those red blotches spreading across his checks the result of not reapplying sunscreen, or—"me driving you there?"

"I'm not getting in a car with a stranger." Sure, he was starting to feel less like one, but still.

A grin stretched across his face. "Who said anything about a car?"

The scooter rumbled louder than the waves crashing on the shore. "Hold on," Javier said.

No need to ask me twice. I wrapped my arms across him.

This feels nothing like the torso I practiced CPR on in PE.

I cleared my throat. Thankfully the roar of the motor masked it when he revved the scooter forward.

Javier had used the term loosely. The "scooter" looked—and drove—more like the love child between a Vespa and a motorcycle.

Air rushed past us. Every curl long (and brave) enough to escape my helmet's confines whipped across my face while the ends of Javier's hair tickled my nose. Did he use lavender-scented shampoo?

I held back giggles, a sneeze, and a swoon in favor of what I did best. "Left at the pier. Right at the base of the hill."

"You got it."

The rumble of the scooter reverberated inside my bones. Beach and beachgoers blurred. Soon, Matteo Beach's pier shrunk smaller and smaller behind us. At every click of a turn signal,

I suggested a better route whenever one presented itself. "That way is faster." Or "Left instead of right."

"I sure picked up a real backseat driver today, didn't I?" He glanced over his shoulder. Rays of sun lit the single dimple deepening his cheek.

"Eyes on the road." I couldn't deny I liked having his eyes—his body—on me, though. "And FYI, this 'backseat driving' is the only reason we're making such good progress."

He laugh-snorted. "The only reason, huh?" He pressed on the throttle and the scooter charged forward.

I fastened my arms tighter around him. For safety reasons, obviously. "Okay. Point taken. Your Lightning McQueen skills—"

"Oooh, I love him."

Same, I wanted to say but didn't. Better to keep the door to a best-Disney-character debate closed. Ha! As if anyone in the lineup could hold a candle to the Fairy Godmother.

"Your driving skills," I continued, "are equally as important as my navigation ones."

But would the duo be enough to get me to the fundraiser on time?

I craned my neck over Javier's shoulders and leaned forward, checking the scooter's time display.

I blinked and blinked. Unless he set the clock to run ahead, I'd arrive late.

To. An. Event. I'd. Planned.

Even worse, I was the (ir)responsible party that'd unleashed the force of Hurricane Po upon it. How much damage had she wrecked already? Could I salvage the destruction?

Like trying to snuff out a hundred birthday candles in one go, I blew a hard sigh. If I couldn't handle a school fundraiser, could I actually plan a magical (and fiasco-free) event fit for Paulina? One that she'd remember forever?

One that would enchant Mandy enough to invite me for an interview?

Right as I was slumping back onto the seat, the scooter drove over a speed bump.

My body lurched forward. My small boobs smashed into Javier's shoulder blades. Helmets knocked together. Everything wobbled. Seconds before I toppled off the seat, Javier's hand latched around mine.

He pulled my body back to his. "I got you," he said, keeping his hand over mine.

Electricity went through me. Thank god for the helmet keeping my hair from standing (more) on end. Who could blame me? This was the most physical I'd gotten with anyone.

Sure, the arrangement of our bodies somewhat resembled the configurations of Po's and my Big Spoon / Little Cuchara.

Except this rumbling motor was anything but sisterly. Same thing could be said about the too-small seat directly over it. I'd never felt flutters like this before.

The breakfast apple must've been cursed. Instead of lulling all my senses into a Snow White–style slumber, the forbidden fruit stirred every cell in my body awake.

I couldn't classify the uninvited sensations as completely unwelcome either. If anything, they tempted me to RSVP *Yes* and *More, please.*

If Po could read my thoughts, or had thermal vision goggles lying around, she'd never let me live this moment down. I couldn't help but giggle.

"What's so funny back there?" Javier asked.

Everything. "Um, I swallowed a bug and it tickled my throat." If my hands weren't latched around him, I'd use them to facepalm.

"Snacking on insects, huh? I mean, they're probably tastier

than those franks you're grilling. What's the special ingredient again? Ten percent anu—"

I squeezed him with the strength normally reserved for wrestling Po. I eased my grip only to let him gulp some air and laugh-snort more. "Left at the next corner and then we're there," I said.

A row of dogs and their owners lined the metal fence. The queue snaked up the hill, double the length of last year. My stomach clenched with nerves. When the scent of burning charcoal and grilled beef franks reached me, the belly growls helped loosen some of its knots.

I took another whiff. Grilled onions? Was this one of Po's "secret menu" items that Callie mentioned? While I was over here sniffing everything, I might as well take one last inhale of Javier's lavender shampoo. Too bad I nearly broke my nose on his helmet when he swerved into the high school's parking lot.

The screech of the scooter's tires made some dogs whip their heads at us. Others barked from inside washtubs.

Wow. SBA did a great job of executing my vision.

Two rows of tubs bordered the sides of the parking lot, the space between them creating a makeshift aisle. Callie paced up and down it, handing towels and refilling shampoo bottles for SBA members lathering dogs. She stopped for a second and snagged her phone from her pocket. Her thumbs tapped across the screen. At the next string of barks, she lifted her head. "Finally! I was just texting you."

Even though Callie beelined toward me, I couldn't tear my attention from Po.

She stood at the far end of the parking lot, behind one of the BBQs. Earbuds in. Head bopping and hips swaying. Wrists jangling with charm bracelets as she stoked the charcoal. She flipped over franks and onions, cooking with an ease that mirrored Mom's.

How had I never noticed the physical resemblance to Mom? Eyes set over high cheekbones. Matching curves. Hair the color of burnt cinnamon. Only, Po's hung so straight nothing could frizz it up. Not an occasional rainstorm or the grill's smoke.

Either because she felt my eyes on her, or the barking finally cut through her music, she looked up from the BBQ. In a very unlike-Mom move, she dropped the cooking tongs onto the flaming grill grate. Thankfully, Wesley leaned over from the BBQ next to hers and picked them up, turning the row of hot dogs over before they met a fiery end.

"I want to give you something for helping me," I said to Javier. "Can you wait here for a second?"

"Sure thing, Castle Towers. It's going to take me a few to unload your bike anyway."

I hopped off the scooter. It had to be the gust of wind that made me shiver. No way I could be missing his body heat this quickly.

I sprinted across the parking lot. Even without me to chaperone the committee—and Po—everything appeared to be under control. Dozens of dogs were getting washed. Double the amount of hot dogs were being prepared.

A huge sigh of relief. Except—

If I was really as relieved as I told myself, why was a lump the size of an ice sculpture forming inside my throat? I swallowed it and reeled off some orders. "Brush in the direction of fur growth, Julie!" I snagged the portable dryer from the backpack's side pocket, handing it off like a baton to Mark. "Wesley, make sure the buns are toasted, not charred!"

I kept running. Closing the triangular space between Callie rushing from the tubs and Po charging from the BBQs.

"You hung up before telling me where to pick you up," Po

panted at the same time Callie asked, "Where's the banner? The photography club will be here any second."

"I had a snafu with the banner—that's why I'm late."

Callie's porcelain skin somehow went even paler. "Will the dogs still be able to tear through it? Repeat customers keep asking."

"Um, about that." I lifted the backpack. Its zipper bulged, on the brink of bursting. "Hopefully this will be as fun for the dogs. And equally Instagrammable."

I motioned for each of them to take one of the zippers. Those cord extenders on Javi's Mickey Mouse sling would have really come in handy. Po and Callie managed to pull them down—unleashing an explosion of newly illustrated flags that tumbled to their feet.

They rummaged through them. Their eyes widened like little kids searching through a broken piñata's bounty.

Please like them; please like them.

Just when I thought my lungs would catch fire, Po's voice cut through my worry. "Little Cuchara, these are amazing. Uber-Banksy."

Callie rolled the edge of a flag between her fingers. "With a touch of Basquiat. They'll look good in photos," she said, frowning a little. "But—"

I put a hand up. "I know. Too thick for a tear-through." I dipped a hand into my backpack, snatched my pencil from inside my utility bag. "But what if we string these together? Turn it into a jump rope that the dogs can hop over?" I flicked the pencil's eraser end at the flags. "Or a limbo bar that they can crawl under?"

Po gave me a round of applause. "Teaching old dogs new tricks! Brava, maestro!" She nudged Callie in the ribs. "This is why she's the best event chair SBA's ever had." Po winked at me.

That tiny gesture felt like a huge gift.

"And why you're going to crush Paulina's party," she muttered into my ear.

My chest filled with more bubbles than the iridescent foam clinging to the edges of the washtubs. "Thanks, guys. But in full disclosure, I didn't make them alone." I gestured over my shoulder. "Javier helped me."

Their heads snapped to him, more accurately his butt, since he was bent over unhooking Po's bike from the back of his scooter.

Po waggled her eyebrows. "Here I was worried about you getting kidnapped by a stranger with candy."

"I'd eat his candy anytime." Pink splotches bloomed on Callie's cheeks before we burst out laughing.

"Okay, less drooling and more working." Even if there were no disasters of apocalyptic proportions to fix or prevent, decorating needed to be finished before the photo club came to shoot the event. I scooped up the flags, pushing them into Callie's arms.

"Do you want me to hang all the flags together? That could look neat," she said.

"Negative. The rectangular flags should go along the fences." I flicked my pencil to the right. "For the triangle ones, let's string them together in the picnic-slash-BBQ area. Over the tables." I pointed the eraser end from one light post to the other. "I want the individual letters spelling *fundraiser* to look like the Venice sign."

"Oooh yes," Callie said. "That's much better."

"Really putting the *I* back in *committee*, eh?" Po said.

I ignored her and kept going. "There are also some deflated beach balls mixed in there." Treasures Javier offered from tower eighteen's lost-and-found bin. "If we blow them up, they can look really cute for the dog photos."

"On it," Callie said.

It felt great to be back at SBA's helm. My cheeks ached from smiling so wide.

Po grinned, too. "Well? Aren't you going to introduce me to your *little friend*?" The last part she said à la Al Pacino in *Scarface*—the worst portrayal of both Cuban refugee and accent in history.

"Fine. But grab me a hot dog first. Secret-menu items and all."

For once, she did as she was told without protest. With an extra spring in my loafers, I headed back to Javier.

"Thanks again for the help," I said, trying to undo the helmet's strap under my chin. Javier leaned closer, taking it between his fingers.

"This clasp always sticks." His hands grazed my jawline on every attempt to undo the fastener. Good thing my tan skin didn't allow blushing. Otherwise, my cheeks would match the school's red bricks.

Finally, the clasp *clicked*. Javier slipped the helmet off. If my hair matched one of the poodles being blow-dried right now, he didn't say anything.

"It's good to know there are still some knights in shining armor," Po said from behind us.

I glared at her. "Javier, meet my sister, *Mariposa* Torres."

She stuck out her free hand. "Older sister, FYI. Feel free to call me Po."

After they shook, I snatched the plastic to-go box from her. "Now that you've met, hot-dog duty awaits," I said, turning her in the grills' direction.

She rolled her eyes but smiled hard, mouthing, *Go get 'em, lion.*

I swallowed a groan, praying Javier hadn't caught that. When she was on the way back to the grills, I said, "Since you missed your lunch break, please take this as a token of my appreciation."

"You don't need to give me anything. I had fun decorating those banners with you."

"Yeah, same here." Drawing on something bigger than the six-by-eight-and-a-half-inch pages in the back of my day planner had been fun. So was working on drawings with someone. Riding his scooter hadn't been too shabby, either.

Heat crept up my neck. Best cool down by bathing some dogs.

"Just take it." I pushed the to-go box into his hands. "No *buts*."

His eyes narrowed over the hot dog topped with sautéed onions, cotija crumbles, and gochujang. "You promise no butts were harmed in the making of this hot dog?"

We both laughed. "Pinky promise," I said.

He licked his lips. I did, too. I suspected it wasn't only because of the mouthwatering food.

Thankfully, Callie shouted for my help. Fixing an event issue took precedence over categorizing these weird emotions. "I gotta go. Thanks again, Javier."

"Wait. Can I get your number?" His voice cracked a little. "That way we could—"

"Schedule the flag drop-off?"

Maybe it was a stray cloud, but a shadow flickered across his face. "Right. Alcohol or nail polish should help get the ink out." He handed me his phone. "Sorry again for drowning your cell," he said as I began filling out the new contact card. "Leave it in a bag of dry rice overnight to help it come back to life."

Here I was, caught between Po's backward pearls of wisdom and Javier's *Farmer's Almanac*. I couldn't help but laugh again. My fingers stopped typing. I deleted a few letters, then returned his phone.

His face lit up brighter than the glowing screen.

"Thanks again, *Javi*."

"My pleasure, *Cas*."

Javi jumped back onto his scooter.

Behind me, Po squealed, setting off an encore of dog barks.

"Cas, I really need a hand with this Saint Bernard!" a voice yelled.

Blame that cursed apple for leaving me standing there, staring at Javi's scooter ride off into the sunshine, instead of helping Julie wash Nana's doppelgänger from *Peter Pan*. Or catching the foam-covered Chihuahua running all over the parking lot.

How did Snow White break the curse again? Before I could mull it over, Po materialized at my side, grabbed my elbow and said, "Debrief, now."

Even from afar Callie must've spotted the stars in my eyes because she suddenly looked less eager to hang flags and more interested in running over to get my personal edition of Hot Goss.

I took a deep breath, ready to dish it to them. But of course, that's when the photography club strolled into the parking lot. Just because things hadn't gone awry so far didn't mean there weren't disasters lurking around every washtub.

"No time for the details," I said, reaching for the next best thing: the lipstick sticking out of Po's front pocket. Whether by luck or destiny, the color was exactly the one I needed.

I swooshed the tube of pink across my lips.

Po turned her phone's volume all the way up. Cuban rhythms and Celia Cruz's throaty voice crooned from its speakers. The Afro-Cuban diva sang about how if you wanted to arrive first, you had to run slow.

No wonder Po always got everything backward.

"Praise the gods," she whooped, breaking out into an end zone dance. "Cas has a crush!"

CHAPTER ELEVEN

Outside on the cafeteria tables, we scarfed down Po's culinary creation. "Who knew cotija and gochujang go together better than ketchup and mustard?" I said. The new toppings, especially the jalapeño and avocado, had been as much of a hit as the new banners.

Po beamed. "In-N-Out's loss is SBA's gain."

I washed the food down with a swig of the pineapple Jarritos we were sharing. "Seriously. It's soo good."

"Ahh, thanks, Little Cuchara." She ruffled my frizzy hair with gochujang-coated fingers. *Squeeze previously canceled hair wash into tonight's schedule to shampoo away fermented red-chili paste and dog fur.* "Teamwork really makes the dream work." She smiled through a mouthful. "Ready to keep working together?"

I tore out a blank page from the back of my day planner. "Kudos on performing well today. As my 'assistant' on Paulina's quince, I expect you to comport yourself with even higher levels of decorum."

"'Higher levels of decorum,' huh?" She snatched the paper away. "Remind me again—how exactly did your phone 'get so wet' it stopped working?"

I aimed a piece of hot dog bun at her head. It landed inside her cleavage instead. At the unexpected bullseye, we couldn't stop roaring. The belly laughs came easier, having just practiced some with Javi.

Po plucked the piece of bun from between her boobs, tossed it into her mouth, and said, "Measure your life in stitches, and I'll tell you how much you laughed."

Stitches. What an odd way to describe laughing, but it fit. I felt closer to her now than I had in the past two years. "I'll tell you about my phone after this call."

My pulse picked up speed. The heartbeats echoed less loudly, almost as if the Mom-shaped hole had shrunk a bit. "Take notes in case I miss anything, okay? A lot's riding on this party for me." *For our family.*

I reached into my backpack, grabbing the box of markers and a tube of sunscreen. I extended both to Po.

She slathered some sunscreen over her reddening face, arms, and strip of belly exposed by her crop top. Made a big show of mulling over which marker to choose. With an exaggerated wink, she grabbed the pink one and pointed at the lipstick coating my mouth. "A crush for a crush."

"So long as this scheme of ours doesn't leave us crushed."

Po chuckled. So did I, even though I wasn't joking.

I tugged at my blouse's collar. Po scooted closer and fanned the blank page at me, as if trying to blow my worry away. "Relax. Paulina's going to love your ideas. The quince will be the bash of the summer. That Mandy woman won't have any other choice but to offer you the internship. Ready?"

"Yes." Maybe. "Are you?"

"Always," she said, tapping the FaceTime app and pulling up Paulina's number.

Between trills, the tip of the pink marker scratched against the page. Po didn't bother to write anything useful, like the date. Only *Po + Paulina 4eva* inside a big loopy heart.

Paulina's face appearing on the screen cut my groaning short. "How are my favorite hermanas doing?" she asked.

"A lot better now that we're talking to you." Po used a soft and squishy voice that I'd never heard before.

"Same." Paulina continued to keep most of her face still, but her faux lashes betrayed her. They fluttered and fluttered, each bat reserved for Po.

Po reached into her pocket and put on more pink lipstick.

That's it. No more flirting. I angled the phone closer to me and said, "Let's recap where we left off yesterday." Opening the *Paulina Reyes Quince* tab inside the day planer, I recited the preliminary checklist. "Party in three weeks." The perfect timeline before the application window for Mandy's fairy godmother internship closed. "Budget—"

"'Enough to make Tía Mari in México jealous,'" Paulina said, imitating her mom's accent again. Although she giggled, it faded quickly. She broke eye contact with Po.

Heat rose to my cheeks. Even Po squirmed on the seat. Neither of us asked Paulina what this tension was. Not surprising since the Torres clan had grown used to avoiding uncomfortable feelings.

Right before the silence became inescapably awkward, Paulina flipped some shiny locks over a shoulder, as if trying to push back whatever bothered her. No wonder she and Po liked each other.

Paulina fixed her face, putting the cool-calm-collected mask on again. Good. I think.

"You also mentioned wanting a 'deconstructed' quince," I said. Time to earn my fairy godmother's apprentice robes. "I came up with some suggestions for what that could look like."

Paulina rubbed her hands together. "Give it to me."

"What about a gender-swapped court?" I asked. "Or no court at all?"

Paulina drummed her fingers across her desk. "Ohh, that's cool."

Po reached under the table to fist-bump me.

"But no," Paulina said.

Instead of circling one of these options, I crossed both out. Moved down the list. "Okay, what about no chambelán?"

"Or maybe . . ." Po chewed the end of the marker hard enough to leave teeth marks. "A chambelána instead?"

Paulina's neck flushed. "I really like both those ideas," she said, much to the delight of my sister. "But I don't know if—" She glanced over her shoulder, to the door behind her, then back to us. "I mean, those don't hit the 'deconstructed' mark as much as I'd like. What else do you have?"

A sinking feeling crept into my stomach. Was Paulina going to be a quincezilla from day one?

Even if she was, I simply needed to manage this fiesta the way I did SBA meetings and events—with a firm hand and lots of vision. I tightened the grip over my pencil. "What about different foods served at each table?"

Paulina scrunched her nose. Okay, then. I drew a line through that idea. "A wild location, perhaps?"

"We're getting closer with that," she said, fidgeting with a dangly red earring.

Red lightsaber? I jotted before Po blurted, "Since you're a Disney vlogger, Disneyland maybe?"

Paulina let go of the earring to clap. Silver and black hilts. Red blades. Bingo. The earrings were lightsaber replicas. Something about the way the miniblades swung back and forth enchanted me.

I skipped the next suggestion on my list in favor of a detour.

"Better yet, what about a galaxy far, far away? In other words, whatever a 'deconstructed' quince means to you, we take that and make it *Star Wars* themed."

"Yes." Paulina's smile flashed brighter than the red glitter lining her eyes. "A million times, yes."

Back in the planner game, baby! My shoulders lifted so high Po's heavy slaps of praise couldn't lower them.

"My mind's running with ideas now." Paulina tapped a manicured finger against her chin. "Oh my gosh." Her finger stilled. "We can go even deeper with the wild location." Like every good performer, she paused for a beat, amping up the dramatic effect. "YouTube. We stream the entire quince on my channel."

Po mic dropped the pink marker onto the table. "That's brilliant." She hit the mute button. "Didn't I say this would happen?" Was she moonlighting as a ventriloquist after school? Otherwise, how was she keeping her lips that still? "Mo' exposure, mo' clients."

"I'll even upload a couple shorts featuring some of the planning parts," Paulina said. "What do you say?"

My mouth gaped open. Normally people only showcased the party. Not the grunt work it took to make a Pinterest board come to life. Fairy godmothers never got a chance to step into the limelight.

Yet here was Paulina, offering to share her spotlight. Perhaps I'd labeled her a quincezilla too prematurely.

I unmuted and said, "I'm one hundred percent taking you up on that invitation. Thank you." I swallowed a mouthful of excitement and let the planner in me retake the wheel. "Streaming the quince on your channel's a fabulous idea. For the bonus planning parts, I suggest filming only a handful of the prep. The parts that may be the most fun to watch?"

"Good call," she said. "That way the shorts don't turn into a docuseries critics call 'a journey into the caught-between-two-cultures rituals of modern Latine life.'" She scoffed before taking a swig of Perrier.

Po giggled. "Too bad I'm not turning fifteen, cuz I'd sooo use that docuseries as my college application. Alma's and UCI's admissions boards would gobble that right up." She elbowed me in the ribs. "Sucks we can't have a quince do-over, eh?"

For once we were on the same page.

Paulina's choking burst our bubble. The Perrier must've gone down the wrong pipe. Po hunched over the phone. "Paulina, are you okay?"

"More than okay, actually." Paulina wiped her mouth with the back of her sleeve. "But also a tad embarrassed you've seen what a klutz I can be."

Polished Paulina seemed the antithesis of that, but whatever. No need to rain on Po's heart-eye parade. "You contain multitudes," Po said. "I like it."

Paulina twirled some locks between her fingers before turning her attention to me. "Let's rewind to before I shot Perrier out my nose. Cas, what parts of the quince prep do you recommend showcasing?"

I moved my pencil over the planner and said, "Dance choreography." Po concurred with a shoulder shimmy.

"Yes, please." I couldn't tell if Paulina was talking about my dance idea or Po's jiggling cleavage.

"Filming the photography session could be super meta, too," I continued.

Paulina's eyes widened. "Love it."

Po's pink marker zipped across the page, this time actually writing a numbered list of my suggestions. I tilted my head for a better look.

Next to *dance* she drew three stars. Next to *photo shoot*, two. Some sort of rating system?

"Decoration rentals and the dress fitting could be super fun," I continued. "Oh! Cake tasting."

"And entrée sampling at Disneyland," Po added.

"Yes to everything. Especially to the Disney tastings. Four birds, one stone!" She winked at Po.

With the tip of the pink marker, Po tapped her temple. "Great minds think alike."

Paulina smiled, excusing herself for a moment to plug in her laptop. While her back was turned, I yanked a makeup wipe from my utility bag and erased the pink dot staining Po's skin.

This party was turning out to be more complicated than I'd anticipated. In my mental checklist, *Paulina Reyes's quince plans* morphed into *wrangle Paulina + Po's flirt fest.*

Although maybe I was being unfair to Po. Because while we waited for Paulina, Po jotted three stars next to decor rentals, cake, and food tasting.

Yup, definitely a rating system. Why hadn't I thought of using one at SBA meetings? Three gold stars for Po.

"Okay, I'm back," Paulina said. "What's next?"

"This is a solid foundation for planning the shorts you want to upload," I said. "Ready to brainstorm the actual party?"

"Brainstorming's not necessary. A vision of my deconstructed quince flashed before my eyes during that Perrier-induced NDE I just had."

Po and I held a collective breath.

"I'll film—and upload—the planning bits only," Paulina said. "Without. Having. An. Actual. Party."

Po sprung from the table to give her a standing ovation.

Paulina basked in the praise. While both gushed about how groundbreaking this concept was, I lapsed into silence.

Down the street, a lawn mower whirred. Nearer still, a car alarm blared. Neither came close to the warning signal ringing inside my head.

Po must've seen my knuckles going white against the pencil, because she sat down again. Underneath the hearts and star ratings, she scribbled, *Crap! Is this going to be a problem for your application?*

100% , I wrote back. Because how the hell could I use Paulina's quinceañera as "party-planning experience" if it wasn't going to be an *actual* party?

"Guys, is your screen frozen?" Paulina said. "Can you hear me?"

Remember how to speak. "Yeah, it's just . . ."

My chances of becoming a fairy godmother's apprentice were in jeopardy. And if Paulina only wanted to film planning segments, did that mean I wouldn't get another shot at writing the quintessential thank-you-Mom speech?

The pencil slipped from my hands. Under the guise of picking it up, I ducked under the table.

Get it together. If I could salvage the banners, there must be a way to fix this. A way to make this party work for both Paulina's purposes and mine.

"Everything okay down there?" Po asked.

"Uh-huh. Just trying to find my lucky pencil," I said, latching on to it. Bringing its eraser-end to my lips, I whispered, "If you want Mandy's fairy dust to turn you into a real pencil wand one day, you'd better help me come up with a rain plan, stat."

I twirled the pencil over the crown of my head, imagining it were already enchanted.

Think, think.

After a flurry of heart sputters, at last, an idea materialized.

Yes, the plan congealed the hot dog pieces sloshing inside my stomach. Yes, it leaned more on the selfish side of things than on the selfless service of a fairy godmother. But this ploy was the only way to keep my family headed down the HEA-bricked road.

I whipped back up and snatched the phone from Po's hands. "First, chef's kiss for the planning-shorts idea. It completely achieves the deconstructed vibes you want. Your viewers will love the very merry unbirthday party content. However—"

"Hold up." *Very merry unbirthday*, Paulina mouthed, as if testing the words. "That's from *Alice in Wonderland*, isn't it?"

I nodded. Who knew all those hours I'd spent on *Through the Looking-Glass* Pinterest boards for Melina would come in handy?

"We're using it. This video series will be called"—the spark in her eyes burned so hot I was shocked her room didn't catch fire—"My Very Merry Unquince."

"Perfection," Po said.

"Cas?" Paulina said. "You don't look convinced."

Drawing on every hour I'd spent in drama class, I said, "It's great. But you've mentioned your mom's a keeping-up-with-the-tías type of person, so . . . wouldn't she be mad if you don't have an actual get-together?"

Paulina slumped in her chair, mm-hmming on cue. "You're right. La Mera Mera's going to be Darth Vader levels of pissed off if I tell her I'm opting out of a super-traditional, over-the-top shindig like she probably envisioned for her perfect Mexican daughter."

My lips twitched. Guilty as charged for trying to coax her into having one exactly like that to add onto my résumé.

I flicked my eyes away from the screen. I couldn't keep staring at Paulina's frowning face. Much less Po's narrowing eyes.

If she suspected I was up to something, what right did she have to judge me?

I wouldn't even be in this position without her having wheedled me into it.

"Thanks for looking out for me," Paulina said.

More like looking out for myself. For my family.

But if this plan let me turn the steering wheel back to Mandy's internship, why did it also feel like something was slipping through my fingers? Mainly my moral fiber. And something else I couldn't place.

"Well, I'm not giving up the unquince idea. I'm still going to upload a series of vlogs on my channel—not a traditional-style quinceañera." Paulina crossed her arms across her black tank top in a way that yelled, *Got it?*

Yep. You're used to having the last word.

Before I could formulate a new internship plan, Paulina groaned. "Argh, but you're also spot-on about my mom. I need to do something to appease her. She'll never get off of my case otherwise." She fidgeted with one of her lightsaber earrings. "What about something small and super fancy? Can you make that work?"

"Not for Mandy," I said but only meant to think.

Paulina's eyebrows knitted together. Po's throat bobbed. Dang it.

After what felt like an eternity, Paulina nodded. "Yeah, that makes sense. Mandy's firm is very prestigious. Why would one of her most promising young interns waste their time on a small dinner? No worries." She grabbed then released a fist of hair. "I get it."

Guilt gnawed at me. At least she didn't suspect something

was off. Not to mention she'd pretty much handed me a get-outta-jail-free card.

I could circle back to plan A and reply to Melina's sweet-sixteen request. Her party wouldn't come close to the exposure I could've gotten with Paulina's. It didn't come with the opportunity to draft a thank-you speech for her mom, either.

But it had the potential to fit Mandy's requirements.

I waited for the happiness to rush in. The gratitude. Excitement. The only thing I felt was my fingers growing cold around my pencil and the truth settling into my heart's hollows.

More than any other event, I wanted to plan another quince. "It's too bad this didn't work out, Paulina." I fought the urge to slump over the table. "I—er—Mandy Whitmore and Associates really wished it could have."

Paulina's hair fell over her face. "Same. It would've been awesome to collaborate with you. Both of you."

Po slapped her palm across the table, breaking up Paulina's and my pity party. "I refuse to let the two of you throw in the napkin this easily. It's completely possible for us to have our pie and eat it, too."

Paulina and I shared a surprised look. "How?" I asked.

"Have your unquince for your channel to scratch your deconstruction itch," Po said. "And have a smaller get-together to appease La Mera Mera. You're a great vlogger and editor, so what if"—Po shot Paulina a knowing smile—"you shot it like that vlog where it looked like you rode every one of Disney's fifty-eight attractions in one day but really didn't?"

My pencil started to move across the page. Me, taking notes from Po? What multiverse had I stumbled through?

Paulina nodded. "If I shoot it in the style of those quince and wedding videos . . ."

"You can make it *look* like you had the quince of the season,"

Po finished for her. "Last night you said your mom doesn't even intend to invite most of your family. Pictures—aka proof of something fancy—to make them jealous is her actual MO."

What? I tipped my face toward Po. Where was I when they'd had this conversation? Paulina must've caught my confusion because she said, "I slid into Po's DMs last night. I told her how I suspect my mom cares more about the *perception* of my party rather than me *experiencing* a quinceañera, so . . ." Instead of looking bummed, like I'd expected, she beamed. "She'll be thrilled to have 'evidence' of the quince to show off."

Po threw an arm around me, pressing her cheek to mine. "And you'll have 'evidence' for Mandy's—"

"Dossier," I said, jumping in before Po possibly blurted *application*.

"Po, this idea's so genius I could kiss you right now," Paulina squealed.

Po's cheeks flared with streaks of pink to match her lipstick. For once, she was speechless.

"What do you say, Cas?" Paulina brought her face close to the screen. Each fleck of glitter twinkled like a star ready to grant my heart's true desire. "Are you up for playing a little make-believe?"

If only she knew how practiced I was getting at the art of fantasy. I curled my toes into my loafers before I could break out into a waltz. "Yes," I said. Real life could wait.

CHAPTER TWELVE

After spending the rest of the afternoon shampooing and flat ironing my hair, I headed to the laundry room to check on my (and Po's) clothes—and Javi's lifeguard flags.

Sounds of slushing water and a whirring motor filled the small room, along with waves of heat pumping from the drying machine. Po's brightly printed nylons tumbled over my neutral cottons in a pirouette of fabrics. With dance on my mind, I tapped a pen against my lips like a metronome.

Which baile would best suit Paulina's deconstructed quince? A sexy but simple salsa? A festive cha-cha? An elegant waltz?

Sitting cross-legged on the floor, I opened the day planner, flipping to the section reserved for Paulina's unquince. I brought the pencil under the word *dance* but didn't fill any of the open slots with a particular type of routine.

How could I when none of these ballroom styles fit her vibe like a pair of lace quinceañera gloves?

With the pre-soaked flags sloshing and the drying machine rumbling, I swapped the day planner for my iPad. "Paulinaland," I said, typing the name of her YouTube channel.

Time for more research.

I fast-forwarded through a few videos. Hmm . . . Jet-black clothing. Onyx nails. Wedged Jordans. The only bursts of color came from her signature red-glitter eyeliner and statement jewelry.

Gold hoops were her go-to. When they didn't flash between sleek tresses and her long neck (always clasped with her nameplate necklace), dangly red lightsabers did. Occasionally, some other type of *Star Wars*–looking earrings.

Sparklers went off inside me, spurring my pencil across the page. *Red lightsabers. Darth Vader. Stormtroopers.* I drew a corresponding sketch below each word.

A laser sword. An outline of the helmet worn by the biggest baddie of the galaxy far, far away. The armor donned by the army of his henchmen. "Holy crap," I muttered, slouching over a paused video.

Despite being built like a Disney princess, Paulina dressed like a *Star Wars* villain. I checked out a few more vlogs to confirm my theory.

Thanks to Dad fanboying over the franchise, we used to have family movie nights where we'd stream the prequels and originals. I recognized Darth Vader's color palette and Anakin's vested silhouettes in some of Paulina's clothing. Were her other wardrobe choices based on new villains' outfits?

After Mom got sick, we never watched the more recent content . . .

The washing machine's loud timer went off. My head snapped up. For a second, Mom's dark brown eyes reflected off the machine's window instead of mine. A flash of her white chef's coats and a blur of the red aprons she'd wear over them replaced Po's clothes clashing against mine.

I scurried backward until my spine smashed into the wall.

When I blinked, none of her things were there anymore.

In the seconds between chest heaves, it hit me again. Like always.

She was gone.

Millions of milestones we'd planned to do as a family, gone with her.

The air in the laundry room went from cozy to oppressive. The smells of detergent and fabric softener, cloying instead of crisp. I scratched at my throat, terrified of drowning underneath it.

Why did some memories dull the heartache, while other times the same ones sharpened the edges of my heart, making every breath physically hurt as badly as it had those first days After?

I sprang up, grabbed the iPad, and rushed into the hallway.

With every step forward I outpaced the pain, shutting my eyes when I neared the family photos. Why add more salt to my wounds?

By the time I neared the kitchen, my pulse had slowed. If Po had glanced in my direction, she probably wouldn't have guessed anything was wrong.

Thankfully, she didn't. She sat right where I'd left her, keyboard clicking and bracelets jingling from behind the laptop. Brows furrowed in concentration as she followed through on finishing college applications. As promised.

As planned. Good. She deserved the chance to make her once-upon-a-time college dream come true. I touched the eraser end of my pencil, tucked behind my ear. *We did good.*

A piece of the Torres HEA clicked into place.

I rolled my shoulders back. Even the *pew-pew-pews* growing louder did nothing to weigh them down.

I turned into the living room, screenshots pulled up on the iPad, ready to go.

A familiar spray of curls, and the headset crowning them, rose from the back of the gaming chair. I edged around it and stood next to the TV.

Did a newbie fairy godmother accidentally cast a reverse makeover after work or something? Because the dad from this morning was long gone.

A five-o'clock shadow stubbly enough to grate Parmesan cheese covered half his face. His lawyer's garb? Replaced by thick white socks in Adidas slides, red mesh Angels baseball shorts, and a white V-neck undershirt. Attire suited for a boxer without any fight left in him.

Probably not the best time to remind him about the family dinner night next week. I pulled up the event on our family calendar and added a reminder alert for a few days before.

I stepped in front of the screen, waving my arms. "Dad? Um, hello!"

"Hey, kiddo." He took a swig of kombucha. "Um, can you move a little to the left? You're in the way of the game."

"I'll move after you help me identify these *Star Wars* items."

He scooted the chair forward. Craned his neck around me, fingers still flying over the controller.

"The faster you let me know what these items are, the faster I'll get out of your way." I held up the iPad and flicked through the pictures.

"Sith holocron, Kylo Ren's saber, and"—his eyes darted from my iPad to the parts of the TV my small frame or big hair didn't block out—"Dark Acolyte helmet."

"Gracias." I stepped out of his way, typing everything he'd listed. "That wasn't too hard, was it?"

"I guess not." He chuckled. "Why do you want to know what they are, anyway? Thinking of becoming a Sith Lord without telling your papá?" He laughed again, not quite the booming laughter from this morning. But enough to make me join in.

"Who knew your Wikipedic knowledge on this stuff would actually come in handy one day?" I added *Sith Lord* to my notes. "This isn't for me; it's for a new client. I'm planning a *Star Wars*–themed quinceañera for her."

His eyes brightened. "First off, it's *Wookieepedic* knowledge. Secondly, wow, kiddo." He paused the game to look at me. "That's super rad."

Now that I had his full attention, I waded deeper in. "What type of ballroom dance fits best for a"—I glanced at the iPad—"Sith Lord?"

His smile from this morning boomeranged back. Yes! Then, oh my Sith Lord—

I put a hand over my mouth, muffling the telenovela style gasp when he set the controller down. *See?!* I wanted to shout. This quest to become Mandy's fairy godmother apprentice really was the golden ticket to getting my family back on track.

"Definitely a toss-up between a tango and a paso doble," he said. I typed both down. "A tango's all about syncopated steps, high elbows, and constant connection between bodies." My face flamed at the memory of wearing Javi like a life jacket. I grabbed Dad's kombucha, held my breath, and chugged, hoping the chilled drink would cool me. Nope.

"There's a looser American style. You kids should opt for that version instead of the traditional dance."

"Dad, stop! Like I said, it's for a quince client. I'm not going to be part of the court. Actually, no one is." Dad quirked his eyebrows. "She wants to do a solo dance as a symbol of empowerment."

"That's pretty awesome."

Yup. Precisely the reason why Paulina wanted to upload this vlog to her Very Merry Unquince series first. Though for her mom—and my Mandy "dossier"—she'd promised to create another video, frankenbiting footage she'd taken from this year's prom to make it look like a traditional quince court swirled around her unaccompanied performance.

"In that case, solo tangos are becoming more popular. An Argentine one would be great for a *Star Wars* dance."

"What song would you pair it with?" I leaned in.

"Remember the song in *Phantom Menace* when Obi-Wan and Qui-Gon battled with Darth Maul?"

I couldn't place the names anymore. I nodded anyway, because this was the longest conversation we'd had in months.

"Duel of the . . ." His voice trailed off like he was waiting for me to finish the sentence for him. When it became apparent I couldn't, he said, "Fates."

"Riiight." I jotted it down. "Duel of the Fates." Little did he know how much my fate, and by extension his and Po's, rested on getting this party right.

"We should do a prequel rewatch this summer." He scratched his stubble. "Put it on our calendar."

I nodded, pulling it up. Two events in one month? I almost pinched myself to make sure this wasn't a dream.

"But a paso doble . . ." he continued.

"Double step? Is that another type of dance?"

"Yup. It can also be performed without a special someone." His voice lowered when he said, "I suppose any dance can." He paused for a beat before continuing. "Its choreography's faster and more complicated than other Latin ballroom styles."

Right before I could grasp what was happening, he reached between the bottle of kombucha and a glass of iced coffee. Picked up the controller—

And turned off the Xbox.

Unable to keep the joy out of my voice, I said, "I've never heard of that dance before. Is it new?"

"Heck no, kiddo. Its roots go way back in Spanish history. Bullfights and military marches." His cheekbones glowed from the ceiling lights. Or maybe from the ill-tended fire inside of him sparking back up. "The name *paso doble* allegedly comes from those marches. You see, tunes were played during marching, and they were set to a very fast tempo."

As fast as the speed of his voice? The only thing Dad loved more than talking about *Star Wars* was chatting about political history. I glanced at the far end of the wall, imagining his Alma University diploma hanging on it. Pictured the embossed *Bachelor of Arts in History* gleaming in gold.

Too bad the only history he didn't discuss was our recent past.

"The music would 'inspire' the troops to take one hundred and twenty steps per minute instead of the standard sixty," he said.

"Double the number of steps."

"Ergo, the name *paso doble*. If you go with this style . . ." He pulled off the headset. "Then Darth Vader's theme song"—he gestured for me to start writing on my iPad; *good looking out, Dad*—"'The Imperial March,' would be da bomb."

Laughter rang from the hallway. "Your vocabulary gives your age away faster than the salt seasoning your pepper hair," Po said, stepping into the room.

Dad chuckled. "Thanks for the reminder, mija."

Then he did more of the unexpected. He sprang from his gaming chair. "But talking to your elders that way?" he tsked-tsked. "I suppose you're too old for a time-out, so doing a demonstration for your sister seems like a fitting punishment." He extended a hand.

Even though Po rolled her eyes, a smile crept to her lips. She was setting her hand inside his when he grabbed it, using her fingers to lift the hem of her duster. "Pretend you're a matador and this is your cape."

He stepped back and began to circle her, belting out, "Pum, Pum, Pum, Pum, paa-ruumm, Pum, paa-ruumm . . ." He pointed at me, then the tablet. "'Imperial March.' Darth Vader's theme song."

I missed this side of him so much. Assertive. Dorky. Laughing. And most importantly, spending time with us.

Exactly like he used to Before.

I pulled the track up, cranking the volume as high as it could go.

The blare of trombones and trumpets swelled and crescendoed. The music must've helped Po and Dad get into character, because their movements, while improvised, became more fluid.

At the next flick of Po's duster, Dad rushed under it and charged toward me. "No!" I yelped, except he latched on to my hand and swung me around anyway. "Just because I plan school dances, Dad, doesn't mean I actually dance!"

"Oh, c'mon, kiddo. You're Cuban. Of course you dance."

I shot Po a pleading look. The traitor yanked the iPad from me and said, "If you can't beat 'em, join 'em."

To reward her for getting the saying right, I did.

Cymbals crashed. Violins trilled. Brass instruments boomed. My loafers stomped across the floor, toes somehow finding the steps to a dance I didn't know.

We looped one another, laughing as we morphed from matador to bull and back again. The song gathered speed. Surged with power and control. Right as I pictured how good the swish of Darth Vader's black cape would look flying around Paulina—with smoke machines shooting fog to curl around black heels—

the percussion and brass gave way to a run of delicate flutes and ethereal xylophone chimes.

Paulina's glitter makeup came to mind, along with the softness in her face when she dropped the YouTube persona. This part of the song fit her perfectly, too.

Would she be as happy about this baile and song choice as I was?

When the faster tempo returned, my heartbeat dashed off to the races. Violin vibratos and percussion booms quickened, sprinting with the brass blasts to see who'd cross the finish line first. The music reverberated against the floors, ricocheting off the ceiling. It went through my limbs. Thrummed at the marrow deep inside in my bones.

Reminded me of just how alive I was.

The notes crescendoed. I turned into the bull again and charged at Dad and Po. At their wide smiles and red cheeks. Every instrument struck in unison one more time, before falling silent.

Our laughter bounced from every corner of the room. The life was finally back inside the "living" room. By the looks on Dad's and Po's faces, they felt it, too.

CHAPTER THIRTEEN

I pulled the first load of lifeguard flags from the drying machine, lifting a yellow one to the ceiling. Only a few traces of the poodle sketch clung to the nylon. I grabbed a red one next. Hmm—the lines of an *F* were barely visible. Rummaging through a few more, I searched the fabric for more evidence of the drawings. On some, the ink had washed off completely. Perfect.

I folded the flags before setting them into a laundry basket, then moved back to the washing machine. One last load of pre-soaked flags to go. Tossing them into the washing machine, I poured Tide Plus into the detergent drawer and pressed the heavy duty button.

The washing machine rumbled awake. Suds began to fill the washtub, the bubbles not unlike ocean water frothing on the shore.

Did doing laundry remind Javi of the beach? His knowledge about laundry tips piqued my interest. The possibility that he may also like watching foam scrub away stains, enjoy restoring things to their former glory, kept it.

When should I return these to him?

If I asked Po for advice, she'd probably say something like, *Don't put off today what you're going to do tomorrow.* This time, I actually agreed. Weird.

Picking up my planner, I scrolled down tomorrow's hourly time slots. Different colors coded various activities.

Green for SBA events. In a few days, the committee would be back in room 237 to finish organizing the art auction—our next summer event.

Gold for Paulina. *Research designers and confirm with Marcus about dance rehearsal.*

Purple for Po. She'd promised to finish her early action templates by 12:45 p.m. I'd proofread them at 1:00 p.m. Confirm that she'd started drafting her admissions essay by 5:00 p.m.

Time slots were wide open afterward. Wouldn't it be practical to drop off the flags then? I tapped the pencil against my temple.

Which color should I fill this block with? Brown to match his hair? Ooh. Blue to twin with his sling bag? Or what about the color of my cheeks whenever his infectious laugh-snort echoed inside my head? Pink.

The *snap* of me shutting the planner burst my bubble. What was I thinking? Lifeguards didn't have evening shifts. Plus, that chunk of free time ought to be reserved for planning Paulina's quince. Not arranging my own after-party.

Setting the planner to the side, I reached for the personalized mug clattering on top of the washing machine. Back when birthdays used to be a big deal around here, I'd gifted this to Mom.

In a contest between Disney and real princesses, Tiana and Diana tied for her favorites. Both of them smiled from the sides of the mug. But none of Mom's café con leche or green tea filled it. Only a huge serving of uncooked jasmine rice covering most of my phone.

Would this cell-phone-in-dry-rice trick work as well as Javi's other tips? I tugged my phone loose. Fought the urge to close my eyes when I pressed the side button.

Oh my gosh. Javi's advice actually worked. "Yes! Yes! Yes!"

"You okay in there?" Po yelled from the kitchen.

"Uh-huh." I flicked through Po's and Callie's missed calls and messages from earlier. Scrolled down the new likes and comments on SBA's Insta page. Whoa.

Classmates loved the flag sketches. The strung-together-triangle-flags-as-a-jump-rope idea was proving to be as repostable as the tearaway banner.

"I'm more than okay, actually." Even on my personal page, new DMs flooded my inbox. No party requests. Only tons of classmates asking if I could sketch their pets in a similar style.

My chest ballooned with pride. Pride over another memorable event in the books, over people wanting me to immortalize their fur babies. *Maybe I should start—*

The washing machine whirred, signaling the next phase of the wash cycle. Signaling me to scrub my former hobby from my mind.

Even back when I used to paint, blank canvases were places to experiment with messy colors and imperfect lines. Not something to exhibit, let alone make for other people.

I began kindly turning down offers, when the phone chimed with a text from an unknown number.

Unknown

Did your phone rebound?

Something prickled across my fingertips. The sensation traveled all the way up my arms, like that wave of pins and needles when sleepy limbs woke up.

I texted back.

It made a comeback.

Thanks for the phone and laundry tips. How do you know about this cleaning stuff anyway?

Almost immediately, typing bubbles appeared on the screen.

My mom's a cardiac nurse at Hoag and works long shifts. Dad usually took care of the housework, so after . . .

After. The magic word to twist my stomach into instant knots.

I took up lots of those cleaning duties.

Though the bulk of my schedule was always devoted to getting our HEA back on track, cleaning came in handy whenever an empty slot in my planner needed to be filled. The less the pages resembled the hollow chambers inside my heart, the better.

Ditto. So many duties all the time.

Oh Sith Lord. Had I said that in person it would've sounded super cringe.

The phone chimed again—with a voice note from Javi. "In the span of three seconds, we've said *doodie* twice. A side effect of those hot dogs, perhaps?"

A belly laugh broke through. I voice-noted back, "You're the worst," saving his message before it vanished.

Typing bubbles rippled across the phone.

PS If you want to drop off the flags, I'll be back at the beach tomorrow 😊

Suds frothed inside the machine. At the possibility of seeing Javi again, everything in me fizzed, too.

I opened my planner again. The empty slots glared harder than football field floodlights. Before I talked myself out of filling it with something Javi-related, I texted, I can drop them off after 5:15 p.m. Will you still be at work then?

The typing bubbles reappeared. I'll be off my shift but . . .

No words or bubbles came. The screen began to dim. I shook the phone and muttered, "But what, dammit? What?"

Po poked her head through the door. "Are you sure you're okay in here?"

I flinched back, nearly dropping the phone. The rice trick had worked its magic on a doused phone. I doubted it'd fix a cracked one. "Yeah, totally fine."

She glanced at the screen. I flipped it over in the nick of time.

Not handing you fodder for cheesy CPR/lifeguard jokes, thank you very much.

"All right, then. Keep your secrets." She wiggled her eyebrows before pounding down the hallway. Her steps clomped loudly like always, but not loud enough to drown out Javi's incoming text.

Do you want to meet up after my shift?

After flipped my stomach again. Only in a happier, more fluttery way. I never imagined that was possible. Not with the Pavlovian response tied to it.

They started a Movies at the Beach right by the pier this summer.

A movie at the beach? Blood rushed to my head. Was Javi asking me out on a date? I wanted to call for Po, have her barge back in here to decode this message ASAP. Except . . .

She'd probably only answer my question with one of her own: *Do you want it to be?*

Hmm. If I had to make a list of qualities for a first date, Javi checked the boxes for lots of them.

Funny. Useful in all sorts of binds. Unflappable (mostly) in the face of Hurricane Po. His philosophy of having a smile wherever he went. And topping the list: his fluency in Parental Past Tense.

This attribute hadn't been on the first-date Pinterest board I'd made way back when: an Italian place for dinner (*Lady and the Tramp* forever!), cute dress, curls styled by Mom, makeup courtesy of Po.

Well, no Italian place graced the shoreline. The constant breeze by the pier rendered a dress completely impractical—unless I wanted to be blasted on Hot Goss as the Matteo Beach Flasher. No Mom around to help me embrace my hair. Sure, Po could apply makeup ten times better than I ever could, only I had zero interest in a spiel about how fast her Little Cuchara was growing up in exchange.

So many of the details weren't matching up to the original board in my head, and yet . . . a flicker of surprise trailed the realization that pieces could be rearranged. Or swapped out for new ones.

My thumbs hovered over the screen.

The red flags in the laundry basket gave me pause. But within the washing machine, the last load beckoned. Lucky for me, most of those swished green.

CHAPTER FOURTEEN

Half of the crowd hunkered in front of a big screen, chattering. Some lounged on beach chairs or beanbags. Others were propped on their elbows, sprawled over colorful beach towels.

More gathered at the far end of the makeshift viewing area for the Movies at the Beach, forming lines in front of different food carts. My mouth watered at the cucumber slices and pineapple spears swimming in plastic bags half-filled with lime juice and chamoy. Whiffs of buttered popcorn and churros wafted over me.

For a minute, I was transported to Disneyland with Paulina.

When the scent of onions sizzling on a grill reached me, I was back at the fundraiser with Po.

Before I looked around for Javi, I tugged the phone from my back pocket. I snapped a panoramic photo, saving it to the *SBA Event Ideas* album.

We had gone over details of the art auction fundraiser earlier today but hadn't picked an overarching theme yet. Would something movie-related like this work?

Display the student artwork like film posters outside a theater. Screen a movie inside the auditorium to raise more cash.

And by having concession stands—including Po's hot dogs—we could triple the intake.

I jotted everything down in my planner when my phone buzzed with a text.

I see you.

I spun around. Little kids darted between the seating area and the food vendors. More people streamed in from all corners of the beach. Then, against the backdrop of the silver screen and darkening sky, came Javi.

Light from phone screens caught on his lifeguard shorts and hoodie. On the Mickey Mouse sling bag he wore as a cross-body. Mickey's smile was big, but it didn't compare to Javi's.

Or mine.

"Castle Towers. You came."

"I did." From my backpack, I retrieved the bundle of folded flags, wrapped neatly in a bow. "Thanks for letting me borrow them. Because of your Mr. Clean tips, most of the drawings came out."

"That's good for my boss. But sucks for you. You're a great artist." During the handover, his fingers grazed mine. Sparks went off in their wake.

"Was an artist." Talking about my past hobby turned the sparks into stings. Then again, wasn't practicing talking about the past one of the reasons I'd come?

"'After Mom'"—I made air quotes—"I had a visceral reaction to how unruly watercolors could be. All those ways to ruin a blank white page?" Bitterness exploded in my mouth. "No thanks."

"Funny how while you stopped something old"—he motioned to his lifeguard uniform—"I took up something new."

He scratched at the sling bag's strap. "'After Dad'"—he mirrored my air quotes—"I researched every med school in SoCal, thinking I could apply and get in." He gave a brittle laugh. The briny breeze snatched most of it away. "Turns out med schools don't accept people who can't operate a motor vehicle yet. Or suck at math." He shrugged. "But that desire to try to save someone stuck."

Even though I was trying to save some*thing* instead of some-*one*, I understood completely.

"I signed up for Junior Lifeguards as the next-best thing." Javi traced the outline of Mickey's smile as if to make his own reappear.

"Ah. Now it makes sense why you helped me yesterday." Po had been right about him. "A damsel in distress is catnip for a knight in shining armor."

Javi's fingers left Mickey's smile. He waved his arms around us. "If this turned into a fantasy realm, I'd be more of a knight in rusted armor." He poked the tip of his finger through a tiny hole at the side of his hoodie.

Together, we giggled.

"And even if you were in distress, you're no damsel."

"Oh, no?" I perked up, touched that he recognized my ability to bibbidi-bobbidi-boo myself out of a fiasco. Hopefully Mandy would, too. "What am I, then?"

Hearing someone call me *fairy godmother* out loud would make it feel more real.

"You're the castle towers, obviously." His face brightened when he said it.

Yes . . . Maybe Mom didn't name me after a specific castle but castle-like qualities.

The ability to weather all storms. To use every stone thrown my way to stand even higher. And to host fabulous parties.

"Yes," I said.

Javi extended an elbow. Good, because the castle realization had left me dizzy.

"Let's get to our spot before the movie starts," he said.

The clouds shifted, covering a crescent moon. Any makeshift aisles were suddenly snuffed out by the dark. I squinted to see through the maze of beach towels and chairs, not to mention the throngs of people rushing back to their groups.

In the darkness, it was easy for bodies to jostle against each other. Easier still for feet to catch on the edges of chair legs and bags. For snacks to slip from hands. For sodas to geyser from cups.

The enchanting scent of his lavender shampoo had nothing to do with me huddling closer to Javi. I only wished to avoid a repeat of yesterday's soaking, obviously.

"It's just over here," he said.

My heart pounded as hard as it had yesterday. Maybe more. Because while yesterday Javi had been driving the scooter, I'd been directing the route. Tonight, Javi did both, steering me around beach chairs and people spread out on towels, escorting me to a destination unknown.

I didn't "offer" any tips this time. I simply enjoyed the ride.

"We're here," he said, stopping at the edge of a large beach towel.

The night sky did nothing to dull its red and purple stripes. Or the symmetrical lines that formed diamond patterns and glyphs between them. The snacks he'd arranged in the middle of the towel were no joke, either.

A huge tub of popcorn served as the centerpiece. Kernels glistened with butter. Seasoned mango spears shimmered from inside a plastic baggie.

Even without any silverware to be found, I had a flashback

to Angie's table settings. Only now, instead of *Javi* and *Cas* in cursive script on fancy place cards, our names were printed across white stickers on Starbucks cups. Despite the condensation dripping down the sides, most of the letters were legible.

He smiled, putting the dimple on display. "If we have another liquid mishap, this combo of letters can't come close to the 'anagram' we formed yesterday."

"Don't you mean 'anusgram'?" I cracked up. If Po could see me flirting!

With a laugh-snort, Javi flopped onto the blanket. I joined him, leaning toward the screen. "I haven't seen this movie before, but I know the basics. Great White terrorizes small town." I covered my mouth. "Oops. Did I spoil it for you?"

"Nope. It's one of my favorites."

"A lifeguard who loves a killer-shark movie? I don't know if that makes you one of the bravest junior lifeguards or one of the worst." I took an exaggerated gulp of water.

"Wow. You really went there, huh?" he asked.

"You did almost drown me."

He snickered, swishing the ice cubes in his cup. "Not on purpose. And sorry to burst your bubble, but *Jaws* isn't about a killer shark. I mean, it is on the surface, I guess. Underneath the 'waters,' though, it's really about a guy trying to save his family."

"Not like I know exactly what that feels like," I said.

Javi traced the patch stitched onto his uniform. "Like I TMI-ed you earlier, yeah, me neither." He laughed. "Which I hope you didn't mind, by the way. My best friend thinks I 'have a tendency to overshare.'"

I shook my head. Sure, it was sorta comical to air some of our dirty laundry with a bundle of fresh flags between us. It also felt weirdly good to air it—period. "I think I'm starting to prefer oversharing—at least about 'After' topics," I said, making air quotes again. "Versus no sharing."

I tried to keep the barbs from my voice when I added, "The latter's the approach my dad and Po—until recently and only sparingly—take when it comes to talking about Mom."

"I'm sorry," Javi said. Whether he meant my loss, not being able to process it with my family, or both, I couldn't tell. He said something about how important it is for him to honor his dad's memory.

"I'm happy you're able to do that. Does your mom also—" My throat constricted, making it impossible to get more words out. What if Dad could never get on board with me wanting to talk about Mom? With me wanting to keep her alive in our house somewhere other than hallway frames?

Javi didn't press when I stayed quiet. Instead, he slid my cup of water closer.

I took a much-needed sip. When I changed the direction of the convo, he went along with it. "Um, so does the guy in the movie . . . end up saving his family?"

"You're going to have to wait to find out," he said.

"Nope." Tonight's plan involved dropping off the flags. Chatting a bit. Leaving before the movie started so I could prep some Paulina-related items ahead of tomorrow's rehearsal. "Tell me what happens."

He shook his head. "First off, no spoilers. Secondly, maybe the attempt to save them is more important than the actual rescue."

"If you're on shift the next time I visit lifeguard station eighteen, please remind me not to get into the water."

"So there is going to be a next time?" His lips twitched with a smile. "I was going to wait until later to ask, but now that we're on the topic . . ."

"Like you said yourself, 'no spoilers.'" I grabbed a piece of popcorn and threw it at him. He grabbed the kernel and dunked it back into the tub. Who knew flirting was an activity way more fun to do than just observe it from the sidelines? "If I'm going to have to wait to see if this dude saves his family, so are you."

Javi's smile dialed up higher than Mickey's. Trying to hide the size of my own, I dropped my gaze to the towel. Focused on it until brain functions resumed.

Hmm. Not terry cloth. But a sturdier material that was at the same time more delicate.

As if reading my thoughts, he said, "It's Guatemalan textile." He brushed his fingers over some of the fabric's diamond-shaped embroidery.

I mirrored his movements. The different patterns and shapes reminded me of an ancient language. Was it? "It's beautiful."

"My dad brought it back from his . . ." He breathed in, his exhale barely audible over the commotion of the crowd and the crashing surf. "His last trip there."

Once more, the conversation traveled from the shallow end of a pool to teetering over the edge of the Mariana Trench. He looked ready to dive in.

A little more prepared to join him, I sucked in some air and said, "Can I ask you something?"

"Shoot."

"I'm two years in." My eyes stung. "Does it ever get easier?"

"Oof." The weight of the question hunched him over. Perhaps the weight kept pressing, because he brought the bundle of flags under his head, using it as a makeshift pillow.

I did the same with my backpack, lying down next to him. Dark purple clouds streaked the mottled blue sky. If I watercolored this blackness overhead, the page would look like a giant bruise. "I'm taking your silence means no."

I'd suspected as much. Sometimes the hole in my chest didn't feel Mom-size—it spanned the length of the Milky Way. How could carrying something that massive ever get less arduous?

"It's been four years, and no, not really." His voice was as thin as tissue paper. "I'm really close to my mom. Dad used to say I inherited the gift of gab from her, so we talk about everything."

Like Mom and I used to.

"When we don't feel like talking," he said, "we'll binge telenovelas or K-dramas."

"Mom and I would do the same thing, but with rom-coms or Disney movies." A huge stab of loss went through me, except . . . I couldn't help but smile at his good fortune. "That's so awesome you have her."

"I know. My best friend is also super supportive. I don't know if having both of them around is like constantly being strapped to a life vest or that time-heals-all-wounds crap is true, but . . ." He rubbed at the Mickey appliqué, not unlike Aladdin coaxing Genie from the lamp to make everything better. "Weirdly, parts of it do get less hard. I don't know if that makes any sense."

It didn't. So I stayed silent. Kept my face fixed toward the sky. Some of the clouds were shifting enough for stars to emerge.

"That's Polaris," Javi said, pointing straight up. "Did you know it takes three hundred and twenty-three years for its light to travel to Earth?"

My stomach twisted. "Great. For all we know it could be already dead."

The night sky was a massive graveyard. I closed my eyes, keeping back tears. Keeping the sight of these massive things seemingly burning with life—but weren't—away. Apparently nowhere was safe.

No. Not true. Special events and parties were safe spaces. They celebrated life and the living. No loss for miles there.

"Some stars explode. Some simply fade away. In the end, they are like us, I guess." The bundle of flags rustled as he shifted his body toward mine. "Just because something—or someone—passes doesn't mean their light doesn't shine on."

After a beat of silence, a small smile tugged at my lips. Maybe it was his words sinking in. Maybe it was that more clouds shifted, more stars emerged. The Big Dipper. And right above it, the smaller but no less twinkly lights of the Little Dipper.

A Big Spoon and Little Cuchara.

Warmth poured over me, filling some of the hollowness inside my chest. The void left by Mom's absence didn't feel so cavernous anymore. The sky didn't feel as vast in its infinite sadness.

Not when it was capable of sparkling against so much darkness.

I reached for my cup. Ice cubes glinted inside like jewels on a tiara. "To starlight," I said.

"And summer nights."

We clinked our cups together and took synchronized chugs.

Whoops and applause boomed from the crowd as the images hit the screen and the movie's soundtrack floated around us. For the briefest moment, I pretended they cheered for me trying to keep sparkling against the dark . . . cheered for the Pinterest board and sketches flashing inside my head.

A belle of the ball making her grand entrance with a swoon-worthy plus-one. Only, it wasn't Paulina or Angie. Or any of the other classmates on my potential-client list. The person under the spotlights, gliding under a swirl of glitter confetti, was me.

For the first time, I imagined what it would be like if I were the girl of the hour instead of the person planning her every minute. My hands itched for the crook of Javi's elbow again. Instead of my fingers skimming his hoodie, I pretended they brushed the satiny finish of a chambelán's tux.

I caught an ice cube between my teeth. Biting down, the *crunch* burst my fantasy. A laugh so small slipped out that Javi didn't hear it. Who was I kidding?

All I wanted was to keep marching down the fairy godmother path. For a second, though, it'd felt nice to walk in a princess's glass slippers.

CHAPTER FIFTEEN

Po pressed her elbows into my stomach. "Wake up, sleepy head." Her eyes shone brighter than the sunshine spilling into "my" room. In what universe did she wake up before I did?

I groaned, pushing her elbows off me. "Need more rest before dance rehearsal with Paulina today." I tried to pull the covers over my head.

Po grabbed the duvet, holding it hostage. "Ah-ah-ah. Don't you even think about it. I can't believe I fell asleep before you got home. Was there any K-I-S-S-I-N-G?" She sang-shouted.

"Nope. More like T-A-L-K-I-N-G." Javi's openness about how difficult this process was hadn't plastered over every fracture running through my heart. But our conversation had filed down some of its jagged edges. Made it easier for me to snuggle against the pillow without fear of slashing it open.

"Details of the date—now!" Po said.

"I wouldn't call it a 'date.'"

"You guys went to a movie. On the beach. You got home after ten." She rattled off each fact like checking items off a list. "If it walks like a date and talks like a date—"

"He needed to get the lifeguard flags back. The place was

packed. The movie was *Jaws*," I said, listing things back. "Maybe it was a friendly hangout."

Po harrumphed. She flopped onto the bed, wriggling under the covers next to me. "Maybe. Maybe not." She drew the covers over both our heads. "The only thing that matters is what *you* want it to be."

"I freaking knew you were going to say that."

She tugged a handful of my tresses. Last night's salty air had transformed the flat-ironed locks back into curls. "Don't sidestep the convo. Do you like this guy or not?"

My body flushed. And not from the heat of us huddling inside this cocoon. "I do," I said. "But . . ."

"No buts! I mean yes, butts! I don't even like guy butts, but his is an anatomical wonder."

I laughed because it was true. Still, cute as Javi was, he'd said it best: I was the castle towers—not the princess pining inside them.

Along with the loads of planning Paulina's party required? Not the ideal time to add another event to my schedule. No matter how badly I wanted to.

"I can hear the gears in your head turning. Don't overthink this, Little Cuchara. Just go with—"

"The flow?"

"Exactly," she said.

I massaged my palms, considering Po's advice. Dang. I'd been doing a lot more of that lately. If the sky fell this instant, at least the duvet would shield us. "Hypothetically speaking, suppose I did dip a toe into 'the flow' . . . Wouldn't it be smart to have a junior lifeguard at the ready?" I asked.

Po broke out into squeals that rivaled the cheer squad. "Absolutely. Imagine having all the mouth-to-mouth you could ever want on standby."

For all her chaos, her sense of humor never strayed far off course. "Took you long enough to make that joke."

"CPR for Cas! CPR for Cas!"

A pounding of steps came up the hallway. The door flew open. "Girls, is everything all right? I heard screaming."

We pulled the covers down. Dad stood in the doorway dressed for work. "Everything's good, Dad," I said.

"Better than good. Cas had a blast on her first date last night."

"That's great." He scratched his stubble. "I think." That earned twin giggles from me and Po. "Listen, I'm running late but I left you breakfast in the kitchen." He slipped his phone from his navy suit pants. His face stayed fixed on the screen on his way out of the room.

A *ping* from one nightstand, a chime from the other. I reached for my phone. Read the new event he'd scheduled on the family calendar.

The Talk.

I sunk back into bed, huffing while Po cracked up.

Although part of me appreciated Dad's interest in dad-ing again, this was one event I was not looking forward to.

With summer classes, club meetings, and sports teams practicing on campus, cars crammed every corner of Matteo Beach High's parking lot. Inside my own car, we ate the pastelitos de guayaba. Washed down the Cuban pastries with the coffee Dad had made.

"Breakfast of champions," I said, relishing the taste of two things that shouldn't pair so well but did.

Po smiled. Flakes of the crisp puff pastry glittered on her lips. The pink lipstick matched the guava paste stuck between her front teeth. Enjoying the cuteness curbed the instinct to immediately reach into my utility bag and hand her a floss stick.

"Where else do you think I get the energy to lead the volleyball team to so many trophies?" She laughed.

"Trophies that will help you get into Alma or UCI," I said.

Her laughter flatlined.

"Hey," I said, reaching across the car's center console to squeeze her knee. "Don't worry. You're going to get in. Your hot dogs were such a hit the event committee will probably be thrilled to have you join this fall. Plus, if this side hustle keeps growing, I'll need a full-time assistant." Until I started Mandy's internship, of course.

"You mean it, Little Cuchara? Because—and BTW, I'll deny this if you ever bring it up again—I put off thinking about college for so long that some fight-or-flight response must've kicked in." Po blew across the coffee although it was barely warm. "I'm grateful you constantly nagged, because now I have a shot." She sat up straighter. "Thanks for also letting me cook for SBA because I really miss cooking at In-N-Out." She took a huge breath, letting it out in a single rush. "I really miss Mom."

I retracted my hand from her knee. Talk about going from zero to a hundred. "Yeah, me too." I turned my gaze to the driver-side mirror.

If this topic was the one I wanted to discuss so badly, why was my jaw clenching to prevent more words from coming out?

Heavy silence filled the car instead of a conversation I thought I'd wanted to have. Why did bringing up Mom sometimes hurt as much as glossing over her absence? Hurt as much as the absence itself?

I slumped into the car seat. Po fidgeted in hers, looking as uncomfortable as me. Relief settled over me when she shifted toward the school's parking lot.

The invitation to keep talking about Mom expired.

Clearly, I needed to practice more Parental Past Tense with

Javi. Learn how to keep dipping a toe into these conversations without drowning. Then I could help Po and Dad build their own fluency.

"C'mon," I said, changing the topic for both our sakes. "Let's go dance with Paulina."

Po's posture loosened. "Yes, please." One benefit of being Hurricane Po, I supposed, was how quickly she breezed from one emotion to the next.

She flipped down the passenger-side sun visor. Checking herself out in the mirror, she gasped at the pastelito crumbs on the corners of her mouth. She wiped them off before applying a new coat of lipstick. "Hey, do you have those—"

"Here you go." I extended a floss stick. Before I released it, I said, "Swear you'll behave."

"Pinky promise." She wrenched it away, bolting from the car across the lot. I got out, loafers pounding as I tried to catch up.

The dance team faced the back wall, perfectly spread out. Each dancer held an arm behind themselves, standing still as statues. An alarm blared through the speakers overhead. When the horns and drums dropped, the team spun around, breaking out into a routine.

Hips rolled. Arms spun and legs swung. Individual dancers took turns springing forward in different techniques—jazz, ballet, hip-hop, gymnastics—for a few beats before their movements synced back together.

Po swayed her hips and motioned for me to join. I shook my head, choosing instead to mouth some of the chorus. I knew it from one of the playlists Mom had listened to while cooking: *Dance the night away, Live your life and stay young on the floor . . .*

The team dropped into synchronized splits. Torsos and limbs did things AP Bio hadn't covered. I angled my head to get a better look.

Would I ever get the chance to dance with Javi? While one guy was on my mind, my gaze drifted to another. Marcus.

The captain of the dance team sure looked happy being at the center of these twirling bodies. When he caught me staring, he winked an electric-blue eye at me.

Corny as it was, so many classmates at Matteo Beach High would kill to be in my loafers right now. Instead of winking back, I gave him an exaggerated eye-roll, followed up by extending both hands and signing "flirt" in ASL.

He gave one of his low, husky laughs before spinning into one flawless pirouette after another. The team fell across the floor on the song's last beat. Panting, they shot their arms up in victory.

Po clapped so hard I was surprised her palms didn't split open. More applause rang behind us. So did the squeak of Paulina's wedged Jordans.

The second her glitter-lined eyes locked on Po, Paulina dropped her serious mask. *That was quick.*

"That choreo was freaking amazing," Paulina said. "So's your idea for the 'Imperial March' paso doble." She shimmied, making the red lightsaber earrings sway.

"The Very Merry Unquince's off to the races," Po said.

A light-headedness swept over me, as if I'd just blown up a dozen balloons in one go. "You really think so?"

"Obviously." Paulina asked. "I'm working with a Mandy Whitmore intern, after all."

I stiffened. "Right."

The second Paulina moved her attention to Marcus, I licked off my sweat mustache. "Well, well, well," Paulina said as he wiped his forehead with a hand towel before telling the team to take a thirty-minute break. Most of the team headed out of the gym.

Gianna and Lee, Gianna's BFF on the dance team, stayed put, aiming their phones at the distracted Paulina—before moving them over to me.

Gianna waggled her phone. A few seconds later, my back pocket buzzed twice.

A notification that she—and also Hot Goss—now followed me on Insta. Another buzz ushered in a new DM. Are you planning Paulina Reyes's Very Merry Unquince? I'm OBSESSED with her channel!

I didn't even bother to hide my smile. YES! I messaged back.

Lee danced all the way out the doors. So did Gianna, even with her face glued to her phone.

Another notification lit up my screen.

Hot Goss tagged me.

Mirror, mirror, on the wall, our event chair nabbed Disney's fairest YouTuber of them all 👀

Between Paulina's promised shout-out and Gianna broadcasting my new gig to the entire student body, my side hustle now had major buzz.

Now *I* had buzz. My entire body hummed in a way it never had before. *Stepping into the limelight is sorta fun.*

More notifications poured in. I wanted to read them to see what people were saying about me, but couldn't. Not with the way Po draped her arms over Paulina and me, squeezing us into a group huddle. "Isn't he a meaty dish?" Paulina said, watching Marcus strut over.

Po shrugged. "I wouldn't know. I have no appetite for that type of meat." Pink streaks went up her neck. "In case you're wondering."

If my face hadn't been so close to Paulina's, I would've missed the way she bit the inside of her cheek. "Good to know. As for me, me gusta de todo . . . in case you're wondering."

At Paulina's "liking everything," Po hiccuped.

Cute as this will-they-won't-they was, Po was my assistant, and Paulina, my client.

Not merely my client, but the key to unlocking Mandy's internship. I broke up our huddle, ready to start rehearsal, only for Paulina to jump in with, "¿Y tú, Cas? What do you like?"

So far it wasn't "what" I liked but who. To bring back some semblance of professionalism, I slipped my phone back into my pocket and said, "Starting practice on time."

"Don't be such a buzzkill, Cas." Po turned to Paulina, opening her big mouth again. "She recently met this—"

Before she mixed more of our business with my (maybe) pleasure, Marcus came to the rescue. He kissed both sides of my cheeks before fist-bumping Po.

"Paulina, I'd like you to meet our school's captain of the dance team, Marcus Bennett," I said.

I'd told her about Marcus being Deaf on our call, so she had her Notes app ready to make communication easier. So excited to get my paso doble on! Cas is a GENIUS! Paulina typed, holding the screen for him to see. She brought the phone back to add, PS Is it okay to film some of our practice for my vlog?

He nodded, giving her a thumbs-up.

"Cas had so many amazing ideas for my party," she said and typed at the same time. "It got me brainstorming new things I want to incorporate."

My stomach sank. What new things? "Like adding an extra dance or something?"

In exchange for help in Spanish class, Marcus had promised *one* choreographed dance. Po assumed I took Spanish instead of another language to get an easy A. Truth was, I wanted to anchor myself to another part of our past that wasn't a staple at home anymore.

I dug my fingernails into my palms to refocus. "Or do you have something entirely different in mind?"

Please don't.

She batted her faux lashes at me, then Po. This time, she didn't let her mask slip. "You know how I wanted to perform a solo dance?"

I parroted back what she'd said less than twenty-four hours ago. "'A solo dance symbolizes empowerment.'"

Paulina nodded. "Well, I changed my mind."

"Change your mind, change your life, I always say."

"Aw, thanks, Po." Paulina tucked a sleek lock of hair behind her ear.

I gritted my teeth. "Yeah, thanks, Po" I said, shooting Marcus a drowning look.

Now that Paulina wanted to change this aspect of the unquince, I'd probably owe him lots more tutoring. Not the worst thing, but my calendar was crammed enough.

I wiped my sweaty palms down the side of my blouse. We hadn't even begun the first dance rehearsal and already Paulina wanted to switch things up. A far cry from demanding live swans to be featured as backup dancers, but the quincezilla meter ratcheted up a notch.

I cleared my throat and said, "So now do you want an entire court?" I supposed that would be better for Mandy purposes anyway.

"Not a whole court," she said and typed at the same time. "I'll still manage to make it look like one's there in postproduction."

A tiny breath of relief. Mandy's application was still safe and sound.

"What I can't add in post is . . ." Paulina looked over her shoulder to the double doors and sighed. Typed something on her phone. "Ugh. Baymoon's late."

Po and I swung our heads at each other.

Baymoon? Was this person conceived at Coachella?

"If it's just me and a partner, we'd still nail the 'deconstructed' aesthetic. Plus, La Mera Mera can finally shut up about"—she fidgeted with her gold necklace—"me having a chambelán."

Marcus pointed to the word on Paulina's phone screen, forehead wrinkling. He tilted his head to sign, What's that?

Escort, I finger-spelled.

Flirting with my sister while her date waited in the wings? So not cool. If Paulina had kept mum on a possible significant other until now, what else was she keeping quiet about?

As if I had any right to judge.

Perhaps some secrets were like presents: best kept under wraps. Still. Poor Po.

"Like we talked about the other day, she really cares what Tía Mari thinks." She sighed. "But the more I thought about it, the more it felt wrong not to include Baymoon." Genuine affection filled Paulina's voice, easing some—not all—of my frustrations.

"I guess this way La Mera Mera can shove her cake in my aunt's face, and I can eat it, too." Paulina gave a small smile. It didn't reach her glitter eyeliner.

"That's great," I said, trying my best to return one.

Paulina held up her phone. I know you two already arranged a solo paso doble, but can we revamp the choreography so my chambelán can join?

Marcus waited for my answer. So did Po.

If there were a *Sisterly Solidarity Handbook*, there would probably be a section about helping your sibling get the girl. Only, I wasn't reading from *that* handbook, but from *How to Become a Fairy Godmother's Apprentice* instead.

I pulled my planner from my backpack. Opened the tab to Paulina's Very Merry Unquince. Crossed out the *solo* in front of *paso doble*. With our family HEA hanging on Paulina's party, what choice did I have? "Anything to make this the very merriest unquince you've ever had."

Paulina beamed. "I knew you'd say yes."

Po scrubbed a hand over her face. "I need to go to the bathroom," she said, stalking off.

"Wait!" Paulina chased after her. "I left my iced coffee in my car and the props Cas wanted for the dance. Help me get them after?"

Po stopped. Her face was caught somewhere between hope and dejection. I motioned for her to get going. "Yes, Po, go help Paulina."

For better or worse, she'd signed up as my assistant on this.

As they left, I turned to Marcus and rubbed a fist across my chest. Sorry, I said, then finger-spelled, Diva.

No worries. Switching the steps should be okay, he said. Help me block it?

The doors flung open. Lee and Gianna rolled in early from their dance break. They hung around the back of the gym, appearing to stretch. But if Gianna was simply warming up, why was her phone pointed at us?

Was she trying to boost me again, or did she want an inside scoop for Hot Goss?

Can't you use someone from your team? Gianna and Lee are back, I told Marcus.

Wouldn't be half as fun as dancing with you, he said. He swept my hand into his. Pulled me close.

Dang his minty shampoo smelled good.

Not as good as Javi's lavender one, though.

Marcus spun me across the polished floors. Twirled me back in. And actually dipped me. As I stared into his electric-blue eyes, the only thing running through my mind was how many coats of brown it'd take to make them match Javi's.

Would he text later? Ask me to the next Movies at the Beach?

The cardio cranked up my pulse. Except the possibility of hanging out with Javi again was what sent my heart skipping.

"May I have this dance?" a voice asked from behind me.

I pivoted around. My breath hitched. It was one thing to make someone else's fantasies come true. Quite another to have mine walk into the building.

With a little bow, Javi extended a hand.

Marcus stepped back with a small smile.

I laced my fingers through Javi's. Whether he started our waltz or I did, it didn't matter. Marcus, Lee and Gianna, the gym—everything faded until it was just us gliding across the floor. "Javi, what are you doing here?"

"Shouldn't I be asking you the same thing, Castle Towers?" His face mirrored both my excitement and confusion. "Actually, there's another question you should answer first. Do you want to go see the next Movies at the Beach on Saturday? We can keep talking about everything. Or nothing."

I lifted my face to the ceiling. The old-school disco ball hung there motionless. The way Javi and I spun around the gym more than made up for it. He drew me close. As close as when we were on his scooter. Even without the motor, a thrill went through my core.

"I'd love to."

His dimple appeared. "Great."

On the next spin, I caught the scent of lavender again. Our waltz eased into a slow dance.

I'd helped plan so many of these dances, and here I was, finally having my first one.

In perfect imitation of what I'd observed countless times, I lay my cheek against his chest.

If he wore an Italian cotton tux shirt instead of this hoodie, would this still feel as cozy?

There I went picturing him in a tux again. I was so caught up in this moment, dancing to the rhythm of our shattered-but-not-completely-broken hearts, I let myself say something off script.

"Before we get into the specifics of why we're both here, there's something else I want to ask," I said.

If Paulina wanted a deconstructed quince, wouldn't she love the idea of her planner bringing a date to the activities?

Sure, I'd have to clear it with her first, but still. "Would you—"

Double doors slammed from the front of the gym. "Thanks for blocking the dance in my absence, Cas," Paulina said. "Gracias for finally gracing us with your presence, Baymoon." She lifted a too-familiar trenta Starbucks cup into the air. The ice cubes clanked against each other.

The iced mocha might as well have splashed me all over again because goose bumps broke out across my arms.

Javi was Baymoon?!

Our slow dance came to a halt. My vision stopped spinning; my thoughts didn't. Each one probably washed over the canvas of my face. Especially the acronym etching between my brows.

WTF.

CHAPTER SIXTEEN

Hola and hello, everyone. It's Paulina!"

Was she smiling wider now than in her previous vlogs?

"If I'm extra bubbly, it's because today I'm kicking off my Very Merry Unquince Series." Her mouth formed a perfect O.

If she wanted her viewers to witness the definition of genuine shock, Paulina simply needed to flip the selfie stick over to me. Or Po. Not Javi.

Why was he grinning? Putting that infuriating dimple on display, business as usual?

"I'm starting off with a sneak peek of dance rehearsal. First, let me introduce you to my chambelán." She pulled Javi into the frame. He gave a huge wave, seeming very comfortable in front of the camera.

Here, I'd assumed he only liked to watch spectacles—not star in them. In the role of Prince Charming to Paulina's Sith princess, no less. The nerve of this dude.

"Say hi, Javier," Paulina said.

"Hi, Javier." He laugh-snorted at his own joke. The ridiculous sound cooled my anger, at least for a second.

"This clown and I've known each other since forever. My mom—" She lowered the selfie stick, dropping her mask in the process. She wiggled her jaw side to side. "Going to edit that part out. Ready, Baymoon?"

He nodded. Paulina lifted the camera (and her frown) and said, "Our parents probably always envisioned my quinceañera as a dress rehearsal for our wedding or something. Cute, huh?" She giggled.

Po cocked her head at me, like she also noticed Paulina's laughter sounded too forced to be true. Then again, who knew what was and wasn't real with her?

Or with "Baymoon."

I dropped my gaze to my loafers. Like I could call their kettles black.

"And this is Castillo Torres." Paulina pointed the camera toward me.

I managed a feeble wave. Not the impression I wanted to make for my first advertising shot. "My lovely quinceañera planner and hashtag-chingona interning at M—"

Po coughed super loudly. Mimed a zipper motion across her lips. Paulina lowered the selfie stick.

Thank you, Big Spoon. What a massive spike and block. No wonder Po helmed the volleyball squad.

"Everything okay?" Paulina asked.

Javi grabbed the iced mocha off the bleachers and extended it to Po. "Need something to drink?"

Po crossed her arms, refusing to take it. Paulina arched a brow.

"Um, Po's trying to cut back on caffeine," I said, scrunching my nose. If it didn't grow like Pinocchio's on this lie, it certainly would on the next. "Also, Whitmore and Associates has first-time clients sign NDAs, so. Can we ixnay on the Mandy stuff, please?"

"Ahh, of course." Paulina face-palmed. "I should've known better. I'll edit that part out before I upload. Sorry."

Could she also edit out the last five minutes of my life? Better yet, the last two years?

"You don't have to apologize." I turned to Javi, glowering. *But you do.* "It's my bad for not sending it yet."

Great. Now I had to commit forgery to keep this facade going.

"Okay, guys, we're going to practice our Darth Vader–themed paso doble. You heard that right. A. Darth. Vader. Ballroom. Dance." This time, she didn't playact her excitement.

It filled the gym, entrancing me enough to inch back into the camera's frame. "It's going to be perfect," I said.

I'd make sure of it. Not only for the sake of her unquince, but everything else that'd follow if it went off without more complications.

"Perfect it will be," Paulina said in a Yoda voice. "I'll upload footage later. Until then, 'ignite the spark.'"

"'Light the fire,'" Javi said.

She stopped recording. Shook out her arms as if trying to fling off her YouTube persona. "Intro done, now the rehearsal. Whoops." She face-palmed again. "I forgot the props." She turned toward the doors. "Cas, can you please stand in for me again so Baymoon can practice?" Her tone made clear this was a command, not a request. "Po, come help me for a sec?"

Po begrudgingly followed her. But not before pointing to her eyes, then to Javi, mouthing, *I'm watching you.* Thankfully one of us had read the *Sisterly Solidarity Handbook*.

Javi's brows creased before relaxing. "Oh, I get it." He chuckled. "You think there's something romantic going on with me and Paulina." The chuckles built to belly laughs, ending with an encore of his signature snorts. "I assure you, Castle Towers, it's not like that." He took a step closer.

I moved backward. In the span of a few minutes, we'd gone

from waltz to slow dance to tango. I shook my head, which only added to my dizziness.

I knew Javi was a jock. How had I not realized he was also a player? "Whatever, *Baymoon*."

Javi opened his mouth to say something. I cut him off with my hand. "I don't have time for an explanation." I tugged my phone from my back pocket and texted Marcus that we were ready for him. "Let's simply focus on the dance, okay?"

Marcus came down from the top of the bleachers, trailed by Gianna and Lee. The dramatic duo sat on the first row. Front and center for this telenovela. Great.

"Um, Gianna, Lee? This dance is a very important part of Paulina's birthday. She was fine with letting you watch her film the intro, but she probably wants to preserve some privacy in rehearsals. There's also the matter of minimizing video leaks before she uploads them herself, so . . ." I motioned to the huge exit signs over the doors.

Lee shook his head. "Marcus asked me to help with the music."

Gianna nodded. "Plus, like I told you, I'm a huuuge Paulina fan. You have my word—I won't post the dance."

My jaw tensed. Interesting that she didn't promise to *not* post anything else.

"Come on, Castle Towers," Javi whispered. "She's a fan and she promised. You could make her day."

"Oh no. I'm not going to fall for your Mr. Nice Guy act again," I muttered. As Po would say, *fool me once, shame on you; fool me twice, I'll kick your ass.*

I need them to start and stop the music and take choreography notes, Marcus said.

My shoulders drooped. "Fine, but no posting," I told Gianna.

She squealed. Marcus gave a single clap, bringing the rehearsal to order. Wait. Wasn't that supposed to be my job?

He motioned for me and Javi to take our places. A drawn-out sigh. It sucked that Javi turned out to be a frog instead of a prince, but no toad would stop me from becoming a fairy godmother's apprentice.

I placed a hand inside of Javi's. At his touch, I tried my hardest not to flinch.

Or melt. *Curse you, body, for betraying me.*

Follow my steps, Marcus typed, holding the screen up to Javi. He gestured to Lee, who tapped something on his phone. A second later, Darth Vader's theme song exploded from the speakers.

Javi followed Marcus's steps as best he could. He stumbled over himself. Nearly tripped on his sandals. He let laugh-snorts loose as he attempted to get the matador steps down—all while trying to avoid trampling on my loafers.

Marcus held up his hand. The music stopped. A huge breath, then he signaled Lee to restart the track. He motioned us to begin again, shooting me a look, then said, You lead.

I side-eyed Javi, smirking. *Mess with the bull, you get the horns.*

I pushed off of him, spinning across the floor. Funneled all my conflicting emotions, and this chaos, into something I could control: this dance's steps.

My arms swung wide. Legs kicked toward Javi's nether regions. "If you don't watch your steps, 'Baymoon,' Paulina can add more family jewels to her birthday tiara."

Javi cracked up. Instead of following my next sequence, he grabbed one of my arms. Tugging me back, he said, "You keep saying that like it's some pet name when it's my actual name."

I wheeled out of his grasp, shooting a fist—er, hand—over

my head like Marcus demonstrated. "You said it was Javier Luna."

"Exactly. Javier *Bae*-Luna." He twirled me back in. "Luna means moon—I thought you knew Spanish."

Although my body was no longer in motion, my mind kept spinning, trying to catch up.

"My mom's Korean," he continued. "She's always advocated matriarchal alternatives to patriarchal traditions."

Oh.

"I like seeing both of their names next to mine when I write my full name. It's a daily reminder that Dad's still with me."

Ooooh.

I swallowed. Maybe I'd jumped to conclusions too quickly. I could take a page from Po, breeze off and forget embarrassing things. But I should also continue to live up to my namesake.

Stand firm. Lower drawbridges only when the guests mean you no harm.

I circled around him, head high and heart still cautious. "Okay, but that doesn't explain why you asked me to the movies. Twice. When according to Paulina, y'all have been practically betrothed since infancy."

"Our parents were friends. More like her dad was friends with my parents. Her mom's sorta, hmm—" He tipped his chin toward the lights, as if trying to find a nicer word up there.

"A tad Mami Dearest?" I offered.

"Accurate and clever." Javi put his dimple on display. "As far as the betrothal—"

Marcus motioned for Javi to dip me. I hated that I had to trust him to bend me backward without dropping me. His grip held sturdy and he lifted me back up gently. "Hardly," he finished.

We stood like that for a few moments. Panting nose to nose.

With no place for my eyes to run to but his big brown ones . . . or his lips, mere centimeters away.

The gathering speed of the instruments perfectly mimicked the wild thumping of my heart. Or maybe it was his, quickening against mine.

For the second time today, Paulina's voice cut through everything. "Yes. That's exactly the passion I want to bring my viewers." She swung two lightsabers over her head. "Brava on the choreo, song, and these props, Cas."

Po did that whistle thing with her fingers. Marcus gave me a thumbs-up. Lee jumped in with applause. But Gianna tilted her head.

Dang. Did she suspect something? I peeled myself away from Javi. Braced myself for the latest Hot Goss story to buzz from my back pocket.

Thankfully, none came. My crushing-on-the-chambelán secret was safe.

More classified info to add to the List of Things to Keep Away from Paulina.

Except—wait.

Why was Po's lipstick smudged all over Paulina's mouth?

And how did Paulina's glitter eyeliner end up smeared on Po's cheek?

Paulina's posture went rigid when she caught me staring. She turned on one of the lightsabers. It hummed to life, casting a red glow onto her cheekbones. "Apparently we all have some explaining to do. Emergency meeting. Parking lot. Now."

Another command from the quincezilla. Only this one, I happily obliged.

CHAPTER SEVENTEEN

The four of us congregated around Paulina's black SUV.

"If we're going to work together, we have to trust each other." Paulina said.

"Uh-huh," I forced from a scratchy throat. "Totally. Trust."

"So for transparency, I'm adding the Very Merry Unquince to my USC application this fall." She swung the lightsaber over her head. "Did you know George Lucas went there?"

Probably due to my jaw unhinging, Javi leaned in and whispered, "He created *Star Wars*. She's talked about wanting to be like him when she grows up since forever.'"

I mentally thanked Javi for the Wookieepedia entry—but no. Pieces of Paulina's or Star Wars's origin stories weren't the reasons for my concern. "You're going to be a senior?" I asked, my voice rising. "Did you skip a bunch of grades, or are you not technically turning fifteen?"

Po turned on the other lightsaber. Its distinctive hum pierced the air. "Chill, Little Cuchara." She pointed the blue saber at my neck. "Age ain't nothing but a número. Plus, people turning thirty are having 'doble quinces' now."

Paulina smiled at her before frowning at me. "Yes, I'm going to be a senior. No, I'm not turning fifteen." She crossed her arms over her chest, restoring her stare to its former stoic glory. "Why? Does Mandy Whitmore and Associates check IDs or something? Will she fire me for being seventeen?"

"No one is going to check your ID." I dabbed my forehead with my blouse's sleeve. "Or fire you—I swear."

Javi rubbed his eyes. "Might wanna wait until the rest of the story before making any promises, Castle Towers. Because in case you haven't guessed by now"—he held up his hands, spreading his fingers wide—"there's more!"

Gulp. So this was what happened to people who put the cart before the horse. They got trampled by hooves.

The sun caught against Paulina's glitter eyeliner as she narrowed her eyes at Javi. Her glare softened only when she turned to Po. "After our first call, I couldn't stop thinking about what you said." Paulina sighed.

Po raised a brow. "Which part?"

"The part about how college admissions boards would eat up a quinceañera docuseries."

Po's face relaxed.

"I discussed it with my college adviser afterward, and we came to the conclusion that a video of me 'experiencing rituals of modern Latine life' will help my application stand out." Paulina swatted Po on the shoulder with her red saber.

"Told ya heritage's like candy to college boards," Po said, swatting her back with the blue saber.

"For all we know, maybe the Force was even at play. Making me put off having a quince until now for this very purpose."

"Oh c'mon, Pau. You held off to piss off your mom," Javi said, laughing.

"Partly, yes. Being La Mera Mera's little puppet to perform our success in el norte is exhausting." She sliced the saber through the air.

The saber's hum echoed inside the hollows of my chest. Angie's mom had also wanted every aspect of her daughter's quince to be bigger, better, brighter. The party had probably been just as much a rite of passage for Angie as a status showcase for Mami Dearest.

But as the quince planning unfurled, there had been several moments of genuine affection between them. Gauging by Paulina's continued hard and aggressive swings of the lightsaber, I doubted she could say the same thing.

Clearly not all moms were created equal. Her complicated relationship with her mother made me miss how uncomplicated mine had been with my own.

Paulina's movements slowed. Her clenched jaw gave way to a smile brighter than both sun or saber. "But performing my Latine-ness to get into my dream school? I doubt the admissions board could pass up this opportunity for allyship and activism. Hell, maybe it will even elicit their guilt."

I nodded, gripping the edges of my planner. I'd assumed parties were about celebrating joy and the start of an HEA. But as I unwrapped the top layers of Angie's—and now Paulina's—quince, I was beginning to find they were also tied to elements of performance.

La Mera Mera wanted a quince to display their family's newfound wealth. Paulina wanted a quince to display her heritage.

She dressed like a Sith Lord, but was Paulina really Machiavelli incarnate? It didn't seem completely right to make a show out of ritual and tradition to game the college system. Still.

Using the unfairly stacked cards life randomly dealt . . . playing them however you needed to . . . it didn't seem totally wrong, either.

Let alone too far off from what I was doing myself.

"I get it, Paulina. I'm sorry about your mom using your party like that." *I'm sorry about using it like this, too.*

"Thanks, Cas. Once I'm a famous director, I won't have to sit through my mom's constant lectures. I won't have to act like I care about what my aunt thinks. Don't get me wrong—I love my parents." She turned off the lightsaber. "But I'm soo looking forward to the day when I have final cut on my choices."

Because of her YouTube platform and persona, I'd assumed she was in the driver's seat of her own life. But maybe she was more like Pinocchio and her mom like Stromboli: while Paulina took center stage, La Mera Mera controlled some—if not all—of her daughter's strings.

An urge to hug her crashed over me. Except, I was her planner, not her buddy. The only hope to keep our lines from getting more muddled than one of my old watercolor paintings was to keep our boundaries intact.

Some boundaries blurred anyway when Paulina turned to Po and said, "In the director's cut of this vlog series, you'd be my chambelána, versus having to throw Baymoon in at the last second per La Mera Mera's 'request.'"

"I'm a person, Pau," Javi said. "Not a food item you throw in last minute like salt."

Exactly. And you're sweeter, like sugar, anyway, I wanted to say but didn't.

Paulina rolled her eyes, but a giggle broke through. "I know. I'm just tying up loose ends with Po and trying to convince Cas I'm not some diva constantly demanding last-minute changes."

Javi bit his lips to keep from laughing. "Whatever you say, Alfreda Hitchcock."

Oh boy. Even I knew Hitchcock had allegedly been one of the most demanding directors to work with. How many more switch ups would she throw my way? Would I be able to keep up?

"Thanks for allowing me to be vulnerable with you two. It's not easy for me to do," Paulina said. Po patted her shoulder.

"You can say that again," Javi said, his voice teasing but brimming with empathy.

She playfully pointed the saber against his stomach. "Now that everything's cleared up, should we get back to practice?"

Before getting to the paso doble, shouldn't I have taken a cue from Paulina? Come clean about my own intentions for this bash? How could I not when she'd been so honest about hers?

I shot Po a look. Considering she was cozying up with Paulina, maybe she also agreed that the time had come to tell the truth.

But her mouth flattened to a thin line. She gave a tiny head shake.

"Oh, come on, Pau. That's not everything," Javi said. "You conveniently left out your idea of us possibly fake dating each other for more views."

Paulina's cheeks went red. "I told you to keep that on the cutting-room floor, Baymoon." She prodded his arm with the lightsaber. "I mean, I won't actively dissuade viewers from believing what they want to believe, but—" She ran her tongue over her teeth. "Not one of my better directorial visions, okay?"

"You know what they say," Po said, staring at me. "'The ends justify the means.'" *Oh, so when it suited her, she could get quotes right*. She jutted her chin at Javi. "Also, 'Perspective can be as easily lost as it is found.'"

Javi waved her quotes away. "As much as I love film facades and performances, I draw the line at actual fraud."

I held the planner up like a visor to shield myself from the harsh sun. Also to hide my guilty face. "We should really get back to rehearsal," I said.

"Seconding that motion," Po said.

Paulina used the edge of the saber to tip up the planner. "Finish what you were going to say a second ago first."

"Huh? I don't think I had anything to add," I said, voice growing tight.

"Yeah, when I mentioned clearing things up. You and Po shared *a look*. What's up?"

One awkward laugh and a warning glare from Po later, I reached into my utility bag, rummaging for my makeup wipes. "Oh, yes. I don't condone mixing business with whatever you two are doing." I handed one wipe to each of them. "So all I ask is for you to not let this"—I motioned to Po's left cheekbone smeared with Paulina's eyeliner, to Paulina's mouth smudged with Po's lipstick—"get in the way of planning a great party."

Paulina's face relaxed. So did Po's.

"You have my word," Paulina said, extending her hand. She shook mine hard enough for the coffee and pastelito from this morning to slosh inside an already-churning stomach.

"Thanks, Cas. You're the best planner a girl could have." She headed back to the gym, Po following a half step behind.

The distance between Paulina and my chance to come clean grew larger and larger. Until it disappeared behind the swinging gymnasium doors.

Javi took off his cap. Raked a hand through his wavy hair. *Lavender.*

"I know this production of hers is out there, but—" His throat bobbed. "She was really there for me After Dad. Especially when Mom couldn't take more time off work. So I need to be here for her now." Our eyes connected. "While she might've called first dibs on these twinkle toes—" He spun around with a sequence of dance moves.

I laughed hard enough to dislodge most of my guilt and worry.

When Javi came to a stop, he flicked the shirt pocket over his chest. *Gasp.* No, over his heart. "—Everything else . . ." His lips quivered a little. "Is free, should someone be interested."

His openness, his nervousness, drew me in. I didn't even realize how close we were standing until the scent of his mint gum rolled over me.

"Since you're not trying to decapitate me with your limbs anymore, I assume your misunderstandings about my relationship with Paulina have been cleared?"

I covered my face with the planner again. Oh Sith Lord. Only a spell could make the embarrassment over my outburst vanish. I almost plucked the pencil from the back of my ear and flicked it over my head. "FYI, I'm not the jealous type. It's more that . . ."

I couldn't be like Snow White's huntsman and hand my heart in a box to just anyone.

Shattered as it was, I needed to make sure anyone else handling it would do so with care.

Javi gently lowered the planner. "I know." His voice was soft. "You're not the only one that's been through the ringer, remember?" How could I forget? "Before we head back to rehearsal, anything else you want to ask? I'm an open book."

He could say that again. Me, on the other hand? Instead of commiserating with a Disney princess, now I related to a Disney prince.

Aladdin, I feel you, bro. Fessing up to your crush about your true identity is a million times harder than it seems. I parted my lips, caught between wanting to get something off my chest and basking in the warmth radiating from his.

"No questions, only an answer." If I couldn't tell him the truth, at the very least I could offer him a nugget of it. "About this." I pointed to his shirt pocket. "Yes. Someone's interested."

Javi beamed, his lopsided grin brighter than any jewel in Aladdin's Cave of Wonders.

So much for keeping business away from pleasure.

CHAPTER EIGHTEEN

"I love the idea of framing some of the artwork as posters for 'coming attractions,'" Callie said. "Having a screening in the auditorium would also bring in more money."

Murmurs of confirmation broke out from the desks across the room. Most committee members nodded.

"Great." Taking a page from Po's rating system, I sketched three stars next to *Movie Night* under the "SBA Art Auction Brainstorm" spreadsheet on my iPad.

"Should we open the floor for movie suggestions?" Callie asked, looking to me.

Before I could answer, Wesley jumped in. Rude.

"What about *Fast and Furious*?" he said.

"Which one?" I asked, only half joking.

"All of them," Wesley said, sparking laughter from the committee.

I hit my pencil across the top of the podium. "Vetoed."

"Fine," he huffed. "May I suggest the original *Star Wars* trilogy instead?"

"You may, except . . ." After rehearsing the paso doble for hours the other day, I needed a break from anything that contained the "Imperial March." I turned to the whiteboard. The marker squeaked against it as I sketched an outline of Darth Vader's helmet. Drew an *X* over it.

While Wesley slumped in his chair, back at the podium, I straightened to my full height.

I couldn't act this autocratic with Paulina. Sheesh, even at home, I could barely put a dent in Dad's gameplay.

SBA was my little kingdom. Here, I retained control. No way I'd give it up that easily. "Any *Star Wars*–related propositions will be rejected."

Wesley's nostrils flared. "Then why don't you pick?" He snapped his laptop shut. "That's what always ends up happening anyway."

Ouch. At the dog wash, Po mentioned something about me "putting the *I* back in *committee*." Echoes of a similar sentiment—alongside smatterings of *dangs* and one *yup*—from people less biased than my sister knocked the wind out of me.

Callie turned to me. "What Wes probably meant to say is, why don't you come up with themes? That way we can gauge what direction you're thinking of going."

I nodded. "How about rom-coms? Musicals?"

"Oh, *The King and I*!" Steph called out from the back of the room.

I created a new tab on the spreadsheet labeled *Movies*. Wrote a carbon copy on the whiteboard. Extending the olive branch to Wes, I said, "If you're really dead set on *Star Wars*, fine. For the love of my sanity, though, none of the movies that play Vader's theme song."

See? Queen of this castle was a far cry from Cuban dictator.

"No need to explain, Madam Chair. I'm a huge fan of Paulina Reyes, so I get it," Steph said. "You must've heard that song so many times."

Excited chatter rippled across the room. Between Hot Goss

and Paulina's channel, everyone at school—aside from Wes, apparently—knew I was planning this quince. "Exactly. Hearing it one more time will probably make my head explode."

Callie giggled, pointing at my phone on the desk right next to us. "Apparently not the only thing that's blowing up."

The screen brightened with new notifications. Squinting, I made out starry-eyed emojis from Po. A dancing woman in a red dress and thumbs-up from Paulina, confirming tomorrow's dress fitting. Yet another DM from Melina: Can you plan my sweet sixteen, or not??

I tensed. Paulina's party would take up most of my time this month. Better not to take on more.

I could almost hear Po saying, *You've made your sheets; now you've got to lie on them.*

"Cas?" Callie said. "About the themes. Anything else?"

I cleared my throat, flicking my gaze away from the phone. "Fairy tales. Old-school Disney animated movies." I covertly flicked my pencil over the spreadsheet. "Anything with a happily ever after."

I turned to the board, ready to jot down suggestions. "Start throwing out movies. Majority vote determines what gets screened." I glanced back to Wes. "If there's a tie, I break it."

After the meeting, Callie headed to the window. Made a big production of looking out of it. "What are you doing?" I asked, stuffing my tablet into my backpack.

"I'm just checking if any motorcycles are coming to pick you up."

"Scooter." I grinned. "Javi drives a scooter." The sensation of riding it shouldn't have surged through me again. But, it did.

She bounced on her feet. "Are you going to take another spin on it?"

I shrugged, tapping my phone screen. Javi's text from earlier glowed.

Still on for the movie this weekend?

"I don't know," I said, answering Callie. And Javi. I slipped the phone back into my pocket. I'd deal with him later.

If only I could do the same with Callie. Her expression yelled she wasn't going to accept my answer without a better explanation. We were friendly. Not really friends anymore. Every single detail didn't need to be dished. Only—

I looked over my shoulder to make sure the door was shut. Before this meeting, Gianna had been sniffing around my locker before she headed into dance practice, so. "If Paulina Reyes's chambelán looks familiar"—I chewed my lips—"it's because he's scooter guy."

No amount of makeup wipes could erase Callie's frown. "Cas, you're too good to be the side chick. Taking 'scooter rides' behind your client's back isn't cool, either."

I curled my toes inside my loafers. Yesterday I told Paulina about a fake NDA to keep the truth at bay. Today, it was Paulina's and Po's truth that needed protecting . . .

I cleared my throat, tackling only half of her assumptions. "Trust me—I'm not a home-wrecker." Our home had already been wrecked by something much worse. "I wish I could explain in more detail, but . . ." I tucked a curl behind my ear. "What I can say is don't believe everything you see on YouTube."

Callie blinked. "Got it. You're bound by party-planner privilege." She sat on the desk next to mine. I lowered onto the edge of the next one over. "Since it's complicated, but not in the way I thought, well, you should see him again. He's super cute and . . ."

She cast a sidelong glance, scanning me from the top of my frizzy hair to the tip of my loafers. "Since the dog wash, you look different."

"How?"

She tugged on a ringlet and said, "You've been wearing your hair curly more, for starters."

"Only because I've been busier than usual lately," I said.

"You act different, too," she said. At that I raised a brow. "I don't think you've ever given us a majority vote on an agenda item before. Or opened the forum for themes in general."

"Really?" I said, feigning ignorance. "I hadn't noticed." Good thing I was on my way to becoming a fairy godmother and not an actress, because oh boy, my acting skills could use a lot of work.

"Uh-huh," Callie said.

I avoided her stare by looking out the window.

Rolling hills rose beyond the parking lot. A realm of McMansions and immaculately kept yards adorned them. Persistent droughts had parched some spaces between lots. The sun, with its Midas touch, sparked them gold anyway, beautifully masking their thirst.

Was the committee thirsting for more participation?

As event chair, most of the responsibility fell on me. Including guiding the committee with a firm hand. But had my "firm hand" morphed into an iron fist?

If my fingers clenched tightly over the sides of the day planner were any indication, the answer was yes.

Noted.

So what now? Instead of looking at the committee as subjects of my realm, should I try seeing them more as knights of my classroom table?

My stomach knotted. So many things could go wrong if I delegated duties.

Then again, the paso doble had only been possible with Dad's help. The banners, with Javi's. Paulina's quince only landed in my lap partly—okay, mostly—because of Po.

I sucked in a breath. Perhaps I *should* ease up control in favor of more cooperation.

Tendons shifted over my knuckles as I loosened my fingers over the planner. Out of practice with easing my grip, I slackened my hold too much.

The planner slipped from my grasp.

I scrambled to grab it. Callie beat me to it. She picked it up, turning it over.

Of course, it'd opened to the back pages filled with sketches.

I considered yanking the planner away, but . . . classmates liked the flag sketches . . . Paulina liked these . . . and way back in middle school, in the Before era, Callie and I had been in art class together.

I kept my hands at my sides, letting Callie flip the page. With every turn, my heart pounded like it was trying to break through my ribcage.

Picasso had his "blue period." I had this: the black pages.

A bunch of charcoal tornados and monster drawings. A collage of black hearts with holes cut from their center. Collections of different-size lightning bolts. Flames. Rain. I'd pressed the pencil so hard on some that little tears etched a few pages, giving the illustrations an almost 3D-like feel.

After a while, I said, "I promise the rest of them aren't like this." I'd stopped adding to this section the second Insta's algorithm led me to Mandy's grid. "There's a sketch of the Matteo Beach pier on the next page if you don't believe me. You'd probably like the beach ones better."

She took in a few of them. "Each style has artistic merit. I like both. As much as I liked your banners." She handed back the planner. I wedged it into my backpack. "We just spent hours going over the art auction but"—she exhaled—"have you ever considered participating in it?"

"No way," I said, balking. My relationship status with events was always planner, not participant. "Sure, I've 'exhibited' my drawings to people recently. But that was a result of necessity more than a desire to share them publicly."

"I think the whole point of art is the necessity of sharing it publicly," Callie said.

Was that the whole point of art? To share it? Or to keep it somewhere safe, like between the covers of my planner?

I squirmed on the desk. Before Callie noticed, I shuffled to the door. "Come on," I said. "Meeting's over."

She flipped off the lights. "Well, you should think about it. You have a *gift*."

"Was that a party-planner pun or something?"

"Maybe," she said, grinning.

The clap of our shoes echoed in the empty hallways. Along with Callie's growling stomach. "Hey, you want to grab an acai bowl?" she asked. "My treat."

For the first time in a long time, I took her up on the invitation.

CHAPTER NINETEEN

I double-checked the event on our family calendar: *Cuban family dinner*.

The ingredients patiently waited in the kitchen. The dad who'd promised to cook it, on the other hand—MIA.

I texted him again. The do-not-disturb notification glared from the bottom of our text thread.

Starting dinner without you, I tapped. The text went off with a *swoosh*.

Still no reply.

I let out a groan, giving Chewbacca a run for his money.

Now this meal became another problem to fix. Usually this gave me purpose. Today, I bristled.

I grabbed my planner. Swung my legs off the mattress. Stomped out of my room.

I didn't shut my eyes going down the hallway this time. It was like rewinding time, ending back when we were all together again. Like the happy families populating Mandy's grid.

I turned into the kitchen. At least Po was here as planned. Laptop open, chewing on the end of a pen with her purple lips. How could she be in a good mood when Dad was hours late and nowhere to be found?

Less than twenty-four hours ago, he'd not only confirmed dinner (good), but he'd also stopped by Sprouts to pick up the ingredients (even better).

And now he'd *poofed,* vanishing like fog-machine smoke.

Under Mandy's tutelage, I'd finally learn how to transform his short-lived spurts of fatherhood into a forever type of deal.

Until then, I tempered my aggravation by flinging open cabinets. Drawers. The fridge door. Yanking out all the stuff needed to make tonight's picadillo and tostones. Piling it all onto the island.

I zeroed in on the onion.

I'd watched Mom slice (or was it dice?) loads of them. Even though I hardly cooked anything outside of scrambled eggs, how hard could it be?

Cutting board: check. Knife: check. Now I had to remember some of her movements. Without peeling the onion, I chopped it in half. The *thwack* of the blade hit the wood. Both halves of the onion rolled down different sides of the island, thudding onto the floor. Peachy.

"I thought you were applying for the fairy godmother internship, not auditioning for the next *Scream.*" Po lifted herself from the chair; her combat boots clomped across the kitchen.

"Har, har, har." I dropped to my knees and reached for an onion half.

Po grabbed the other one. "Hey, what's going on?" she asked, her voice breezy as ever.

I should've expected as much. Here I was, a disgruntled daughter, while Po wore her purple lipstick. As much as I wanted to unload some of my feelings, I swallowed them.

I shouldn't ruin her good mood by going Eeyore on her. Not when she exuded Tigger energy.

"Attempting to cook dinner," I said. "What's going on with

you? Flirting with Paulina?" I refrained from reminding her not to let things get too steamy until after the party.

"Sadly, no. I was checking out Alma's website again. I think I prefer it to UCI. Thanks again for badgering me about college."

"De nada." At one section of my family's vision board sharpening into focus, I exhaled more of my frustration.

Po placed the onion on the chopping block. "I thought Dad was supposed to do this for us. Don't you want to wait?"

I shook my head. "He's not answering his phone and I'm too hungry." I got back to dicing. Redirecting my icky feelings into *chop-chop-chops*.

Po scrunched her face.

"So what if my techniques are slasher-like?" I asked. "It will still get food into our bellies."

I brought my attention back to the onions, totally not in the mood for Po to start excusing Dad's bad behavior. To say some nonsense about *"three steps forward, one step back."*

A step back was still going backward. Not pa'lante. And all I wanted was for us to move toward the HEA sketched in my head.

My eyes burned. Tears pooled. I wiped them away with the back of my sleeve before they made a grand entrance.

"It's okay, Little Cuchara." She placed a hand on my shoulder. "Go sit down. I'll cook."

"I'm fine," I said. "It's just the onions."

She took her hand from my shoulder and grabbed my wrist "Picadillo calls for 'diced' onion, not onion puree. I think you can move on to this." She pressed a smaller chopping block and green pepper into my hands.

I traced a finger over its firm, waxy skin. "This shade of green would look good on you." It would be the perfect color for the art-auction invites and fall-inspired Pinterest boards.

Or as a stroke of watercolor across a blank canvas.

The onions hissed when they hit the oiled pan. While I'd been in my color-palette reverie, Po had already peeled and minced the garlic. "Get cracking on the green pepper. I also need oregano and the cumin," she said.

Curls of steam and scents began to wrap around her. A pink glow burnished her cheekbones. Probably from standing right over a burning flame. Except something about the way she glowed made me think the fire came from within her.

Whether excitement over college or her crush stoked it, I couldn't tell. In case it was the latter, I didn't press. That'd simply open the door for her to ask about Javi.

Hmm. Should I tell her about him anyway? I bit my lips.

No. Telling her now would be like layering on a coat of paint before the last one had dried. Best to wait a little longer. Make sure the picture between Javi and me was more in focus before I showed it to her.

I set the spices and herbs on the counter.

"Thanks," Po said. In a thick Cuban accent, she added, "Now, don't forget the second most important ingredient."

One of Mom's lines. Whenever we'd helped her cook, she'd always said that. I expected the impersonation to cleave into my rib cage the way I'd hacked into the poor onion.

Most times, I couldn't even bring myself to replay Mom's sayings inside my head. So hearing them from someone else's lips . . . uttered by someone who, until recently, sailed past most mention of her?

A pang of hurt went through me, yes. Except it was more like when I ran the tip of my tongue over the spots where I got my wisdom teeth pulled. It sucked to rediscover the gaping holes left behind. It was more odd to discover relief.

So much of Mom had been lost. Now her words were being

spoken again, inside her happiest place after Disneyland. A twinge of joy fluttered inside me.

"Second most important ingredient coming right up," I said.

Good thing Po's back was turned, because my hands shook when I approached the tablet propped upright against a stand. The iPad technically belonged to the family. In reality, the sole owner had always been Mom.

It housed her recipes. Organized her spreadsheets. Compiled her playlists.

With two super-traditional Cuban dishes on tonight's menu, should we play something from her guajira list? I tapped Benny Moré's "Bonito y Sabroso."

The sway of congo drums and brass danced with the scents filling the kitchen. Benny's bright voice followed next. He crooned about people who danced beautifully and deliciously.

Like Javi.

Po browned the beef. And apparently also read my mind. "Thinking about your guy, are you?" she said.

What was the point in lying to her? "Maybe. Are you thinking about your girl?"

"Maybe." She grinned. Before I could warn her about the danger of us playing with fire, she said, "Bring me the—"

I handed her the cups filled with the olives, raisins, and capers, my arms' muscle memory springing back to life.

"When are you seeing him, BTW?"

"I guess the same time you're seeing Paulina." I poured the sherry vinegar into a tablespoon. It hissed when it hit the skillet. "At the quince dress and tux fitting."

The pink on her cheeks deepened into a crimson. It clashed with her purple lipstick. I sighed. "You're seeing Paulina before, aren't you?"

She winked. Yes, I was happy for her—for both of them—and

yet . . . "Po, don't you think you should wait to date until after the party?" I said, part plea, part prayer. "Because if things get messier—"

She pointed a wooden mixing spoon at me. "Yeah, yeah, I know. Your internship. Paulina's film school." She went back to stirring. "I won't screw that up for either of you. I swear." Her face lit up. "Did you know the dance-rehearsal video has almost more views than any of her Disney corn-dog challenges?"

I snorted. "Jeez, I wonder why those are her most popular videos." She playfully swatted my hand with the spoon. "Ow!" I brought my hand to my mouth in faux pain, pressing my tongue to the spot where she'd whacked me.

Wow. The spices really enhanced the savoriness of the beef. The sweetness of the raisins offset the olives' saltiness. "This is good, Po. Better than any picadillo Dad's ever made."

"Really?" She flashed a smile, the wattage brighter than all the kitchen lights combined. "I got so many messages about the hot dogs the other day." She turned back to the skillet, lowering the heat. The beef simmered. "What's the next SBA event?"

"The art auction."

"Cool." She pressed her fingernails into the wooden sides of the spoon. "Um, do you think I can help cater that, too?"

"We are going to be making it bigger this year, so yes, catering will probably be involved." Why hadn't I thought of this before? "I'll pitch your services to the committee. Between us, though, consider the gig yours." My lips quirked upward. Sometimes an iron fist did come in handy. "Do you want to make the hot dogs again?"

She shook her head. "Hear me out before you say no . . ."

❧

Po had the idea of shaping the tostones into small cups and stuffing the insides with spoonfuls of the picadillo. To prove it could work, she made a few prototypes.

She set a platter on the kitchen table. Mouth watering, I lifted one for closer inspection. Ground beef glittered with seasoning. I gave the sides of it a squeeze. Who knew twice-fried plantains could be so pliable?

I popped one into my mouth and groaned from the deliciousness. "Perfect hors d'oeuvres for the auction."

She jumped up and down, clapping.

"But they are also perfect for"—I sprang from the chair, darting across the kitchen to grab the iPad—"this." I extended it to her. "You should add it to the recipes."

Her cheeks flushed. "You really think so?" she asked.

"I do." After hearing Mom's music, her words, and now enjoying her food again . . . I remembered what Javi had said the other night about stars.

Mom's starlight kept shining. If Po and I tended to its fire, we could make sure it always did. "Take it."

She cracked her knuckles and massaged her palms the way she often did before volleyball matches, then took it. "What do you think about calling them PSTs? Picadillo-stuffed tostones?"

"I love it," I said.

Her fingertips moved across the screen. Right when she hit Save, a text pinged.

I took a sidelong peek. Sorry, got stuck at work. On my way.

"Well, well, well, look who finally decided to make an appearance," I said, biting into another PST.

Po set the iPad on the table. "I can hear that eye-roll," she said through a mouthful of her new creation. "Have you ever thought about cutting Dad some slack every now and then?"

My mouth fell open. A half-chewed raisin landed onto the table. After hooking her up with two summer jobs, she really had the nerve to ask? "You're joking, right?"

"No, I'm not." She swallowed loudly. "People do the best they can with the tools they got."

"Well, Dr. Phil," I snapped. "If that's true, Dad's got no tools."

"That's exactly my point, Einstein."

"Then he should make a pit stop at Ace Hardware. I could drop him a pin; it's on the way home." I stuffed another PST into my mouth, preferring to chew than discuss this any further. If these weren't so damn good, I would've lost my appetite.

"Fine. Forget I said anything. Should we at least save some of these for him?" She motioned to the last few PSTs. "But I'm also still hungo, sooo. I'm down to finish them if you are."

"Finally, a plan I can get behind."

Po shook her head, trying hard not to laugh. She picked up the tablet again, checking out the family calendar. "Him being late is a good thing, ya know."

I tilted my head.

"He's missing dinner, but we're missing the birds-and-the-bees talk," she said, pointing to the event Dad had set.

I bit my lips, but a laugh broke through anyway. Thank you, Universe, for silver linings.

CHAPTER TWENTY

Of course Po had to go to the bathroom the second we pulled into the school parking lot. "Paulina's going to be here any second," I said, slamming the car door shut. "We've got a day full of fittings and no extra time to spare."

"Tell that to my bladder," she said, running toward the gym. On her sprint through the double doors, she almost knocked over Gianna and Lee. Gianna did a double take at Po sailing past, then turned in my direction.

"Hey, Cas!" She beelined over. "Marcus didn't mention you guys were practicing today. I would've worn something"—she frowned at her gray cropped sweatshirt—"befitting of a local celebrity."

"I don't think Paulina would care about your clothes." Why would she if her eyes rarely left Po? "But don't worry—you'll probably miss her altogether," I said. "We're about to head out on more party-planning business and only meeting here for carpooling purposes."

"Stylish and eco-friendly? Paulina's the best." Carpooling had been my idea, but whatever. "Also, 'more party-planning business,' eh?" Her eyebrows arched, inviting me to say more.

I looked over my shoulder. "It may or may not have to do

with—" I ran my hands over my blouse and khaki shorts, extending them into the shape of a gown.

Gianna barely contained her squeal.

There. Just the right amount of insider scoop to satisfy her desire to sniff around. I brought a finger to my mouth, then gestured to the gym. *Move it along.*

"Thanks for that tidbit, but I'm so bummed you aren't practicing today. If Paulina needed a break for a dance or two, I would've loved to sub in." She crept closer. A dizzying mash of rotting flowers and baby powder clogged my nostrils. Whatever body spritz this was, it made Dad's kombucha smell like freshly scrubbed puppies.

"You know exactly what I'm talking about." She winked. "You and Prince Charming looked awfully cozy twirling all over the place the other day."

I forced an awkward laugh. "Darth Vader's theme song really lights a saber under your feet."

"If you say so." She blew a tuft of hair off her face. "How do you like working with Paulina, by the way? Is she different behind the scenes than on her videos?" She snagged her phone from a pocket on the side of her leggings. "Off the record, is she a secret diva?"

"What? No!" Sure Paulina had thrown some curveballs, but I wouldn't consider her a diva. And hopefully never would.

"C'mon, spill," Gianna continued. "Your secrets are safe with me."

Gah, how many times had Po warned me? *You give people an inch and they take a kilometer.* I should've kept my mouth shut.

At Po's combat boots crunching against the gravel, I let out a sigh of relief. "Hey, Lady Hot Goss," Po said. "Marcus said to get your butt back to practice."

Gianna huffed, turning to the gym. "Chat later, Cas."

Uh, we better not. "Marcus didn't really want her back in practice, did he?"

Po shook her head. "It looked like you needed a lifeline."

"Thank—"

No point in finishing. Not when her head was swinging toward Paulina's approaching SUV. The second the driver-side door cracked open, Po sped forth.

Her pink duster billowed against the summer air, each flap fluttering in a way I thought only existed in rom-com running scenes.

Paulina and Po wrapped their arms around each other in a tight embrace. I coughed before their hugging and whispered chattering turned into something more than friendly.

Surprisingly, they broke apart.

"Now that we're all here, I want to quickly go over the agenda." I opened the planner. "Today we're doing fittings."

Po clapped and Paulina nodded.

"We have three places to visit for your dress, starting at the Nordy in South Coast, then Neiman Marcus at Fashion Island—"

"I loved the ones you set aside there." Today, Paulina made no attempts to put on her serious mask. I looked over at Po. Their Cheshire Cat grins matched perfectly. "But I absolutely adored the boutique you DMed last night."

My chest lifted, filling with pride. "Great. There's an up-and-coming designer there who's branching out from her bathing suit line, *Beaches Love Me*, into evening dresses. You've worn some of the one-pieces as bodysuits in some of your vlogs so I figured you'd like her gowns."

Paulina draped an arm around me, pulling me in for a quick squeeze. We'd graduated from smiles to hugs now? "Picking up on details like that is why you're the best planner a girl could have," she said. "Isn't she the best, Po?"

Po shot me a smirk. "She has her moments."

I rolled my eyes in faux annoyance. "After your fittings, we'll meet Javi later in the afternoon for his tux fitting. Any questions?"

I'd posed the question partially out of courtesy—but mostly, rhetorically. Because I really wanted to mentally shout, *See, Gianna? No teen prima donnas here.*

But then, Paulina spoke. "No questions, only a few requests."

My throat constricted. Before I could ask what she had in mind, a familiar motor roared into the parking lot.

A screech of wheels. Javi's scooter pulled up a few parking spots away. He slipped off his helmet and threw his head back. Rays of sun sparkled across each swish of dark tresses, across the Mickey appliqué on his sling bag.

When he glanced over, his eyes found mine. I couldn't look away.

"Po and I will take my car, and you and Baymoon take his scooter," Paulina said.

Now this was a change I could get behind.

"Also I'd like to do decor hunting today, preferably before my fittings," Paulina continued. "Can you get them moved to later in the day?"

I turned to her and blurted, "What?" Reschedule the fittings that were about to start?

"Um," I tugged my phone from my back pocket. Searched for available time slots on the stores' styling portals. "Neiman Marcus's and Nordstrom's gown salon appointments are already booked today." My shoulders tensed. "In fact, they don't have anything open for two weeks. So to have your party at the end of the month like planned"—and for me to apply to the Mandy internship before the application window closed—"we have to keep this fitting."

"You'd think stores would part the seas for a Mandy Whitmore client." Paulina narrowed red-glitter-rimmed eyes. Even Javi tilted his chin.

My mouth opened in an awkward smile. "Mandy can set plexiglass over pools so her clients can dance on water, but parting the Pacific during wedding season?" I chuckled, trying hard not to choke on it.

"Huh, I didn't think of that." Paulina nodded. Javi lowered his guard. Po let out a slow exhale. "Fine. I'll keep the dress fittings as is, but I need you to squeeze the decorations in today, too."

"But I . . . um—" I slipped the phone back into my pocket, opened the planner back to the *Paulina* tab. "I have us scheduled for decor rentals . . ." I turned the page over. "Next weekend."

She stared at me unblinking. Had she drawn her glitter eyeliner's wings extra sharp this morning? Because today they were edged extra scythe-like, capable of cutting through whatever stood in her way. I swallowed. "What I meant was, what time is best for you?"

A smile bloomed at the corners of her mouth. "You know what they say, 'there's no time like the present.'" Probably because of the confusion painting across my face, she said, "Po and I will tackle dresses. You and Baymoon can gather decor. Afterward, we meet up at the tux studio."

"Great idea," Po said.

Javi turned to face me. "Pau's plan makes sense," he said, a bloom of pink creeping up his neck.

"Next weekend I'll be MIA filming the new food items dropping at Disneyland," Paulina said. "Like you said yourself, it's wedding season, so it's probably smart to lock down decorations early anyway."

Between Paulina's newest change-ups and Javi's glances, my concentration fizzled. I plucked the pencil from the back of my ear. Drummed its eraser end against the planner to refocus. "What about filming? Aren't you uploading this to your channel?"

She waved off my concerns. "A director doesn't really film, Cas. I mean, they can if they want, but mostly, they bring the vision. You're already familiar with the vibes I want. Baymoon's been my second unit director since day one." She shrugged. "Think of this as a team project. Get some footage. Remember my skills in postproduction? None of my viewers will know I wasn't there."

Javi scoffed but let that single dimple loose. "You're really shooing us off like your B unit?" he asked.

"Uh-huh," Paulina said, crossing her arms. "Do you have a problem with it?"

Javi shook his head. "I don't have a problem. Do you, Castle Towers?" he asked, edging closer.

Extra time with him? Yes, please. I hugged the planner to my chest. Was that pounding the sound of my pulse? Or today's schedule knocking against the cover, reminding me that swapping out fittings for camerawork wasn't part of the plan. "Are you sure you don't need me at the fittings?"

Paulina's eyes locked on me. Po's too, that turncoat. Together, they scanned me from the top of my air-dried-and-only-mildly-frizzy hair to my button-down pink blouse and khaki shorts before landing on my loafers. That kicked off a string of low whispers. I caught smatterings of "law intern slash golfer" and "OC real estate agent" but couldn't tell who said what.

"I'm positive," Paulina said sweetly. "It's settled. You and Baymoon take decoration duty. Text me pics and videos. I get final approval of flowers and rentals. By the time we pick a dress, it'll be time for Javi's tux fitting anyway. We good?" Her tone indicated the conversation was over.

Javi motioned to his scooter. The sunlight caught on the ends of his hair. Like a moth drawn to a photo-booth bulb, I hurried over.

Po swept to Paulina's SUV, shouting, "Get in, loser; we're going shopping."

Paulina responded with an equally loud "Woo-hoo!"

When I hopped on the back of the scooter and wrapped my arms around Javi's waist, nothing boomed louder than my heartbeat. I brought my chin to his broad shoulder, inhaling oceans and lavender fields. Yup, nothing.

Javi did a double take at the etchings on the glass doors. "You're taking me into PP Celebrations? What type of party are you throwing for Paulina again?"

"It's short for Pelican Point Celebrations." I trembled with laughter, shaking my phone's camera all over the place. "It's one of OC's premier banquet halls, boasting both indoor and outdoor ballrooms. Last year, we had prom in the lake garden. I came up with the idea to put color-changing tea lights inside the lake."

"You have a track record for combining unusual items and school events so I gotta ask: Was this lake filled with freshwater or PP?"

"You're making me ruin the video for Paulina," I said, laughing.

Javi sucked in his round cheeks, making duck lips. His gaze went through the lens—through me. "Make sure you get my Blue Steel pose."

That pulled cackles from both of us. I hit the record button, stopping this video to start a new, nonchaotic one.

Something about the thumbnail made me not delete it. The light glinting off the Mickey appliqué resembling a shooting star, maybe? Or how the sun-lightened ends of Javi's tresses cast a golden halo?

This moment could be great to sketch. Or watercolor.

I shook my head. I was supposed to be focused on Paulina's quince, not my once-upon-a-time hobby.

"As I was saying, PP Celeb—" I couldn't help but crack up again. As much as I wanted to keep dissolving into fits like this, decorations needed to be locked down. "Pelican Point Celebrations also has an entire section of their building dedicated to rentals. That way, you can rent some of the decor, even if you decide to have the party somewhere else."

So many of OC's—even LA's and San Diego's—party planners came here to scope out the goods. Whenever I came for SBA duties, I'd always kept an eye out for the fairest godmother of them all. Sadly, I'd never spotted her. Her apprentices probably did the legwork for her. *Sigh*.

Javi pushed a few locks of hair out of his face, eyes fixing on me. His gaze was warmer than the summer air. Heat poured over me. Pooled into the void inside my chest. I stored it the way a wishing well collected secret desires.

"C'mon," I said. "Follow me."

We walked under the rose archway leading into the florist room. A mosaic of fresh and dried flowers dangled from the ceiling like chandeliers. Javi's nostrils flared. "It smells so good."

"It does." I wanted to keep inhaling lavender fields, but it'd be smarter to get the scoop on the roses instead. "Hey, can you text some of those flower arrangements to Paulina while I chat with the head florist?"

"On it." He moved to the tables stacked with fragrant centerpieces fit for luxury hotel lobbies, weddings, and everything in between.

I headed in the opposite direction, toward Himari, PP Celebration's botanical genius.

"Hey, Cas," they said, adjusting the straps of their orange overalls. "Isn't it a little too early to order centerpieces for homecoming?"

"The audacity," I said, grabbing my chest. "It's never too early to start planning. But no, I'm actually prepping another quinceañera."

"Look at you go, rock star." Himari high-fived me. The slap sent a thrill up my arm. "I just stocked the foliage wall in the back with seasonal flowers; go check it out."

I inhaled. Sure enough, fresh eucalyptus and lemon leaf perfumed the air. "Will do."

I half turned on my loafers, only to be grabbed by my elbow. "Not before you tell me—who's the cutie?" they whispered.

"Trust me—the less you know, the better."

"Oh, to be young," they grinned. Their smile slid off their face when a reedy woman stepped through the archway.

She wore her hair in a perfectly sheared bob. The auburn hue pulled at images of fire. More the wildfires that decimated mountains than cozy flames inside a fireplace.

Himari pushed a clipboard into my hands. "Gotta go see what she needs before I get fired." They plastered a smile on their face and rushed toward Blunt Bob. "Soraya, what a pleasure it is to see you again."

Riiight. Drawing the pencil from the back of my ear, I wrote *Matteo Beach High SBA* on top of the order form strapped to the clipboard. Jotted potential flowers for Paulina's party underneath.

Gold cymbidium orchids? Their long stems stretched the length of a lightsaber. Their gold petals also glowed like the light beaming from one.

The last thing I wanted to do was text Dad, but fairy godmother duty called. I pushed down my irritation and pulled out my phone. Do yellow sabers exist?

The phone vibrated.

Yes, but if this is about the Sith Lord party, your friend would prefer red sabers instead.

Huh. Paulina was going to use a red lightsaber for the paso doble, so . . . Which red flowers evoked Sith saber vibes? The cardinal flowers covered with spiky red blooms Javi was holding? I tucked the clipboard under my arm and hit Record, capturing him strolling to the vases filled with lilac roses. The thin cotton of his white shirt clung to the muscles in his back. The dark shorts clung just as snuggly to his—

Javi must've felt my stare—er, phone lens—because he turned around. "My eyes are up here, Castle Towers."

My stomach lurched with embarrassment. Another wave of humiliation crashed over me when Blunt Bob chuckled from an aisle over. "What? No. I wasn't checking you out. Just your outfit."

Sadly, he wasn't buying my excuse. Face on fire, I turned away from him. Wedged myself between two huge vases of roses. Added two new tasks to today's agenda.

No more checking out Javi for the rest of the day. Focus on procuring the perfect decorations.

"Find anything Paulina would like?" I asked.

"What about this? It's very quinceañera-y." He picked up a

polyantha rose. Small blossoms. Fluffy petals colored a pink so pale some shimmered white.

"It's beautiful," I said. "Perfect for lots of birthday girls, but . . ." Sidestepping the vases, I plucked the stem from his hand. "Too cloud-looking. And Paulina's no cloud. She's a star." I put the rose back into the vase. "One in a galaxy far, far away."

A rustling behind us. Soraya's steely eyes flicked down to her clipboard, gold pen scribbling across the page. When she looked up again, her mouth puckered. Sheesh. Judgmental and nosey?

I shuffled past her and a pink peony wall to a vase containing super-dark roses.

"Black Baccaras," I said, lifting one. "See these edges?" I skimmed the top with a finger.

Javi nodded at the almost-black petals.

"This is the darkest rose. As the blossom unfurls, though . . ." So what if I sounded like Isabela Madrigal right now? If Mandy was going to hire me as a fairy godmother's apprentice, best to practice flower talk whenever the opportunity presented itself. "The interior petals open to a velvety, burgundy red."

"So gnarly," Javi said, inching in. "In a good way."

"Exactly why . . ." I patted the rosebud against my chin. Before I spiraled into calculating how many layers of watercolor paints it would take to get this effect, I wrote *Black Baccara bouquets* on the order form. "They're perfect for Paulina. Sending her pics for approval right now."

Moments later, the phone buzzed. Paulina's string of heart-eye emojis, along with the *Ratatouille* chef's kiss GIF, boosted my confidence. I pointed the screen at Javi, sharing the good news.

"Excellent. But, wait—" He tapped the top of the order form, pointing to *Matteo Beach High SBA*. "Instead of your school's student body association, shouldn't it say the fancy event firm you work for? Don't want to have the order go to the wrong place because of a mistake, ya know?"

My knuckles twinged against the pencil. "Muscle memory, I guess. Thanks for looking out." His helpful nature tugged at my inner Jiminy Cricket. I toed the floor with my loafer as if squashing the sanctimonious bug. The only voice worth listening to was Mandy's.

Happily ever afters are our business.

"Crossing out Matteo Beach High SBA"—I drew a line through it. "And putting the correct firm, Mandy Whitmore." I scribbled her name. "There. All fixed."

High heels clicked to a halt behind us. Some crunching noises joined the party. Sure, Soraya appeared to be sifting through decorative stones with her hands, but her attention fell on us—er, me.

Or rather the rose in my hand. Hmm. Was she also throwing a party for a Sith Lord? Did she want to copy and paste my ideas to her client's aesthetic board?

Before the intensity of Soraya's stare—and the guilt of lying to Javi—burned me to a crisp, I said, "Come on. Let's get out of here."

Thankfully, I knew the perfect spot to cool down.

CHAPTER TWENTY-ONE

Rows of recessed spotlights beamed over beautifully crafted ice sculptures. Some figures even contained LEDs inside them, sparking the ice from within.

"Welcome to the Arctic Art Studio," I said through chattering teeth. "Since Paulina approved—" I cleared my throat. *"Loved* the Baccara roses, the pressure's on to find the perfect ice decor."

I let Javi walk ahead to get more footage of him. For Paulina's channel, obviously. I zoomed in on the back of his head. Anyone who ever called brown basic had never seen hair color like his. Soil after rain. Smoky quartz. Chocolate diamonds.

Focus.

I lowered the phone's camera. Angled it over the soles of his Vans, stopping midhalt every time Javi stopped to stare at an animal sculpture, especially the dolphins.

I moved nearer to capture the visible puffs of his breath. Weird how a canvas of cold air was necessary to see it. Po would undoubtably have a quote about this. Something like, *"Things are there even when you can't see them."*

The Poverb could be the opposite of the starlight wisdom Javi dropped the other night at the beach. Both philosophies found their ways to my heart's hollow spaces.

"Oooh." Javi pointed to the sculptures at the far end of the room. "Are those rotating?"

"Yup," I said. "Motor-powered and mirrored pedestals."

"No way." With the speed and bounce of a puppy, he ran over to check them out.

I practically fainted. "Javi—"

His shoes squeaked against the floor as he stopped. He glanced back. Despite the cold, there was a fire in his eyes.

It burned away the rest of my sentence: *there's no running allowed in this room*.

A quick scan of the room to make sure we were alone. Then I did something I never thought I'd do here.

I sprinted after him. "Wait up!"

The *thump-thump-thump* of my loafers against the floor mimicked the piñata-like poundings Mom would give the hallway carpet every spring, clobbering away the year's accumulation of grime.

Maybe the run had shaken off some of the emotional muck piled up since After . . . because by the time I reached Javi, the spring in my loafers could out-bounce Tigger's tail.

Together we headed down an aisle. Javi pointed out the Eiffel Tower. He told me about going there the year before his dad got sick. When they'd climbed to the top, his dad joked that he liked the views from the heights of Tikal's pyramids better. "Mom and I are gonna go this Christmas to find out if he was right." There was no regret in his voice that his dad wouldn't be joining them on that family trip. Only excitement that he'd get to go.

Stopping at the sculpture of Olaf, he said, "For bingeing, Mom prefers telenovelas. Dad opted for K-dramas. Disney movies were their middle ground. *Frozen* being their fave." He let his signature laugh-snort loose. "Fun fact: he almost named me Sven."

I shivered partly from the cold, mostly from holding in laughter.

"What?" he asked. "You think Sven suits me better?"

"Maybe," I teased, although if Javi resembled anyone in the franchise, it'd definitely be Kristoff. Huh. Was talking about his dad so freely Javi's way of holding on to pieces of him? Was each memory a layer of plaster patching up his heart fractures?

I breathed in the cold air and gave it a try. "Fun fact: my mom's favorite place was Disneyland. I think she named me after the castle."

He narrowed his eyes. "I can totally see that." At the next sculpture, a towering number 21, he shared that it had been his dad's lucky number. We traded little tidbits of info like that as we walked down the aisles.

As the carved ice glittered around us, I felt a glimmer of hope that maybe one day, I could have similar talks with Po and Dad. For now, I was beyond grateful to be practicing with Javi.

I'd been so caught up in the convo I didn't notice I'd led us into a row of different-size statues of David . . . plus lots of other less famous but equally chiseled (and naked) torsos.

Javi caught me staring at them. My cheeks flamed. "None of these scream 'Paulina,'" I said, looking away.

"Or *Star Wars*."

"Um." My throat tightened. I pushed out words that rarely saw the light of day. "Do you have any suggestions?" Yielding control didn't come naturally. But I was quickly finding out that, like with anything else, practice made it easier. "You're her best friend and the unquince's 'chambelán,' so . . . I want to take your thoughts into consideration."

Javi beamed, putting each ice sculpture's LEDs to shame. "Actually, yes."

He headed to the elephant a few aisles down. Plucking the phone from his pocket, he searched Google Images for an AT-AT.

"Behold. The All Terrain Armored Transport," he said. "The baddest ground vehicle in the Imperial Army."

I yanked the phone, enlarging the picture. My eyes flicked to the sculpture, then back to the screen.

If elephants had an evil stepsister, this trunkless mecha pachyderm was it. "Huh . . . They fight for the 'dark side,' too, à la Paulina's theme."

"Plus, they make their debut during a battle on Hoth, an *ice* planet," Javi said.

"Okay, this is genius."

I pulled the clipboard from under my arm. Under *Ice Sculpture Custom Order Requests*, I wrote, *2 four-foot AT-ATs*. My adrenaline spiked at hitting the jackpot on another idea Paulina would (fingers crossed) love. Or it was from standing in the middle of Javi's spotlight. Before I melted into a puddle, I handed the phone back.

Our hands brushed. I shuddered.

"Dang, Castle Towers. Your hand's a glacier." Javi cupped my hand between both of his. Lifted it to his lips. Blew hot breath over it. "Let's get you out of this room before you get hypothermia."

Freeze when I was on the brink of spontaneous combustion? Impossible.

He turned toward the door, tugging me forward.

"Hold on," I said, keeping a grip on his hand. With our fingers linked, it was almost as if we were gearing up to start dance rehearsals again. "Paulina's quince needs to be perfect. The sculptors here probably have the skills to carve this, but in case they can't, please help me pick a plan B."

I tugged Javi back.

Except—

Curse you, iron-fist tendencies. And ice-cold air for stiffening my limbs. Because when I drew him in, I used a lot more force than intended. We moved like we were paso doble-ing all over again.

Only he was the one flying inward.

We slammed against one another. The collision rocked us backward. My spine hit the 8 of a towering 18. The base of the sculpture wobbled on the platform, shifting across the floor.

And right when I thought the entire thing was going to topple over, Javi swung an arm around it, righting it in the nick of time.

"That was an awesome rescue," I said. The wetness of the sculpture seeped through my blouse. The ice didn't pull a single shiver. Not with the heat of Javi's body warming mine.

"Rescuing's my summer job, remember?" His quick hands had saved the sculpture. But in that moment, all I cared about was how they drifted from the curves of the 8 to the sides of my waist. "I had to make up for ruining the banners somehow."

I blinked up at his single dimple. Oh my gosh. Hardly any space separated our lips.

Wait. Are his actually parting? Or is it my imagination?

What better place for a first kiss than right here? In the middle of a velvet room surrounded by glittering ice and twinkling lights, as if hundreds of fairies were sprinkling pixie dust around us.

Was it magic that lifted me onto my toes? Or the result of having spent so much time with Po lately? While I was all about plans, she was all about participating. Maybe Dad was right. Being more like her once in a while—especially now—could be a good thing.

I angled my chin higher.

Javi tilted forward.

Drawing on every inch of my iron-fist tendencies, I pulled the neck of his shirt. Brought him closer so my lips could finally claim his.

I tasted minty ChapStick on his mouth. Mangos on his tongue.

Watching on the sidelines hadn't prepped me for all the breaking apart to giggle, nose bumping, and forehead knocking. Our movements didn't mirror the slow-motion French kisses in movies—the perfectly angled lip locks on Pinterest boards even less.

Forget 'em. If perfection looked good, practicing getting there with Javi felt better.

By the way his heart thudded against mine, he probably agreed.

One of my hands skated up his back. The clipboard clattered to the floor. I left it there to skim muscles I'd only read about in AP bio.

The room went fuzzy. Like the oxygen had been swapped with helium. I pressed my mouth harder to his. He wrapped his arm tighter around my waist.

The sculpture behind me rocked again. Okay, maybe our choreography was getting a little out of hand. Good thing Javi had those quick reflexes—

The cold firmness against my back suddenly vanished. A millisecond later—

CRASH and *SHATTER*.

We broke apart, the magic spell over. "Please, party gods," I whispered. That sound of one hundred plates smashing? *Please let it be an impromptu Greek party on the other side of the door.*

What little air remained in my lungs whooshed out when I peeked over my shoulder.

"No, no, no!" I dropped to my knees, scrambling to assess the damage to the 8.

Javi sucked air through his teeth. "At least the bottom half survived the fall."

"Yeah, but the other half—"

Fragments of it sparked down the length of the aisle. Other bits had ricocheted off the ground, glittering from different parts of the floor.

My pulse hammered against my temples. Each heartbeat thumped, *Fix this*.

But the heels on the other side of the wall pounded louder.

"We have to fix this before someone comes in. Hurry." I grabbed some of the smaller shards. Only, they kept slipping from my fingers, landing on the floor and breaking into even smaller pieces. GAH!

"Plan B: start collecting the bigger chunks," I said, pointing my pencil down the aisle. "Then we glue them together."

Javi's eyebrows scrunched together. "How are we gonna glue ice—"

The door creaked open. Oh no.

Soraya barked orders from somewhere farther down the hall. "Yes, ma'am," another voice said, followed by an exhale. "I'll take care of that right away."

The door shut. The heel clacks receded.

Safe. For now.

I tucked the pencil back behind my ear, reaching into my utility bag. "We fix it with this." I yanked out a tube of Krazy Glue. "This can put anything back together."

Javi's jaw clenched, as if stopping short of saying, *That's not going to work*. He sprung forward to lend a hand anyway.

In his eagerness to help, he didn't watch where he stepped. His shoes crunched on ice splinters—then he slipped on one of the bigger cubes.

His arms flailed. A yelp not unlike the Chihuahua yips from the fundraiser escaped from his lips.

Copying some of Po's volleyball moves, I hurtled forward, snatching the back of his shirt before he crashed headfirst into an elephant sculpture.

For a few seconds, both of us stood as frozen as the ice around us. Javi heaved out clouds of breath inches away from the elephant's tail.

"You okay?" I asked, trying hard not to laugh. Or cry.

"Uh-huh," he said, chuckling as he steadied himself. "You can let go."

Good thing, because with the voices growing louder from the other side of the wall, four hands would work faster at fixing this mess than two.

I grabbed two broken pieces. "Here, pour some of the glue over it," I said. But instead of fusing them back together, the glue froze over and turned into a weird sticky film. There went that idea.

My knees knocked into the floor. The glare of the shattered ice shot straight into my eyes—no, into the mom-shaped hole.

Javi's hand draped over my shoulder. "Hey," he said. "Sometimes things can't be put back together." His voice lowered, like he was speaking from a deep-rooted pain. "No matter how badly you want them to. No matter how hard you try."

No. It was possible to fix broken things.

It had to be.

No matter how much I tried to blink back tears, a few slipped out. They rolled over my cheeks and splashed onto the floor.

Unlike Rapunzel's tears, mine didn't contain any hidden powers. The sculpture didn't magically right itself upon contact.

"What if we just pay for the damage?" Javi said. "Like a we-break-it-we-buy-it deal?"

I shook my head. "People forget that there's usually a third *b*. Break, buy, ban."

If my application made it to the interview round, how would being banned from Pelican Point Celebrations look to Mandy? Hire a teenage delinquent? Never. "Which can't happen because of SBA and—"

"The firm you intern for?"

I mumbled something in response, grabbing at some of the bigger shards. The icicles began to melt. No matter how much I tightened my hold, my family's HEA dissolved with them.

Another tear spilled. Then a few more. At this rate, I might as well ride the current of the waterworks straight out the door.

No.

If fairy godmothers didn't give up when the going got tough, then neither would I.

I wiped my eyes with my sleeve. "Plan C," I said. "We clean this up. Bolt before anyone comes back." Even if this sculpture couldn't remain intact, at the very least my PP Celebration privileges could.

"I'm on board with that," Javi said.

Plucking the pencil from the back of my ear, I flicked it to the smaller sculptures atop linen-covered tables. "We shove the smaller bits under those tablecloths. The bigger chunks we scoop up and drop over there." I pointed the pencil to the ice platters and bowls sparkling over ice-carved bar tops. "Now, move."

Curls of breath ribboned around us as we hustled. On the next leg of our sprint, Javi stretched out the bottom hem of his shirt. "Pretend this is a kangaroo pouch," he said.

I shoveled handfuls of ice into his makeshift apron. Stole only a few glimpses at his lower abs.

He poured the fragments onto a platter. When he let go of his hem, I broke out into belly laughs, gesturing at the wet patches on the front of his shirt—now draped perfectly over the fly of his shorts.

His neck flared. "Brilliant," he said, laughing.

"I don't have toilet paper," I teased. "But I have these." I wrenched out two hand towels from my utility bag. "Dry yourself, then help me mop the floor."

Our fast-and-furious wiping would have given Cinderella serious competition.

"Now, let's lift what's left of the 8," I said. He nodded, bracing one side of the circle, while I grabbed on to the other. "One, two, three."

We lifted it back onto the platform.

Javi chuckled. Which quickly built to snorts.

"What's so—" My heart stopped. The way the lower circle of the former 8 pressed against the shaft—er, base—of the upright 1 . . .

The day we'd met, the ice mocha accident had formed an "anusgram." And now? Now because of our kissing accident we'd created a—

"Mommy, what's that?" A voice squeaked behind us.

I glanced back. A customer gaped at the new, but definitely not improved, "member" of the sculpture family. She covered her child's eyes with her handbag.

I discreetly kicked some ice pieces under the table behind us. "Yeah, what is it, exactly?" I scratched my head, trying to sound innocent.

"A different type of wiener than the franks Po grilled at the hot-dog fundraiser, if you ask me," Javier whispered, his body vibrating with held-in laughter. I elbowed him in the ribs, biting the sides of my cheeks to keep from cracking up.

"I need to speak to a manager immediately," the lady said. "Better yet, I'm going to write a letter."

"Ooh, someone's going to get in trouble," the kid said.

While the mom dragged her child out the front door, I pulled Javi to the emergency exit. Adrenaline coursed through my veins, spurring my legs to keep up with my wildly beating heart.

Perhaps this was why hearts were built from muscle—not bone, not ice.

Even when they shattered, when holes the size of people were pierced through them, those fist-size organs kept pumping.

Our hands reached the long door handle. We flung it open, stepping outside.

Bringing a hand to my forehead, I shielded my eyes. Whoa. Did the sun always shine this brightly? Or had me kissing Javi broken some sort of hex?

Sunshine glistened over Javi's cheeks and nose. Sweat started to sprout from his pores. Instinctively, my fingers moved to the utility bag, specifically for the oil blotters inside.

I reached for my phone instead. Took a video of Javi's shiny face, snorting with laughter. And a photo of the wet patches on his shirt and shorts. On Javi's next round of cackles, Po's words from the other night echoed: *If you can't beat 'em, join 'em*.

So I did, laughing until my eyes pooled with wholly different types of tears. My laughter tapered into gasps, and while technically breathless, my body hummed with so much life.

I moved the camera to the baby-blue sky dipping into sapphire waters. To the sunshine glittering against thousands of car windows as the vehicles sped on PCH in the distance. To the palm fronds shimmying like pom-poms in the breeze.

Colors always blazed this brightly inside Mandy's grid. Had they always burned this brightly outside of it, too?

"Are those pics for Paulina?" Javi asked.

"Yes." Some I'd already attached to her text thread.

I pressed the phone to my chest. The rest I'd keep just for me.

If I ever found myself sliding back into a grayscale world, I'd have these videos to guide me along the Technicolor brick road back home.

CHAPTER TWENTY-TWO

The soles of my loafers and Javi's Vans crunched against the parking lot's gravel on our escape. "We have ten minutes to get to B Spoke," I panted. "Their late policy is vibranium-clad."

His waves bounced off his cheekbones as he ran next to me. "Fingers crossed traffic won't be too bad."

This was SoCal. Traffic always sucked, but I nodded and picked up my pace. "Good thing your scooter drives faster than Cinderella's pumpkin coach."

Halfway to the scooter, a voice shattered my wishful thinking. "Castillo Torres!"

I halted midstride. Slowly, I turned.

Sun sparked on Blunt Bob's hair. And on the—er, my—clipboard she waved overhead.

Every muscle in my body locked. In my hurry to take off, I'd not only forgotten to drop off the rose order and the AT-AT request—but also managed to leave evidence behind.

"Should we just mad dash to the scooter and hightail it outta here?" Javi whispered.

In the Before era, Dad would always bring Po and me to take-your-kids-to-work day. Some of his courtroom tactics had been stored in my long-term memory. "I did the crime, so let me see if I can get out of the time." A huge breath. "But have the scooter ready for our getaway in case. I'll be right back."

The dimple popped out. "That's what people in slasher movies say right before they get stabbed, BTW," he said.

"Not helping." I headed toward Soraya before I lost my nerve.

"I was looking all over for that." I batted my eyes, doing my best Bambi impression. "Where did you find it? The balloon hall? Or the linens room?" I asked, reaching for the clipboard.

Soraya kept it away. "I found this at the base of a sculpture. One I'd never seen in all my years of visiting this establishment."

The more her gaze bore into me, the more my throat went dry. After an eternity, she lowered the clipboard, tracking everything I'd written on the order form with a burgundy-painted fingernail.

How much cadmium-red, ultramarine-blue, and true-black paints had to be mixed to match her nail polish?

Get it together. No time to blend colors in my head. Not when her Rolex *ticked* and *ticked*, winding down on precious time to get to B Spoke. Or worse, counted the seconds before she turned me over to the front desk.

I reached for the clipboard again. "I must've dropped it there by accident. Thank you so much for returning it. It was nice to meet you—"

"Baccara roses are bold, yet classically romantic." She shifted the clipboard away from me. "Admittedly, I had to look up an 'AT-AT.'"

She pronounced it *ay tee ay tee* instead of *at at* the way Javi had. "Party planning is so much about organizing details and being a therapist to the clients that a coordinator can forget to hone their creativity." Her eyes leveled with mine. "Erecting a new sculpture to add to the studio's rotation takes, well, balls."

Wait—was that a pun? I muffled my laughter in case she wasn't joking. Only the corners of her mouth lifted, so maybe . . .

"It's proving to be quite popular, too," she continued. "In the few minutes I spent inside the Arctic Art Studio I overheard three orders. One for a bachelor party. Two for a bachelorette."

"Our phallus in wonderland is a hit?" I blurted. "Um, I mean—"

She lifted a hand to cut me off. A full smile broke across her face. It emboldened me enough to ask, "If you're not going to bust me, may I ask where you're going with this?"

B Spoke waited for no one. Paulina Reyes didn't, either.

"In the floral room there was talk about you working for your high school's student body association. Yet your beau over there—" She gestured to Javi.

"Oh, he's not my . . ." I pressed my lips together. Aftershocks of our kisses surged through me. Whatever our relationship status was, it'd certainly leveled up.

"He indicated you also worked at Mandy Whitmore." The steely look in her eyes returned, eyebrows lowering like velvet curtains.

"I'm my school's SBA event chair. As far as working with Mandy . . ." A wistful sigh escaped me.

Blame it on the heat. The mind-numbing cold inside the Arctic Art Studio. The filing down of my heart's sharpest edges. Or a combo of all of the above.

After everything I'd done today, what was divulging my wish-upon-a-star dream to a stranger? "I'm hoping to apply to her fairy godmother's internship before the application window closes this summer."

"In that case, let me formally introduce myself. I'm Soraya

Hashemi, senior party consultant at Mandy Whitmore and Associates." She extended her hand.

I grabbed it, mostly to steady myself in case I passed out. "You work with Mandy?"

"I do." Soraya's expression brightened. "As should you. You clearly have a strong vision for your events. You're also capable of whipping up a rain plan in the face of an emergency." She snickered. "One that surpasses the original."

She handed the clipboard back. "I highly encourage you to send your application. Tonight, if possible."

"Tonight?" I pressed the clipboard to my chest, feeling it cushion the empty places. "I only have one big party under my belt. I'm hoping the quince I'm currently in the middle of planning will get me on Mandy's radar. But it won't be done for another few weeks."

She flicked her hand, waving away my concern. "While you've got instincts that can't be taught, you still have a lot to learn, my dear." She gestured to the clipboard. "I placed my card under the clip. Email me your resume along with your application, and I'll make sure they land on Mandy's desk tomorrow morning."

My stomach fluttered, as if diving down every Space Mountain drop.

"Now, I have to run or I'll be late to my next appointment," she said.

Holy crap—same here.

"Thank you, Ms. Hashemi. You have no idea how much this means to me." How much it will mean to my family, inching nearer to our HEA.

Soraya's auburn hair swooshed on her strut to one of the many European imports studding the lot.

I'd gotten so used to being the fairy godmother I'd overlooked the possibility of having one of my own.

Thank you, Fairy Godmother, I mouthed. *Thank you.*

The scooter's speed and Soraya's fairy dust couldn't ward off the blight of rush-hour traffic. I paced outside B Spoke's storefront. "How pissed do you think Paulina will be that we blew the appointment?" I asked.

Javi scratched the back of his neck. "Do you want me to be optimistic or realistic?"

Sweat prickled my hairline. Great. If she'd flip over this, how mad would she be if she found out about the internship?

Soraya had just sped up the clock on preventing that problem, but the sinking feeling didn't go away. "Maybe she'll be more forgiving considering I managed to rebook the fitting for tomorrow," I said. Scoring a last-minute cancellation was nothing short of a miracle. "Make sure you put this in your schedule for mañana."

He frowned. "Um . . . you know how I mentioned Mom and me marathoning stuff? Tomorrow we're going to be watching more *Crash Landing on You.*"

"As much as I support you and your mom spending time together, if you're not here mañana the only thing crash landing on you will be my foot," I teased. Sort of. "I suspect Paulina's will, too. And her wedged Jordans look a lot heavier than my shoes."

"Sheesh, okay," he said, staring at my loafers.

"Po's always making fun of them." Did her quips make me self-conscious? Hardly. The footwear was part of my fairy godmother's uniform as much as the pencil-wand tucked behind my ear.

"Hey, I never underestimate the versatility and dependability of a good loafer," he said. "They are perfect for any occasion."

Something about the way he smiled made me feel like maybe he wasn't only talking about footwear. A thrill rushed through me. "Agreed." I said. "Imagine if Cinderella wore loafers instead of glass slippers. She would've never lost her shoe in the first place."

Javi edged nearer. There was that scent of lavender. "But how would the prince have found her?"

"Ummm, by looking at her. Hello. It's not like she was wearing a disguise."

Javi leaned against B Spoke's window display. Only a thin sheet of glass separated his beach-casual outfit from fancier wools and silks. "Yeah, she was."

"What?" I scoffed.

"The soot, the rags? The handkerchief?" He gestured to the pocket square on the dress form. "She wore them for so long she forgot her true identity. When she put the slipper on," he said, rocking back on his heels, "she remembered."

As much as the topic of "true" identities made me tug at my blouse's collar, curiosity got the best of me. Who was this guy who saved lives, smashed sculptures, but also theorized about Cinderella? "And who was she really?"

Javi gave a lopsided grin. "A princess."

"No. She married into the title."

"Says you, Castle Towers." Tinker Bell's pixie dust had nothing on the sparkles in Javi's eyes. The way their glimmer fell on me, I felt like I could lift off the ground and fly.

I shook my head with a laugh. "Speaking of princesses"—I glanced down the sidewalk—"where's ours? Can you text Paulina and get an ETA?"

He snagged the phone from his back pocket.

"While you're at it, remember to put tomorrow's fitting on your calendar," I said.

He sighed, but a small smile crept to his lips. "I will. Between

Pau's collection of lightsabers and your no doubt equally impressive one of loafers, I can't get on either of y'all's bad side." His fingers tapped across the screen. "Guess I'll have to double up on episodes with Mom tonight."

In classic Javi fashion, he went deeper. Telling me how they didn't have much extended family here. Watching shows became a default (and fun) way to keep up with their Spanish and Korean.

The love dripping from his voice made my heart flutter. I couldn't pretend I didn't feel a couple of pangs alongside it. I breathed through them, focusing on Javi's joy. On his invitation to talk about my mom as freely as he was able to talk about his.

"Watching movies was how Mom learned English," I said. "Lots of cheesy rom-coms." The things I'd give to be able to watch some of those with her again. Another ache. I kept going. "But mostly tons of Disney movies."

"She loved a happily ever after?"

"She didn't just love them." I plucked the pencil from the back of my ear, rolling it between my fingers. Mom not getting her HEA only made me more determined to make sure the rest of my family did. "She believed in them more than the healing powers of caldo."

"Huh," he said, tipping his chin up. "Mom and I sorta adopted shows as our chicken soup for the soul, too. Now that I think of it, we also gravitate to shows with an HEA." He fidgeted with the Mickey appliqué on his sling bag. "Do you still watch movies with Po or your dad?"

"Oof." I slumped against the window display. "Short answer is no."

"And the long one?"

"I doubt I can share that version. Paulina and Po will be here any second."

"Give it a shot. You know how bad traffic is," he said. A massive delivery truck zoomed down the street. The shine of its side-view mirrors strobed off our skin like magic dust from a wand.

Enchanted by it, or the opportunity to get my frustrations out, I said, "After Mom, Dad's either working or playing *Star Wars* video games twenty-four seven. Which is why I'm familiar with some things related to a galaxy far, far away." I shifted on my loafers. "And Po's got the attention span of Geppetto's goldfish now, so neither of them are the ideal movie buddies anymore."

He pushed some hair off his face. "That's too bad. You know how Mom and me talk about Dad a lot?"

I hugged the planner to my chest, nodding.

He cleared his throat. "Well, bingeing's good for when we don't want to talk, in any language."

My fingers twitched. I'd never considered that not talking didn't have to be such a bad thing . . . so long as there was someone by your side to not talk with.

"Plus, you can still get your weekly fixes of HEAs that way," Javi added.

Without missing a beat, I said, "I still get them through Mandy Whitmore. 'Happily ever afters are our business' is her motto, after all."

I pictured her Insta grid, imagined each of her beautiful photos as a layer of stucco. Working for her would plaster my heart's fractures in ways the Krazy Glue wasn't able to with the ice sculpture.

"Interning for her must be very fulfilling," Javi said.

The earnestness in his voice nearly broke my resolve to keep his assumption intact. But if I fessed up now, wouldn't he just run to Paulina and tell her everything? More the actions of a concerned friend than a snitch, but still. The fallout would jeopardize my chances with Mandy.

"Yes," I said. "Interning with her is the best." I tried to channel Po's "believing is seeing" philosophy. *If I'm manifesting tomorrow, I'm not really lying today, am I?*

Wrong. Guilt slithered through me. I closed my eyes, wishing for the cars rumbling past to squash it.

A bell-like chime. For a second, I thought the sound came from the flick of Soraya's fairy godmother wand, granting my desire—not an incoming notification on Javi's phone.

"You're not going to believe this," he said, laugh-snorting. He turned the screen around, showing me a text from *Pau AKA Sister from Another Mister*:

Bro, can't make it to the fittings. Something came up 😉

"What?" I squealed. The guilt stayed lodged inside my belly, but at least I didn't have to tell Paulina I'd screwed up. Spared—no, saved—by Hurricane Po. I cracked up at the irony.

Another chime.

Considering I'm not going to miss watching you squirm in a penguin suit, please have your crush reschedule the tux fitting for same time tm, por fa.

The world went fuzzy when I reached "your crush." And when Javi's eyes glittered unabashed, inviting and caring, it encouraged me to cup the back of his neck and pull him in for a kiss.

Once more I was swept off my loafers.

This time, I made didn't try to plant myself back on Earth.

CHAPTER TWENTY-THREE

Back at home, I was still keyed-up from the day's events. Epic first kiss, check. Applying to Mandy's internship faster than anticipated, check.

After I hit Send, the application flew off to Soraya with a *swoosh*.

I sunk back into the kitchen chair. Late-afternoon sunshine spilled through the windows, gilding the room with more shades of gold than our school's trophy cases.

So what if I couldn't add today's personal wins to the case? The urge to celebrate closing in on the internship—and our HEA—surfaced anyway. Begging me not to ignore it.

With Po still out "trying on dresses" with Paulina, and my annoyance levels with Dad—who was working late again—peaking higher than the palm trees outside, I'd have to throw myself a mini-party of one.

I crossed the kitchen. Grabbed Mom's iPad. Wouldn't a *Star Wars* playlist be the perfect soundtrack for hammering out more details on Paulina's quince?

Probably.

I lowered the tablet. Wouldn't one of Mom's playlists work just as well? Maybe better, considering the location?

Before I lost my nerve, I flicked through some of her playlists until I hit one called *Best of JLo.* I tapped an oldie but a goodie called "Waiting for Tonight" to kick it off.

The kitchen filled with guitar, keyboards, and the Puerto Rican diva's voice.

To feel your lips on my fingertips took on a different meaning now.

I couldn't wait to feel Javi's mouth pressing on mine.

It took a moment for reality to catch up to the daydream.

As much as I loved mixing business with pleasure, the best course of action was probably to pump the break on "pleasure" until after Paulina's party.

Today, luck—or magic—had been on my side. I sighed, knowing too well that sooner than later, luck, like fairy-light batteries, ran out.

I sulked back to the kitchen table. Pulled up some of the photos of tuxes I'd bookmarked for Javi's fitting tomorrow. "Which one of these will help make Paulina's dress look fairest of all?" I said to myself, enlarging the pic Po texted me of Paulina wearing her front-runner gown.

The fabric covered in black sequins mirrored a star-dusted sky. A sweetheart neckline perfectly showcased her long neck, clasped with her signature *Paulina* necklace. The high slit on the side and her sleek hair imbued the gown with cape-like vibes.

Darth Vader would be a very proud papi.

Would he feel the same way about these tuxes?

More importantly, what would Mandy think? Now that Soraya was going to hand deliver my application to the fairy godmother herself, the need for "perfection" on this party ratcheted up to "perfect-plus."

My mouth went dry. I chugged some water. I reached the bottom of the bottle, and ugh—still parched.

Was it the pressure of nailing the quince that pressed heavy on me? Or the song playing?

Once upon a time, it'd been one of Mom's favorites. And she wasn't around to hear it.

She wasn't around to get the inside scoop on my first kiss, either.

Disney movies and rom-coms nourished her soul as much as yucca fries and mamey shakes. More, even. Yet I couldn't tell her about my starring role in my budding romance.

I scratched at my blouse. Better to feel the burn of my nails against my skin than the emptiness inside my chest.

When that didn't work, I turned the music off. Snagged the phone off the table. Scrolled through Mandy's grid. All its brilliance chased the darkness away. "Happily ever afters are our business," I whispered.

A few seconds of relief before Dad barged in. "I come in peace, kiddo." He extended a huge box from Folks Pizzeria, lifting the lid a little.

Gasp. A margherita.

"Your favorite," he said.

The red sauce sparkled. The flour dusted the crust's charred and chewy parts. No wonder the Evil Queen tempted Snow White with food.

Opening the cardboard sides of the pizza box, Dad took an exaggerated inhale. "Mmmm, this sure smells good. Too bad no one is around to share this with." He waved the top flap through the air.

The smells of hot bread and cheese wafted over. Pangs of hunger temporarily replaced my indignation. "Fine. Hand it over."

"Does this mean I'm forgiven for missing dinner the other night?"

"No." Javi's openness had been the perfect backdrop for practicing expressing things rarely vocalized. Apparently, our convos hadn't helped me talk only in Parental Past Tense, but in Present Tense. "And you can't keep missing our dinners."

Dad looked as shocked as I felt at actually speaking up. I straightened my posture, steeling myself to keep going. "You can't keep missing our lives." The words came out hard, yet polished. Like stones used to build castle towers.

After a moment's hesitation, he rewarded my boldness with a nod. "You're right." He slid into the chair next to me, setting the pizza box onto the table with shaky fingers. "I'm sorry, kiddo. I've just been so swamped with work."

I bit my lips, holding back about his constantly blasting off to a galaxy far, far away after work. I didn't want to overwhelm him. Or myself.

All this talking made me feel as if I'd been poking a bruise. Not excruciating, but not comfortable, either. As Po would say, *It's a marathon, not a horse race*. This amount of sprinting was good enough for now.

"I really want to make it up to you." Dad sounded so serious I actually believed him. "Homework help, a Costco run, more pastelitos for breakfast—anything?"

"Actually, there is something," I said, reaching for one of the cheesiest slices.

Color returned to his cheeks. Happy that I'd taken his olive branch? Or relief that his citizenship to Dadland hadn't been revoked? "Should we wait for Po before digging in?" he asked.

Whoa. First, he sounded like a dad, and now he was acting like one?!

My heart squeezed. Its edges didn't cut my chest as deeply as before. "Hmm. Let me get an ETA first." I picked up my phone. I flicked away one notification from Callie, two from Javi. Tapped on the dozens of unread ones from Po.

"'Having dinner at Paulina's!!!' String of heart-eye emojis."

Considering Dad clammed up at any mention of *mom*, I skipped reading the next part aloud.

Her mom's got a VERY strong personality btw . . .

My fingers flew across the phone: Strong like Queen Elinor from Brave? Forcing her daughter to follow traditions? Or does she put the "bear" back into overBEARing like Mrs. Ming Lee from Turning Red?

I licked my lips, suddenly hungrier for details about Señora Reyes than pizza.

Before hitting Send, I brushed a fingertip against the words her mom's. Flinched back as if they'd paper cut me. Was it even my place to ask? Especially if I intended to keep some parts of the party strictly professional?

I deleted the text and continued reading aloud Po's: "'She's shocked I haven't seen *Rogue One*.'"

"What?" Dad's eyes widened. "I never screened it for you girls?"

I shook my head and finished Po's text: "'It's her new mission in life to convince me it's the best *Star Wars* movie of all time. BUT HOW IF THERE ARE NO EWOKS?!'"

While Dad cracked up, I found the perfect GIF of Ewoks dancing. Followed it up with a bunch of party-popper and confetti-ball emojis.

"It looks like it's just us," I said, lifting the slice.

We toasted with the pizza and took synchronized bites. Our groans of delight swirled through the kitchen.

I darted to the fridge to get another bottle of water, anticipating my throat pinching closed. Tasting some of our go-to meals from Before usually triggered this. A visceral reaction to enjoying our best-loved foods when Mom couldn't.

Weirdly, it hadn't happened last night when I'd chowed down the PSTs with Po.

Seconds passed. It didn't happen now, either. Instead, my stomach grumbled louder than the emotions churning it. Made it easier for the old saying to rush back.

Food is meant to be enjoyed and shared. It might've come from Mom. Or Po. I honestly couldn't remember who said it first.

All that mattered was that it helped unlock my jaw. I left the bottle of water in the fridge. Grabbed the ranch dressing and headed back to the table.

"I like this Paulina," Dad said, his voice muffled by dough. "It's a good thing you're hanging out with friends again."

I slumped into the chair. Sure, Paulina had shared some personal stuff. But only to help me understand what she wanted from her Very Merry Unquince, right?

"She's more Po's friend. I'm simply helping her plan the *Star Wars* party I told you about. She loved the idea for the paso doble, by the way, so thanks." I dipped my head in gratitude.

"If you need access to more of my *Star Wars* knowledge, it's yours. Pro bono."

"That's exactly what I need your help on."

While he beamed, I cracked my knuckles. Stretched my fingers the way I used to before sitting down to paint. The tendons and ligaments in my hands relaxed a little.

As did everything else. Achy chest included.

I turned the laptop toward him. "This is the front-runner for Paulina's dress. And these"—I took a bite of pizza then pointed it at three tux contenders—"are the top picks for her chambelán. His name is Javi." I hoped he didn't hear the swoon spilling from my voice, or if he did, that he attributed it to the mouthwateringness of the food. "I mean, he's going to look hot no matter what."

Dad's eyebrows drew so close together they almost touched.

I dipped the slice in some dressing, stuffing my mouth before anything else plopped out. I swallowed. Loudly. "Um, what I meant to say is, I'm not feeling these anymore. I want"—*need*—"the outfits to scream galaxy far, far away. This all-black option here comes close, but I don't know. It's not perfect."

"Firstly, if your friend's going for a glam Darth Vader look, you nailed it, kiddo."

The slap of his high five reverberated on my palm. Party planning really brought people together. After the wave of happiness came a surge of hope.

If he and Soraya thought I was cut out for this, then (fingers crossed) Mandy would.

"Secondly . . ." He pulled the laptop closer, fingers clacking against the keys. "Whenever you see Lord Vader, a stormtrooper is never far behind." He turned the laptop back toward me.

An image of a stormtrooper beamed between the pic of Paulina and the collage of tuxes.

"See these sleek, white body plates?" He trailed them with an edge of pizza crust. "It's armor seamlessly attached to a black body glove."

If being evil meant looking this good, conscript me to the Dark Side ASAP. He went all Wookieepedia again, droning on about the use and function of the armor and helmets.

My attention zeroed in on how much this streamlined, white outfit with black accents would pop next to Paulina's gown, and vice versa.

Like Po would say: *Light can't exist without shadows.* Plus—I scooted to the edge of the chair because—stormtroopers wore utility bags?

This had to be a sign.

Reaching for the backpack slung over the chair, I dug out my day planner and pencil. Flipping to some of the empty pages in the back, I sketched the black pants from one suit. Paired them with the white jacket from another. Shadowed in the lapels. Added the black bow tie from the third option. In place of a utility bag, I drew a black cummerbund. Doodled a hidden Mickey on it.

B Spoke probably didn't have smiling Mickey appliqués to patch onto their rentals. I could rummage through Po's old trading pins and find a tiny one to stick to the cummerbund. That way Javi could still bring an extra smile with him to the party.

"Ta-da." I showed off my rough design like it was the *Mona Lisa*. "How does this look?"

A spark ignited in his eyes, burning away more of the haze usually clouding them. "Like Trooper Javi's going to this quince in style."

Images of Javi wearing the outfit jumbled in my head and short-circuited the wires responsible for tethering my good sense. "He's going to be the hottest chambelán OC's ever seen."

Oh Sith Lord. Not again. Part work, part excuse to keep my flaming face away from Dad, I texted Paulina a picture of my sketch.

The phone buzzed in my hands.

Not a response from Paulina, or an email from PP Celebrations that the AT-AT sculptures were a go. It was a new event on the family calendar.

The Talk rescheduled.

Well, at least he'd remembered to get it back in the books. "Ugh," I groaned, then surprised myself by how quickly grumbles could turn into belly laughs.

Dad laughed with me. The corners of his eyes crinkled. Except not in the way they did after gaming all night, or working all day. He simply looked like himself again.

Our laughter spilled out the archway, down the hallway. I hoped that whether from the framed portraits or somewhere out in a galaxy not so far away, Mom was watching.

CHAPTER TWENTY-FOUR

Paulina sat on a bench in B Spoke's tailoring area, configuring her camera's setting. Behind one of the fitting room's velvet curtains, Javi slipped into part of his tux. To keep my gaze from burning holes through the drapery, I slipped the phone from my utility bag.

I discreetly refreshed my inbox for the hundredth time.

Nothing from Mandy. I slumped against the rolling rack. Had Soraya given her my application already? Was Mandy on the fence about me? How much longer until a response?

I shivered as a horrific possibility crept up my spine: What if Mandy rejected me?

No fairest fairy godmother of them all to take me under her wing. Teach me how to turn Dad from wannabe Jedi to prince. How to keep Hurricane Po sailing toward our previously programmed destinations.

I hugged the planner to my chest like it was a life preserver. Keeping me, and our HEA, afloat. Without it, how else would Mom know everything had turned out okay?

Javi threw the curtains open, slashing through my waking nightmare.

As he stepped onto the fitting platform, Paulina sprung from the bench to start filming. "Looking good, Baymoon."

Now, that was an understatement. The crisp shirt under a white tux with black lapels fit him perfectly.

Paulina frowned as she moved the camera from his torso to his cargo shorts and flip-flops.

"Caaaaas." She lowered the camera. "I know I said I wanted 'deconstructed' vibes, but please tell me this isn't the full outfit. If it is . . ." She crossed her arms over a black faux-leather vest. "The bottom half of this outfit stays on the cutting-room floor."

Javi and I shared a glance and some giggles. "This is not the full look." I pushed off the rolling rack. "Since the outfit choices are pretty 'classic,' I figured why not 'unquince' it up by having Javi try on one piece at a time? That way your viewers can have a reaction for each part of the outfit."

And not get hit with the full stormtrooper reveal until the very end.

A smile grew across her face. "That's genius. I love that so much."

"Perfect." I tapped my pencil across the top of the planner. The gold ring encasing the eraser twinkled against the soft bulbs strung around B Spoke's showcase area. *Patience, apprentice; you'll become a magic wand soon.*

"Let me film you getting footage of Javi before we layer on the next piece," I said.

Paulina leapt into action. "Chin up, Baymoon. Higher. No, too much!" She rounded the circular platform where he stood. "Find the light to get the best angles."

I tried to keep my phone locked on her. But as she barked more orders, I kept drifting it to three wall-length mirrors wrapping around Javi.

He turned the tiniest bit. Staring into one of the mirrors to meet my reflection, he said, "What about here?"

If Paulina hadn't had her back turned, she would've spied my goofy grin.

Concentrate. Enough filming this section. Onto the next. I pushed the rolling rack filled with jackets, pants, and cummerbunds to the fitting room. Red herrings, all of them. The real clothing already waited inside.

I glanced back at Javi. Our eyes met. We beamed. Hopefully not only because of our stormtrooper surprise.

"There. Perfect. Don't move," Paulina said. "I'm going in for a single shot." Paulina looped around the platform. "Yes. You're serving it. Adjust the bow tie. Run your fingers through that mop of yours. Then at the count of three, look into the camera and brood."

"What does 'brood' even look like?" he asked.

"Like your stomach hurts," Paulina said. "One, two, three."

Javi doubled over. Clutched his stomach, moaning.

"Grr. Not that type of stomachache, Baymoon. This is for my unquince, not a Pepto Bismol commercial."

I held in so many giggles I was surprised my lungs didn't explode. "Pretend you bit into a lemon," I said, heading to the bench. "Or better yet, do your Blue Steel pose. Only lower the intensity by fifty percent."

Javi nodded. Thankfully, I was sitting when he went into model mode. Over here, my knees could wobble as much as they wanted to without making me stumble over dress forms.

"Got it." Paulina huffed a satisfied breath. "Next shot."

"Allison," I called out to our assigned tailor. "We're ready."

Paulina stepped aside to let Allison hop onto the platform and take Javi's measurements. Camera in hand, Paulina lowered onto the bench next to me, pointing the lens around the space.

She captured a column of flawlessly folded shirts. The gentle sway of the lightbulbs riding invisible currents of AC. The way the light sparkled in Javi's hair. I could fill an entire page in the back of my day planner with a matching palette of brown hues and still not have enough room.

Paulina moved the camera to a dress form but left out the tiny scraps of cloth strewn across its base.

I narrowed my eyes at her viewfinder. Did she employ the same strategy I did when creating Pinterest boards?

Showcase the best. Crop out the rest.

As if reading my mind, she zoomed in when Allison measured Javi's biceps. "I don't know much about film techniques," I said, "but I presume that's the money shot?"

Javi must've heard because he flexed his muscles. I clamped my jaw to keep from cackling. The laughter had nowhere to go but out my nose via a loud snort.

Paulina chuckled. "Po was right—you can be funny when you loosen up." The softness in her voice when she said my sister's name kept me from scoffing.

Po would get an earful later. She couldn't get away with throwing me under the party bus in front of my most important client. Then again, I wouldn't have scored this gig without her, so . . .

"I'm sorry she couldn't make it today to help out," I said. "Our school's volleyball team is the real deal, so they pretty much practice year-round." I put up a hand in Scout's honor. "I promise I can handle this fitting solo." The second the words left my mouth, my eyes drifted to Javi.

Nope. Ojos back on the prize. I cleared my throat and said, "Paulina, are you ready for Javi to try on the next piece?"

No response.

"Paulina?" Nada. Her face stayed glued to her phone screen.

No need to squint at the name above the texts. Only one person would be sending her Ewok-cooking GIFs.

Paulina didn't even notice when Allison left. Or when I got up. Much less when I peeked inside the fitting room to double-check that the rest of the outfit was stashed inside.

I stepped onto the platform with Javi. Stealth was probably not required with the way Paulina's thumbs were tapping across the screen. I whispered anyway. "You, fitting room, stat. I'll whistle when I'm ready for the big reveal."

"Gotcha." He grabbed my hand. "Hey, are you coming to the next Movies at the Beach with me?" Electricity shot up my arm. I peeled it away before my hair frizzed more.

"Let's work now. We can discuss play later." Before he could protest, I nudged him off the platform and headed to Paulina. Hormones and heartstrings would not wreck today's agenda.

"While Javi's changing, we still have the venue, menus, and photo shoot to plan," I said, lowering next to her.

I flipped open my planner. "Have you checked out the spreadsheet I sent? The one with all the banquets halls and hotels I've used for SBA—er, Mandy Whitmore—events?"

The air froze. She looked up, her expression serious.

Blood rushed to my ears. Goodbye, internship. Adiós, HEA—

"Sorry, Cas, did you say something?"

Thank you, Hurricane Po, for coming in with another massive save.

I let out a slow breath. "Um, yeah. Have you looked at the potential locations yet? Or menus?"

She slapped the side of her black jeans. "I stayed up so late watching *Rogue One* with Po I completely forgot." Her phone buzzed.

She giggled and disappeared into the screen. She looked up a second later. "Sorry, sorry. We were just coordinating times for me to come watch her practice."

Po only made plans—and stuck to them—when I forced her to. Yet here she was, scheduling future events with Paulina? Things were getting more serious between them than she'd let on. Which was good for them, I guess, but why hadn't Po told me anything?

Paulina's ringtone blared, pulling me from my thoughts. The two ominous notes from *Jaws* sped up. The hair on the back of my neck stood on end like it had the other night on the beach.

Paulina's serious mask quickly replaced her swoony face. "Sorry, I got to take this. It's La Mera Mera."

Who had this ringtone for their *mom*?

"I told you I had fittings today," Paulina said in perfect Spanish. I couldn't catch her mom's exact words. Only her hard and barbed tones. The shark comparison started to click."Yes, I'll ask her." Paulina exhaled. "Yes, I'll tell her that, too." An eye-roll. "Okay, I'm busy. Got to go."

She stuffed her phone into her pocket, wiping her hands down the sides of her vest as if to wash them of the conversation. "Sorry about that."

"Is everything okay?" I asked.

Paulina shrugged. "Yeah. Since I had Po over for dinner last night, she wants you to come over soon. I already planned on asking, but now the invite seems like it is *her* idea. You in?"

I rubbed at the pearl button in the middle of my blouse where there was a sudden ache. Heartburn from too much Cuban coffee, not my heart burning to hang out with another Latina mom, obviously.

"Yes." I cleared my throat. Sure, accepting the invitation could potentially lead to more muddying of our business/buddy waters. *Keep it professional. Interact with La Mera Mera strictly for the purposes of writing Paulina the best thank-you-Mom speech ever.* "Gracias. It's really kind of you both."

"Yeah, well, wait until you hear this before you label her 'kind.'" Fidgeting with her necklace, she said, "When I mentioned the NDA Mandy wants me to sign"—ugh, I was hoping she'd forgotten about that—"she had her attorney draw up one for you to sign, too." Great. "An exclusivity agreement as well."

My shoulders tensed. "Exclusivity agreement?"

"She doesn't want you to take on any other quinces or similar parties for classmates. Last night Po said there's a girl that's been DMing you about doing her sweet sixteen."

I flicked my gaze to my loafers. "Melina."

"Yeah. La Mera Mera wants the dinner party to be your sole focus considering you're 'only an intern,'" she said, using air quotes. "Po thought it best, too. That way, 'Little Cuchara doesn't burn herself out.'"

Breathe in. Now, out.

Exactly how much of our personal life had Po shared?

Although I wasn't the one getting undressed behind the fitting-room curtains, I felt exposed. Vulnerable. A tightness wrapped around my chest, as if I wore a corset three sizes too small.

This was Disneyland all over again . . . when Po showed Paulina my sketches without permission. Except now it wasn't my messy pencil lines that were on display—it was me.

I balled my hands into fists.

"I'll send you both documents this weekend, and don't forget to send me Mandy's," Paulina said. "If it's okay with you, can you turn down the other offer to tide La Mera Mera over until she gets the signed docs back?"

I shifted on the bench. "Like, right now?"

"If it's not a problem," Paulina said, studying me.

I gave a brittle laugh. "No problems here ever." I finally messaged Melina back, politely declining her sweet sixteen.

Well, there goes my backup plan. The fairy godmother's apprenticeship now completely hinged on nailing Paulina's un-quince. I painted a tight smile on my face. "All done."

"Thanks. I'm sorry my mom's so damn extra." The serious mask began to fall away. "But I'm also not sorry because I'm having so much fun doing this. Aren't you?" She gestured to the curtains.

Maybe they had some type of BFF mind meld, because Javi's voice boomed from the other side of the velvet, cutting through the jumble of emotions coursing through me. "Ready or not, here I come."

Argh. As if things weren't already chaotic enough, this wasn't the cue.

The phone nearly slipped from my hands. I somehow righted it, managing to press the Record button right as he stepped through the curtains.

No! I twisted back toward Paulina. *Capture the birthday girl's reaction, not her chambelán!*

Thankfully, I caught every glorious second. From her leaping off the bench to her shrieking with joy as her camera captured Javi's outfit. "Cut," she yelled.

She flung her arms around him. Before I knew it, her arms looped around me, too. "You've turned my bestie into a stormtrooper," she whispered. Her voice was softer than any silk inside this store. When she pulled away, her eyes sparked brighter than the glitter lining them.

Was this another glimpse of the real her? A *Star Wars* villain in the streets but a Disney princess in fitting room suites?

"You've listened to me blab about my life. Never once have you judged the more questionable choices I've made with this party." A shaky breath. "You've also been so gracious with sharing Po, especially when things have been tough at home."

Paulina drew me in for another hug. She didn't embrace me like her planner.

She held me like her friend.

While her body radiated warmth, mine prickled with cold. Not the good ice-sculpture kind, either, but frostbite.

Would she keep clinging to me like this if she knew I'd lied about Mandy's internship? What about me hitching my cart to her horse in order to get it?

If she found out the truth, she'd never hug me again . . .

Or by proxy, Po.

"This is going to be the best unquince ever," she said with a Po-like shimmy. The swinging lightsaber earrings scraped my cheeks.

She who lives by the machete dies by the machete.

With the Poverb resounding in my head, I really didn't think the moment could get any worse. Then Javi bounded over, tapped Paulina on the shoulder, and said, "May I cut in?"

Paulina winked, stepping aside. He swept me into his own bear hug. His arms wrapping around me did nothing to warm me up this time. "Seconding what Paulina said."

"Yup," I croaked. "Best unquince ever."

CHAPTER TWENTY-FIVE

Green-blue waves rolled all the way out to the horizon. Gold beams of sunlight pierced through thick clouds. Loafers in hand, I trudged through the sand.

Salty air raked through my hair with every step. The curls I'd spent time deep conditioning frizzed around my shoulders. By the time I neared the volleyball nets next to the Matteo Beach pier, my hair spiraled less like Botticelli's *Birth of Venus* and corkscrewed more like Princess Merida's.

Except I didn't feel like a princess. Or even the castle towers where they lived anymore. With the awful feeling slithering through me, *dragon beneath castle* suited me best.

Wasn't my entire job to anticipate and prevent terrible things from happening? Not that getting closer to Javi or Paulina was bad. Some of the best things since After Mom had happened while planning this unquince, except—

Now there was more on the line than Paulina's party or Mandy's internship. What if I screwed it all up?

I tore a hand through my hair. My fingers got stuck. Ugh.

Unbelievable that I was rushing to Po for advice. Then again, she'd pushed me into this mess. She'd better help pull me out of it.

I gulped some briny air, ready to shout across the sand to get Po's attention.

Her kicking ass on the court spellbound mine instead. With the heel of her palm, she smashed the ball over the net. The *slap* rivaled the surf pounding the shore, eliciting a chorus of *daaangs* from her team on the sidelines.

Po brought her arm behind her back. Flashed a hand signal to her teammate. I stepped behind Cynthia and Brandi. "Eeek, they're going for a big dog!" Cynthia said.

I didn't speak enough Volleyball to know what that meant. It didn't stop me from being captivated by my sister's speed and raw power. Each curve of her body glowed with sweat. Particles of sand stuck to her skin, shimmering like confetti.

Po owned the court. No matter where the ball flew from, she sprang to find it.

Maybe this is what a leap of faith meant. Believing that with either the help of her team or solo, she'd knock the ball over the net.

A collection of *oofs* rippled from the squad when she didn't hit the ball over. In classic Po fashion, she brushed the sand off and kept going.

My entire life's philosophy was avoiding "dropping the ball." Po shrugged it off when things fell. Gah, how this tendency of hers irked me, my irritation probably anchored by the resentment over her disastrous quince. By the subconscious grudge I'd held at her glossing over how bad it'd actually been.

Now, though?

Each time she rose on sand-coated knees and tried again, the indignation and frustration deflated a bit. Who knew they'd been taking up so much space inside?

The sun shifted, spotlighting Po. Her shaking off more sand endeared her to me. Inspired me in a way her Poverbs never could.

She hit the ball back and forth. Grunting with fury, like she wanted to punish the ball. Banish it over the net. Win this grueling game at all costs.

The hard slaps and battle cries cracked through my tower of assumptions. Maybe she didn't blow past things as easily as I had thought.

I edged between Cynthia and Brandi when the set wound down. Cynthia pulled me by the utility bag's strap. "We saw you on Hot Goss. Tell us details of this YouTuber's quince." She pronounced it *kwins*.

"It's pronounced *keenseh*," I said. "You know, since it's short for quinceañera?"

Brandi swatted Cynthia with a towel. "Told ya you should've taken Spanish."

Cynthia swatted back, then draped the towel over my neck, hauling me in. "I watched the video of the dance you and Marcus choreographed." She clutched her chest. "The passion between Paulina and Javier is out of this world."

I had to bite my tongue to keep from laughing. "Yep. Super passionate, those two." Just not with each other.

"I hadn't ever watched her channel before, but Gianna keeps reposting clips to her socials and . . . swoon." Brandi fanned herself with a towel. "So far the ones from the ice-sculpture place were my fave."

"Same here." I counted on my dark skin to hide the way my face flamed. Judging by the way Cynthia tilted her head at me, perhaps the melanin didn't conceal that much.

Thankfully Po strode over, pointing at her and Brandi, then two other teammates. "You're up." She motioned to the court. "Let's go." Her voice spilled over with assertiveness.

"Yes, Captain," they said in unison, scrambling to the court.

WTF. Why didn't *this* Po show up at home more often?

Between the both of us, we could've forced Dad to hang up his Xbox controller months ago. No Mandy fairy dust required.

Her voice softened when her gaze landed on me. "This is the most pleasant of surprises, Little Cuchara. Need me to go shopping with you before your second movie date with—"

I stopped her by coughing loudly. "Cynthia watches Paulina's channel. Let's go talk over there," I whispered into her sweaty ear, gesturing to the cement benches above the strand.

"Why? What's up?" she asked.

Taking a page from her playbook, I coated my mouth with red lipstick.

Po blinked and blinked. "Team, family emergency," she yelled over her shoulder. "Be back in five."

"Make it ten," I corrected.

Pacing in front of the bench where Po sat, I said, "I'm second-guessing this pretending to be a Mandy intern with Paulina and Javi."

Clouds rolled in from the horizon, scudding across the sky. "'Going with the flow' didn't seem so bad before."

Before so much business got tangled with pleasure. Before the dynamics in the unquince court had changed. My loafers crunched on the sandy gravel. "But now I'm drowning."

"Good thing you're falling for a lifeguard, then." She wiggled her brows. "His CPR will revive you in no time."

"I hate it when you make valid points." I dropped beside her. The cement hit my spine. The sting throbbed with the guilt of lying to Paulina and Javi. With the worry of turning into a pumpkin before I became a fairy godmother's apprentice.

"Don't *you* feel bad about this? I mean, you and Paulina are more than friends." Like me and Javi. "Shouldn't we . . ." I frowned into my lap. "Tell them . . ." *Brace yourself.* "Maybe they'd underst—" But the rest of the word shriveled. "Never mind. The truth would only complicate the mess."

Po blinked. Impressed, or taken aback by how reality won out over wishful thinking. She draped a sweaty arm over my shoulder. "Yep. Can't risk rocking the sails now."

Cold hard facts. Too many kisses had gone by. Too much familial history shared, linking the four of us together. Added to the dilemma was Paulina's preference for *Star Wars* villains over Disney princesses.

Could I really afford to piss off a Sith Lord? Especially if her lightsaber could burn my bridge to Mandy. And blasting me on her channel could destroy my chances at booking future clients.

My chest caved. Then there was Javi. A guy who preferred theatrics playing out in the telenovelas and K-dramas he watched with his mom—not in real life. He'd had enough of that already.

As if sensing the regret pressing heavy onto my shoulders, Po gave them a little squeeze. "I know this situation sucks, but we can't make huevos rancheros without breaking a few eggs."

I scoffed, trying hard not to think about a very broken huevo.

Humpty Dumpty had a great fall. All the king's horses and all the king's men couldn't put Humpty together again.

My head dropped to my hands.

Oh Sith Lord, what had I done?

Po rubbed my back the way Mom used to whenever I'd get upset. Despite everything, her touch eased some of my tension. "You're going to get the internship, okay? If you get it before the party, then everything you told Paulina—"

"Everything *we* told Paulina—" I squinted at her.

Matching the expression, she said, "And everything *we* told Javi wouldn't really be a lie."

Logic began to overpower my conscience. "Technically, I guess."

"Have you ever screwed up an event?" she asked.

"Obviously not."

"Then all you have to do is keep your head above water until Mandy hires you."

Po spoke with such confidence it started to dispel the worst of my fears. "I only sent Soraya my application last night." A flock of gulls circled overhead, wings fluttering to the tempo of my heart. "Would an interview request come in this quickly?"

"Anything's possible." She leaned back into the bench, stared into the horizon. The entirety of the Pacific Ocean twinkled before us.

Her newest quote paired well with her Poverb from Disneyland: *Believing is seeing.*

Together they drowned out the noise of beachgoers zipping past. Of waves rumbling. Of whirring wind that stretched whitecaps of saltwater to infinity and beyond.

Had I gotten so caught up with trying to prevent the worst that I'd completely forgotten how to anticipate the best?

I pulled my phone from my utility bag and my pencil from behind my ear. "Believing is seeing, right?"

I twirled the end of the pencil over the screen. The gold ring holding the eraser flashed against the sun. "I'm a Mandy intern," I chanted, part special request, part fairy godmother incantation. "I'm a Mandy intern."

Po wiggled *abracadabra* fingers toward my phone. "In the name of JLo, Celia Cruz, and both Selenas, please make Little Cuchara Mandy's intern."

A deep breath.

If you're out there, Soraya, I need you.

Mom, if you're listening, I need you more.

Here goes everything.

One new email gleamed from my inbox.

Mandy Whitmore Internship Interview Request.

My chest lifted, as if a bounce house inflated inside of me all at once. I read the email twice to make sure my eyes weren't deceiving me.

"I can come in for the interview the week after Paulina's party," I squealed. "Or, because of a last-minute cancellation—" I sprang from the bench and broke into a happy dance, not caring that I was in full view of everyone on the strand. "I can come in a few hours!"

Po leapt toward me. "Told ya." She circled me in an impromptu version of the paso doble. At the next jogger jetting by, Po yelled, "My Little Cuchara's on her way to becoming OC's next big party planner!"

Gulls wheeled overhead, flapping their thick wings south toward Pelican Point. Most of my worries flew away with them.

A pair of sunbeams began to pour from a fluffy cloud decorating the sky.

Perhaps I didn't have one fairy godmother looking out for me, but two.

CHAPTER TWENTY-SIX

People pushed rolling racks through the foyer. Others hustled through hallways, flipping tabbed day planners and scrolling tablet screens. Everywhere inside the lobby of Mandy's office was a flurry of making fantasies come true.

I curled my toes inside my loafers to make sure I really stood there. Inside the fairest fairy godmother's real-life grid.

Soft lighting gleamed across pastel-colored decor. Fresh flowers bloomed inside crystal vases. Silver frames glinted across the high-reaching walls, showcasing special events. Every picture-perfect moment held the promise of a great, big, beautiful tomorrow.

"Yes," I whispered to myself. "All that glitters is, in fact, gold."

I hurried to the reception area. "Castillo Torres," I said to the elegant person behind a white lacquered desk. "I have an appointment with Ms. Whitmore."

The last stop before turning around the not-a-real-intern situation. The final test before Mandy sprinkled me with her pixie dust, imbuing me with the power to fix the mess at home.

"I'll let her know you're here," the receptionist said. "Please take a seat."

Sinking into the white-tufted couch, I glanced back at the

receptionist. At her pin-straight hair cascading over her back. Reflexively, my fingers went to my waist.

"Ahh," I muttered, unzipping my utility bag and reaching inside. *There you are.* Since I hadn't had time to flat-iron my hair, anti-frizz serum would have to do. I ran a few drops through the ends of my hair. Using the phone's screen, I gave myself a once-over.

Years of straightening had flattened some of the spring from my natural hair. Some curls frizzed; others hung a little limper than I would have liked. Still.

The ringlets were beginning to reclaim the space across my shoulders. Slowly remembering how to corkscrew instead of falling in straight lines. And as jarring as it was to see Mom's texture inside of my own tresses, I cracked a grin.

"Something old, something new, something borrowed . . ." I whispered, happy that part of her would be joining me in this interview.

Must wear it curly from now on, I added to my personal agenda. That way, part of her could join every other important event.

I uncapped the coral lip gloss I'd borrowed from Po and smoothed it over my lips. Her version of liquid courage. It felt right to take a piece of her into this interview, too.

"Miss Torres." Soraya's throaty voice pulled my face from the screen. "It's good to see you again."

"Not as good as it is to see you." I rose from the couch. "Thank you so much for expediting my application and squeezing me in last-minute."

"Of course." She led me down a hallway flanked by glass walls. On one side was a conference room big enough to fit every Disney princess. On the other were smaller but no less beautifully decorated offices.

"I bet that one's yours." I pointed to the room with red

abstract art on the walls and a massive throne / office chair behind a mahogany desk.

She glanced back, the corners of her mouth curled. "Right you are."

We approached a set of double doors at the end of the hallway. Keeping up with Soraya and the excitement and nervousness of finally meeting the woman behind the bejeweled curtain left me breathless.

"Ready?" Soraya asked.

I quickly added another layer of the coral gloss. "Always," I answered.

She knocked three times before flinging the doors open.

A small gasp escaped me.

I'd always sketched Mandy's office like a SoCal modern art museum meets Beast's library. Instead, I stepped into something pulled less from a fairy tale and more from a beach-cottage Pinterest board.

Patchwork cushions framed window seats. A cozy spot for perfect views of PCH. Of seaside homes dotting both shoreline and the rugged hills above it.

A small desk took up the space near the back wall. In the middle of it, her signature diamond-studded stylus twinkled like a real fairy godmother's wand.

One flick of the wrist could turn any life around. This was everything I'd wanted. Everything I'd worked for. So why wasn't I stepping forward?

Or falling as deeply under its spell as I thought I would?

Did the desk being awash in an expanse of perfume bottles, empty glasses, and party favors dilute the stylus-wand's magic? This mess reminded me too much of Dad's console table.

Her bookcases were no better. Where were the style books and the photos of VIP ceremonies from the lobby to crown these shelves? Only mismatched frames encasing faded pictures reigned on each ledge.

What was so special about sitting on a park bench or drinking a Big Gulp? Wasn't Mandy supposed to be the patron saint of crafting *magical* memories?

Mandy motioned us over to a big couch. Clearing the tickle in my throat, I headed over.

Up close, she looked even more like Michelle Obama's doppelgänger than in her grid photos. If Cinderella's mice cut up Glinda the Good Witch's pink dress to create a pantsuit, that's what Mandy wore. Diamonds studded her earlobes and wrapped around both wrists. Even if her office didn't look the part, she did.

She cupped my hands like we were long-lost sisters. "It's so nice to meet you, Castillo."

"Ditto, Ms. Whitmore." I gave her a firm handshake, pulling away before she felt my pulse picking up speed. "I'm a huge fan of your work."

"Please call me Mandy." She grinned, putting deep dimples on display. Double that of Javi's.

"If you insist . . . Mandy." Her name rhymed with candy and tasted like it inside my mouth, too. Excitement began to eclipse my first (not-so-impressed) impressions of this room.

"Soraya told me you're quite the planner already." The diamonds on her wrists glittered as she waved for me to sit. Notes of honeysuckle and lavender wafted from her.

Mom's perfume and Javi's shampoo. The main ingredients in a bravery potion, apparently. The second I breathed it in, I took my place on her couch and said, "I'm the youngest event chair Matteo Beach High's student body association has ever had. Recently, I started a side business where I help classmates plan birthdays."

Mandy and Soraya nodded approvingly.

Maybe Po was right. I should celebrate myself more.

Soraya sat on the pleated arm of the sofa and handed Mandy a gold folder. She opened it, slipping out my application. I took another inhale of the valor perfume.

"Your last, and current, parties are both quinceañeras," Mandy said.

"That's one type of party that's been growing at our firm exponentially," Soraya said.

"That doesn't surprise me," I said.

Soraya scooted to the edge of the sofa arm. Mandy tipped her chin up. "How do you mean?" she asked.

For years I'd been prepping for this moment. "People like honoring traditions as much as creating new memories . . ."

The monologue came out as polished as silverware. What I didn't expect was for the words to land in the pit of my stomach. Or have memories of Mom's Disney pins float to the surface—much less for them to pull up thoughts of Paulina's and Angie's moms. I tugged at my blouse's collar and continued with my sales pitch. "Quinces are a bridge that connects kids to countries their parents left behind."

Soraya and Mandy exchanged pleased looks. *Please let my sigh of relief go unnoticed.*

Mandy handed me a glossy photo from the folder. "Thoughts on a quinceañera who wants her court to wear these?"

The fourteen damas wore gowns in an array of neon taffeta. "This quinceañera is *not* afraid to let her court shine as brightly as she does," I said, sitting straighter.

A flicker of approval danced across Mandy's eyes. If I continued to bibbidi-bobbidi-blow this test out of the water, I'd transform from faux intern to the real deal.

"What about one that wants to play Cardi B's 'Be Careful' for the main dance routine?" Soraya asked.

I winced. "Sheesh. The chambelán wasn't simply a friendly escort to the party." Like Javi was to Paulina. "But a boyfriend who cheated." I tapped my finger against my chin to the beat of the song. "And the birthday girl wants the entire party to know it."

"Bingo," Soraya said, sparking giggles from Mandy.

"I'm so happy to not be fifteen anymore," she said through a wistful exhale.

In none of my wildest dreams would I have ever thought to add two unsolicited cents to this interview. Let alone want to interject based on the Poverb barging in, *Go grande, or return to your casa*.

I couldn't go home. Not until I nailed this.

"Actually, you don't need to be fifteen to have a quince anymore," I said.

The wheels of rolling racks, clicks of stilettos, and orders barked on headpieces crept in from under the door. The clangor was like their minds collectively churning. "Oh, no? Please illuminate us," Mandy said.

"There are double quinces now, for people turning thirty. Or whenever they can afford to have one." My heart sputtered. *Stay on task*. "My current client, a Disney YouTuber with over one hundred thousand subscribers . . ." I didn't have to pause long for the numbers to sink in. For Mandy and Soraya's eyes to widen on cue.

I hated using Paulina's platform for my benefit. Then again, she was doing the same thing. I unclenched my jaw and continued. "Paulina Reyes, also known as Paulinaland, is having a *Star Wars*–themed 'quince' even though she's turning eighteen."

Mandy's fingers drummed against the folder. "Are you saying she probably feels more rooted in her young adulthood now than she did at fifteen?" *More like she's gaming the admissions board to get into a prestigious film school*. "That she wants to be the one who decides when she leaves her adolescence behind?" she asked, rolling the diamond bracelet around her wrist.

All those twinkling diamonds, combined with the way the sun sparked on her stylus-wand . . . at last, I began to fall fully under her spell.

The air turned heavy. Squeezed my chest until my heart contracted.

No. Expanded.

The expansion caused something to unlatch. Almost every time I met with Paulina, she offered up another reason for wanting a quince. If I peeled back the layers of her motivations, would this ultimately be why she wanted one now, deconstructed or not?

To be in the driver's seat—er, director's chair—of her adulthood?

Something wedged in my throat. Mandy was right. People should get to decide which parts of themselves to shed, and when to cast them away. Versus being forced to let go because of an arbitrary timeline.

Because here's the rub: on a person's fifteenth year, not everyone is ready to make that leap at the stroke of midnight.

Sure, I had to jump into adulting younger than fifteen. Our family needed a grown-up. Speaking more on my behalf than Paulina's, I answered, "Yes."

"It's a lovely sentiment, Castillo. I hope this becomes more popular in the party-planning community."

How different would Po's quince have turned out if she hadn't rushed it? No mistakes, no absent tilde. No disaster.

"I hope it does, too," I said, scooting closer to Mandy.

This was why I needed to get the internship.

Not just to transform the lie into the truth, but for these nuggets of insight that she sprinkled like fairy dust. Mandy sifted through pages inside the folder, most likely looking for a harder question to throw my way. "You know what?" She shut the folder. "Why don't you just tell us why you want to be a party planner?"

The clouds outside shifted, flooding the room—me—with light. The answer I'd written on countless index cards buzzed at my lips.

"My older sister had a quince a few years ago," I said. "It was a disaster—namely, because the banner person forgot to put the tilde over the word años." Retelling the story never got easier. "So instead of wishing her happy fifteen years, it encouraged her to celebrate her fifteen happy buttholes."

Their eyes rounded in disbelief.

"Yeah, I know." Still cringeworthy. "In that moment, something switched inside me." Slam-dunking this interview loomed on the horizon. "If I could help prevent a special event from being ruined, I vowed I would." A pause for dramatic effect. "Crafting special events are about attention to details, hard work, and sticking to plans. Parties are a science."

As soon as the words left my mouth, though, they clashed against images flashing inside my head.

The fundraiser banner. Darth Vader's paso doble. The new "member" of the sculpture family inside the Arctic Art Studio.

Soraya and Mandy looked at me with expressions that yelled, *Is that all party planning is, though?*

"But parties are also magic. And maybe . . ." I pushed past the lines in my monologue for something new. "Magic sometimes also needs spontaneity for it to spark."

Mandy's and Soraya's nods synced up. "Now, can you tell us why you love parties?" Mandy asked.

I squared my shoulders. "They celebrate new beginnings and transformations. They are keys that unlock happy endings." Although I was back to my scripted answers, I believed each word with every atom of my being. "They're the best way to share joy. With so much fun and beauty swirling on the dance floor, how could anyone feel anything but happiness?"

There. The end of my monologue.

Mandy and Soraya both smiled at me like I'd crushed it. Except . . . Blame it on Mandy's stylus-wand, twinkling from the middle of her desk, bewitching me with another spell. One that compelled me to go off script again.

"Lately, I've realized sharing other emotions is equally important."

Too chicken to see what reactions painted their expressions, or maybe afraid of them spying mine, I looked out the window.

An oil tanker and a cargo ship floated in the teal waters, rippling all the way to the horizon. Not only did my heartbreak weigh more than these ships, its hurt heavier than the *Queen Mary* harbored a few beach cities up PCH—my family's grief had been a shipwreck.

One that left us marooned in an archipelago of pain.

Po, Dad, and I all occupied different islands of it.

Until recently. Add that to practicing Parental Past Tense with Javi, getting to know Paulina better, and rekindling my friendship with Callie . . .

Under the guise of fixing a pearl button on my pink blouse, I pressed my hand to my chest. The fractures running through it still cut. But the Mom-shaped hole ached a little less, its depth no longer bottomless.

"Tears of joy, tears of sadness? Parties are a safe canvas to let emotions out." Saying it out loud was like breaking another curse.

Or like casting my first real fairy godmother spell. One that let my heart refill space left by Mom's absence.

"If you hire me, you'll get an apprentice that's the love child of a fairy godmother and a scientist. I'll help make events look good enough to post on a grid"—I pulled the pencil-wand from my tote, pressing the gold-ringed end to my chest—"and memorable enough to stick here."

My pulse pounded strong. It could've come from the way Mandy nodded, from her eyes flicking to Soraya before landing on me. But maybe it came from letting parts of myself out of the castle towers. From allowing pieces of me to crash my own party and become honored guests.

CHAPTER TWENTY-SEVEN

I flung the classroom door open. At the committee's smattering of gasps at my sudden appearance, Callie turned from the whiteboard. "Ah, Cas, I'm glad you could join us." She shot me a knowing look, as if she suspected what—er, who—had held me up.

I couldn't help but chuckle. "Apologies for the holdup, everyone." Sure, I was late, but after the interview a few days ago, it felt like I'd finally arrived. "Actually, you know what? I'm not sorry."

Mumbles and giggles rippled through the room. "I trusted you'd take care of business." I didn't know if I completely believed the words coming out of my mouth. But the excitement on everyone's faces made me think that I should.

"We've gotten through the first half of the final art fundraiser details," Callie said, extending the red dry-erase marker to me.

I shook my head. If my job was to make the belle of the ball shine as brightly as possible, shouldn't I make sure the committee members sparkled once in a while, too? "You stay up there. Finish the list," I said, slipping into one of the empty desks.

Callie's cheeks flushed. "Okay, then." In beautiful cursive, she wrote *Catering & Artwork*. "Cas's sister, Po, chef of those yummy hot dogs from the dog wash, offered to cater the event for us. I have her proposed menu of finger foods. I'll email it to you now, and we can vote on it."

A cacophony of buzzes and pings chimed through the room. I didn't need to pull out my phone to read the menu. Picadillo-stuffed tostones. Cuban sandwiches. Yucca fries.

Stomachs growled. Lips were licked. Not surprisingly, everyone voted yes for Po's catering. And when Wesley suggested a popcorn stand, I said, "That's a great idea."

Wes folded his arms against his chest. Defenses still higher than the walls of a castle, eh? Not that I blamed him. "I'm serious, Wes. Do you have any more proposals?"

"Raspados," he said, garnering more approvals. "What about having a shaved-ice stand?"

This topic pulled up memories of the Arctic Art Studio. I'd rather be kissing Javi among ice sculptures instead of planning to hand out scoops of shaved ice. I shook those thoughts from my mind. "Everyone in agreement?" I asked.

While the group voted on the art auction's final touches, I texted Po about the committee green-lighting her menu—and checked if Mandy had done the same for the internship.

I pressed the screen. Nothing.

I was about to refresh the inbox when Callie moved to the next item on the agenda. "Lina won't be able to finish the painting she'd pledged. No one has replied to my email regarding donating another art piece, either."

My hands tingled. Leftover adrenaline still coursing from Mandy's interview? Or were the sketches in the back of my planner goading me on?

"It is summer break," Wes said. "Plus, the art auction is so soon."

Callie's arms flapped at her sides. "Someone here must know at least one design-inclined classmate interested in providing last-minute artwork. C'mon, people. Anyone?"

It'd been so long since I'd painted. Painful memories of that time crept in, followed by the trepidation of putting something imperfect on display.

Except—

Wasn't this too perfect of an invite to decline? Before I lost my nerve, before this portal of possibility closed, I raised my hand. "I'll do it."

Callie stared at me. "You sure?"

No. I still preferred the straight lines of a planner. The easy-to-fill slots on a phone calendar. Hard-to-control paints that resulted in messiness still made me shudder. But I wasn't going to let that stop me from trying this once.

"I'm sure."

"Great. And FYI, just have fun with it," Callie said. "It doesn't have to be perfect."

Go with the flow. Just have fun. Two sides of the same nickel? Life lessons I needed to practice more, or a coin best left inside the ruins of an ancient kingdom?

I swallowed, exhilarated—and terrified—to find out.

Callie and I were almost through the main entrance door when she dragged me into the bathroom.

"If you needed a tampon, all you had to do was ask," I said, reaching into my utility bag.

"No period, but since it's the second time you've been late to something SBA related, I still consider this a red alert." She twirled blonde locks around her finger. "Please tell me the lifeguard hottie held you up again."

I tilted my head and gave an exaggerated chin scratch. "Maybe you're the one who is really behind Hot Goss."

Her chuckles grew wispy, like the Beast's enchanted rose losing petals. "But seriously Cas. Tell me. I need to live vicariously through you right now."

Before I protested with *Trust me, you really don't,* I had a flashback to middle school art class. Callie telling me bits and pieces of going to therapy, solo and family. More memories rushed in, uninvited. Walking into a classroom early (unlike now). Finding Callie huddled in the corner of it, talking to one of her parents on the phone. The sleeves of her jewel-toned cardigan brushing away tears.

I shouldn't blame myself too much for blocking out so much of that time period. For forgetting that once upon a time, Callie and I had a friendship outside of school.

Not wanting to lose out on that anymore, I reached for her shoulder. "Is everything okay at home?"

Her face clouded over. "My parents are finally divorcing." She gripped the sides of a sink. "It sucks, but I don't know. Part of me is super relieved." She covered her face with her hands. "Jeez, that's the most screwed-up thing to admit out loud. Forget I said it, okay?"

I patted her back, the way Mom used to do to me. "I know that feeling."

Time stretched. "When my mom first got sick, my sole focus was her getting better." I looked down at my backpack, picturing the day planner inside of it. My chest went tight. Wait . . .

Did my obsession with planning start before discovering Mandy's grid?

The sicker Mom got, the more medicines were added to her treatment plan. More chemicals and compounds than those inside an AP chemistry textbook. I didn't necessarily like keeping track of the meds.

But I loved drawing lines through long lists of unpronounceable names the second she took them. Loved filling in the lines inside the daily schedule.

They were *eff-yous* to every unknown hour—to each horrible what-if those sixty minutes could usher in. Tallies of small victories, or so I thought. Because in the end, a collection of wins did nothing to prevent us from losing the war.

"When it became clear 'better' wasn't going to happen, the thing I dreaded most was the moment it would finally end."

Now I held on to the sides of one of the sinks. "Po took me surfing once. Waves pummeled me from the top. Sand hit me on the bottom."

Phantom saltwater burned my nose. Real tears stung my eyes.

"Occasionally I'd stand up and take a huge gulp of air." I exhaled. "That's how it felt right after. Not this overwhelming sadness like I'd expected, but being able to breathe again."

Thankfully every sliding window lining the far side of the room was propped open, because the air soured. "It's horrible, isn't it? Me finally taking a breath the second after Mom's last?"

The abhorrent confession continued to fill the bathroom. Proceeded to trample on my chest like a stampede of wildebeests.

"I'm sorry, Cas." I was grateful for Callie's words, unable to muster any of my own. "What I'm going through isn't remotely the same, but, yeah. The back-and-forth, the emotional whiplash. It sucks. A huge part of me can't wait until it's over." She blinked up at me. "So, no. What you said isn't horrible. You felt that way because your mom wasn't suffering. You, your dad, and Po didn't have to watch her go through that anymore."

My chest heaved in and out. And then, that overwhelming crushing sensation, that stampede of emotions, receded.

The sharp edges pressing into my chest retracted.

I wished it could've been Dad who had helped file them down. Wished Po had drizzled my skin with messy goops of Neosporin. Wrapped up the wounds with lopsided Band-Aids.

In the end, perhaps all that mattered was that the pain had been defanged.

That way, its venom couldn't travel through my veins and poison me.

Relief settled over me like it did that horrible day.

Only this time, guilt didn't join the party.

By the way Callie's eyes started to brighten again, I suspected this convo had also helped take the sting off some of her conflicted emotions. "Jeez, here I thought I dragged you in for some guy gossip, not a share circle," she said through a small laugh.

The energy inside the bathroom flipped.

"I can still tell you about the guy gossip." A friendship-bricked road formed over the yearslong gap between us. I took a step onto it. "I'll start at the beginning if you swear not to tell anyone."

"Pinky promise." She extended her finger.

We shook. I talked. Mom always said that's how Cubans connected. A plate of food. Or dishing out chisme. Preferably eating and gossiping at the same time.

I told her about how Paulina assumed I was a Mandy Whitmore intern when we met. In hindsight, an assumption I should've tried harder to correct.

Except Paulina's party wasn't even what got my loafers through Mandy's door. The happy accident at the Arctic Art Studio did.

Callie's eyebrows rose higher with each revelation. At the

"phallus in Wonderland" part, she laughed so hard she had to wipe tears from her eyes. Happy ones.

"Well, I'm glad things are working out, and if"—she shook her head—"*when* you get this internship, Paulina will be none the wiser."

"Great minds think alike." There I went, sounding like Po again.

This time, I liked it.

We walked out of the bathroom. My heart a little lighter and loafers bouncier. When we strolled outside, past the bathroom windows, a toilet flushed.

My loafers halted midstride. I nearly fainted when Gianna—of all people, GIANNA—strutted out of the door and waved.

The blood in my veins froze colder than any sculpture housed inside the Arctic Art Studio.

What Paulina didn't know wouldn't hurt her. But if Gianna had been in the stall eavesdropping on our conversation, Hot Goss certainly could.

Sunlight faded into shadows. I tried calling Po again, but my calls went straight to voicemail. I think Gianna overheard me talking to Callie about the whole faux-intern thing, I texted.

No reply. I told myself the silence was probably because *"no news is good news."*

We watched her come out of the building with wired headphones on. The noise-canceling ones Dad used for gaming. So there's a chance that she hadn't heard anything.

Did someone swap out Matteo Beach's regular sand for quicksand? Because my loafers sunk deeper and deeper with every step.

With a *swoosh,* another text flew from my phone.

There's nothing on Hot Goss, either, so 

Who was I trying to convince, Po or myself? The way my fingers stiffened after every text, probably the latter.

I shoved the phone into my utility bag before I spiraled further. I continued to limp toward the pier, to the Movies at the Beach where Javi waited.

The same food vendors lined the north side of the setup. Sweet and savory scents mixed with the salty air. Apparently, stomachs could growl through tons of churning.

I scuttled around the maze of chairs and beach towels. Headed toward the front corner of the screen. The glint of the Mickey appliqué on Javi's sling bag eased the chill running up my spine.

His long limbs stretched over a different Guatemalan textile. Tonight's blanket was more sarape style. Bright blue and green stripes. Yellow arrows embroidered between the bands of colors. The colors a perfect backdrop for Javi's red uniform.

He must've sensed my eyes burning holes through his hair, because he propped onto his elbows. Tipped his chin over his shoulder. Our eyes met. His face brightened.

It lit me up in return, chasing more, but not all, of my worries into the shadows.

"Hey, Castle Towers." Javi sprung to his feet, wrapping his arms around my waist. That they stayed there—instead of trekking up to wring my neck—had to be a good sign.

While locked in his bear hug, I snuck one more peek at Hot Goss.

Nada.

Relief laced with anxiety lowered me to the blanket. If I couldn't shake off every trace of uncertainty, at the very least I could rid myself of the other chafing mess.

I slipped off my loafers, pouring sand out. The tiny grains, especially the quartz, sparkled. "How could something so small and pretty be this meddlesome?" I said, mostly referring to Gianna.

"I don't like sand," Javi said through a chuckle. "It's coarse and rough and irritating, and it gets everywhere."

Yup. Exactly like chismosas.

When I didn't join in his laughter, Javi added, "It's an Anakin Skywalker quote from *Episode II*, by the way."

I managed a weak smile. "He wasn't wrong."

"Rough day?" He scooted in. The scent of his lavender shampoo paired so well with the ocean air.

"It's getting better," I said, sticking to some of the truth.

"We've got time before the movie starts." He motioned to the blank screen and chattering crowd. "You want to talk about it?"

"Okay, but only the good parts." I put my loafers back on. "As SBA event chair, I usually plan the summer art auction. But . . ." I tipped my chin up to the sky. Should I paint something like this for the auction?

Only a smattering of stars twinkled among the shadows. No Big Dipper or Little Cuchara to pierce through the darkness.

The blank pages in the back of my planner seemed small now compared to the vastness of the sky. All at once, my fingers itched for a bigger canvas.

"This year I also signed up to donate an art piece."

"Wow, Cas." Who needed a galaxy of stars when Javi's smile lit up the entire shoreline? Its brilliance burned away more unease. "First the banners, now this. It's awesome you're putting your art out there again. It takes grit to do that."

Huh. I supposed it did. It still felt a little dizzying to be under a spotlight. But I was starting to get used to it. And I couldn't deny it felt pretty good.

"How should we kick off celebrating?"

His words rippled through me, sinking deeper and deeper. I'd been so focused on other people's celebrations that I'd probably been missing out on lots of my own. "Let's start with snacks." Celebrations and food paired together like Timon and Pumbaa. "I'll grab something from one of the vendors."

"Nope. I got us covered." He reached for a small cooler at the edge of the blanket. Slid it between us and rolled the top open. "Ta-da."

Two Double-Double In-N-Out burgers bookended two orders of animal-style fries. The gooey sauce, melted cheese, and charred onions on top glimmered.

We clinked fries. Some people might have preferred them extra crispy. But "soggy" only meant they'd soaked up more of the toppings.

"And for the main course—" From a cardboard cupholder beside him, Javi presented two trenta-size Starbucks cups of water. The order on the side sticker read *Extra Ice*.

I cracked up. He joined in. Our laughter floated around us, mixing with the sounds of the crowd and the roar of the sea.

I leaned forward. "No, not the main course," I said, claiming his lips with mine.

Exploring his mouth felt magical. Wait. Was this kiss really magic? Because like Pinocchio, every inch of me came to life.

If celebrating felt like this . . . I kissed him again, kicking our party into high gear.

CHAPTER TWENTY-EIGHT

"If I ever consider going on a cruise, remind me about *The Poseidon Adventure*," I said as the movie's credits rolled.

"It's got a happy ending, though," Javi said. "I thought you liked those."

"I do and it does—for six people. And only after escaping one catastrophe after the next." I raked a hand through my hair.

Ugh. Nearly every scene in the movie had made me do this. Too much hair grabbing—never mind the sweat-inducing chaos of the day—resulted in extra frizz.

Fine—if this mane refused to stay behind my ears, into a top-knot it'd go. I grabbed a fistful of hair, twisted it up into a bun. Tried to contain it with a hair tie.

Watching me wrestle with it, Javi said, "That's the whole point of a disaster flick, Castle Towers."

The hair tie catapulted from my fingers. Hair tumbled across my shoulder blades. I stuck my hand into my utility bag, fishing for a spare but finding none. "That's a thing?"

Javi nodded.

When Paulina became a director, she should direct a movie called *Frizzy and Tieless*. A disaster flick for the ages.

"There's an entire genre of movies that revolves around impending and ongoing disasters," he said.

Didn't life already ensure a quota of bad things? Why would people want to watch more calamity unfold? "How do you know so much about this stuff, anyway? Are you going to film school like Paulina?"

Javi shrugged. "Don't get me wrong—I love me some movies and TV. It would also be fun going to college with Pau, but I don't know." He took a sip of the water. "Film? Accounting like my dad?" He tracked one of the blanket's blue stripes until it merged with a green one. "Nursing like my mom? I have no idea."

My mouth gaped open like Flounder. For a moment, I was as voiceless as his bestie, Ariel.

"What?" he asked through a chuckle. "Is not having the details hammered out yet a crime or something?"

I'd had my hospitality major and PR minor picked out since After Mom. "In the eyes of a future planner, it's a capital offense."

"Before you report me to the authorities, need I remind you that we've got lots of time before applying?"

"Um, sir, we have a little over a year!"

"My point exactly. 'Over a year' is a long time. I'll figure it out."

I dropped my gaze to my lap. Time slowed to a crawl After Mom. The Torres family's dark tunnel seemed to stretch endlessly. Ergo my attempts at fast-tracking us out of it. I pushed another fistful of hair behind my ear.

Javi pulled at his hoodie's drawstring. "By the looks of it, I suspect this rebel-without-a-major-yet is a problema for you."

His agenda was light-years ahead of Po's "Hakuna Matata" life philosophy. But not having his future 100 percent mapped out wasn't ideal, either. "It's, um—"

Truth was, if my true identity got out, I'd have a much bigger problem at hand than this frizz so . . . Shouldn't I make some allowances? "It's only a bit of an issue."

Javi clutched his chest in faux hurt. "Well, I'm hoping it's one that can be solved."

Same here, same here.

He removed the hoodie string, handing it over. "For what it's worth, I like it curly. You look uncomfortable wearing it like that, so here ya go. It's yours if you need it."

For so long, I'd been the one doing the rescuing that being on the receiving end of help disarmed me.

The helping hand, paired with the conversation we were having, made me want to break the what-they-don't-know-won't-hurt-them pact I'd made with Po.

Javi was a compassionate person. Wouldn't he have sympathy for my devilish ways—especially if I told him the entire story. I tied my hair up with the string. "Javi, I need to tell you something."

He gave me his full attention. "What is it?"

Breathe. If things started to go south, simply scuttle back to the shallow end, no harm done. "It's a cautionary tale. A PSA on the dangers of not hammering out the details." And hopefully, a solution to my Pinocchio problem.

I told him how after the funeral, Po and Dad became intent on throwing a last-minute quince. His mantra became something like *This party is what our family needs right now.* While she played the ultimate trump card: *It's what Mom would've wanted.*

In their rush, they'd ordered a banner from someone who didn't understand the ramifications of a missing tilde.

My chin quivered throughout the next part of the story. I expected to feel the stab of embarrassment that accompanied it, but Javi's face remained free of judgment, free of horror.

He just kept listening.

"I've never admitted this to anyone before—" First with Callie, now this. Apparently, Mandy's stylus-wand had spellbound me with some type of Mom confession charm. "But as horrible as the party turned out, it also felt like a fitting punishment for celebrating a milestone without her."

"General survivor's guilt," he said. *Must google the term later.* "I felt it whenever I'd go swimming without my dad. When I first started to use these, too." He bunched a portion of the blanket between his hands. He let go and tugged his sling bag closer. Skated a thumb across Mickey's smile. "Have you felt it after experiencing other important moments?"

"No." I squirmed on the blanket. "I haven't celebrated anything big since Po's party."

Night air goose-bumped my limbs. After Po's quince, I *had* celebrated momentous occasions—for other people.

Never for myself.

Was being a planner a way for me to experience important moments sans the guilt of doing so without Mom by my side?

I covered my legs with the blanket and kept going. Told him about how the video of the banner made the rounds on Hot Goss. "Details matter. Plans matter."

He nodded, like my story made sense. Like he was taking it all to heart. "Is the moral of the story that I need to pick a major by the end of summer in order for us to keep dating?"

Us. To. Keep. Dating.

Butterflies in the stomach? More like butterflies in the entire body.

Would they fly away the deeper I waded into the truth?

Then again, it didn't feel right to keep building our relationship with fantasy either.

The movie's last title card scrolled across the screen. The high casualty count flashed behind my eyelids. Even if Javi and I survived the fallout, it didn't guarantee that Paulina and Po would.

"Fake it till you make it" it is.

"A major is preferred but not necessary," I said, unable to shake my conscience.

"Should we get going?" Javi asked, gesturing to my night-chilled skin. "It's getting pretty cold."

"I should get home before I turn into a pumpkin."

"Or freeze like Olaf." He rubbed my arms, attempting to warm them. They didn't. "While we pack up, tell me what you liked most about the movie."

I rose, glancing at the empty screen. "Watching characters take charge and kick ass in the face of impending doom was weirdly cathartic." We gathered the empty In-N-Out trays and wrappers. "I mean, they had to work together to survive, but . . ."

"Isn't that the only way to ever make it out of a calamity?" Javi moved to a nearby trash can, dunking the empty cups in. "Teamwork?"

Over the last couple of years, I'd navigated life without anything except Mandy's grid as my guiding light. But—

Every recent would-be disaster had only been averted by letting other people help. "You might be onto something," I said.

"Next week's screening is also a disaster flick." Did Javi's penchant for these movies remind him that he could survive—even thrive in—tragedy as long as his MVPs were by his side? "You in?"

"Yes," I said, RSVPing without hesitation.

"Awesome. Thanks for giving me a reason to use these blankets more regularly." We walked back to the blanket, lowering down. He tugged the edges of it over my shoulders. The cold (but not the guilt) vanished.

Returning the favor, I zipped up his hoodie. Only, my fingers stalled in the middle of his sternum.

Was the thumping coming from the tips of my fingers or deep within Javi's chest?

Was his Dad-size hole as big now as it was a few years ago? Did summer beach days and saving lives help patch it the way parties and Mandy's grid did mine?

"If you're wondering if it still works, the answer is yes. Corazón is still ticking. Squeakier than before, but trucking on, nonetheless." He undid the zipper a bit, pressing my fingers against his rib cage. "See?"

I extended my fingers. His pulse beat steady across the fleshy part of my palm.

I swallowed hard. *His heart is in my hand.*

As if responding to my thoughts, Javi said, "With everything it's been through, my only request is that you handle it with care."

A tight nod. Until my lies became a reality, I'd have to simply stomach the deceit. Keep quiet about things, despite how much his honesty demanded my truth. "I promise." I found his lips. Sealed my pledge with a kiss.

Po screaming my name cut the kissing short.

She shouldered through the swarm of people gathering their belongings. She stopped at the edge of the blanket. Bent over her knees, hands gripping her thighs as she tried to catch her breath.

"Your phones—" As she sucked in air, my own breath quickened. "Are off."

"Yeah, they make us turn off our phones at the beginning of the movie," Javi said, brows meeting together in concern. "Is everything okay?"

Ignoring Javi, she panted, "Castillo, check your phone."

Po uttering my full name was a kick to the gut so brutal I couldn't speak. With trembling fingers, I fished the phone out of my utility bag. Powered it back up.

A flurry of notifications exploded across my screen. My vision blurred until—

The subject line on top snapped everything back into focus: Mandy Whitmore Internship Program.

I tapped the email.

> Dear Miss Torres,
>
> It is with great pleasure that I welcome you to our fairy godmother apprenticeship program. We are very excited to have you on board with us!

The blanket fell off me as I jumped up and down.

I got it! I got the internship!

No more lying to Paulina and Javi. None of these shenanigans getting back to Mandy. Happy Ending master class obtained.

Ha! No wonder Po was as breathless as I felt.

Hold on. Blood rushed to my temples. My ears rang like alarms.

How could Po be this gaspingly excited for me about the internship, if I hadn't told her I'd gotten it yet?

"The Torres sisters better spill the beans on whatever's so epic," Javi said, eyes twinkling.

Po pushed herself off her knees, straightened her shoulders to face me. Her lipstick shined bright in the darkness.

Red.

My stomach dropped to the ground, disappearing under a million grains of sand.

Paulina.

She knew.

CHAPTER TWENTY-NINE

I tapped IG's notifications. Most of them were DMs sending me Hot Goss's latest "scoop."

> Has local Disney YouTuber been spending so much time inside the House of Mouse that she didn't recognize a rat when she spotted one? According to sources, Matteo Beach High's resident party planner isn't who she says she is. Might want to follow up on those references, Princess P, before Ratatouille steals your big (c)hunk of cheese!

Before my fingers gave out, I DMed Gianna, His name is Remy!!!

As I went back to her profile, the phone slipped from my hands.

It landed on top of my foot with a hard *thud*.

I yelped in pain. The loafers were no glass slippers, and yet my toes—my entire leg—felt on the brink of shattering. Served me right.

Once again, Javi came to the rescue. He did the princely thing of not only picking up the phone, but also rubbing the top of my loafer as if to ease the hurt.

He brushed the sand away from the screen. Before he handed

my phone over, the bright screen—no, the flashing post—grabbed his attention.

With the words *chambelán* and *cheater*, with the names *Paulina* and *Javier* strobing before his eyes, how could he not read the caption? Let alone refrain from reading the comments.

His lips flattened into a hard line, jaw clenching tighter with every finger scroll.

"Javi, I—" Words failed.

He lifted his gaze from the phone. His brown eyes, once so warm and vulnerable, became impenetrable, like drought-hardened soil. "What's this talking about? What references?"

Any attempt at an explanation crumbled at his expression recalibrating. Like he'd misjudged me, realizing now that I was less upright than castle towers and more shadowy than its dungeons.

"You've been lying to Paulina?" His words thrummed taut in the humid air. The unspoken ones hit harder: *You've been lying to me, too?*

"Javi, I know this looks bad, but I . . ." Was there anything I could offer to get me out of this mess unscathed? I shot Po a desperate look.

She chewed her fingernail, as frozen to the sand as I was. Okay, then—no spiking this over the net forming between me and Javi.

He'd been so open about himself. Shared his past. Invited me onto his blanket. Into his heart. *Fix this.*

I turned back to him. Pressed a sweaty palm to my forehead and said, "I swear I didn't—"

Only I did lie to Paulina. I did lie to him.

My stomach contracted so hard, I almost threw up.

He gave back the phone. Our fingers touched. I couldn't tell whose were colder.

"I guess I have my answer," he said.

Why did disappointment cut a million times deeper than anger?

"This post. It's not true anymore—"As much as I wanted to paint over the lie with Mandy's acceptance, the look on his face screamed it was too late.

As the words for why I'd done the wrong things for the right reasons withered, my phone started ringing.

The screen flashed with Paulina Reyes.

"When it rains, it pours." Even though Po got that one right, her voice shook. "Please answer it. She's refusing to talk to me."

I glanced at Javi, but he averted his eyes. I took mine to the sky; I searched for the brightest star to wish upon. Begged for a perfectly crafted apology. For Javi and Paulina to forgive me and shrug off this misstep à la Po.

I tapped Accept. "Hey, Paulina, I was just about to call you," I said, my voice cracking.

"Uh-huh," she scoffed. "Since you're probably with Baymoon and your sister." She sniffled. *Allergies—please let that be allergies.* "Might as well put me on speakerphone."

I did as directed.

"Care to explain this post everyone at your school's tagging me in?"

My grip tightened on the phone, as if by squeezing its edges, I could hold on to my relationship with Javi. And my burgeoning friendship with Paulina. "When we met, I wasn't interning at Mandy's yet—but I am now, you can even call to check," I expelled in a single breath.

"No need, and don't worry—I won't bust your cover."

I swallowed. For now, the internship remained on steady ground. Plus, Paulina not exposing my lying ways had to mean something. An invite to fix our working, and personal, relationship?

"I should've been truthful from the beginning." I directed it to both Paulina and Javi. Eyes darting to him, I said, "I promise no more misunderstandings moving forward, okay?"

When Paulina didn't correct me, Po leaned over the phone. "All's well that ends well, right, Pau?"

Seconds stretched. Javi dipped his head to the ground, frowning at the sand. My shoulders sagged. Po shifted from side to side.

"No, Po, nothing's well. I trusted both of you. And for what? For you to ride my clout tails?" Barbs filled her voice, not unlike the thorns on the Baccara roses Javi and I'd chosen for her party.

Javi half turned away from me, ready to make his exit.

Speak up now or forever hold your peace.

"That's not how it went down," I said. Except, who the hell was I kidding? A part of it unfolded exactly as she'd described. "Okay, maybe it was a little bit like that, but only in the beginning."

Paulina laughed. The venom inside it pricked more than Maleficent's poisoned spindle. "Even if I did believe you, you really think that makes any of this any less screwed up?"

Her question punched me in the gut because it rang true. Even with all the fairy dust Mandy could sprinkle, wrongs would never transform into rights.

My knees buckled; I dropped onto the blanket. Javi shot me a look like my presence on it was no longer welcomed. Noted.

I shifted onto the cold sand, exiled from our kingdom.

He began rolling it up. It felt like he was rolling up his feelings for me alongside it.

My knees sunk deeper into the sand. I'd sullied this party.

I'd spoiled my chance at creating something magical. Not just for Paulina, but for myself.

"You're right. I'm sorry." Even if it meant having to wait longer for the internship, I should've been up-front. Instead of being the fairy godmother of this story, I'd become its villain. "I should've been more proactive in correcting you."

"Both of you, you mean," Paulina hissed.

"Yes, both of us," Po said, wrapping her duster around herself tightly. "Since we're coming clean with everything, I need to fess up about pushing Cas into this scheme."

I turned my head to Po. She helmed the volleyball team. But was she also ready to step back into the role of big sister and take one for the Torres team?

For a second, I was tempted to let her, except—

I was done navigating emotions and situations—good, bad, and ugly ones—solo.

We'd done enough of that After Mom. If we were going down with the ship again, the disaster movie I'd just watched taught me that survival depended on banding together.

"If Po fueled my fire on this, it was only because I gave her the matches to start it. I'm at fault here, too." The lines on Po's forehead smoothed a little.

"Why didn't you tell us the truth from the beginning?" Javi asked, his chin quivering. Unable to find the perfect words, I stayed quiet.

He pivoted, leaving for good this time.

"Wait." Tears wet the corners of my eyes.

I'd hurt two people who'd trusted me.

One with his broken heart, only for me to add another fissure. The other with her party to shed her childhood, when it was me who desperately needed to grow up.

"I told you the beginning of my planner origin story. And

I wanted to tell you what happened next. How Mandy's grid became the only thing that could make me forget Mom was gone." My chest ached; I pushed past it. "All those happy endings made me believe one was still possible for me." My eyes flicked to Po. "For us." I exhaled long and slow. "So when I met Paulina and she was so impressed I was an intern there—"

Paulina cut in. "I was impressed by you, not your internship. I wanted to work with both of you because of your creative vision and Po's energy."

"Oh." I hated that it was the only thing I could manage to say. Hated how she spoke in my least favorite tense: past.

"Look, before I go, I gotta know . . ." Her pause lasted a lifetime. "Was any of this real?"

I couldn't tell if the question was posed to me. To Po. Or both of us.

Javi looked at me, waiting for an answer. He zipped his hoodie up. Clutched the rolled-up blanket close to his chest. Probably protecting himself against my words, my actions, from finding any cracks in his rusted armor.

"All of it was," Po and I said at the same time. Po's eyes locked on the screen, while mine fixed on Javi.

"Look, I'm sorry about what happened to both of you, and I'm sorry about this." Paulina's voice broke. She steeled it again, like a proper Sith Lord. "But in case it wasn't obvious, you're uninvited to dinner. You're both fired from the quince. Lo siento, chicas." She disguised a long sniffle as a cough. "I'm really sorry."

The line went dead. Javi's cue to resume stepping away. "Javi, I'm so sor—"

He put up a hand. "I've got to go check on Pau," he said.

"Thanks," I said. "That's a good plan."

"I'm not doing it for you." He turned away. "I'm doing it for my friend."

His words thrust into my chest. People always talked about getting stabbed in the back. Getting stabbed in the heart cut a million times deeper.

Between the darkness and the tears blurring my vision, Javi quickly disappeared into the thinning crowd. The vendors started to pack up their carts. Two guys began dismantling the screen.

Po slumped down next to me. After what felt like both an eternity and a millisecond, only she and I remained on this stretch of beach. We sat in silence, looking out into the dark horizon until we both shivered. She draped the bottom half of her duster over me.

I curled myself into a small ball, hoping the fabric could cloak me from this pain.

There was only one other time when I'd done this. Only one other time when she'd gone this long without talking.

I cried into her collarbones. Her tears seeped into my curls.

Together, we added another event on our shared calendar of Hurt.

CHAPTER THIRTY

Po rose up and extended her hand, helping me onto my feet. We limped through the sand, across the bike path.

The world of downtown Matteo Beach carried on: families going in and out of restaurants, nighttime joggers zipping by, people taking their dogs on evening strolls down the pier. Except the colors looked muted, the silence between Po and I growing thicker by the second.

Before it got so thick not even a lightsaber could slash through it, I said, "Don't worry. I'm going to fix this. I swear."

"What's done is done, Little Cuchara," she said through her teeth.

I shook my head. "If you care about Paulina as much as I do about Javi, you'd want to fix this as much as I do."

She halted, sand crunching under her combat boots. "Tell me you didn't just go there." She massaged her wrists like she was gearing up for a volleyball match. "Tell me you didn't diss my feelings for Pau like that."

"Look, that came out wrong." Sweat pinpricked the back of my neck. "All I'm asking is for you not to give in to this tendency of yours to shake things off so easily." At last, I'd said it.

She leaned against a parking meter as if considering it. Finally.

Shaking her head, she said, "Wow." Her cheeks flushed a flaming red to match her lipstick. "You are making things soo much worse."

"I'm trying to make things better." She should know by now this was what I excelled at, until recently. Why did she want to take this chance away from me? From us? Especially after everything we'd lost already? "Just let me try, okay?"

"Some things you can't make better, Cas!"

Both of our chests heaved. The heartbroken sobbing from the beach quickly morphed into something I couldn't quite place.

"Sometimes . . . lots of times . . . if it's broke, don't fix it."

Her words echoed against the pavement. Against my hollow places.

No. I tore a hand through my hair. Didn't give a damn how many fingers got tangled in the frizz. "You're wrong."

She shrugged.

Heat shot up my throat, seconds away from spouting fire out of my head like Hades. My eagerness to fix things was probably forged as a result of her constantly breezing past difficulties and Dad constantly hyperspeeding away from them.

What chance did our family have of staying anchored in our past or sailing into the future without someone steering our ship through life's storms?

I had accepted the role without complaint. Until now.

Until she'd doled out another Poverb as if she were a modern-day Rafiki.

"If you're so intent on speaking in aphorisms, the least you can do is get them right. It's 'If it ain't broke, don't fix it.'" I spit the words out slowly.

Maybe they'd stick in her long-term memory that way.

"I know perfectly well what the 'right' way to say it is, okay?" She pushed off the parking meter, charging up the street toward the parking lot edged with bike racks. "I also know, unlike you, that some things can't be fixed."

Those words slashed deeper now than when Javi said them inside the Arctic Art Studio. But this situation was *not* a broken ice sculpture. Or Mom's death. "This can be salvaged."

She cracked her knuckles, continuing to bulldoze through the crowd.

I took a breath and chased after her. "You know that's the whole point of me being event chair. I pretty much have a bachelor's in planning. And a minor in finding a rain plan when things go south."

After Mandy's internship, I could add a master's degree in "Happily ever afters are our business."

My feet stopped moving.

Wait.

Now that Paulina had fired me, would Mandy revoke my internship? I shook my head.

Tackle one disaster at a time.

Peeling my loafers from the ground, I went after Po.

"No, that isn't the point of you being event chair, actually. Much less the point of your obsession with that internship." The acid in her voice nearly melted the concrete sidewalk beneath our feet.

Right before she entered the lot, I grabbed her by the duster's sleeve and spun her around. "What the hell's that supposed to mean?"

She tugged the duster free, flapping her arms to her side. "You really think you can handle the truth, Little Cuchara?" Her voice rose an octave. "I sure hope so because I'm soo sick and soo tired of handling you with kiddie gloves."

"You—handling me?!" My laughter bubbled over with disdain. "That's rich." Where was the Evil Queen's magic mirror? Po needed it ASAP to take a hard look and see who was handling whom with care. "If I can manage your life on top of mine, bring on whatever crap you'll spin to sound like wisdom, Yoda."

She scoffed, started clapping. Each slap stung like a smack to the face. "And there it is." She stepped forward, the pointy nose she inherited from Dad inches away from the round one Mom had given me. "Ever since my 'disastrous' quince, you think everything—scratch that: *everyone*—is a 'problem' for you to fix."

Although the ocean breeze snapped our hair, not enough air filled my lungs. Not with how fast my breath quickened.

"First off, your party was a disaster! The missing tilde? Happy fifteen buttholes? Hello?!" Perhaps being officially taken under Mandy's fairy wings was already working wonders on morphing my pencil into a magic wand. Because as I pressed the utility bag into my side, the pencil's tip poked into my stomach, transforming my contempt into an anger that made the Beast's fury seem like annoyance.

I unleashed more. "If it weren't for me always being on your back, no college prep on time." I stuck out a finger, then another. "No extracurriculars to put on your resume to get into said colleges. Wake up, Po. You are a problem!"

"Thank god I am, huh?" Her breath sped into rasps. "If not, how would you even exist?"

I opened my mouth to protest. What the hell? Did a bee fly into my esophagus and sting it or something? Because my throat swelled, making it impossible to get anything out.

"You can't escape your own life by fixating on someone else's," Po continued.

My skin crawled, her accusation sticking to every inch of me. "I don't need to take this crap from you. Not when I've only ever tried to help you avoid a gap year—a gap life." I spun on the ball of my loafers, forcing myself to bolt.

Except she dragged me back by the utility bag. "I know you think I breeze past stuff. I don't." Her voice softened. "I simply know how to adjust my sails." A few tears rolled down her face; she did nothing to brush them away. "You, on the other hand, think you can escape what happened with Mandy's grid."

Everything she said fell straight into that chasm inside my chest, her words resharpening every jagged edge, making me flinch with every heart sputter. And just when I thought this battle royale couldn't get any worse, Po unzipped the top of my utility bag. Yanked out the Pikachu walkie-talkie. Pressed the button on the side.

"Earth to Cas: you can't control the uncontrollable. Collecting all these happily ever afters won't erase what happened." Her eyes filled with more tears. I hated that mine did, too. "Nothing will."

Why couldn't she stop talking? Every new word felt like vines shackling me in place. Before they kept me there forever, I wrenched the walkie-talkie out of her hands. "That isn't why . . ."

Was she right? About all of it?

My attempts to get our past plans back on track, my efforts to make our HEA come true—were they masquerades for control? How could that even be a bad thing? Give into chaos when I could take charge of it? Never. And why did she care if I stocked up on happily ever afters?

She should be applauding—not criticizing—my figuring out how to pack the emptiness inside my heart. Sure, I'd been using some of my own events to stuff it lately . . . Was that why the void had felt fullest since After Mom? I chewed the inside of my cheek. Dang it.

Maybe Po's points were a little valid.

Telling her would only set her higher on that self-righteous horse. Not that she looked particularly smug at the moment, wiping her runny nose with her duster's sleeve.

The same duster she'd wrapped around me at the beach. Flapped around Dad at home. Cocooned around Paulina whenever she thought no one was looking.

"And as far as the quince, it wasn't a missing tilde that ruined it," she said. Under the bright lights of the lot's lampposts, the tears rolling down the sides of her face glittered. "It was a missing mom."

A missing mom.

Hearing the words out loud was like both the curse and the spell trying to lift it.

The grief I tried my hardest to keep at bay rushed in. The pencil-wand didn't have enough power to undo this feeling. And the other way curses were typically broken? Slim chance kissing Javi was ever going to happen again.

A flurry of blinking didn't hold back my tears. More fell when she whispered, "And a missing sister. Instead of being present with me, you went into fix-it mode. You missed the good parts of the party because of it."

She freed her bike from the rack, hopping on. "You're still missing good parts now." Palm trees threw shadows onto the concrete, black slashes dividing us. "Tell Dad I'm staying at Brandi's tonight."

She rode away.

Her words floated in the air long after the bike disappeared over the hill.

If this were a fairy-tale realm, I would've pegged Po for the court jester, me the fairy godmother. Had she really been the philosopher this entire time? And me who'd acted the fool?

I quietly closed my front door. Shut my eyes at the foot of the hallway. After the havoc I'd wreaked, I couldn't make eye contact with the framed photos of Mom. For once, I was glad Dad *pew-pew-pewed* in a galaxy far, far away because—

"Hey, kiddo, another party tonight?" he asked from inside the living room. "Was it the *Star Wars* quince you're planning for your friend?"

"No, Dad. I've already told you: Paulina isn't my friend." Not anymore.

Her relationship with Po and mine with Javi were over. I tugged the utility bag away from me to keep the tip of the pencil-wand from stabbing me in the side. Only the sharp truth kept piercing.

After Hot Goss's "story," who would hire me? "And as far as the party goes, that's dunzo," I said.

When I informed Mandy about getting fired, would clipping my fairy godmother wings come next?

Dad sucked air through his teeth, not because of the enormity of my troubles. But probably because his character got hit by a laser blaster. "That's too bad, kiddo."

Everything I'd worked so hard to get since After Mom—gone in a span of hours. And *too bad, kiddo* was the best he could do?

That's it. I stomped into the living room, purposely blocking out his precious game.

"It's not 'too bad,' Dad." My vision blurred with tears. They didn't spring from sadness or laughter. "It freaking blows, okay?"

His posture stiffened, like whenever I mentioned my period. Or anything Mom related. Then, his face did that thing that reminded me of blinds shuttering.

For a second, a part of me wanted to give him the benefit of the doubt again. Hiding his feelings was probably his way of shielding us from any more negative emotions, especially pain. But . . .

I was too exhausted to bury more feelings inside the depths of my heart's core. Or hide them behind its jagged corners.

"I lost this awesome client. A guy I really liked. Probably the internship I've been dreaming about since freshman year." With every loss, I took a step forward. "I got into a huge fight with Po. I haven't watercolored in forever." Everything went quiet except for my pulse hammering against my rib cage. "Not since Mom."

His mouthed opened as if he wanted to say something, but he closed it. Took his attention back to the game, fingers twitching across the buttons of the controller.

Perhaps my time with Paulina had set me on the Sith Lord path, because my fury eclipsed everything else. "Dad! I'm trying to talk to you about this!" I said, reaching for his controller.

My fingers latched on to its plastic side. He refused to let go. Game on, then. "I've been trying to talk to you about a lot of things." Holding back on the truth got me into this mess. Maybe spitting it out could get me out of it. "I've been trying to talk about Mom."

That only made him tighten his grip over the controller. I clutched the plastic even harder.

We kept playing tug-of-war. Pushed and pulled. The wheels of the gaming chair squeaked in our tango for the controller.

No. For control of this situation.

"At every chance, you hyperdrive off to a galaxy far, far

away—" My voice cracked, like glass slippers fracturing. "But you disappearing also means you've missed out on so much of what's been going on lately."

The words stuck to the roof of my mouth.

Oh no—hadn't Po just said the same thing?

What if Dad jumping to light speed was the twin of me becoming a fairy godmother's apprentice? Both well-intentioned but ill-equipped ways to bypass heartbreak?

So much for that working out. I'd only hurt Paulina, Javi, Po—

And managed to crush my already-shattered heart.

Po *was* right. I couldn't avoid my feelings. I couldn't control the uncontrollable. Hell, I could barely keep ahold of this freaking controller.

So I let go. Of everything.

The controller either slipped from Dad's grasp, or he let go of it, too.

A blur of black flew over his head. Shot straight toward the accent mirror hanging on the wall behind him. Po's quick reflexes would've caught it. But she wasn't here.

A series of sickening *cracks*, then pieces of the mirror tumbled from the metal frame. A downpour of glass smashed against the floor.

Dad peeked over the gaming chair.

Busted pieces of plastic. Jagged slabs of mirror. The ceiling lights bounced off the glass, glittering back the destruction we'd caused.

I spied parts of my face in the glass's reflections. The dark skin passed down from Mom. Her curls. The high cheekbones and wide mouth I'd gotten from Dad. Dark eyes pooling with emotions.

Feelings over what'd gone down tonight . . . feelings that I'd been holding back since Mom died.

Regret. Anger. Guilt. Shock. Sadness. Everything in between.

Mirror, mirror, on the floor, which one do I feel more?

With so much strewn around me, it was impossible to tell. Not that it mattered. What mattered was that these broken pieces cast back my emotions. Made them inescapable. "I'm so not sorry we broke this," I whispered.

He blinked, mouth hinging open. I couldn't tell whether he was gearing up to bemoan the destruction or lay into me for my lack of remorse.

Instead, he laughed.

Had we inadvertently fallen through this broken glass? Only in Wonderland could his laughter build to chortles that doubled him over the gaming chair.

The deep belly laughs cut through some of the tension. Plus, it was so infectious. My confusion gave way to giggles, quickly swelling to cackles.

More tension fell away.

"You know what? I'm not sorry, either," he said. And that's when the truly unexpected happened.

He knocked over the kombucha bottle. It tumbled off the tray table. Landed with a *thwack* and a *crunch* before splitting in half.

"Dad! What's gotten into you?"

Our eyes met. Without the usual faraway look clouding his expression, that big face of his showcased everything.

It wasn't what'd gotten into him, but what he needed to get out. Dad picked up a piece of the bottle. "I hate the way this crap tastes." He hurled it at what remained of the mirror.

The bottle half hit the biggest chunk of glass. So that's where Po got her athleticism.

More of the mirror crashed to the floor. He jutted his stubbly chin at the other half of the bottle, inviting me to do the same.

Lifting the other half, I threw it. "I hate the way this smells!"

It bashed a corner of the frame. Dislodged some glass still stuck inside.

Dad grabbed the empty coffee mug from the tray table. Pitched it at the opposite corner. More of the mirror tumbled free.

I chucked the marble coaster next.

We laughed, screaming all the things we hated—Hot Goss, traffic, environmental destruction—until a single shard remained. But what to fire at it?

Dad hurried to the entertainment console underneath the TV. Slid open its drawer. Walked back and handed me an extra controller.

Such a small piece of plastic and metal, yet it felt like a million pounds inside my palm.

I could hardly bear the weight of it, much less the immensity of fixing my family. The burden had never been mine in the first place.

My attempts at controlling situations and people hadn't helped anyone. And they certainly hadn't healed me. The time had come for me to let it go.

I took a deep breath, ripping off the final Band-Aid.

"I hate that Mom's gone." My voice came out as a whimper. I cleared my throat, projecting louder. "I hate that she's dead."

I flung the controller as hard as I could.

Bullseye.

The last mirror piece shattered against the floor, a cue for our last round of laughs to morph into weeping.

The crying cut through the light-years Dad had traveled in a different galaxy. Washed away every filled line cramming my day planner. Wiped out the collection of Mandy-curated happily ever afters I'd used to buffer our tragic ending.

I couldn't stop my reservoir of sobs.

Even if I could, I wouldn't. Not anymore.

The grief Dad had been avoiding similarly found its way out of his eyes. His body buckled to the floor. My own limbs grew heavy, like every inch had filled with wet sand. I dropped to my knees, joining him on the floor.

"She was the love of my life." The crying muffled his voice. "God, how I miss her." There was now a bright chime to his tone, ringing more magical than the flick of a fairy godmother's wand.

I couldn't tell how long we stayed there, holding each other. Long enough for my tear ducts to run dry. Long enough for my heart to explode like the last firework at a pyrotechnic show. The blast ripped me apart. Burned me to the core. But I trusted that one day, the smoke would clear.

Until then, I'd find a better way to help—to heal—myself.

I turned my head to the window. Outside, the clouds had shifted. Stars dusted the velvety sky, two constellations brighter than the rest.

The Big Dipper. And the Little Cuchara.

I tightened my grip on Dad, and for the first time, that hole in my chest didn't ache for Mom.

It ached for Dad, for Po . . .

And finally, for me.

CHAPTER THIRTY-ONE

The alarm didn't wake me. The scents of coffee and plantains that wafted over the covers did. Another first.

Dad popped through the doorway, stirring a sizzling pan. "Good, you're awake." He smiled. It actually reached his eyes. "I gotta head to the office but I've left you breakfast in the kitchen." He half turned toward the hallway before pivoting back. "Oh, and it's still a mess inside the living room. Be careful. I'll clean it up later, okay?"

"I'll help you," I said, yawning and stretching my arms over the headboard. My limbs felt looser, not like streamers pulled so taut they'd snap at any second.

On the nightstand, my phone buzzed with a new notification. The Talk rescheduled.

Ugh. Those relaxed muscles tightened again.

"What is it?" Dad asked.

I waved my phone at him. "Our little chat's supposed to start in five minutes."

He shrugged, the corners of his mouth tugging upward. "Nope. We had it last night, remember?"

Yeah.

I guess we had.

❧

I pressed my phone's screen.

No texts from Javi, Paulina, or Po. The only thing that stopped my stomach from sinking further was the one from Callie. At least I still had one person other than Dad in my court.

I saw Hot Goss. Everything okay?

Perfect, my fingers typed reflexively. With a sharp breath, I erased the lie. Just because it was a white one didn't make it right. No, I sent instead.

I recapped everything, fingertips clacking as if this were a pop quiz I knew every answer to. She responded to every message with emojis. Starting with the open-mouthed one and ending with the exploding head.

Totally the correct responses. Even if they punched hard in the gut. The phone chimed again. I'm so sorry, Cas. I feel like this is my fault!

I sat up, rubbing the sleep from my eyes. It would be nice to have her shoulder the blame with me. But Callie had served as only one of the domino tiles in yesterday's disaster. And as much as I hated to admit it, same with Gianna.

Hot Goss would've had nothing to expose if I'd been honest from the start.

Don't feel bad; it wasn't your fault, I texted back. The primary color in this messy painting was me.

Does this mean you've started on your art-auction piece? she texted.

Oof. Another item on this morning's agenda I hadn't started. My gaze drifted past Po's empty bed to the spot inside my closet underneath the shoeboxes storing my assortment of loafers.

How much dust covered the outsides of the ArtBin housing

my art supplies? Did fingers retain muscle memory? Was painting like riding a bike?

The time had come to find out.

The last mouthful of plátano frito melted across my tongue when my phone and Mom's iPad pinged in unison.

Sweet fried plantain congealed in my stomach at the new event on our family calendar.

Family therapy session.

The only thing I knew about therapy were the bits and pieces Callie told me: *It feels like washing a cut*.

It burned. It stung. It wasn't comfortable.

Except, hadn't I been feeling this, and worse, for far too long?

If Dad believed this could help our wounds scab over, I'd conjure Jedi Knight bravery and give this a shot. Hopefully, Po would, too.

My phone buzzed. Po flashed across the screen. Relief at her calling extinguished the worst of my nerves.

Some things could never be fixed. I finally understood that.

I only prayed our bond wouldn't fall victim to that reality.

I answered the call. My phone was halfway to my ear when she shrieked, "Did I just step into an alternate universe or did Dad really add this event to our calendar?"

"Trust me—I feel like I just got invited to the Mad Hatter's tea party. But yeah." I swallowed to keep my voice even. "He really did."

A pause on her end of the line.

Should I apologize now? Where would I even begin?

"It's about time," she said. "What the hell happened last night?"

"It's probably better if I show you." I headed to the living room. Snapped a few pictures of the rubble and sent it to her.

A ping on her end of the line, followed by a gasp. "You threw your first kegger and you didn't invite me?" she huffed between laughs.

"Yeah, right." I giggled despite myself. The chuckling stitched a lot, but not all, of the tear between us. "I'm actually going to put parties on ice for a while."

The quiet on her end of the line confirmed this was the right decision.

It ached to give up something I'd clung to for dear life. Except hurting the people I cared most about pained more.

"I'm sorry, Po." Air left my lungs; some of the guilt over trying to micromanage her life rode out with it. "You were right about everything."

When life came crashing down, I became a castle, all right. Built my walls thick. Ruled from the towers with an iron fist.

Yes, it helped me survive. But by going into survival mode, I'd forgotten how to live. Donning fairy godmother robes was more comfortable—and safer—than wearing glass slippers, after all.

"It's scary to learn how to live again after Mom," I said. My chest heaved in and out. Light-headed, I braced myself against the wall.

"It's super scary." She quieted long enough for our breathing to sync through the line. "But don't you think we owe it to ourselves to try?"

Memories washed over me. Laughing with Po. World history lessons with Dad. Acai bowls with Callie.

Rehearsing with Paulina and kissing Javi.

Even if I couldn't do those last two activities again, I wanted more.

I wanted to be part of the world again, not behind the curtains. "Yes. I do," I said.

"Me too."

"Hey, are you coming back home tonight?"

She exhaled. "Probably staying at Brandi's for the entire weekend."

"Yeah, of course." I clenched and unclenched a hand, relaxing my fingers. "Take your time. Get some space. And remember to always go with the flow."

She cracked up. "That's it! Aliens definitely abducted Dad and my Little Cuchara."

The rift between us threaded closer. So what if we weren't completely stitched back? We might not be perfect right now—or ever—but we were going to be okay.

Hefty bag in one hand and dustpan with a whisk broom in the other, I crouched down, sweeping up some of the smaller pieces of glass. Morning sun hit the bigger shards, bouncing light onto the living room's walls and ceiling.

Pieces of the first Movies at the Beach with Javi rushed back to me. Mostly our conversation about stars shining long after they'd winked out of existence. Every ounce of me wanted to snap a photo of the glittering walls and text it to him as a reminder of that night.

But I was still very much feeling the aftershocks of Po's words. "If it's broke, don't fix it." My mouth puckered as I picked up one smashed piece of mirror after another. "What's done is done." Nope. "Correct" and all, this idiom tasted acidic, too.

The more pieces I chucked into the trash while repeating the sayings, the less they tasted of poison. "If it's broke, don't fix it. What's done is done." The words started to go down like an antidote for lying to myself, to others.

That Pinocchio life I'd been living was through.

I tiptoed over more glass, reaching for one of the controllers. "Into the trash you go."

A *click* when I grabbed its busted middle. "Huh?" I lifted it to my face, examining the controller from all angles.

Yes, there were dings. The joystick stuck out a little funny. But for the most part, it'd survived the impact. Unlike its destroyed twin.

Controller in hand, I bolted to the entertainment console. Turned on the TV and Xbox. I pressed the home button, shoulders tensing. And loosening.

Oh my Sith Lord. It worked.

I pressed each button, trying out Dad's game. *Everything appears to be in order.* I turned off the Xbox before I did the truly unforgivable: lose his battle against the Galactic Empire.

I glanced over my shoulder. The mirror, like so many other situations in my life, could never be made whole again. The controller hummed between my palms. Still—

Some things *could* be fixed.

Instead of striving for perfection, maybe what I needed was practice. Practice sifting through wreckage. Accept what needed to be tossed. And salvage what could be restored.

I stepped back into the mess, tossing more pieces into the Hefty bag. On one of the broken mirror slabs, I glimpsed a smile more lopsided than the controller's joystick.

I set the trash down to pick up my phone. I texted Callie: I'm going to Disneyland tomorrow. Want to meet up at Downtown Disney for ice cream after?

CHAPTER THIRTY-TWO

The pink turrets and blue bricks of Sleeping Beauty's castle gleamed under the sunshine. As I walked toward it, that familiar swell of grief knocked against my chest. Only not as hard as the last time I'd stood here.

Po had been right about a lot of things. So had Javi.

Grief didn't get any easier. Maybe it never would.

But now that I didn't have to shoulder the burden of fairy-godmothering everything, of forcibly patching up this Mom-size hole . . . I could stand inside the happiest place on earth and feel a glimmer of joy alongside the hurt.

I stopped at the foot of the castle, tipping my face up. I'd never know if Mom named me after this specific one. Even if she hadn't, I wanted to live up to my namesake to make her—and myself—proud.

I'd rise to the occasion. Never let my walls get so thick they become impenetrable. Lower my drawbridge. How would I ever get inside my own castle to enjoy soirees if I didn't? Never mind inviting others to share in my life's celebrations. To help me survive my life when calamities took it under siege.

I let out a long exhale, the *whoosh* echoing Aladdin letting Genie out of his lamp.

Showtime.

I pushed forward, dodging a horse-drawn cart and sprays from bubble wands. Hurdling over a momma duck and a line of waddling ducklings, I rushed through the iconic set of fort-style gates made from ponderosa logs, their tops sharpened into spikes. Hurried under the carved FRONTIERLAND sign hanging overhead.

It was fitting that Paulina was filming her latest food vlog here—the themed place Walt Disney built as a tribute to faith, courage, and ingenuity. Three things I'd need in droves to get her to listen to me.

My pulse pounded faster than my loafers. My soles skidded to a stop in front of the tiled entrance of Rancho del Zocalo Restaurante.

The summer crowds faded away as I zeroed in on Paulina, tucked in the back corner of the Spanish-mission-style courtyard / eating area.

Her hair shined so brightly some strands gleamed like indigo streamers. She stood over a table, camera hovering above a plate of enchiladas drenched in red sauce. She moved it to the SoCal-style street tacos, before landing on a pink concha ice-cream sandwich.

Her face scrunched when some of the whipped cream dribbled down the sweet bread's sides. She wiped the bottom of the plate with the tip of a napkin before recording again.

Paulina and I shared more similarities than I could've ever imagined: a burning desire to focus on the best. A tendency to crop out whatever mess pooled around the "perfect" parts. But didn't whipped cream taste just as sweet on the bottom as it did on top?

I approached.

Paulina clocked me. Her face hardened with a stoic mask. She set the camera down and crossed her arms over her black vest. "If you're here with a message from Po, save your breath."

"She doesn't even know I'm here." Sweat pooled at the back of my blouse. "We got into a fight after the call with you."

Paulina's nostrils flared. In the event she was about to lay into me again, I jumped in with, "I'm sorry for ruining your Very Merry Unquince—"

A scoff turned into a snort. "Although I want to kill you, I really should be kissing you. Ew, no, that would be super weird considering—" Her cheeks flushed red; she shook her head. "What I meant to say is, people love romance. But what they really want is drama. A quince turned telenovela? Irresistible."

My jaw hinged open. "Wait. Are you saying this—"

"This charade of yours doubled my views. The comment section's on fire. My college adviser said USC's in the bag, so yeah." A flash of a smile.

The tiny gesture untangled some of my stomach's knots.

"In the end, your farce turned out to be a good thing," she said.

The lip wobble betrayed her. Plus, I was too well practiced in acting like things were fine when they weren't.

Paulina lowered herself into a chair. I sunk into the one across from hers. "No, Paulina. I ruined your party."

She flicked some locks over her shoulder. "Not really. As pissed off as La Mera Mera is over the drama, I finally had a valid excuse to cancel the dinner party." She rubbed her hands together like a Sith Lord and continued. "With all the planning you did, I only have to finish filming this food segment and pick up the AT-ATs from that PP place you went to with Baymoon."

Javi. My knight in rusted armor.

"Pose with them in our outfits for a photo shoot, and that's a wrap on the vlog series." She shrugged. "As much as you and your sister screwed up, worry not—the show will go on."

Her voice sounded too rehearsed, the delivery too chipper. Once again, she focused only on the "good" parts.

"This isn't a 'show,' Paulina. It's your quince."

At that, she paled.

Too much time in the director's chair probably led to this leave-everything-bad-on-the-cutting-room-floor mentality. It struck very close to my Pinterest-board cropping. That similar coping mechanism helped me survive. For a while.

Turned out, mess always found a way. Instead of preventing it, or pretending like it wasn't there, maybe it was better to face it head-on.

"Deconstructed or not, you won't have an actual get-together to celebrate with your mom, um, parents. Or your escort."

Paulina slumped into the chair. Lapsing into an awkward silence, she dropped her head into her hands.

Seconds ticked by before she looked up. Her glitter eyeliner had smudged a little. "I could care less about having La Mera Mera there." Her chin tipped up, as if proud that she'd finally voiced something long resounding in her head—and heart. "As for Baymoon, it's been great having him around to film these videos. But now that you mention it, it would have also been great if . . ." She swallowed, quickly replacing her stoic mask. "Forget it."

Leave it to me to put the *ass* back into *ass*uming.

I always thought a quinceañera required a mom's presence. The person cheering loudest during the grand entrance. The VIP, helping the belle of the ball find her footing if she stumbled. The guest of honor sitting at the best table, watching her daughter plant seeds of dreams that would one day reach higher than magic beanstalks.

Paulina didn't want her mom there at all. It seemed like Javi—and Po—would have been enough.

And I screwed half of that equation up for her.

I ran a cold hand through my curls. Fingers got tangled in knots. Another problem that needed to be smoothed over.

After apologizing to her.

"I really wanted to throw you the best party I could. Except I wanted the internship more," I licked away the sweat mustache. "I'm sorry."

"I wish you would've been up-front about it," she said.

"Same here." I closed my eyes, picturing the red-velvet birthday cake I'd insisted I didn't want this year. I exhaled sharply, as if blowing out its sixteen candles, and made my wish.

If she can't forgive me, at least let her forgive Po.

I opened my eyes slowly.

Paulina's face remained guarded, so I continued. "I don't know if Po told you what happened at her quince."

"She might've mentioned something."

"Instead of 'fifteen buttholes' crashing your party, it only took one asshole to ruin yours."

That earned me a laugh . . . and a grin. Maybe my unused birthday wish worked its magic, after all. Or it was a gift for finally being real with her.

What I should've done from the start.

"I just got so caught up with the fantasy of how perfect things could be again." All of Frontierland went fuzzy as my vision blurred with tears. Weird, considering I finally saw some things clearly.

In my obsession with fixing things, it became easy to skip

over the parts of myself that needed mending. And celebrating. Easy to shut out the layers of Dad and Po that I should've been applauding.

Dad's Wikipedia-style brain with an imaginative flair. The grit it took to drag his butt to work every day, even though he deserved every break from the world to heal himself. Po's effervescence. Her ability to kick ass—on the court and inside the kitchen. A heart bigger than the Matterhorn. And while hers was as mangled as Dad's, as mine, she never kept it from shining anything but gold.

"Whatever Po told you about this situation, I guarantee she exaggerated her role to cover for me."

"Even if you were the leading lady, she was your supporting actress in this melodrama." Paulina dug her nails into her palms, indenting half moons on her skin. "She's not some little ángel."

"Firstly, I'd consider this more of a dramedy." My attempt at a joke stilled her hands. It would probably be smart to stop there, but no. "Secondly, you're right. She's not 'some' angel." A loud group ran by, giving my head time to sync up with my heart. "She's my guardian one."

And just like that, another spell broke.

What—who—I needed to paint for the art fundraiser became crystal clear. Along with so many other things. "She's also my sister, my best friend, my number one cheerleader."

To me, she'd come off as scattered. In reality, she'd tapped into all the different parts of herself, used them to stay afloat amid this grief. Buoyed me in the process without me even knowing it.

I wiped my nose with the sleeve of my pink blouse. "She can be all of those things to you, too—well, except the sister part—if you give her another chance."

Slowly, the shadows lifted from Paulina's eyes. Was she actually considering everything I'd said?

Hope bubbled. If Paulina gave Po another shot, would Javi give me one, too?

"I know you don't need me as a planner anymore, but if you ever need a friend, I'll be here for you," I said, rising from the chair.

Paulina's voice stopped me from taking another step. "There's another Movies at the Beach next Saturday."

The twinkle in her eyes—encouragements not to miss it.

Latine prayer candles are traditionally made from white wax, encased in a long, cylindrical glass, and plastered with a saint or archangel sticker down the middle. Recently, the stickers have started featuring new "saints" and "guardian angels."

Taylor Swift blessing her Swifties, Oprah anointing her devotees. Dad had one of Ruth Bader Ginsburg in his home office. Whenever he needed guidance for work, he'd light it up and ask, "What would RBG do?"

Callie loved my idea for doing a prayer-candle-style watercolor portrait of Po. After stuffing ourselves on double scoops of sea-salt-and-caramel-ribbons ice cream at Salt & Straw, I rushed home to get to work.

Sprawled on my bedroom floor, I started by googling images of guardian angels. I filled the college-ruled lines of the day planner with a checklist of common elements: a billowy gown, golden halo, huge wings.

I sprung from the floor, laughing as the pieces clicked together.

Over *billowy gown*, I wrote *quince dress*. I crossed out *golden halo* and jotted *tiara*. I tapped the pencil against my lips. Velvet curtains or Po's duster to sub as wings?

A sketch of my idea bloomed over the page. I turned to the closet.

Go time.

When Po moved into my room, I'd made some space for her clothes inside my closet. Of course, she hadn't stuck to the designated area. I lifted armfuls of brightly colored crop tops and leggings, curbing the urge to fold them and put them where they belonged.

"Where did she put you?" I muttered, rummaging through the closet. Grabbing a chair, I stepped on it, lifting to my tiptoes. Searched the shelves above the clothing racks.

"Ah-ha!" My heart leapt at the ArtBin and watercolor paper pad behind it. I scooped both into my arms. And that's when I saw it.

The Danish tin Mom used to store our Disney celebration pins. After the funeral, Dad pretty much went into Mr. Clean mode. Anything of Mom's not nailed to the wall he threw away or moved into the garage.

I'd looked for the pins there but found nothing. Now I knew why.

Po had dived in for the save. Once again.

My knees unlocked and I stepped off the chair. Eased the tin and the art supplies onto the floor. My fingertips skirted the rim of the royal blue lid. With my thumb, I tried to pry it open.

The lid made a sharp *pop*, like a needle straight to the side of a helium balloon—or an exhale after holding your breath for over two years.

Afternoon sunbeams slanted through the window. Stretched across the room, casting a spotlight on so many memories.

Metal clinked over metal as I sifted through the buttons illustrated with Goofy holding ballons. Underneath him: I'M CELEBRATING and words and phrases we'd filled in.

I pulled out some pins written in Spanish, all featuring Mom's neat cursive. *Catering another party.* I set it beside me. *Cebollas.* Yes. Onions definitely needed to be commemorated. *Another Cuban playing in the Major League.* My chest swelled with secondhand pride.

Mi familia.

Closing my eyes, I conjured Mom's face. Pressed the button to my chest. My heart didn't sputter. It continued to beat slow and steady.

Rifling through more, I grabbed some penned by Po. *Three-day weekends. Cutting an avocado perfectly around the pit.* Cheers to that, for sure. *Toes!*

I picked up some of Dad's, too. *Making partner. Finding a parking spot at South Coast on Black Friday. Jedi Knights.*

Of course, I had to grab some of mine: *My first day at school, Christmas Eve, Straight A's.*

I spread the buttons all around me, arranging them into my own sort of grid.

The realization started slowly, but when it hit, it filled every inch of me.

Unlike Mandy's, these celebrations didn't highlight very important events. Those were bound to be inside the tin, too, and yet . . . I got an inkling that most of these honored everyday moments.

Being "everyday" didn't make them less magical. Any less worthy of praising.

If anything, they deserved to be revered more. Life was a

collection of moments like these. The fairy-tale events sprinkled in simply provided an extra sparkle.

I snatched my phone, flicked past texts from Dad, Po, and Callie. Clicking on the Mandy Whitmore and Associates IG page, I scrolled down her feed. One spellbinding moment after the next. My heart still leapt at them.

Except—

In trying to keep up with her feed, in trying to create my own Pinterest board of my family's HEA, I'd completely overlooked all of Mom's—all of our—happily ever nows.

I'd stocked up on a wealth of storybook moments already. And although our time was cut short, I was so grateful I'd shared so many of them with Mom.

I hit *Unfollow.*

I didn't need Mandy's grid anymore. Not when I'd always had my own.

Not every new event would be happy. Some occasions would rip my heart open. Or stitch it back up. Others would take my breath away because they were so unexpected.

Like this moment right now, writing an email to politely decline Mandy's offer.

My fingers shook, excited to find out what I'd be celebrating next.

CHAPTER THIRTY-THREE

Po would be proud. My side of the room doubled the chaos of hers. Curled-up tubes of paint, some butterflied down the middle, littered the foot of my bed. Scraps of paper took up lots of the floor. Whirs, beeps, and clicks rang from the middle of the mattress. More accurately, from the printer I'd set up on the duvet, shooting out photos.

They were mostly older family pictures. And a handful of newer ones, taken over the course of unquince prepping.

I rolled a photo of Javi at the tux fitting between my fingers. I grabbed the scissors and cut around his outline carefully. "I'm sorry," I whispered, part rehearsal for the real apology and part mea culpa for moving the blades over his waist.

Slice. That cut was the easy bit. Chopping off the ends of his sun-lightened locks became a little harder. Then again, what was a bad haircut when I'd already stabbed him in the heart?

Moving the shears over his neck gave me pause. "This is going to hurt me a lot more than it's going to hurt you."

Snip.

While Javi's head fluttered into the small mound of picture fragments, I swiped the back of the white jacket with a glue stick. Since he'd always made me feel so light and floaty, I added this portion of the pic to the photo collage of clouds.

With a wistful sigh, I brushed another layer of blue watercolor on the sky. While the paint dried, I cut more colors from pictures. Glued them over the edges of the V-neck plunging down the bodice of the dusty-rose, watercolored gown. I repeated the process, adding more definition on the tiara crowning Po.

Should I also use the photo-collage technique to cover the pencil marks? Or add more layers of paint to hide them?

I shook my head. No more covering up what came before with "prettier" things.

Besides, there was something about letting past techniques connect with the present ones: Glitter next to charcoal line work. Photo collages alongside paint. The hodgepodge of media cast an unsuspecting type of spell.

For so long I believed only a fairy godmother's wand was capable of doing this. Like Dorothy in Oz, I'd forgotten that magic lay as close as the loafers on my feet. As close as the wooden brush in my hand.

I readjusted my grip on the brush when I started filling in Po's mouth. Halfway through, my hand slackened. Why use watercolor when I could use the real deal?

I jumped off the floor and snagged Po's cosmetic bag. Combing through it, my fingers closed over the glittery pink lipstick she wore when she wanted to feel "extra dressy."

"A little bit here," I said, daubing the makeup over the bow of her lips. Hmm. This shade would also be great for outlining the feathers flowing down the length of the gown. My eyes darted between the tube of lipstick and plumage demanding a darker silhouette.

Go grande, or return to your casa.

I hatched lines with the lipstick. Crosshatched those with a darker shade of another lipstick. *That's it.* Now the feathers really started to pop. I'd have to buy her two new lipsticks now, but screw it. Ruining these would be worth it.

With a palette knife, I transferred some Hansa Medium Yellow into the well of the palette. Poured in a few drops of clean water. Stirred with the end of a brush. And voilà.

The dried-up watercolor paint came back to life.

Hope filled me. But it fled quicker than Cinderella leaving the ball. Reviving old paints didn't come close to rekindling my relationship with Javi.

I didn't let the pang of loss stop me from grabbing another brush. I added more yellow to the tiara. While it dried, I hot-glued some of the Disney celebration pins around the edges of the painting, creating a makeshift frame.

I stroked a few more layers of Quin Gold inside the scroll/banner flying over Po's tiara. I blew on the paint to make it dry faster, then grabbed the bottle of Elmer's liquid glitter glue. The red sparkles could double for Paulina's eyeliner.

I brought the bottle's tip over the scroll and wrote *Feliz quince años, Po!*

Fireworks went off inside of me, and when the emotions settled, I grabbed my phone. Snapped a pic and sent it to Callie.

Not exactly the plan we talked about earlier, I texted, laughing. What fun was always going down the perfectly planned path? Especially when detours could lead to something like this.

I sent the picture to Po next. Not a second passed before the phone chimed. Little Cuchara, you just gave me the quince of my dreams!!! More explosions went off inside my chest.

An ellipsis bubbled at the bottom of the screen. Then—WAIT! IS THAT MY LIPSTICK?

A great scholar once said you can't make huevos rancheros without breaking a few eggs 😉

Great scholar, huh? I could get used to that.

Yes! Finally, we were on the same page. I promised myself not to turn over this moment too quickly. It was okay to linger inside this chapter for a bit longer.

I'll see you tomorrow night, Little Cuchara. We can go over the final menu for the art fundraiser. Miss you.

I miss you too.

I set the phone next to the mixed-media portrait of Po, smiling at the quinceañera she deserved to be.

My eyes flicked between the painting and her text: Little Cuchara, you just gave me the quince of my dreams!!!

My breath hitched. I turned to my utility bag. My eyes burned holes through the fabric as I pictured the ex-pencil-wand inside.

Maybe I'd hung up my fairy godmother robes too quickly, because what if . . .

Before I lost my nerve, I texted the portrait to one more person. Followed it up with I have an idea, but I'll need your help.

At Angie's quinceañera, I'd tried to rush her out of the bridal suite. Forced her to face her birthday guests and recite an unrehearsed speech, all before she was 100 percent ready.

Now the glass loafer was on the other foot. Sweat dotted my

forehead, although I only had to face one person. Although I'd practiced my apology all week.

I reached for my utility bag, fishing for the oil blotters. Great. No blotters. Only an art chamois. The cloth couldn't absorb the extra sheen. It mopped up my clammy armpits nicely, though.

I tipped my head toward the horizon. Late afternoon sun gilded cresting waves. "Mom, if you're on fairy godmother duty today, can you help your girl out?" I whispered.

An ocean gust blew around me. Or was it my wish being granted?

Like pulled curtains, the crowd parted. It became easier to shuffle through the moviegoers to find Javi.

He sat on the same Guatemalan textile he'd brought to the *Jaws* screening. My heart skipped a beat at the forlorn way he gripped the trenta-size Starbucks cup of water.

Okay, fairy Mom-mother, tell me you have another miracle up your robe's sleeve. I filled my lungs with briny air and yelled, "Javi!"

He turned toward me. His jaw flexed. The rest of his face hardened, taking in my appearance.

I lowered my gaze. So this patch of shoreline hadn't transformed into a bog, after all. It was only me, my hope, and I, sinking with another possible loss.

Unrooting my feet, I rushed forth. Stopped at the edge of his blanket. "Um, can I sit?"

He bit on the straw. After a long sip of water, he shrugged. "Be my guest."

My lips buzzed with *Beauty and the Beast* jokes. Except, no more hiding my feelings behind Pinterest boards. Or comedy. Not to mention, time waited for no one.

"I can't stay for long. I have to be at SBA's art fundraiser later." I inched down onto the blanket. So cozy, familiar. Him letting me stay unraveled some of my nerves. "You know how I told you I entered a piece? Do you want to see it?"

He nodded, a smile tugging at the corner of his lips. Not as big as the one on the Mickey appliqué on his bag, but both grins helped me hope.

I pulled out my phone to show him. Sharing my work sent ripples of nervousness and excitement up my limbs. *Two sides of the same nickel*, as Po would say.

"It's of Po. At her quince. What her quinceañera should've been, anyway."

I extended my phone. His fingertips knocked against mine when he took it. Maybe there wasn't the full blaze of fireworks from before. But there was definitely still a spark. At least on my end.

He zoomed in on the picture. "It's awesome," he said, tracing the parts where one medium became another.

I perked up. Yup. People with broken hearts knew where to look for busted seams. Where to find the new stitches patching old tears.

When he studied the portrait's clouds, he looked up. "Is this part filled with my stormtrooper suit?"

I nodded. "I couldn't dive into painting again without including some of my favorite people as, like, personal floatation devices."

A small laugh. "Is that a lifeguard joke?"

I shrugged. So what if I'd promised myself no jokes? Progress, not perfection.

"If you look at the rest of the sky, you'll see photos of my dad's blue ties. And here," I said, pointing to the slants of sun, "I used pics of Mom's catering truck and her favorite yellow dress for the sunbeams."

He lowered the screen, setting it between us. "I'm sorry for your loss."

"Me too." A stab inside my chest.

I didn't run from it like before. I let it rip through me. Let it run out of steam instead of allowing it to fester. "I'm also sorry about us," I said. "I promised to not hurt you seconds before I did. If you can't forgive me, I'll understand." I exhaled, releasing some guilt and shame.

Yes, I'd fallen way short of acting perfectly. And although I was prepared to accept the consequences of my actions, I was also ready to cut myself slack for making mistakes.

But that didn't mean I'd resigned myself for this to be the way our tale ended.

"Before you make that decision, I want to tell you more of the story. If that's okay with you," I said.

He didn't say he'd forgive me no matter what. Or that he'd accept my past pain as a hall pass for bad behavior. Instead, he offered a small nod.

I took him up on the invite and told him everything he didn't already know.

I told him about making lists for Mom's medications. Keeping track of them gave me a sense of control over her illness, over the impending tragic ending. Once Mom's dark, bronzy skin started to blanch, the watercolors went straight into the closet.

Po helped me realize a missing mom . . . and a non-present sister . . . had ruined her quince. Not a missing tilde.

I told him how Po had been looking out for me this entire time in such a low-key way I hadn't even noticed. How could I when I had become so obsessed with Mandy Whitmore?

I told him how I really believed that with the fairy godmother's apprenticeship, I could patch up my heart permanently.

I'd learn how to transform my family's messy life into a real-life version of her grid.

If I wanted to fix the "problems" at home, though, I should've started with myself. And while the Mandy Band-Aid alleviated the pain inside my chest, it would never heal it.

It would never heal the hurt of having watched my mom wither away so slowly.

Or make up for the time I'd spent in limbo since she'd passed.

Much less help me mourn the lifetime of moments we had—and those we never would have.

Once upon a time, I thought it was a random algorithm that led me to Mandy's grid. In reality, the only thing that'd escorted me there was me. My unconscious desire to live out the milestone moments I'd never get to experience with Mom, and my conscious wish to learn from Mandy how to plan a happily ever after.

That way I could prevent another hole the size of a person from cutting into me. No more hurting. No more catastrophes. Living in a state that swung between earthquakes, fire seasons, and a never-ending drought, I should've known that disasters would always spring up.

This moment was proof of that.

My entire body relaxed when I finished talking, deflating like week-old helium balloons.

Javi scooted in. The floral notes of his shampoo wafted over. *Must paint lavender fields before the summer ends.* Would that be the last party favor from our time together?

"Have you ever heard of kintsugi?" he asked, grabbing his cup of water. I shook my head. "My mom told me about it after my dad died. It's the Japanese art of repairing broken ceramics with powdered metals, mostly gold."

"Is it more about fixing the pot? Or about highlighting the cracks inside of it?"

His eyes crinkled over the rim of the cup. Taking a sip, he said, "You tell me, Castle Towers."

Huh. I glanced down at my palms, picturing the lines overlayed with glitter. I imagined the edges of the Mom-shaped hole beginning to glow. Lights at the end of the tunnel. Rows of lighthouses ready to lead me out of the dark if I ever fell in again.

"I'll have to think about it. Can I text you a hypothesis later?" I asked.

"Okay."

Cheers erupted from the crowd. Not because Javi was maybe giving me another chance, but because the previews hit the screen. My cue to exit stage left. I rose to my feet.

"Sucks you can't stay. This is one of my all-time favorite movies," Javi said.

"What is it?"

He leaned back onto the Guatemalan textile, arms butterflied behind his head. "*Cast Away*."

"Synopsis, please, sans spoilers."

A smile bloomed, then broadened, finally matching the size of the one on the Mickey appliqué. "Control freak gets stranded on an island where nothing's in his control."

Oh boy. "I don't have to stay to watch it—I pretty much lived it."

He laugh-snorted. Gosh, how I'd missed that sound. "You should watch it this weekend."

"I will," I said, gulping before continuing. "And Javi? Thanks for listening."

He nodded. I turned and walked away, a little lighter on my loafers.

Not a perfect resolution between us tonight. But hopefully, a new start.

CHAPTER THIRTY-FOUR

I arrived at the SBA fundraiser fashionably late. Well, more like *late late.*

Every cell in my body didn't mutiny at being tardy to my party. Nor did my stomach flutter at the size of the crowd. Which, from the looks of it, had grown from last year.

People packed every inch of the parking lot. James set up more line partitions, organizing the queue to the auditorium screening the latest *Spider-Man* movie. Wesley stood at the front of the doors, taking tickets. Callie directed the swarms of people from one art piece to the next.

The rest of the SBA didn't miss a beat. Even without me directing—er, controlling—from the helm, everyone shined their own light. I had no desire to throw a damper on it.

Especially Po's. She wasn't even officially a member of the event committee, but she was definitely having her moment under the moonlight.

Her body swayed behind one of the grills. The silk duster billowed with the ocean breeze, smoke swirling around her like magic tendrils. She looked up. The only thing beaming brighter than her face was her orange-yellow lipstick.

I'd never seen her wear this shade before.

The vibrant colors instantly conjured golden yucca fries, warm sunshine, and spring crocuses.

She waved huge tongs, motioning me over.

Later, I mouthed. *You've got this.* I didn't go and check on her grilling skills to make sure.

She flashed a huge smile, mouthing back, *I do.*

As the event wound down, Callie and I walked between the canvases. Loaded the ballot boxes in front of each art piece onto our rolling backpacks. Tons of pet photography. Lots of Matteo-Beach-pier-backlit-by-the-sunset paintings. A few abstract sculptures. None as interesting as the one Javi and I created in the Arctic Art Studio, though.

At the other end of the parking lot, a small crowd gathered in front of my portrait. Could it hold a candle to *Phallus in Wonderland*? I tugged at my blouse's collar.

Unlike Cinderella's coach, the portrait didn't turn into a pumpkin the closer time ticked toward midnight. Quite the opposite. Under the glow of the spotlights and the gaze of admirers, the painting-collage of Po sparked with life. And not because of the obscene amount of glitter I'd used.

"You did good, Cas," Callie said.

Yeah, I really did.

"Oh, before I forget, Po saved us food for while we're tallying these up." She patted a ballot box. At the stomp of combat boots behind us, we glanced over our shoulders. In the middle of the parking lot, Po and Marcus had broken out into an impromptu cha-cha. "Speak of the devi—"

"Angel," I corrected her. Guess there was a little bit of Madame Iron Fist inside of me still.

Callie grinned. Leaning in, she whispered, "So . . . is everything ready for tomorrow night?"

"Glow sticks, check; Angie's tiara, check. I'm also bringing portable chargers." *I suppose leftover fairy godmother swirled inside me, too.*

Taking a page from Po, why throw all the bathwater out with the baby?

Parties brought joy to people. I wanted to keep ushering in that joy. Only, this time, I wanted to join in on the fun. I wanted to celebrate making new memories for myself, not simply plan them for others in an attempt to bury the ones I didn't want to remember.

"Okay, what about desserts?" she asked.

I popped out my phone and showed her the concept photo for the cupcakes I'd ordered. A chocolate Darth Vader mask and red lightsaber topped a cracked red surface resembling lava.

"Oooh," Callie said. "That looks so yummy."

"One hundred percent." When I'd googled *best bakery in Orange County,* Rubi's Bakery topped the list. The shop was owned by a guy who was not only a Cuban immigrant, but the recently crowned winner of the second annual OC Bake-Off.

His daughter, Rubi, placed third last year.

She'd answered the phone when I called to place my order for a dozen vanilla and a dozen chocolate cupcakes. When she asked if these were for a special occasion, I said yes.

A quinceañera.

Drawing from Javi's Latine-granny-style openness, I followed up by telling her whose. Casually threw in that I was also Cuban-American.

After a brief silence, she'd said, "In that case, I'm making you something extra special."

And she did—at the family discount to boot.

"It's going to be chocolate lava cake on top," I told Callie. "A chocolate-cherry mousse inside a pâte à choux in the middle. With salted cajeta pudding on the bottom." My mouth watered. Callie licked her lips. "Rubi said *Star Wars* fan or not, everyone at the party will think these cupcakes are the 'Chosen Ones.'"

Callie cracked up. "If her desserts are as good as her puns, I believe it." She cleared her throat, motioning to Po rushing over.

Po slung her arms over us and said, "This was way funner than the dogs-and-dogs event. Hey, do you guys have a catering chair on the committee?"

Callie shook her head.

"But we should," I said. "I'll bring it up at the next meeting."

Po winked. "Looks like I'll be adding an extracurricular to my resume, after all, eh?" Sarcasm didn't tinge her voice. Only excitement. And a hint of gratitude. "Thanks for letting me do my thing, guys."

"Our pleasure," Callie said. "You'll be an asset to the group." I nodded in agreement. "I'm going to get started on counting these," she said, jutting her chin to the ballot boxes.

"I'll join you right after I show Po the finished portrait and collect the rest of the ballots," I said.

Callie headed one way. Po and I another.

My loafers synced to the steps of her boots. We stopped at her portrait. The label next to it read,

Artist: Castillo Torres
Once upon a Quinceañera
Mixed media on paper.

Dozens of emotions beamed on her face as she took in the artwork. "Little Cuchara, it's so much more beautiful in real life." The pride in her voice lifted my shoulders.

It felt like the concrete under our feet had been replaced by Aladdin's magic carpet. As I floated to a whole new world, a series of Pinterest boards I'd created flashed in my mind.

Those would-be moments didn't come close to this one right here, right now. "I guess everything is more beautiful in real life," I said.

Po grabbed my hand. I squeezed it. The spaces and jagged edges between us melted.

"I wish I would've bid on it," she said. "It would've been so awesome to bring it home."

"I'll make you another one." That made her start clapping. "Hey, since you're in such a good mood, I have a proposal," I said.

Po raised a brow.

"What about we hit up Disneyland tomorrow?"

"Disneyland?" Her darkening expression gave me pause.

Wiping my palms on the sides of my blouse, I kept going. "Tomorrow night. To celebrate this." I motioned around us. "Both of us need new *I'm Celebrating* pins, and it's been forever since we've watched a fireworks show." My nose didn't grow, because this was true.

Channeling some of Paulina's cool, calm, and collected veneer, I added, "Oh, I checked the calendar, and guess what? It's Princess Nite tomorrow."

Throughout the year, the park held various themed after-hours events, one of them being a night when the park immersed guests in stories of Disney heroines—and tons of sparkly decor. Mom loved tasting all the special treats for the night. And it always gave Po an excuse to dress up.

"Well . . . whaddya say?" I asked.

She chewed her orange-yellow lips. I could almost hear the gears in her head turning.

Paulina never filmed at night. She needed the sun to light the food featured in her vlogs. If Paulina *were* to attend an after-hours event, it would be *Star Wars* Nite—not one where tiaras outnumbered lightsabers.

Slowly, a smile unfurled across Po's face. When it reached Jack Skellington proportions, she said, "Count me in. But only if you dress up with me. Khaki shorts and a button-down aren't befitting of royalty."

"Can I keep my loafers on at least?" I asked, sparking her laughter.

Bingo. The second part of my plan had liftoff.

Inside room 237, Callie and I went through the bids for each piece. My heart doubled when I found out who won *Once upon a Quinceañera*.

Diego Torres.

I let tears flow unchecked. Dad must've come when Po was behind the grill and I was inside the auditorium introducing the movie.

Because of him, the portrait would be coming home. Exactly like Po wanted.

Like I wanted.

When I got home, I found Po in the kitchen with Dad. They were both laughing at something over the stove. The sweet-and-savory scents of Po's now-famous PSTs curled around me for the second time today. Songs from Mom's playlist shuffled in the background. They didn't boom full blast like Po and I would've preferred, but they played nonetheless.

I threw my arms over Dad's neck.

"Hey, what's that for, kiddo?"

For the painting, I wanted to say. For letting Mom's music come back to her happiest place after Disneyland. Only that wouldn't encompass the full truth. "For everything," I said, my eyes flitting to Po. He brought a finger to his lips.

I nodded. The portrait was a secret worth keeping.

I inhaled more scents of Cuban food, listened to more nostalgic melodies. "Since we're still up, what about a movie to pair with this late dinner?"

"Do you have any cinematic suggestions?" Po asked, looking up from stirring the browning meat.

"I do," I said.

The three of us sniffled back tears. Not because we were still uncomfortable or unpracticed in sharing our emotions with one another. But because we didn't want to add more salt to Po's PSTs.

She'd perfected the seasoning mix already.

Between mouthfuls of Po's twist on the Cuban dishes, we debated *Cast Away*. "Chuck needed to let go of Wilson to survive," Dad said.

Po hurled a raisin at him. He shielded himself with a throw pillow, peeking over the edge. "Why do you think the movie title is spelled with two words, not one, Po?"

She flung another raisin. Dad caught it, peppering it over his last PST. "Chuck is a castaway," he said. "But the only reason he survives is because he literally 'cast' his baggage 'away.'"

Po and I swung our heads toward each other. Twin *oooohs* flew from our lips. Some of my heart's jagged edges eroded.

Po elbowed me in the ribs. "Looks like we have to up our brainpower to get into Alma, eh?"

I was so thrilled she'd found the path back to her old college dream. Happier still that she'd rediscovered her joy on the way there, without additional prodding from me.

I uncrossed my legs. A few heartbeats ticked by before I heard myself say, "Um, I've been thinking about checking out other schools besides Alma or UCI. Ones with bigger art departments."

A week ago, I'd nearly fainted at Javi's college plans not being laid in stone. Now?

Now the possibility of going to different schools, of adding new colleges to my Excel spreadsheet, didn't feel like a betrayal of my previously planned path. I needed to trust that my journey would eventually lead me to my destination. And if there were roadblocks, or pit stops, or detours along the way, I'd still get where I needed to be.

"What do you both think?" I asked.

Po gave me a high five. Dad's face flashed with pride.

Feeling floaty from all of it, I said, "Did anyone pick up on the angel-wing motif through the movie?"

Po immediately launched into wanting wing tattoos for her next birthday. Dad swiveled on his gaming chair. Apparently, the thing had more uses than supporting his gaming habit. Nudging the conversation from tattoos to the movie's ending, he said, "I can't tell if it's supposed to be happy or sad. Thoughts?"

"Happy," Po said. "I mean, what's better than closure with one great love of your life, only to immediately meet the next one? You know what they say. 'As one chapter closes, another begins.'" She wiggled her brows. The hitch in her voice, coupled with the fact that she got the quote "right," gave her false bravado away.

"Can't the ending be both?" I blurted. "It's sad that Chuck and Kelly don't stay together forever, but it's also happy that Chuck made it back . . . and that there's more love waiting for him." My eyes darted between them. "If he wants it."

A big tear rolled down my cheek. Bigger than the one about to fall over Dad's. Po rose from the couch and pressed her cheek to his. "Little Cucharas grow up so fast," she said, sniffling.

"So do Big Spoons," he said.

Po's eyes glistened. After a few moments of wiping our faces, the conversation veered off to the importance of dental hygiene.

As Po and Dad's conversation grew more animated, I slipped off the sofa and headed into the hallway. Leaning against the wall, I texted Javi.

> I watched Cast Away. So many thoughts. I can share some with you tomorrow night if you're interested. I'm sure Paulina invited you to the special event already, but I'm extending the invitation personally to you as well.

I turned off the phone, raised it in a toast, and let my eyes drift over every photo of Mom.

"I love you. I miss you," I whispered. "Here's to being one of the great loves in my life. To being a part of so many happily ever nows."

I walked back into the living room, ready to make a few more.

CHAPTER THIRTY-FIVE

Po's eyes bulged when I came out of the bathroom and twirled. The satin silvery-blue skirt swooshed around me. I extended a silver loafer. Adjusted the silk magenta-bow headband keeping (most of) my curls off my face before curtsying. "How do I look?"

"Wow," she said. "The spitting image of a Caribbean Cinderella."

"Close but no Cuban cigar." I pressed my lips to keep from laughing. "I'm Disney-bounding as Cinderella's fairy godmother." Even though I'd cast off the fairy godmother robes, tonight I needed tons of magic to pull off this surprise party.

"Then you're cheating because she's not a princess!" Po said. "It's Princess Nite, not Madrina Nite."

"I guess you'll have to 'princess' for both of us." A deep breath. "I know you have something picked out, but I also bought you something."

She sighed dramatically, as if to say, *Here we go again.*

"You don't have to wear it if you don't want; I only wanted you to have an extra option. Come look."

Grinning, she followed me back into *my* room. *Mine* because she'd finally moved back into hers. I threw the door open and said, "Behold."

She gasped at the sunset-orange puff-sleeved crop top and matching shorts laid out on the bed. "Oh my gosh. This is next-level Princess Jasmine stuff." She rushed forward, fingers skimming the gold foil stars stamping the tulle mesh fabric.

"I wanted to get you a present to make up for some—er, most—of my past behavior. No matter how *dic*tatorial I acted, you always had my back." Technically true, so not a breach of my never-lie-to-anyone-I-care-about-again rule. Still. I kept the other reason behind the star-print motif under wraps.

Po brought the top to her chest, checking herself out in the floor-length mirror. "The colors perfectly match my new lipstick, and this will look kick-ass with my boots." Bouncing on her toes, she scooped me up for a giant hug.

As I caught a glimpse of us in the mirror, my mind flashed to Angie's quince, when she and her mother embraced as equals—the moment when Angie stepped into her adulthood.

This hug marked a similar rite of passage. We held each other not only as sisters, but as friends. Po's voice lowered as she said, "Thank you, Little Cuchara. For the outfit, for always having my back, too." She squeezed me tighter, lifting my loafers from the floor.

Fitting, considering how my overwhelming love for my sister—and hers for me—sent me soaring.

We walked down Main Street, elbows linked. We bought hot kettle corn at the popcorn cart. Took pictures with Princess Minnie and Daisy. Ran up the stairs leading to City Hall.

Inside, I snatched a handful of *I'm Celebrating* pins, stashing them into my utility bag.

Po lifted a brow. "What?" I said. "Just making sure we uphold Mom's traditions." A non-lie.

"I love that," she said. "But do we really need this many?"

"Um—" I gulped. Sheesh. Was my secret plan up in smoke already? "We have a lot of happy moments to catch up on." My words echoed against the wood-paneled walls decorated with photos of Walt Disney and his family.

She nodded in agreement. "We do."

"Let's fill them out later," I said.

"I'm down with that," she said, bounding out the building and down the steps.

Back on Main Street, our laughter floated over the murmur of the crowd, the squeals coming from rides, the ambient Disney songs streaming from invisible speakers.

She hooked her arm around my neck. I relaxed into her, giggling to myself. Despite things being far from perfect, I was here, decked out in something other than a button-down and shorts . . . and I liked it.

"What's so funny?" Po asked.

"Dressed like this, I feel like a glamorous sister duo," I said. "You know, like Anna and Elsa."

"Or sisters from other misters, like Thelma and Louise," Po said.

So she'd also felt our reforged bonds of sisterhood, our strengthened links of friendship. Beaming, I said, "As long as we don't go over a cliff together, okay?"

"We already did, and look," she said, her eyes darting to her combat boots and my silver loafers. "We're still standing."

As always, Po had a point. I kissed her cheek, careful not to leave my clear gloss on her skin. When we approached the castle, I said, "Let me take a pic real quick."

I pulled out my phone, quickly flicking away the notifications from Callie informing me that everyone was in place.

No messages from Javi. My chest tightened. A little.

I took a deep breath, focusing on the beauty of Sleeping Beauty's castle. On being here, having a great hair day with the best sister/friend at my side.

Every detail of a plan didn't need to fit together for the big picture to click into place.

The *thump-thump-thump*s of my heartbeat slowed. Pulsed with the Poverb *"Don't lose what you've got to what you've lost."*

I snapped a photo of the towers. Like them, I'd remain strong but not so thick that I could never be dismantled to build something new. I moved the camera to the bricked turrets. When life got low, I'd let my support system keep me high. I took a picture of the wide-open drawbridge.

Stay open to the unexpected. And host one hell of a party.

I turned back to Po. "Ready for a ride?"

She gave me a thumbs-up, clueless about the one I was about to take her on.

Every asset's in position, Callie texted as we stepped off the *Star Wars* ride, Millennium Falcon: Smugglers Run.

ETA in T-minus 60 seconds, I texted back, following it up with a dancing Pikachu GIF. A happy compromise since I couldn't use the walkie-talkies without giving myself away. Grabbing Po's hand, I led her outside the ride's building.

"Let's go on it again," she said.

"After we get something to drink," I said, even though I wasn't remotely thirsty.

"Too bad Dad isn't here."

"Yeah, too bad," I said, biting the sides of my cheeks.

The second the evening air hit me, I spotted Callie leaning against the Rancor's gate. I couldn't tell which would make

Rapunzel do a double take faster: Callie's corseted, pinkish-purple dress, or her long locks, plaited into an epic braid.

Three, two, one, she mouthed.

I slipped the pencil-wand from my utility bag. One last bibbidi-bobbidi-boo for the road. Taking a huge mouthful of air, I yelled, "A big round of applause for tonight's quince court!"

I flicked the eraser end of my makeshift wand at Callie.

She held a mini speaker into the air, blasting an air horn soundtrack.

Po's volleyball team rushed from behind the crates decorating the *Star Wars*–themed area. They cracked their glow sticks. Each stick glowed a different shade of neon; the colors blurred as the team circled us.

Po's mouth fell open. "What the—"

"A round of applause for the father of the quinceañera, Diego Torres!" I said, flicking my pencil-wand again. Dad sprung from behind a trash can, clad in Jedi robes. He whirled a blue saber through the air. "And give it up for the belle of the ball, Mariposa Torres!"

Her head jerked toward mine. A small gasp escaped from Po's wobbling lips. Brandi, wearing a green velvety dress similar to Princess Merida's, ran up to Po, crowning her with Angie's tiara.

"What in the world"—Po's eyes brimmed with tears; she grabbed my shoulder to steady herself—"is happening?"

I flicked my pencil-wand to Callie again. Like magic, the air horn sounds morphed into the piano, brass, and string melodies of the most iconic quince waltz of all time, "Tiempo de Vals."

The volleyball team broke off into pairs, dancing around us. And right when Po couldn't look more shocked, her eyes fixed on something—someone—behind me. Her belly heaved in and out as she said, "Paulina."

Clad in her sparkly Darth Vader–inspired gown, Paulina strutted over. She bowed in front of Po, her sleek hair spreading over her shoulders like a Sith Lord's cape.

"May I have this dance?" Paulina asked, extending a manicured hand.

Po pinched herself, as if trying to wake up from a dream.

"It's all real, Po," I whispered. "If you don't believe me, take Paulina's hand."

The team erupted into cheers when Po did.

Callie joined in on the applause. So did Dad and every cast member and guest who happened to be walking through Galaxy's Edge at that moment.

I cheered, loudest of all. My palms stung from clapping when Po melted into Paulina's arms. My throat burned from woo-hooing when Paulina gently kissed both of her eyelids.

Dad came over and gave me a hug. "I'm proud of you, kiddo."

I grinned, tipping my face toward the coming nightfall.

Soon the darkness would drape over the neon-pink clouds and the ocean-blue skies. Only against the night sky could stars wink into existence. The moon would shine brightly.

And so will we.

Callie wedged between me and Dad. "You guys ready for round two?"

Dad pulled the red saber strapped on his back, extending it to me.

I tucked the pencil-wand behind my ear to take it. I twirled the saber at Callie. "In three, two, one—"

Callie's mini speaker boomed with the percussion and cymbal blasts of the "Imperial March." I turned on the saber. Whoa. Its glow painted my skin with a beautiful shade of red. No wonder Dad and Paulina loved this universe so much. "And give it up for the second quinceañera of the night, Paulina Reyes!"

"What?" Paulina's eyelids could have become mini strobe lights with all her blinking. "Cas, this wasn't part of the script," she huffed, sounding shocked—and ecstatic.

Once more, applause thundered. Even Chewbacca, taking pics with fans in front of the *Millennium Falcon* a few feet away, roared.

Without missing another cymbal crash, Po spun Paulina again. "You remember how to paso doble?"

"A Sith Lord never forgets," Paulina answered.

Together, they performed the dance. Weeks had passed since the first rehearsal, yet they didn't miss a beat.

With each turn, I could tell they let more of this *Star Wars* land melt away . . . until they were left in a party of two. After the last percussion boom, they laughed in each other's arms.

Paulina glanced in my direction. *Gracias amiga,* she mouthed. *Gracias*.

After the introduction dances, we ran to Frontierland to ride Big Thunder Mountain Railroad. We broke into impromptu steps whenever we wanted. Waltzing with Callie, Dad, and Po may not have been like rehearsing the paso doble with Javi. But it was just as fun and equally memorable.

The cardio worked up our appetites. Paulina gave us the inside scoop on all the treats we needed to eat: The Cocoa-Puff-and-sweet-cream-cheese-topped cold brew at Docking Bay 7. The pineapple soft serve, aka Dole Whip, dusted with Tajín seasoning in front of the Tiki Room. The grilled-cheese-sandwich-and-tomato-soup combo at Jolly Holiday on Main Street.

And of course, we devoured the delectable cupcakes from Rubi's Bakery for dessert.

In the (very long) line for the Indiana Jones ride, I opened the box of cupcakes. Only three remained.

The specially decorated one I'd been saving for Dad. And the two I'd been saving for me and . . .

I closed the box.

Great. Paulina must've caught me wallowing in my pity party, because she broke away from Po. She leaned against the railing next to me and said, "Thanks for showing up with an extended cut of my Very Merry Unquince." Her voice was teasing. But also grateful.

"De nada," I said. "I know the last segment of your Unquince series is still happening later this month—but I figured Po wasn't the only one who deserved a party do-over." I cleared my throat. "One not for your subscribers, USC's admissions board, or La Mera Mera." I grabbed on to the railing. "But one for you."

Paulina's eyeliner twinkled under the lampposts. "I'm sorry about Javi not showing up. I really thought he'd come," she said.

I stood there, not knowing how to respond without my voice cracking.

"If it makes you feel any better, he did say he needed to help his mom fix something." She shook her head. "'Life seems so much simpler when you're fixing things.'"

"That's an Anakin Skywalker quote," I said. "*Episode II—Attack of the Clones.*" That set her faux lashes batting. "Don't look so surprised. I did my homework." I looked over her shoulder at Po. "Anakin's wrong, by the way." I turned my attention back to Paulina. "The line should be 'Life's better when you're living things.'"

The fire in Paulina's eyes turned up a notch. "I couldn't agree more."

Walking out of the ride, I said, "It's almost time for the fireworks. Should we head out to the end of Main Street to secure prime viewing spots?"

"Actually," Paulina said, "what about watching them from the First Order headquarters back in Batuu? It's way less crowded, and from there, it's like the fireworks are exploding right over your head."

The entire team oohed and aahed. Including Callie and Po. Outvoted, I nodded.

On the walk back to Galaxy's Edge, Dad squeezed my shoulder. "I forgot how awesome this place was." There was a tiny tremor in his voice. Nervous as he looked to be back here without Mom, a little smile crept to the corners of his mouth.

He was a Jedi, after all. And Jedis didn't give in to fear.

"Would you be mad if I bailed on the show to get on Rise of the Resistance, kiddo? I've watched the ride-through a hundred times, but—"

I put up a hand. "Go. Oh, before I forget, take this." I flipped open the cupcake box and handed him his special treat. A cupcake decorated with a scroll that said, *Happy Thrice upon a Quinceañera, Dad.*

He wrapped me in a bear hug. Kissed me on top of the head. "How did I get so lucky with you girls?" he said, voice cracking.

I shrugged, even though we both knew the answer.

Before both of us started bawling—I shoved him in the direction of the rebel base. "May the Force be with you."

He turned with a swish of brown Jedi robes, holding both saber and cupcake up high.

Although he slowly disappeared into the costumed crowd, it was obvious he was reappearing into our lives. Into his life.

I was excited, scared—and ready—to follow his lead.

"Cas, let's go," Callie said, dragging me forward.

I pressed my silver loafers into the ground. "Actually, I'm gonna watch in front of the castle. That's where I'd always watch with Mom, and I—"

"Say no more," she said. "We can rendezvous at Space Mountain after the show."

With Dad in a galaxy far, far away, and Po and Paulina inside their own bubble, they wouldn't mind me leaving the group for a bit. "Thanks, Callie. For all the help on this and everything else, too. Want to get acai bowls during the week? My treat?"

"Perfect plan."

"Speaking of plans, that reminds me—" I opened up my utility bag, gesturing to the *I'm Celebrating* pins I'd grabbed back at City Hall. "Hand these out as party favors and have everyone fill them. We can take a group pic wearing them later."

"Gotcha," she said, stuffing most of the buttons into a *Tangled* Loungefly backpack. "But keep one for yourself." She winked at the one she'd left inside. "You can add 'making up with Javi' or something like that to yours."

Because I was at the place synonymous with fairy-tale endings, hope tiptoed in. "In that case, I'm also keeping the last two cupcakes." I hugged the pastry box to my chest, wishing for Javi to show up.

If he didn't, that was okay, too.

I had lots of things to celebrate already.

People sat on printed blankets and beach towels across all of Main Street. Most of the crowds gathered around the circular hub in front of Sleeping Beauty's castle. The scents of sugar and butter floated alongside collective murmurs.

Anticipation for the show charged the air.

This resembled the setup at Movies at the Beach, sans ribbons of saltwater turned inside out by the wind. It was also missing one special guest.

I'd be going back to my Pinocchio ways if I told myself I didn't care that Javi hadn't shown up. Obviously, I'd wanted him here. And him not showing up stung more than I anticipated.

But not so much that I'd miss out on this moment.

I pulled the brand-new Cinderella beach towel from a plastic Disneyland bag. In all of today's planning, I'd forgotten to pack something to sit on for the fireworks.

Me. Forgetting to bring something on the items-to-bring checklist.

Proof that I was indeed letting go of my planning ways? Or had I been subconsciously clinging to the dream of sitting on one of Javi's Guatemalan blankets tonight?

Since that wasn't going to happen, I'd swerved into plan B: bought this towel—and another souvenir—on the walk from Galaxy's Edge.

I turned each side of the towel. One surface featured the pink dress Cinderella had intended to wear to the ball. The other sported the blue one she ended up donning.

Fairy godmothers could perhaps custom-make glittering gowns. But no amount of wand flicks or pixie dust could guarantee a happily ever after.

I knew that now. But that didn't mean I had to stop believing in magic. My life teemed with so much proof of its existence.

I spread the towel over the pavement, blue-dress side up. I lowered down. Basked in the day's heat radiating from the cement. I rolled each edge of the towel between my fingers, letting both the empowerment of princesses and the power of fairy godmothers soak into my skin.

I moved my hand into the Disney bag again, reaching for the other present I'd gifted myself.

A necklace with a glass-slipper pendant.

I lifted it from the bag. The moonlight caught on the charm's curved edges.

I brushed my mane over a shoulder, looped the silver chain around my neck. The glass charm hit just above my heart.

It wasn't that the charm didn't echo against the void left by Mom's absence—it did.

But so did her love for me.

So did my love for her.

The glass-slipper charm fits, and I'm sooo going to wear it.

As soon as this damn clasp hooked.

That's when two large hands draped over mine. I would've panicked had their warmth not been accompanied by the scent of lavender. I gulped. "Javi?"

He fastened the necklace and sat next to me. "Sorry to keep you waiting, Castle Towers." His eyes tracked me from the tips of my silver loafers to the top of the bow crowning my curls, before settling on my necklace. That lopsided smile broke out across his face. "Looks like you found your glass slipper after all."

"Not entirely on my own. I had help from a knight in rusted armor." Under the lampposts' lights his quince-slash-stormtrooper tux jacket glowed. Contrasted exquisitely against his tan skin and dark hair. No need to ask the magic mirror, *Who's the fairest of them all?* "Although you look anything but rusty. I mean, you always look good, but tonight especially." I bit my lips to stop before I embarrassed myself further. "Even if I do miss your Mickey sling bag."

Javi laughed, his cheeks flushing. "Thanks," he said, flicking the jacket's lapel. "Not as comfortable as my hoodie, but it's good to try new things."

And to try things again. Those unspoken words hummed in the air.

"As far as my sling bag, I don't need a constant reminder to smile," he said. "I have plenty already."

I perked up. Did this mean . . . ?

Before my hopes flew higher, I said, "I'm glad you came." I fidgeted with the charm necklace. "The fireworks are going to start any second now."

A small laugh-snort. "Oh, they've been going off since day one, Castle Towers."

I nodded. They totally had been.

He scooted in. Our arms touched.

Yup. The electricity was still there.

Projection lights shot across the castle. The music kicking off the show swelled. During a decrescendo, I said, "I'm sorry I lied to you. I just got too caught up playing make-believe that it got hard to tell you the truth. I know this sounds clichéd, but I swear everything between us was always real."

"I know." His jaw tensed. "Trust me—I understand what it's like to want to live in a fantasy world."

"I do trust you." My throat bobbed. "Question is, can you trust me again?"

"Yes," he whispered. "I think I can." He leaned in. *Repositioning himself because of the thickening crowd?* His mouth parted slightly. *Or an invitation to kiss and make up?*

The promise of a reconciliation angled me closer and closer, until I found the warmth of his lips.

The kiss was far from gentle. It was me burying another apology.

It was him accepting it.

Fireworks exploded overhead. I ran a hand up the side of his neck. The booms reverberated there, thrumming to the tempo of his pulse. And mine.

His fingers trailed the chain of my necklace. He followed each link down to the spot inside my rib cage that would always ache. To the glass slipper reminding me of love and magic persevering.

Folding my hand over his, I kissed him again. Our movements synched with the firework bursts and the soundtrack floating from the overhead speakers, quickening to the songs of our broken-but-beating hearts.

Each kiss didn't break curses or lift spells. But they spun their own type of magic.

I surrendered to it.

No thoughts of the past. No plans for the future. Nothing but giving in to this moment.

No wonder *present* was a synonym for *gift*.

I pulled away, breathing hard against his lips. "I think the fairy godmother slash frog just became a princess."

"Oh, you've always been a princess, Castle Towers. You didn't need any kisses from me."

Explosions lit the sky every color of the rainbow. Tendrils of gold twinkled from the heavens like tumbling fairy dust. The shimmers flashed in his eyes. Glittered on my skin.

Yes. All this time, underneath the fairy godmother robes, a princess gown had waited to be worn.

Smiling, I drew him in by the lapel of his stormtrooper tux. The crowd cheered as the music and booms crescendoed. Or maybe they were rewarding me for reclaiming his lips.

Behind my eyelids, the night sparkled.

I sparkled with it.

EPILOGUE

The Pacific Ocean glittered beyond the rolling hills. Oak trees provided a perfect canopy. Blooming flowers decorated the entire sprawl of grass. There was no other way to describe this venue other than beautiful.

A word I'd never thought I'd use for the cemetery where Mom was buried.

I polished her marker until it gleamed. Rearranged the yellow roses until not even Mandy Whitmore could present them better. And when old instincts pressed to clear out some weeds, I reminded myself of something.

Weeds were flowers, too.

"You could never pass a dandelion or four-leaf clover without making a wish, so . . ." My lips trembled. "I'm leaving them wreathed around you, right where they are."

I took my hands back to her marker, brushed my fingertips over *Lucia Torres*.

Over *Beloved Wife* and *Mother*.

"I'm sure Po caught you up on the chisme yesterday." Po started coming here regularly. She said she liked telling Mom about her newest SBA fundraiser recipes, the classes she was excited to take at Alma next fall, and her Disneyland adventures with Paulina. "I'm sure Dad will tell you about his LARP updates when he comes to visit you before work tomorrow."

My phone chimed from my back pocket. "Speak of the Jedi," I said, smiling at the picture of Dad at Galaxy's Edge, building a new lightsaber. One with a yellow blade.

"As for me," I continued, "SBA's putting the finishing touches on winter formal prep." I pulled my legs to my chest, resting my cheek against a knee. "Yes, I'm going with Javi. And no, I didn't get the dance to be *Frozen* themed." I flicked at blades of grass. "Somehow Wes got everyone to vote for it to be *Fast and Furious XV* themed."

My sigh transformed into a chuckle.

"Guess I can't get away from quinceañeras, huh? Speaking of quinces, I'm formally inviting you to one, but first"—I pulled a small birthday candle and lighter from my utility bag, setting them on the grass before reaching back in for a folded page—"I was hoping we could practice this together."

Through misty eyes, I read, "I want to thank everyone for coming and helping me celebrate my unquince. Tonight, Dad put a new pair of loafers on me. I'm sure Po tried her hardest to hide my planner—

"Pause for laughter," I told myself, drawing the pencil from the back of my ear. It'd transformed into a magic wand anyway, not with Mandy's fairy dust, but with my new drawings. With this new thank-you speech.

I skimmed the eraser end over my tightening throat and continued. "After finding it, I'll set it aside for the rest of the night." A deep breath. "These rituals will mark my transition from child to adult. Even if we didn't have these traditions, I know I'd still be standing here in all of my adulthood. Because one person, above all, has taught me how." My heart stretched. "Mom, your light illuminates everything it touches . . ."

I lit the candle, reading her the rest of the speech. The candlelight flickered on Mom's marker until I got to the end. I thought of Po, of Dad . . . of me.

I blew the candle out.

The flame was gone. Mom's light wasn't.

I folded the speech back into my utility bag and grabbed hold of the invitation to my unquince. I set it on her marble marker. "You'll be there, right?"

All at once a flurry of birdsong rang from the trees, exactly like when Princess Aurora danced to "Once upon a Dream" with the forestland critters.

I cracked up, pressing my palm to the earth.

"I'll take that as a yes."

ACKNOWLEDGMENTS

In the Latine community, the quinceañera's godparents provide stalwart support as the birthday girl journeys into adulthood. In so many ways, my sophomore novel felt like a belle who needed ALL the help on her way to the ball. Mil gracias to all the madrinas, padrinos, and godparents of this book who came to the rescue and got her there!

First up I got to thank my Madrina of Magic: Jen Azantian. You're part rock star agent, part fairy godmother, and I'm forever grateful to you and the ALA team—Alex Weiss, Brent Taylor, Zuko, Ben, and Ollie—for sprinkling some of your ALA pixie dust on me.

Thank you to my Madrinas of Story: Alex Sehulster and Vanessa Aguirre. Your unwavering belief in this story, coupled with your extraordinary passion and vision (and patience), made it possible for me to get my heart onto the page. You not only championed QUINCE—but me—and for that, I'm so thankful.

Godparents of Libros: Gracias to the team at Wednesday Books. Special shout-outs to Cassidy Graham, Rivka Holler, Zoë Miller, and Brant Janeway for helping share this book with readers. To Kristin Nappier, Cassie Gutman, Eric Meyer, Kerri Resnick, Olga Grlic, Devan Norman, Mallory Heyer, and everyone on the team who so lovingly cared for and supported this book.

To my Chambelána de Honor: Cindy Parra, aka, Tiiiindy, the most booraful one. Even though you're the little sister, you hold it down like an older one. Thanks for always having my back and encouraging me to dream—and live—boldly.

To my Corte de Honor: Carolina Flórez-Cerchiaro (we did it, baby! Representing NA/SA LOL), Karin Lopez (can we go to SOCO yet?), Brandon Wright (#sithlife), Chris Pinto (*flying walnuts dance*), Jonathan Osterbach (Perra x Otterbocker), Jonathan Meister (show Mark), Hoda Agharazi (small or xsmall?), Stephanie Dodson (nachos for life), Sara Hashem (podcast incoming), and Gretchen Schreiber (are we blocked out this weekend?)—your friendship has meant the world to me, and I love you so much.

To my Godparents of Community: Thank you to Pitch Wars, AMM, Las Musas Books, Class of 2023 Debuts, Angela Montoya, Melanie Schubert, Courtney Kae, Falon Ballard, Melanie Thorne, Molly Cusik, Gabriel Torres, Nina Moreno, Kalie Holford, Elle Taylor, Peace Zodanou, Lyssa Mia Smith, and Clare Edge, you've fueled and inspired me in more ways than I can count.

To my Godparents of Blurbs: A million thanks to Eric Smith, Jason June, Adriana Herrera, Racquel Marie, and James Ramos, thank you for your kindness and generosity. There isn't any fandom I'd rather be in than yours!

To my Padrinos and Madrina de Meow: Javert, Lestat, and Claudia, thank you for being my new court jesters.

To my Padrinos de Imaginación: Gracias Walt Disney and George Lucas. Your worlds and stories have been food for my soul—this book is very much a love letter to your creations.

To my Godparents of Libraries and Education: Thank you

to all the librarians and educators who continue to uplift marginalized voices. I'm so grateful you share stories with the readers who need them most.

To the Padrinxs and Madrinxs in the Latine Community: Thank you for reminding me to evolve and celebrate!

And lastly, I wanted to raise a glass to YOU! I'm eternally grateful to everyone that picks up this book. I hope the story encourages you to accept life's impromptu invitations. Unexpected detours sometimes lead us exactly where we're meant to be.